PRINCES OF MARAZUR

DONNA ALWARD

Princes of Marazur

© Donna Alward 2021

Second Editions

By payment of required fees, you have been granted the *non*-exclusive, *non*-transferable right to access and read the text of this book. No part of this text may be reproduced, transmitted, downloaded, decompiled, reverse engineered, or stored in or introduced into any information storage and retrieval system, in any form or by any means, whether electronic or mechanical, now known or hereinafter invented without the express written permission of copyright owner.

Please Note

The reverse engineering, uploading, and/or distributing of this book via the internet or via any other means without the permission of the copyright owner is illegal and punishable by law. Please purchase only authorized electronic editions, and do not participate in or encourage electronic piracy of copyrighted materials. Your support of the author's rights is appreciated.

No part of this book may be reproduced or transmitted in any form or by any electronic or mechanical means, including photocopying, recording or by any information storage and retrieval system, without the written permission of the publisher, except where permitted by law.

THE PLAYBOY PRINCE AND THE NANNY

Donna Alward

**ABOUT THE PLAYBOY PRINCE
AND THE NANNY**

The bad-boy prince returns...

When the future queen of Marazur is killed in a car accident, Prince Diego Navarro knows it's time to step up and leave his playboy past behind. His brother, the crown prince, needs him, and so do his niece and nephew, who are now left motherless and afraid.

His first task is to hire a new nanny for the children; someone who can give them the love, attention, and gentle support needed after such a traumatic time. Rose Walters is the perfect candidate. Her references are impeccable, her manners firm, but kind. She's just what's needed at the castle... Diego will just ignore his surprising attraction to her. He'll be gone back to his own life soon enough.

Rose isn't intimidated by celebrity or the opulence of the island castle. She is, however, thrown off her stride by the playboy prince with the racy reputation. It isn't long before she realizes that beneath the charm lies a heart of gold and a man who would do anything for his family. But he's royalty and she's staff. He's constantly in the tabloids and she lives behind the scenes. And neither of them stands a chance when two adorable children decide to play matchmaker.

CHAPTER 1

The noise and hubbub in the West Sussex pub was so deafening that Diego nearly missed the silent flash of the Breaking News banner across the TV behind the bar.

But he saw it out of the corner of his eye. Frowned. Turned his head away for a moment, then felt a queer lift in his gut, as if something was very, very wrong.

"Diego. Hey, Diego." His pal Ryan elbowed him in the arm. "Shite. You'd better look at this, mate."

He turned back to the screen and the lift in his stomach dropped to his feet.

The headline scrolled along the bottom of the screen; white words against a blue background, innocuous compared to the aerial scene that filled the picture. He didn't need to read the banner to recognize the mangled car, one of the black limousines his father insisted they ride in when home in Marazur. If there were any doubt, it was banished by an up-close shot of a small red and yellow flag with the green coat of arms, hanging limply from the front corner of the crushed vehicle.

"Diego." Ryan's voice was gentler now, his hand resting on Diego's arm rather than elbowing him roughly. "It's not your da. Or your brother."

Diego dragged his gaze to the flash along the bottom of the screen. No, it wasn't his father or his brother. There was no need for Diego to worry about them, or who was next in line for the throne. But tears stung his eyes as he read the names. Cecilia Navarro. Mariana Cortez.

His sister-in-law, and the nanny to his niece and nephew.

His phone buzzed. It had been doing that all night and he'd chosen to ignore it, wanting to avoid another argument with his father and instead spend the evening kicking back with his friends to celebrate the start of the UK polo season. Now he felt unbearably guilty as he pulled his mobile out of his pocket and looked at the screen.

Lucy, or rather, Princess Luciana. His half-sister, who was visiting Marazur right now during one of her biannual trips. He took a deep breath, then hit the talk button. "Give me two seconds to go outside where it's quiet," he said loudly.

Leaving the gruesome news report behind, he pushed himself away from the bar and weaved his way through people until he reached the door. Outside, the English spring evening was gentle and mild. He closed his eyes and let out a breath.

"How bad is it, Luce?"

"Bad." In that one word he could tell she'd been crying. Oh God…

"Ceci?"

"Gone, Diego." Her voice caught on a sob. "Mariana, too."

For once the news had it right. His heart stuttered. He'd hoped there'd been a mistake. The paparazzi couldn't be trusted with the truth, as he well knew. What a time for them to be right.

"The children?" he asked, and said a silent prayer that they hadn't been in the car. He couldn't think about Max and Emilia too much; he kept them at the edge of his mind and heart right now. The thought of losing them was terrifying and he steeled himself against the emotion.

"Bruised. Scared. But alive."

He let out his breath, felt a sob escape and gulped it back. He couldn't lose his grip.

"We tried calling you for the last hour," she said. "Your brother…"

His brother would be a wreck and justifiably so. His wife had just died. Perhaps a lot of royal marriages weren't based on love, but Raoul's had been. He'd doted on Ceci and the kids. Mariana, too, had been like part of the family. Hell, she'd been with the palace since…

Since Diego and Raoul had lost their own mother nearly twenty-five years ago. Mariana had raised them. She treated Raoul and Ceci's children like grandkids. Grief struck him, sharp and sure, a painful ache around his heart. Mariana had been family.

"I'm sorry," he replied, pressing the fingers of his left

hand to his temple. Those were two words he said often when it came to his family. Now, though, he really meant them. "I'll be home as soon as I can."

"I know you will," she said gently. Of the whole family, Lucy was the one who was easiest on him, who understood him best. Maybe because she hadn't been raised in Marazur. It afforded her a clarity that others didn't have. "I'm so glad I'm here right now. Papa…" Her voice broke again.

"Is Brody there with you?" Lucy and her family made their home in Canada, on Brody's ranch, but visited often. Right now Diego found himself beyond thankful that she was there now to help his father and brother navigate the next few days. Papa would know what to do…he'd been here before.

A man shouldn't have to face this kind of tragedy more than once in a lifetime.

"Brody's here. And little Alex, too."

And Lucy would be keeping everyone cared for and fed and nurtured, because that's what she did. Diego rested his shoulders against the brick wall of the pub and sighed. Raoul, the crown prince, the responsible ruler-to-be, fair and just. Lucy, the mothering figure who cared for their simpler but no less important needs. And then there was Diego. Where did he fit? In the stables. At parties. In fast cars.

In other countries. With firm admonishment to not be an embarrassment to the family.

"Diego?"

"I'm here. I'm going to go, though, Lucy. I need to make travel plans. I'll be home as soon as I can."

"What should I tell Papa and Raoul?"

"Nothing. I mean, just tell them you were able to reach me. I'll look after the rest."

There was a pause and Diego wondered if his sister was making that terrible disapproving face he hated or if she was simply emotional.

"I love you, Diego. Please fly safe."

Emotional, thank God. He wasn't sure he could take criticism right now. He nodded even though she couldn't see him. "I will. I promise. See you soon."

"Email your plans and I'll have a car waiting for you."

"You worry about yourself, and not me," he ordered. "Love you."

He hit the button on the phone, ending the call, and when he looked up he saw Ryan standing by the back door of the pub, watching him sadly.

"It's bad, eh?" he asked, his brown eyes wide and too-knowing.

"Cecilia," Diego admitted. "And the nanny. The kids though…" Emotion swamped him and he drew in a shaky breath. "Thank God the kids are okay."

Ryan came forward and clamped a hand on Diego's shoulder. "Looks like you have to go back to your castle then, doesn't it?"

Diego smiled grimly. "I can't stay away forever. And they need me. Of course I'm going back." It had nothing to do with duty and everything to do with family. Of course, many believed that Diego didn't value the idea of family as much as he should.

They couldn't be more wrong.

He looked over at Ryan. The two of them had been best friends since he'd gone to Cambridge for his postgrad and joined the polo club. Diego, in a moment of hubris, had made an offhand remark about an Irishman playing polo and the next thing he knew he'd been dusting the dirt off his perfectly creased trousers. Then Ryan O'Toole had held out his hand, pulled Diego to his feet, and said, "Come on, Your Highness. Let's go get a pint."

It had been many years since then, but the offer had been made several times, particularly when Diego needed it most. Tonight, though, it wouldn't help.

"Anything I can do for you?" Ryan asked.

Diego smiled grimly. "The blonde at the bar. Go buy her a drink. I'm going to duck out early."

Ryan nodded with a crooked smile. "Call if you need anything."

"I will."

Ryan went back inside, while Diego lifted his phone again and scrolled through until he found the number of his assistant. Not that he gave her much work when he was away from home, but tonight everyone on the staff would be up and alert.

And Diego would be going home.

One Month Later

Rosalie tried to focus on the words on the page, but they were all a blur. With a sigh, she closed the book and rested her hands on the cover, then turned to look out the airplane window. She wasn't usually nervous before meeting a new family, or the children she'd be caring for. This was different, though. When the agency had called about her new placement, she hadn't expected the job to be for the Royal Family of Marazur. She'd worked for minor nobility and rich families, traveling with them when the occasion warranted, but she'd never been to Marazur and she'd definitely never worked for a prince.

She knew of the island principality, of course. And she'd even had an encounter with the younger of the princes once, though he wouldn't remember. Diego, she recalled, and shook her head. It wasn't Diego she was going to work for. It was Raoul. She had been hired as a nanny to the crown prince's children. The heirs.

"Ms. Walters? Make sure your seatbelt is on. We're going to begin our approach soon. Can I get you anything before we land?"

Rosalie looked up at the sharply-dressed attendant. Raoul hadn't sent a royal jet or anything, but he had chartered a private flight. It was beyond anything Rose had ever experienced. "No, thank you," she said with a smile. "I'm fine."

"Very well. We should be on the ground shortly."

Rose sat back in the comfortable leather and looked out over the Mediterranean. It had been nearly a month since the televisions and papers had been abuzz with the death of Princess Cecilia. They'd shown pictures of the funeral at the cathedral in the capital, a week after the accident. It had nearly broken her heart to see the crown prince, looking harrowed and drawn, holding the hand of his daughter while his son rested on his arm.

King Alexander had looked tired, and Prince Diego had been uncharacteristically solemn as he sat with Princess Luciana and her family.

Once the funeral ended, though, so did the news story, and very little was heard of the family, left to heal their wounds in relative private. The media had moved on, but Rose knew the royal family were people like anyone else. Children who, when it came down to it, had lost their mother. All the wealth and privilege in the world couldn't make up for that, and Rose knew she had her work cut out for her.

The plane landed smoothly at the relatively small airport. When she unbuckled her seatbelt, the flight attendant was at her side once more to collect her carry-on bag. Rose only had to grab her purse before she exited the plane, holding on to the railing as she descended the stairs to the tarmac.

"Miss Walters?"

A liveried man waited at the bottom of the stairs, and he touched his hat as he greeted her. "I'm Marco. I'll see you through customs and on to the palace."

Good heavens. This was a tad surreal, wasn't it?

She smiled politely at him. "That would be lovely, thank you, Marco." The warm, moist air was perfumed with the scent of salt and flora that she knew must be present but couldn't be seen here in the secure, paved area of the airport. The aroma clung to the warm rays of sun that were somehow far more penetrating than any in England.

It reminded her of the school trip she'd taken when she was twelve—four days in Rome, and she'd loved every colorful, rich, vibrant moment of it. It had been a long time since she'd visited the Mediterranean, and she was more than ready to leave the damp and fog of England behind for time in the sun.

She was here to work, but couldn't escape the thought that this was also a bit of a fairy tale, really. Her assignments through the agency had been posh indeed, but nothing on this scale.

"Miss? If you're ready."

Marco had both of her cases and waited for her to make her way through the doors. To her continued surprise, she was escorted through customs without any wait or trouble and in mere minutes found herself ensconced in the back of a limousine.

My word.

She was starting to get nervous, now, and twisted her fingers together. Drew them apart again and wiped them on her black trousers, then regretted that too. She had to keep calm, cool, professional. This was her job. It wouldn't do to be flustered and nervous.

The airport was on the outskirts of the city, and she peered out the window at the narrow streets and charming houses stacked on the hillside. On one of her days off she'd have to come down here and discover all the nooks and crannies. Have coffee or a glass of wine at a little cantina along the cobbled streets. She was still thinking about it when the car began to climb and wind its way out of the urban area and along some of the most beautiful landscape she had ever seen.

Marco slowed and stopped at a huge set of gates, which swung open at their arrival. They crept at a sedate pace along a paved lane flanked with what looked like some sort of oak. Then she caught sight of it. The castle—home of King Alexander of Marazur. Turrets rose up, pinky-beige against the blue of the sky and the green of the manicured grounds. A hedge formed a kind of maze in the "u" shape of the curved drive, carefully trimmed and pruned. It was smaller than some of the manor houses she'd visited in England, but there was a grandeur to it just the same. And a hominess that she hadn't expected. Perhaps it was due to the color of the stone, more warm and welcoming than the cold, gray-white granite she was used to.

She ran through names in her head, desperate to make sure she adhered to the proper forms of address. King Alexander—clearly Your Highness. And how often would she see him anyway? Hardly ever. She'd be with the other household staff. She'd have to communicate with Raoul, she supposed. She would be required to curtsy. He was the crown prince and would be addressed as Your Highness as well. If the press was to be believed, Diego wouldn't be home much and was unlikely to be around. The Sun had just posted pictures of him in South America somewhere.

Marco pulled to a stop and her door was opened by another liveried staff. "Good afternoon, Miss Walters. Welcome to Marazur."

She pasted on a smile and let out what she hoped was a centering breath. "Thank you."

"His Highness is looking forward to meeting you at four o'clock in the blue salon." Perhaps he'd noticed her shaky exhale, because the man dropped his stiff formality for a moment and smiled. "Don't worry, Miss." He held out his hand and gallantly helped her out of the car. "The prince is really very nice. And we're all so glad you're here."

Before she could ask what exactly that meant, he dropped her hand and moved to collect her bags. She looked around her, marveling at the calm beauty of the grounds. It was like a beautiful oasis, more lush than the surrounding countryside, with shrubs, graceful trees, and gardens of rioting blossoms. She gawked around her as they made their way down a neat path leading to the far side of the castle. And when the man opened the door to the north wing, Rose was relatively sure she'd just arrived in paradise.

Diego had spent the three weeks since the funeral in England and then Argentina, ostensibly looking after Crown interests, while conveniently distracting the press. Dammit, he'd been gone less than a month, and now it felt as if the household was falling apart. His act as a decoy had been meant to give the family some private time to get things together. Not crumble into pieces.

Diego ran his hand through his hair for the third time as he left the stables to go back to his private apartment. Maybe Lucy should have stayed to help. She'd offered, but Brody was needed home, in Canada, and Diego had known that Lucy would hate being apart from her husband for any length of time. Diego'd assured her that he'd return within a few weeks, and he'd expected his father and Raoul to have adopted the legendary Navarro upper lip by the time he got back.

Oh, the lip was stiff all right. But as far as getting on with things...not so much. The palace had been a happy, welcoming place before the funeral. Now it felt like a tomb.

Cecelia had made the castle a home with her love and laughter. Now it was occupied by widowers and a couple of children who didn't understand where their mother or nanny had gone. Between the children crying and his brother staring in a daze, Diego wasn't sure how much longer he could keep things going. This was the first situation he'd ever been in where he couldn't bluff or charm his way out.

As his stomach growled loudly, Diego detoured from the family living quarters and headed to the north wing. He'd missed lunch, and dinner wasn't for several hours. Besides, he'd always been far more comfortable in the kitchens than in the more formal parts of the castle. He'd just pop in for a snack rather than call for something to be brought to him.

He whistled a little as he made his way down the corridor, nodding at one of the maids who blushed and dipped in a quick curtsy as he passed. He smiled back, charmed, but felt that the protocol was so silly. He much preferred how it was with his friends and he was just Diego. No rules or airs. Just an ordinary guy.

He stepped inside the kitchen and put on his sweetest, most boyish smile. "*Buenos dias*, Señora Ortiz," he called to the cook, who'd been supplying him with in-between meals since he'd been about five years old.

"Diego." The voice came from the other side of the cavernous room. "What are you doing here bothering me in my kitchen?"

He grinned. No protocol here. Just the way he liked it.

He stepped further into the room and peered around the corner. "I missed lunch. I thought maybe you'd have something you could feed a poor starving boy?"

She came bustling around the corner, a huge bowl in hand, her eyebrows raised nearly to her hairline. "And that poor, starving boy would be you?"

He followed her into the room where the staff usually ate and stopped short at the sight of a young woman sitting primly at the table, a cup of tea in front of her.

"Oh, hello," he said.

The look on her pretty face was priceless. Clearly she recognized him, and there was a fleeting expression of horror and embarrassment that flashed across her features until she schooled it away. She rose to her feet quickly and affected a small curtsey. "Good afternoon, Your Highness."

He rolled his eyes. "Oh, that sounds so formal." He smiled at her, trying to put her at ease.

"Then what shall I call you? Prince Diego?" Her cheeks pinkened. He was delighted. Young, blond, blue-eyed, fresh-faced, and dressed in flowy black trousers and a tailored white shirt. Hmm. New staff? They kept getting prettier.

"You could try just Diego," he replied.

Señora Ortiz swatted his arm. "No flirting," she scolded.

He knew he should be embarrassed, but he wasn't. Neither did he mind that he was a member of the royal family and he'd just been swatted on the arm by the cook.

He stepped forward. "I'm sorry, how rude of me. I didn't even ask you your name."

She swallowed, then smiled and held out her hand. "I'm Rosalie Walters. The new nanny."

Her accent was delectable. He took her fingers in his, doubly happy to see her. "Oh, of course! I'm so glad you're here. My niece and nephew need some happiness and light. It's been so dreary around here for them." He looked at her closely, cocked his head a bit. "That accent. Surrey?"

She smiled then, a real, genuine smile and not the polite curve of lips of a moment ago. "Guildford, actually. My mum and dad still live there."

"I went to school at Cambridge."

"I know." The acknowledgment put a little of the awkwardness back in her eyes, but she recovered nicely. "You've hardly any accent at all, Your Highness."

"Diego," he corrected, finally dropping her hand. "I sometimes forget English is actually my second language. I speak it far more often than I do Spanish these days."

"Diego, are you going to talk to the nanny all day or have something to eat?" There was a sharp edge to Señora Ortiz's voice that Diego didn't mistake. Friendliness was one thing, but fraternizing with the staff would be severely frowned upon.

"Eat, of course." He turned his charming smile on the cook and took the plate she'd prepared from her hands. "You're an angel, Señora Ortiz."

She raised only one eyebrow this time. "And you are as incorrigible as ever." She took a second, smaller plate, and placed it in front of Rosalie. Cake. If he was right, it was the cook's signature orange cake. His mouth watered.

"Thank you," Rosalie said softly, and picked up her fork.

"May I join you?"

She looked up, her eyes wide with surprise. The flush on her cheeks deepened. "Oh. Of course."

What else was she going to say, anyway? He was a prince. As much as he might act otherwise, he was now third in line to the throne. It irritated him that people were often nice to him out of obligation. He'd rather earn their regard on his own merits.

He put down his plate, pulled out a chair, and sat. Señora Ortiz had fixed him a basic chicken sandwich with a few olives and some cheese to the side. He spread his napkin on his lap, picked up the sandwich, and took a good-sized bite. Lord, Miss Walters looked like she was wound tighter than a spring, her back all ramrod-straight and not a hair out of place. There was some-thing about her, though, that reassured him. She was probably nervous—who wouldn't be? But she looked like she'd be kind. Sweet. Patient. He chewed thought-fully and watched her take a dainty bite of cake. Max and Emilia would need those qualities in a nanny.

"Orange cake is Señora Ortiz's specialty," he said quietly, wiping his fingers on his napkin. "She's trying to make you feel at home."

Rosalie looked up at him and gave him a wobbly

smile. "I'll confess I'm a bit nervous. And anxious to meet the children. I'm…I'm very sorry for your loss." She tucked a little strand of disobedient hair behind her ear. Her ears were pierced, he noticed, with little pearls in the lobes. Totally appropriate. Classy, and beautiful.

Her voice was sweet and clear, and one hundred percent genuine. If he were anywhere else, he might like to talk to her for a good long while. And then stop talking altogether. But that would be inappropriate here and she was far too important for him to trifle with.

"Thank you," he responded. "It was such a shock. I'm afraid my brother is very grief-stricken. I'm glad you're here, Miss Walters." He looked down at his plate for a moment, then back up. "Max and Emilia need to smile again and get back into a normal routine."

"Of course. To lose their mother and their previous nanny…their whole world has been turned upside down." She took a sip of tea and placed the cup precisely on the saucer again. "Did you know that most children actually thrive on structure? It gives them a sense of security." Then she laughed a little, a breathy little sound that was unexpectedly sexy coming from such a tidy package. "Oh, that made me sound like a stick in the mud. I promise I'm not. Consistency is good. Kindness is better, with a little fun thrown in for good measure."

Her manners were impeccable. And she was highly trained and recommended. He'd seen that for himself. There was something more, though. She would be firm, he suspected, but also gentle and loving. And that smile… When she forgot to be nervous, it lit up her whole face.

"Your last employer was very happy with you," he remarked.

She nodded. "Gregory was a sweet boy. But he got too old for a nanny and he's off to school now. I was there for two years and honestly, quite sad to leave."

"And you traveled with the family as well."

"Yes." She frowned. "You're awfully well-versed in my qualifications."

"That's because I saw to the hiring of you," he replied, popping an olive into his mouth. "Well, along with my sister, Luciana. Lucy. She helped before she went back to Canada."

"I see." She put down her fork, then looked up at him again. "Actually, no, I don't. I wouldn't have thought that it was your job to hire household staff." Her brows pulled together in puzzlement.

He eyed her somberly. "Well, it would have been Cecelia's," he said quietly and shrugged. "I have connections in London, you see. I did some asking around, and your agency came highly recommended."

"Oh. Of course that would have fallen to…Princess Cecilia."

He held her gaze. "In the days after the accident, I felt very helpless, especially when it came to the children. This was one way I could ease my brother's burden."

"Hiring someone to care for two small children, sight unseen?" she asked.

It struck him as curious that she'd challenge him;

after all she was the one benefitting from his decision. But he respected her for it, too. He needed someone who'd put Max and Emilia first. He leaned forward, still holding her gaze. "Miss Walters, rest assured you were thoroughly vetted before we offered you the position."

A pink stain spread over the crests of her cheeks and she dropped her eyes. "Of course, Your Highness," she replied.

He waited for her to look up and when she didn't right away, he cleared his throat to prompt her to do so.

"Can you call me something else, please? If not Diego, then, I don't know, Mr. Navarro?"

Her clear blue gaze was utterly guileless. "But you are *Your Highness*. Or at the very least, Prince Diego. You are in no way, shape or form, a mere mister."

"Couldn't you pretend?"

She suddenly focused on her tea cup. "No, I could not."

He wondered why. Wondered if it was some stupid, silly class notion of aristocracy that he hated. During official functions he wore the appropriate clothing and sash but the rest of the time he preferred to be more casual. A regular suit with or without a tie when he was on charity business, and khakis and button down shirts for casual, like he was wearing now. Complete with wrinkles.

That didn't explain the lack of eye contact, though. He'd almost think she was shy, except there'd been a few moments where she'd dropped her guard and he'd actually felt as if they'd connected. He chalked it up to first-day nerves.

She finished her tea, took a last bite of cake, and put down her fork. There was still a corner of the piece left on the china, and he thought she looked at it rather regretfully before checking her watch. "It's three forty-five," she said, placing a hand on her belly in a tell-tale gesture of nerves. "Perhaps someone could show me the way to the blue salon?"

Señora Ortiz came around the corner. "I'll have one of the maids take you," she said. "Don't worry, Miss Walters. You'll learn your way around in no time." She smiled reassuringly.

Diego frowned and got up as soon as Rosalie stood and smoothed her blouse. "Don't trouble the staff. I'm going that way anyway. I'll show you."

"Thank you," she replied, and he was grateful she'd left off any form of address this time.

He led the way out of the kitchen and toward the offices at the back of the castle. But when he looked over at the young woman beside him, he realized the agency had left out one thing when they'd spoken about Miss Walters.

They'd left out how pretty she was. And not in a drop-dead gorgeous, glamour sort of way. No, she was the kind of woman who emanated simplicity and calm, like a fresh spring day. Like the spray of tea roses on the china set Mariana had always used—beautiful, classic, timeless.

She was the kind of woman who could cause a man all sorts of trouble…without consciously doing a thing.

He'd have to watch out for that.

· · ·

HE DIDN'T REMEMBER HER.

Rose followed Diego through the castle, a half-step behind him as they made their way out of the north wing and toward what she figured was the back of the building. It was interesting how the different areas of the building had different vibes. The kitchen had been spotlessly clean, beautifully modern, and yet warm and welcoming. Her room was in the family wing, next to the children should she be needed and keeping her close to her charges. It was the most beautiful room she'd ever been able to call her own, perhaps a bit more finely appointed than she was used to, but light and airy with sheer panels at the windows and a bedspread of sage-green leaves and pink rosebuds. Not only was there a huge bed and an attached ensuite complete with a stunning clawfoot tub, but she had her own sitting area too, with a sage-green sofa and chair and polished end tables.

Now they were marching toward the business area of the castle, where presumably the king, his sons, and his staff had their offices. The nerves in her stomach were tumbling over themselves now. She hadn't considered coming face to face with Diego so soon, or her gut-reaction to him. His insistence on being so familiar threw her off. He was just as gorgeous as she remembered, but there was more, too. When he talked about the children, there was a softness around his eyes that spoke of deep affection. And a surprising steel in his voice when he'd informed her she'd been vetted before being hired.

He was the playboy prince. She'd expected charm,

and he'd had that in spades. The rest, though…she wasn't sure what to make of him. Or her fluttering in her stomach when he smiled and a half-dimple popped in his cheek.

Now she was on her way to meet Raoul and she pushed aside her thoughts of Diego and ran through the protocol in her head yet again. Hopefully she didn't have any crumbs on her collar or anything.

They stopped outside a massive oak door and Diego smiled at her reassuringly. "Don't be nervous. He doesn't bite. He'll probably try to ply you with more tea."

She nodded. "Thank you. Sir." There. Sir might work. Less formal than a fussy title and yet respectful and delineated their difference in station.

He smiled, a crooked little flash that made her pulse give a solid thump. She wouldn't berate herself for that; Diego was and always had been unfairly sexy and reputably charming. She was human, after all. That was the problem.

"I don't like it, but it'll have to do," he said. "I don't know what it is, but I can't shake the feeling that you look familiar."

She laughed, but inside she was squirming. She had taken the proper training, passed all her accreditation and had been working for five years now. But she hadn't forgotten that at nineteen she'd been struggling to put herself through school and Diego had swept through her life. She'd made an entire weekend's worth of wages in the time it took for him to get off one train and catch another.

"I have one of those faces," she supplied. "Sir."

"I take it back. It's no better than the rest. We'll have to work on it." He had the audacity to wink at her.

She was working up a suitable response when the door opened. "Ah. Diego. Why am I not surprised?"

She goggled at the sight of the crown prince. Raoul Navarro was older than his brother and even smiling, his countenance was far more serious. There were lines beside his eyes and mouth, and just a hint of dark circles suggesting lack of sleep. Where Diego wore tan trousers and a light blue shirt, Raoul was clothed in a perfectly tailored charcoal gray suit, complete with white shirt and flawlessly knotted necktie.

It was a terrible time to lose her carefully rehearsed words.

"This is Miss Rosalie Walters, your new nanny." Diego smoothly performed introductions.

"Yes, Miss Walters. Please come in." He stood aside. "You've gotten settled, I hope?"

She hastily bobbed a curtsy. "Yes, Your Highness. Thank you. The room is beautiful and I'm looking forward to meeting the children."

To her dismay, Diego followed her into the room. Now she felt outmatched and outnumbered.

Raoul gave a short nod, then gestured towards a small seating area. "Would you like some tea?"

She caught Diego's eye and nearly smiled at the impish expression on his face. He'd definitely called it.

"Tea would be lovely, thank you," she replied. She shouldn't have been surprised when an assistant immediately came in with a tea tray, but she was.

"Thank you," she said to the woman, who placed

the tray on the table in front of her. "Shall I pour, then?"

There were only two cups on the tray. Diego held up a hand. "None for me, thanks."

Raoul took a seat in a china-blue chair, looking absolutely regal as he did so. "I assume you're joining us, Diego?" He looked over at Rose. "Diego took on the job of searching for a nanny," he explained. "I found in the days after the funeral I was very distracted. Now I'm trying to catch up on state business as well as get on with…"

He cleared his throat. Rose's nervousness was temporarily forgotten as her heart softened. "I'm so very sorry for your loss, Your Highness," she said quietly. She handed him a cup of tea and he smiled and took it gratefully.

"Miss Walters, I think you'll find that amid all the formalities here, our family is a close one. I'm at a loss with the children." He put down his teacup and met her gaze. "I don't know the right thing to say or do. If I should talk about Ceci or not, if they need hugs or space. I apologize for being so personal but…I'd like it very much if you could give me your thoughts as you care for them. I'm depending on you to understand what they need and help me provide it." His expression was one of extreme humility. "I'm the heir to Marazur, but I'm also a father."

Oh, she was doubly impressed now. Of course, it added to her pressures but at least she felt as if they could work together to ensure the children's happiness.

"Of course," she replied, resisting the urge to reach

out and pat his hand. "I'm looking forward to meeting them both. Getting them back into a normal routine will help a lot. And so will knowing that there are people who love and care about them. I've only been here a little over an hour and I can already see that they're very loved."

Diego had been silent so far, but he leaned ahead a little and looked at his brother. "I'm here to help you, too, Raoul."

Raoul smiled thinly. "Thank you. But I'm fine, really. Work is the best thing for me now. As Miss Walters said…a normal routine."

Rose looked over and saw Diego frown, but she didn't have time to think about it as the next ten minutes were filled with Raoul asking various questions about her and her plans. When he was seemingly satisfied, he stood and offered his hand.

"Thank you, Miss Walters. I don't want to keep you from settling in or meeting Max and Emilia. Perhaps we can talk again tomorrow."

"Of course." She took his hand briefly, and bobbed another quick curtsy.

For the first time during the meeting, he smiled. "Miss Walters, it's going to be tedious if you keep bobbing up and down all the time."

Her cheeks heated. "Yes, sir."

"Good. Do you need someone to show you where to go? Señora Romero is our housekeeper. She'll provide you with household schedules and the like."

"I'll take her," Diego offered. "I promised Max we'd kick the ball around in the garden before dinner."

She held her smile, torn between being annoyed at Diego's continued nearness and grateful for his assistance. It was nice to have an ally, but she couldn't allow herself to be too familiar with the family. The truth was, she needed to get settled in her place, which was not drinking tea with princes but in the nursery with children and with the other household staff.

Where she belonged.

CHAPTER 3

Diego led her back to the nursery, and she was glad of it as she would have taken a few wrong turns otherwise. He knocked on the door next to hers and a maid opened it, stepping aside and smiling. "Good afternoon, sir," she said respectfully. "And Miss. I'm Ernestina. I've been looking after the children since…" She halted as her speech stumbled. "For the last few weeks. We're so glad you're here."

"Thank you, Ernestina." Rose held out her hand. "I'm Rosalie, but you can call me Rose."

Squeals interrupted what conversation they might have had and Rose saw Ernestina wince. The maid was easily in her mid-forties, and Rose guessed she'd been nominated as temporary nanny and preferred her household duties to those of child minder. Diego came around the corner with a small boy tucked under his arm and a little girl only a step behind, looking up at him like he hung the moon.

Oh dear. She really shouldn't have to remind herself

to be professional, but men with kids… Not to mention *hot* men with kids. She was human, after all. And a woman. A woman who cared for children for a living. Knowing that his niece and nephew loved him—and he loved them—said a lot about the kind of man Diego Navarro was. In only a little over an hour, her preconceptions of Diego had melted away one by one. The charm was there, but she hadn't expected the warmth, or the honesty of his emotions with his family.

Ernestina's voice interrupted. "The children were just about to have tea. Dinner is promptly at seven. Unless there is a function, the children eat with the family. That's how their mother preferred it." Tears glimmered in Ernestina's eyes. Cecelia had been well loved, by family and by the staff, it seemed.

"I'll be sure to have them ready," Rose assured her.

"Señora Romero asked me to tell you to come to the kitchen for your dinner once the children are in the dining room. She'll give you the household schedule then. I've written the children's schedule out for you as well." She went to a small desk and picked up a moleskine book.

Ernestina then turned around and faced Diego and the children. "Emilia, Max, this is your new nanny, Miss Walters."

The room went quiet. Emilia looked away from Diego and stared at Rose, and Max, who Rose understood to be four, popped his thumb in his mouth. A telling reaction for a boy his age. She'd have to tread gently.

"Hello," she said softly, and offered a smile meant to reassure.

Emilia's dark eyes hardened with resentment. "I want Mama Mariana. Not you."

Diego was the one to issue a reprimand. "Emilia. Manners," he said sharply.

At the sound of Diego's snappish voice, Max started to cry, little heartbreaking sobs shaking his body.

"It's all right," Rose assured Diego, and stepped forward toward the children. She knelt down a little and looked Emilia in the eyes.

"I am so very sorry about your mama and also Mariana. Of course you wish they were here instead of me. I wish they were too, Emilia."

Emilia appeared very astute for a six-year-old. "If they were here you wouldn't have a job."

"Emilia!" This from Diego again, but Rose held up her hand.

"I would have a job somewhere else, that's all," she replied. "But as unhappy and sad as you are, Emilia, that was a bit rude. And I don't think you are generally a rude little girl."

Emilia looked away, a determined set to her jaw, but she looked chagrined, too. Lord, the poor things were too young to know how to deal with grief. Most adults didn't know either, but for children…

Max was still whimpering, held against Diego's shoulder now. Rose let him stay there; he was comfortable and being comforted. "Hello, Max," she said to him as she stood. She put a hand gently on his warm little back. "My name is Rosalie. And I'm here to look after you and your sister. Is that okay with you?"

Huge brown eyes glimmered at her and he nodded a little, taking his thumb out of his mouth.

"You like your *Tío* Diego, don't you?" She used the Spanish term, thinking Max might find it a bit comforting, hoping her limited Spanish would be sufficient over the coming weeks.

He nodded and clung tighter to Diego's neck. Her heart was a big old pile of goo now, seeing both the tenderness in their relationship and also how sad and upset the children were.

"Do you want to stay for tea?" she asked Diego quietly, thinking that having someone familiar they cared about nearby might ease the way a bit.

Diego's gaze touched hers. His eyes weren't like Max's, or even Raoul's, she realized. They were more of a hazel shot with gold flecks. He had a way of looking into her eyes as if nothing and no one else existed. That day years ago on the train platform, she'd been too shocked and starstruck to really notice. But he'd been with her all afternoon today, and they'd worked as a team. They'd also looked into each other's eyes more than was prudent, she realized.

"I did promise some football in the garden," he said quietly. "One more cup of tea won't kill me. I hope."

Rose turned to find Ernestina laying out the light meal. "Thank you, Ernestina. For everything. May I come to you if I have any questions?"

The maid looked rather pleased Rose had asked, which had been Rose's intention all along. "Of course,

Miss. Señora Romero will know where to find me if you need anything."

Ernestina then took her leave, shutting the door with a quiet click behind her.

"Well," Rose said, putting her hands together and smiling. "Let's see what there is to eat, and you can tell me all about yourselves."

DIEGO TIPPED HIS HEAD BACK AND LOOKED UP AT THE stars. Thousands of them were out tonight, pinpoints of silvery light in the inky blackness. There wasn't much in the way of light pollution on the castle grounds, and lots of evenings he found his way to the upper balcony, away from the constraints of his title. Up here he could just *be*.

Today was the first day he'd felt truly useful in quite some time. He'd offered, yet again, to help his brother, but he'd been brushed aside with a quick "I'm fine." Well, if Raoul wouldn't accept his help in the running of the country, the least Diego could do is help with the family. And it hadn't been a hardship spending time with the new nanny, Rosalie.

He let out a long breath and rested his hands on the stone balustrade. *Rose*, he remembered her saying to Ernestina. Miss Walters was proper and she'd made sure he knew it. She was quite prim in some ways, but strangely relaxed, too. And gentle, which he appreciated. Her admonishment to Emilia, though, had been bang-on. Rose wouldn't tolerate rudeness. All in all, he suspected she was just what the duo needed right now.

Routine, rules, leavened with a lot of kindness. It didn't hurt that she was beautiful, either. All in all it had been an enjoyable afternoon.

"Tea" in the nursery had consisted of milk, bread, and slices of salami, followed by little almond cookies. She had sat with the children and nibbled on a cookie, but mostly she got them talking about themselves. Max loved football, so she told him stories about watching matches in England and then listened intently as he explained, in his halting four-year-old way, how he'd scored a goal against Tio Diego. And Emilia enjoyed dance, so when Rose spoke of taking ballet lessons when she was a child, Diego could picture it in his mind. She would have been adorable—all arms and legs in her leotard, her blond ponytail swinging as she danced. Within fifteen minutes both children had relaxed and were utterly engaged.

Diego had then made good his promise to kick the ball around with Max, and Rose had asked Emilia to give her a tour of the garden.

Maybe that was what struck him so profoundly. Rose didn't patronize the children, even though they were so small. She made them feel valued. Just a small gesture like asking for a guide to the garden had changed Emilia's attitude completely, and Diego guessed it was because it made his niece feel like she had something to offer rather than simply being told what to do or being dismissed as unimportant and in the way.

It was a sad statement that he, at thirty, could understand exactly how that felt.

There was a movement below, and he squinted to

make out the form walking in the shadows along the path among the shrubbery. A woman, he realized. Not just any woman, but *her*. Miss Walters. Except he found it impossible to think of her that way. She still wore the black trousers and white shirt of what he supposed was her "uniform." He hoped she wore other outfits as well. The black and white was somewhat…boring. Despite all that, there was something about her that was beautifully simple. The name Rose suited her perfectly.

He watched as she ambled through the winding paths, finally stopping by a fountain that spilled its water with a steady *burble*. The moonlight shone off her light hair, no longer twisted up in a bun but flowing loosely around her shoulders. Rose reached into her pocket and took something out, then he watched as she flicked her thumb and a tiny splash bubbled into the pool. Diego smiled then, loving that she had a little bit of whimsy about her. Had she made a wish before tossing the coin? And what would a woman like Rose wish for?

He shouldn't go down there. He should just leave the balcony and head to his apartment and pretend he hadn't seen her. But when did he ever do what he should? He went inside, along the silent corridor, and down the stairs, his shoes tapping on the stone steps as he let himself out onto the grounds at the back of the palace. The least he could do is thank her for today and see how the evening had gone with the children.

She didn't hear him until he was nearly upon her. When she turned her head and saw him standing there, she jumped a little, and put her hand to her chest. He grinned. "The sound of the water, I guess." At her puzzled expression, he elaborated. "The reason you didn't hear me," he said.

"Ah." She frowned a little. "Are you sure it's wise for you to be out here, sir?"

That sir business again. He shrugged easily. "I don't know what you mean. I'm pretty sure it's safe enough."

"That's not what I meant." She bit down on her lip, and he watched as her teeth changed the shape of the soft, pink flesh. Awareness flickered between them, and he knew what she'd implied even without her having to explain.

"Is it wise for you to be out here, Rose?"

Her eyes widened at his use of her first name.

"I'm sorry. I should go in. It's late and tomorrow's a busy day…" She jumped up from the stone ledge of the fountain, but he reached out and grabbed her arm to keep her from running away.

Damn. She lurched to a halt and looked up at him, and his lungs felt as if they were squeezing together. Her chest rose and fell with fast breaths, and he could see the same uncertainty in her eyes as he was feeling inside. It was the damnedest thing. Maybe it was her position within the household. She wasn't a girl at a club or some aristocrat's daughter. He knew how to deal with those kinds of women. Rose was different somehow. Diego was used to games that he was certain she didn't know how to play.

"Not to be impertinent, sir," she said breathlessly, "but you've kept rather close all day. And it's probably not appropriate for either of us. I'm the nanny. You're a prince. I'm the help, Dieg… Sir."

But he caught the slip. "You were going to call me by my name."

"Yes, I was. And that would be really inappropriate. I appreciate all your help today, I do. But it's…it's not right that you're so…so…"

She was stuttering. And it wasn't because she was cold in the balmy night air, and it wasn't because she was afraid. It was because she was mere inches away. So close it would take hardly anything for him to pull her against him. He was no stranger to instant attraction, but this threw him for a bit of a loop.

"If I let you go, do you promise not to run away?"

Her gaze blazed into his. "Don't you understand? All it takes is for you to order me to stay."

He released her arm, hating that she'd played the power card. He would never use his rank in that way. "I'm not ordering. I wouldn't do that. I'm asking."

She remained where she was, but he knew that she could be gone in a flash. He knew that she should be, for that matter.

And yet she stayed.

"Tell me about yourself," he suggested.

She tilted her head to the side, just a bit. It was amazing how she could point out their difference in circumstance in one breath and challenge him in the next, without even trying.

"You read my CV. And I'm sure you spoke to the agency about me. You already know the facts."

He was equally amused and frustrated. "They told me about Miss Rosalie Walters, Nanny," he replied, shoving his hands into his pockets. "I want to know about Rose, the person."

"Why? Begging your pardon, sir." He saw her swallow and a flash of uncertainty flitted across her face. "Why does my personal life have to do with my job?"

She was utterly right. What difference did it make who she was other than the nanny? It wasn't like got up close and personal with any of the other staff. There were boundaries. Boundaries he hadn't crossed since he'd been…oh, about nineteen, if memory served.

He looked at her for a long moment. She met his eyes directly, but not with any antagonism. She was, he realized, one of the most serene women he'd ever encountered. She didn't shy away from tough questions and she'd had an answer for every question and a solution for every problem today. Unflappable, that's what she was. And he liked it. So much of the household had been in chaos for the last month. Unflappable was hugely appreciated.

But there was something else, too. Something he'd felt for a long time but hadn't admitted to anyone else. He was lonely, and in one afternoon Rose Walters had made him feel like a human being and not a title or a news item. Of course he'd want to know more about her.

"Maybe," he said quietly, "because I could use a friend."

She laughed. Not really at him, but more an elegant outburst of incredulity. "You? Come on. You're Diego Navarro. Social butterfly. Charming as the devil himself, by all accounts."

"Including yours?"

"I've only just met you."

He smiled, just a little. "First impressions?"

She frowned. "Okay, yes. Charming."

Something inside him was pleased she thought so. But there was more to him than some…playboy. He guarded that inner part of himself fairly closely, because in his position the truth made a person vulnerable. That she'd seen it and somehow tapped into it today made her very different from anyone he'd ever met, except for maybe Ryan.

"Do you have family, Rose?"

She didn't correct him on the use of her first name. Instead she turned from the fountain and began walking along the path, slowly, her shoes making little shushing noises against the finely crushed rock. "I do, yes," she answered. "My parents are both living, and I have a brother and a sister and…several cousins."

He smiled. Did she realize there was a warmth to her voice when she spoke of them? "That sounds very nice," he replied, falling into step beside her.

"My brother's a vicar," she said, and chuckled. "Which came as a big surprise as he was always getting into trouble when we were kids. And my sister lives in London and works in insurance." She angled a look in his direction. "We're very firmly middle class."

There she went, using labels again, pointing out how different they were. It was getting quite annoying, really. "And what do they think of your line of work?"

She shrugged, then tossed her head a little, her hair flipping over her shoulder and out of her way. "My brother teases me because I work for posh families. My sister thinks I'm crazy to want to be around children all the time, and my mother fears I'll raise everyone else's kids and never have any of my own, though she also thinks it's lovely that I get to travel now and then."

It sounded so refreshingly normal. So many times over the years he'd longed for that kind of family. Not that his wasn't great—they were. But there was a whole different expectation and a whole different way of living when you were under a microscope. Every transgression, every mistake was documented and publicized.

"Do you? Want some of your own?"

She hesitated and looked over at him. "I suppose I do. I'm twenty-six. Nothing's ticking loudly yet, and I haven't met the right man, so I don't worry too much about it."

She looked away, but something was off. A little twist of her lips, perhaps, or the way her gaze shifted downward. There was something to that story, but he wasn't going to press. He knew that they had to have *some* boundaries.

They started walking again, beneath an arbor of wisteria that surrounded them in sweet scent.

"This garden is beautiful. Emilia showed me a lot of the flowers today. She's very quick and has a good memory."

"Cecilia was very hands on with them. Even though Mariana was always here, Ceci was a wonderful mother. I think that was one of the reasons Raoul loved her so much." He paused, then figured he might as well say what was on his mind. "Mariana brought us up, too, after our mother died. It's not a huge stretch to understand why Raoul was attracted to someone with a soft and nurturing heart."

She nodded, then grinned at him. "That's not *your* type, though, is it?"

She was referring to the tabloid stories, he supposed. "I believe the correct term is 'arm candy'," he said. "I don't even know if I have a type. Perhaps the uncomplicated type, if any."

"I think you want me to feel sorry for you. It's kind of difficult, considering where we are."

She was so blunt. He liked that about her. Liked it even more that she had a little half-grin on her lips. She was teasing, he realized.

"Not working, then. Damn."

She laughed, a warm, sultry sound that was unexpected. It hit him square in the gut and he reminded himself that she was off-limits.

"I like your laugh," he said quietly. The night and the intimacy of the garden prompted hushed tones. It was as if there was no one else in the world right now. No divide in their station, no official family duties, none of the grief that had permeated the palace lately. He nudged her elbow with his hand. "There hasn't been much laughter here lately. It's nice, even if it is at my expense."

She stopped, turned to him, and looked up into his face. "I'm sorry. I shouldn't have teased you about your life of privilege. You put your pants on one leg at a time, like the rest of us."

He chuckled. "Now I'm going to have to try putting both legs in at once, so I can be special."

But her face remained serious. "No, I mean it. You have feelings like anyone else, and of course this is a difficult time. And you live in the public eye, which makes it even harder." She put her hand on his arm, her fingers warm and sure. "Is there a right or wrong way to grieve? And is it really anyone's business?"

That was it exactly. In addition, Diego was really worried about his brother, and his father, too. Alexander was the king, but it seemed he'd aged a good decade since the accident. He rarely smiled anymore, and he looked so tired. Raoul, on the other hand, had become something of a workaholic.

"I'm really glad you're here."

She released his arm. "Yes, you mentioned that."

"No," he said, stronger than he'd spoken before. "It's not just the children who need you. I think we all do."

Her eyes widened. "That's a tall order for a new nanny on her first day on the job."

"Don't worry. I just mean… you've got a sweetness to you. A steadiness. And a great smile. Just do what you do, Rose. That'll be enough, I think."

"And you? What will you be doing?"

"What do you mean?"

"Now that I'm here, will you be jetting off again, resuming your normal life?"

He frowned. "What makes you ask that?"

She took a step backward. "Emilia said you aren't here often. That you're too busy traveling all over and having fun. The kids miss you…sir. They think the sun rises and sets on you. If you want them to have stability, perhaps you need to focus on being there for them on a more consistent basis."

Ouch. It wasn't anything he hadn't heard before, and Rose was a stranger, really. Her opinion shouldn't have the power to hurt him, but somehow it did.

"*Miss Walters*, I do believe you've overstepped."

She lifted her chin. "I beg your pardon, *sir*, but you overstepped when you came out here tonight and approached me, rather than leaving me to enjoy my walk alone. I don't mean to be insubordinate or overly blunt, but I'm here to do a job. Not make friends."

It burned that she was right. Completely right. Truth was she was pretty and he was lonely. He'd opened up to her, crossing the line between prince and nanny. Then she'd been honest and he hadn't liked what he'd heard.

She wasn't sending mixed signals, despite what her gorgeous eyes said, despite the little shiver of attraction that ran between them. She was here for the job. He was the one blurring the lines.

"I beg your pardon." He stepped back and sketched a quick bow. "I won't disturb you any longer. Goodnight, Miss Walters. *Buenos noches.*"

He turned on his heel and started back along the path, leaving her alone beneath the arbor. Maybe she expected him to leave again. Maybe they all did. But someone had to lead the family through this crisis, and Diego figured he might just surprise everyone. This was one time he'd stay.

Rose watched him walk away, his shoes crunching against the fine gravel. She let out a huge sigh. This had never been an issue before. At each house where she'd worked, there'd never been any blurring of lines between employer and employee. Parents had been employers, not friends, and they'd worked together to see to all the needs of the children. No meddling uncles or family members. Especially incredibly attractive ones with a well-documented reputation.

She'd offended him. She understood that much, and when he spun to walk away, she longed to call after him and apologize. But she didn't. The line had to be drawn and it had to be clear. Might as well do it now.

Still, she thought, as she finally left the shadows of the wisteria, it might have been nice to have a friend here. He certainly cared about the children, and his brother and father, too. He seemed…lonely. Which was ridiculous, of course. He had lots of friends—the papers were full of them. There was no reason why their conversations today should play on her sympathies. She imagined what it would have been like tonight if they'd just met at the fountain as an ordinary man and woman. Maybe she would have flirted back with him, just to see that teasing gleam in his eye. Maybe she wouldn't have forced herself to ignore the ripple of awareness that had rushed through her when he grabbed her arm and asked her to stay.

But they weren't regular people, and she'd do well to remember it.

She found her way back to her room, and wondered where Diego's was. Close by? In another section or wing? She let herself in quietly, and first went to the door that joined her room with the nursery. She peeked in and saw both children sound asleep, exhausted their time outside today.

She closed the door and let out a long sigh. It was nearly midnight. Her day would begin at six. She really needed to get to bed.

Instead she went to her window and opened it, letting in the perfumed night air. She sat on the window seat and looked out over the dark grounds, a world away from where she'd been this morning.

She didn't know how long she'd be here, but she could hardly discount the influence this job would have on her future. On top of that, it paid extremely well, and she could send more money home. Nothing meant more than looking after family.

Nothing. And so, when she finally crawled into bed, she knew that sending Diego on his way was best for everyone involved. Because screwing this up would have ripple effects she didn't even want to think about.

Six hours later she rose and showered and dressed for the day; went to the kitchens and ate and then saw to the preparation of Emilia and Max's morning meal, then went back upstairs and started them on a morning routine that they'd follow most days. It wasn't until one o'clock, when the midday meal was served, that Rose learned that Diego had left that morning for Paris.

She'd been right about him after all.

ROSE COULDN'T REMEMBER A MORE PLEASANT JOB.

She'd been in Marazur for two weeks now, and for the third day in a row she sat in the garden on a blanket, watching the children as they kicked a ball around after their al fresco lunch. The weather was stunning, the summer heat softened by the breeze from the sea that swept over the island. Perfect for picnics and play. She smiled as the duo ran along the level stretch of lush grass. Emilia had long, thick curls, and Rose had plaited it in a "Dutch" braid, which was Emilia's favorite. Both children wore ordinary, but fine quality clothing—shorts, T-shirts, and trainers.

Raoul seemed determined that his children have "normal" childhoods. It wasn't just in their casual dress. Other than a television in the nursery, there was a distinct lack of electronic devices at their disposal. Instead they were encouraged to play, and each morning after breakfast they worked on lessons, at their father's orders.

The schedule suited her just fine, she mused, plopping a berry into her mouth. Max had a hard time sitting still, but the playroom was full of things to keep him busy. At his age "school" consisted of blocks, creative projects that worked on his fine motor skills, early math manipulatives, and lots of stories. With Emilia, things were a bit more structured. Before long, Rose figured a tutor would be brought in to see to the children's education. For now, Rose followed the curriculum that Mariana had been teaching.

The best part? The children reciprocated by helping her with her Spanish, which was more than a bit rusty.

She sat cross-legged on the blanket and watched as Max kicked the ball past Emilia and between the orange markers they'd arranged as goal posts. As he jumped and put his arms in the air, Rose laughed. He was all boy, but he was a sweetheart, too. Emilia looked over and tried a crinkly-sort of wink—she'd let the goal in on purpose, Rose knew. The siblings were close, which was nice. She supposed that was because they had to rely on each other.

Rose took a sip of water as Emilia and Max switched places, and she thought about her own family. She and Devon and Haley were somewhat close now, but it hadn't always been that way. She'd been twenty and nearly through her schooling when Haley had gotten pregnant. Devon, as the oldest, had been hard on Haley, especially as he was new to his parish and very conscious of appearances. And Haley had assumed that

Rose would be a nanny to her baby when she was born. When Rose had said no, everything had blown up. The tight-knit family had unravelled and Rose was still hoping they could be stitched back together again.

She sighed. Those hadn't been the most pleasant years. And things were still strained between her and her sister at times. It was hard to put the pieces back together when they were now so spread out and disconnected. Diego wasn't the only one who felt lonely now and again.

"If this isn't a sight."

Before she even turned her head, she knew it was him. Warm, soft, and just the hint of an accent flavored his voice. She schooled her features and turned to see him striding across the grass, casually dressed in khaki shorts and a T-shirt. The cotton stretched across broad shoulders. *Wow,* she thought. And kept her mouth firmly shut.

He approached the kids first. "Ah, *mi rayito de sol,*" he announced, picking Emilia up and giving her a bear hug. "*Como estas?*"

The response was a rapid fire of Spanish that Rose couldn't keep up with. With a hearty laugh, Diego put Emilia back on the ground and reached for Max. Max, with a devilish twinkle in his eye, began to run away, his giggles filling the garden with childish joy. Rose watched as Diego, his smile wide, raced after him, caught him under his arm, and proceeded to hang him upside down by his feet.

"*No, no!*" shouted Max, giggling and gasping the

whole time. "*Tio Diego! No!*" The giggling turned to full-on belly laughs, and Rose found herself grinning.

"Diego, really," she commented dryly, but inside she knew this was exactly what Max needed and was grateful to Diego for providing it. While Emilia was more than happy to be active and play outside and get into her share of dirt, Rose knew it wasn't the same as having "guy time."

And it wasn't like Raoul would be out here in a pair of shorts, horsing around. She understood he had duties, but he'd hardly seen the children. She was lucky if he popped in once a day to say hello. She'd been both surprised and disappointed by that, particularly after what he'd said the first day. Now Diego was here, laughing, playing, bringing his incredible energy to their picnic. Not just energy... Love. He genuinely loved these children and made it hard for her to remain annoyed at him for leaving. He kept surprising her, and she suspected that beneath all the obvious charm there was a warm, generous heart.

Diego put Max down, made sure he was steady on his feet, and then stood. "It's good to see them out playing," he said to Rose, coming over to the blanket and plopping down in a most unceremonious manner.

It was as if that night in the garden had never happened. Rose looked at him for a moment, trying to puzzle him out. "You know," she said, a contemplative note in her voice, "you're rather like the Cheshire Cat. You appear, and then you disappear. You appear..."

He laughed. "I know. And then I disappear."

"You've got the same grin, too," she pointed out, her lips twitching.

"Alice in Wonderland," he mused, making a humming sound. "Haven't read that since I was in short pants." He looked down at his bare knees. "Oops."

She did laugh then, she couldn't help it. "We've been reading it at night," she said. "I started them with *The Wind in the Willows*. It was my favorite when I was little. And then Emilia picked out Alice. I'm not sure what we're going to read next."

"It's wonderful that you're reading to them," he said, resting on his elbows. Looking far too comfortable for her liking. And far too alluring.

"Of course I am. It's my job, but even so, I've always loved reading to children before bed."

"It's very Mary Poppins."

"Book or the movie?"

He looked over at her. Goodness, he had stunning eyes, and it was unfair that a man have lashes that lush and dark. "The movie. Ceci made us all watch it when the anniversary edition came out a few years ago." He raised an eyebrow. "That's a few hours I won't get back."

She looked over at the children. They too had flopped on to the grass and Rose smiled as she saw Emilia lift her hand and point at a cloud floating past.

"Emilia's quite a little mother to Max," Rose observed. "She really looks out for him."

"That's sweet."

Rose nodded, but met Diego's gaze. "It is, but it's something I want to watch. She's so little. I don't want her to feel like she has to take her mother's place for him. It's probably helping her with her grief, but it should never become a burden to her or an obligation, you know?"

Diego was quiet for a few moments. She looked over at him and his face wasn't as relaxed and open as it had been just a minute before. "Did I say something wrong?" she asked.

He shook his head. "No, you didn't. You're absolutely right. It's not good for her and it's not good for Max, either."

"For Max?"

Diego's voice had a strain to it she hadn't heard before. "When one sibling takes responsibility for the other, it's easy for them to take over and want to do things for the other. Helping, protecting…on the surface it seems admirable and good. But sometimes the other sibling can feel…incompetent. In the way."

"A burden?"

He nodded. "I guess."

"And you're speaking of you and Raoul now, yes?" She lifted a shoulder when he stared at her. "Come on, Diego. It's pretty thinly veiled."

"When our mother died, Raoul was a great big brother. But then he was so determined that my life not be difficult that he did everything. There was nothing for me. Raoul was the crown prince. Raoul was the heir. Raoul was good at diplomacy and business. I was…not in the way, exactly, but not useful."

Was that why he traveled so much, got his face in the tabloids? He was bored? Uninspired?

"Anyway, I don't want that to happen to Max. They should both be their own people. And understand me too, Rose, that I know the situation wasn't easy for Raoul, either. He dealt with all the responsibilities."

"So much for a life of privilege," Rose murmured. Now Max's stubby finger was pointing at a butterfly. They were so sweet. A little stubborn, and Max was terribly cranky when he got overtired, but sweet kids. Remarkably unspoiled, considering.

Diego sat up, crossed his legs so he was sitting like she was. "Did you realize you called me by my first name?" he asked.

Heat rushed to her cheeks. How could she have forgotten herself so easily? It was his fault. He kept ignoring the line between employer and employee. "I-I'm sorry." She stammered a little, but Diego shook his head.

"Rose, about the garden that night…"

"I really should pack up the picnic."

She moved to open the basket and tuck away the dishes, but Diego put his hand on her arm. "Stop. And hear me out."

His fingers were strong, and warm, and felt entirely too good as they circled her wrist. She closed the lid on the basket and sat back hesitantly. "Of course." She obeyed because he'd told her to, and he was her superior. It certainly couldn't be because of the low note of entreaty softening his voice.

"I thought a lot about what you said. You're right. There is a status difference between us, and you are here to do a job and not be a friend." He laughed a little and shook his head. "I'm a bit too old to have a nanny. But life is hardly ever black and white. I hate all the formality, if we're being completely truthful. And this place has been so dreary, you came in like a ray of sunshine on a cloudy day."

She was touched by the compliment, even understood his perspective. "Hate it or not, Diego, it's how it is."

"You're infuriating." He ran his hand through his hair and she resisted a smile. He was adorable when he was agitated. Max was a lot like him, she realized, with a catch in her heart.

"Rose," he said again, and she gave him her full attention.

"I'm sorry I interrupted. Go on."

"You were right about me overstepping. After Paris, I was in South America again the last few weeks and I couldn't stop thinking about being home. That's unusual for me. Normally I can't wait to get away. Something's changed."

Don't say it's me, she thought, her stomach clenching. That would be…God. Cliché and horrible and…so ridiculously fairytale-ish. Ugh.

His jaw was set in a stubborn line. "I'm needed here. Whether Papa or Raoul realize it, I'm needed. And I'm not going away again until I'm convinced things are fine." He met her gaze. "Rose, someone has to keep the family together. Family's always been the most important thing. And it feels like it's all crumbled to bits in the last two months. Most of all I worry about those two." He nodded toward Max and Emilia. "What

I'm saying is, when we're, I don't know, in public, call me sir or Your Highness or whatever your sense of protocol demands. But please, when we talk about the children, when we work together...let me just be Diego."

His plea touched her. She knew all about trying to keep family together. He could have used other arguments, but he'd chosen the one that had a guarantee of success. Did he know? Did his research into her include her relationship with her sister and niece? Her parents and brother? And yet, looking into his eyes now, she saw sincerity. Honor. And humility.

"They need you," he said softly, and his eyes were on the children, not on her. "And they need me. Let me help. Please."

"You love them very much," she stated, wishing his plea hadn't gone straight to her heart.

"Has their father been around often?"

She shook her head. "He's been busy. He stops in once each day, though."

Diego frowned. "That's not parenting."

"It's not my place to judge," she replied. "It's my job to care for them and meet their needs. All their needs," she added, as Diego looked over. "His Highness is struggling, that's all."

"Emilia looks like Ceci," he murmured, softly so neither of the children could hear him say their mother's name. "And I'm sure right now reminders of her hurt a lot. That's no excuse, though. I'll speak to him."

"Diego, please..."

He reached over and squeezed her fingers. "I'm his

brother. It's not overreaching if I say it. Besides, he needs my help, too."

And what about Diego, she wondered. What about his grief? Or maybe he hadn't been home enough in recent years to feel the loss the same as the others. He certainly seemed okay.

A whiny shout diverted their attention, and Rose quickly slid her fingers away from Diego's. Team or not, there were still rules. Maybe they weren't written down but it was a simple matter of what was appropriate and what wasn't.

"What's the matter?" she asked, kneeling on the blanket as Max came rushing forward, big tears in his eyes and his lips set in a line that told Rose that a tantrum was in the offing.

Out came a rush of Spanish that left Rose scrambling and Diego chuckling. "He says that Emilia won't let him go to the pond to see the fish and he says, in effect, that 'she's not the boss of me.'"

Rose struggled not to laugh. It was such a typically childish thing and more reassuring than troublesome. "Max, darling," she said gently, "Emilia knows the rule is you can't go to the pond without a grown-up with you."

"*Si*," Emilia said, but the tone was belligerent and very "I told you so." Rose sent a quick look in Emilia's direction, and the girl was quiet.

"Why don't we all walk to the pond together, see the fish, and then we'll go inside for a story?"

"And a nap," Max grumbled. "You will make me take a nap. I hate naps."

She touched her finger to the end of his pert little nose. "And you're very grumpy if you don't have one. Come on, let's see the fish first."

She grabbed the basket while Diego folded the blanket, and together the four of them walked down the grassy hill toward the pond. It wasn't particularly huge, but a cute little stone bridge crossed it, and from the apex they could look down into the clear water and see the flash of koi swimming around.

Rose put down the basket and leaned over to peer into the pond, while Diego lifted Max into his arms so he could see better. Then Rose began a game. She started a story about a koi fish, and each one of them had to add a line to the story. When it was Diego's turn, he passed, but Rose shook her head.

"Nope. You have to play or you can't stay at the pond."

The koi had names of Eduardo and Maria, thanks to the children. Maria was being bossy and Eduardo wanted to go play with the other koi.

Diego sighed, frowned, and thought for a moment. "Eduardo told Maria he was hungry for a snack. And when she turned to get him one, he swam away to join the other koi who were playing…"

He faltered, and Max jumped in. "Football."

Rose shook her head. "Nope, sorry Max. It's my turn." Max's face fell a little, so Rose smiled and said, "Polo. The koi were playing polo."

Max's smile disappeared as he giggled. "Fish can't play polo!"

"Why not?"

Emilia, keen on the game, jumped in with, "Eduardo's polo pony was Flash, because he went so fast. He held his mallet in one fin and the reins in the other and they went flying over the grass, chasing the ball."

"Well done, Emilia!" Rose grinned, and the story continued. By the time Maria had come back with empanadas and churros, Eduardo had scored the winning goal. But he took a terrible scolding from his sister.

"Eduardo explained that sometimes a boy needs to get out and blow off some steam," Diego said. "And Maria, seeing everything had turned out okay, said she'd try to be more understanding in the future."

Rose chuckled. It wasn't too hard to imagine Diego as Eduardo.

"What's 'blow off some steam'?" Emilia asked, wrinkling her brow.

They picked up their picnic materials and began walking to the castle again. "Well," Rose explained, "back when trains were first invented, they ran on steam. When the pressure in the boiler got to be too much, they'd have to let some out to release it before it blew up." She ruffled Max's hair. "Sometimes little boys —and girls—need to blow off some steam before they blow up."

"Miss Rosalie?" Emilia reached over to hold her hand and the girl looked up at Rose, her dark eyes shining. "You are very clever. I want to be smart like you."

"Aw, thank you sweetheart." She was touched by the compliment. "And if you study, and ask questions, and want to learn things, then you will."

"I'm smart," Max said defensively.

"Indeed you are," she replied. Diego hid a smile.

Together they got the children up to the nursery. Rose supervised hand and face washing and then took Max into the bedroom where he was to nap.

"I'm too old for naps," he protested.

"Nonsense," replied Diego. "Everyone likes a good siesta."

"Not me."

"Well, I do." Diego sat on the edge of the bed. "I'll bet Rose is going to read you a story, too."

Max was lying on the bed now, his lids growing heavy. "Don't want Miss Rosalie. Want *Tio* Diego."

She shrugged at looked at Diego. "You're literate. I'm sure you can read a story or two."

He laughed outright, and the sound made her feel all warm inside.

"Emilia and I are going to work on her letters and numbers for a while," Rose said. She always looked forward to this part of the day. "If you read to Max, we can get started right away."

"*Por favor, Tio*," Max said, sitting up a bit, giving Diego the biggest set of puppy eyes Rose had ever seen.

"How can I resist this face?" Diego replied, grinning. "Pick out two stories, Max."

Rose left the door open part-way as she and Emilia went to the polished table where they did their lessons. She put out pencils, crayons, and stickers along with several worksheets of the alphabet and numbers to ten. Emilia's printing was improving each day, and after a few practice sheets they'd work on a little spelling and maths.

Emilia had finished the whole alphabet and was in the midst of her numbers when Rose realized she hadn't heard Diego's deep voice in quite some time. She got up and went to the bedroom door and paused on the threshold, her heart melting just a little bit as she looked at the pair of them.

Diego was lying on the bed with Max, a forgotten storybook open between them, and Max was curled into the much larger figure of his uncle, his head resting on Diego's shoulder. Both were fast asleep.

That's how it should be with their father, she thought. Oh, she understood that the demands of Raoul's position were unique, but these kinds of moments were precious and few. Maybe Diego was right. Maybe he should speak to Raoul, because despite the prince's assurances on the first day, he really hadn't been involved with his children much at all.

Unlike Diego. He'd been gone for two weeks, but in one afternoon he'd shown them fun, love, affection. He'd given them time and made them feel important.

Diego—renowned playboy, palace bad boy and notorious womanizer, would actually make a very good father.

The world was just full of surprises.

CHAPTER 5

That afternoon set the pattern for the days ahead. Diego found himself increasingly busy between checking in at the stables and his office, and he had no trouble sleeping at night, except that he thought far too often of Rose just before nodding off.

On the day of his return, he'd awakened from the shared siesta after an hour, his shirt sticky from where Max's head rested. Carefully he'd extricated himself from the awkward position and tiptoed out of the bedroom and to the main room where Rose and Emilia were doing lessons.

Emilia's little head had been bent over her work, and Rose was watching, a smile of encouragement on her face as Emilia printed and spelled aloud as she went. They hadn't seen him yet, and he let the scene before him sink into his memory. She cared about the children. He'd hoped that whoever they hired would, of course, but with Rose it was genuine affection. Her honey-gold hair was twisted up into a knot at the back of her head, and her ivory complexion had already mellowed a little from the Mediterranean sun, giving her a glow. She'd relaxed from her severe black trousers and white blouses too, opting for softer, pale linens in deference to the heat.

She was beautiful. She was damn near perfect. And that scared the hell out of him almost as much as it drew him to her.

"Very good," she praised softly, and Emilia looked up at her with something akin to hero worship.

Max was asleep, Emilia was studying and both were happy. He wasn't a fool; he knew it was because they were getting attention, and the good kind of attention. What children needed were two parents. In the absence of that, they were getting Rose and Diego as substitutions for the real thing.

In that moment he promised himself that as long as he was needed, he'd be there for the children.

The first thing he'd done was go to Raoul and make his case. Raoul had dark circles beneath his eyes and he'd been short with Diego, firing back that a bachelor who was rarely at home had no business telling him how to raise his children. It was no less than Diego had expected. He stopped at Raoul's secretary's desk on the way out. "Stephani, is he getting any sleep?"

"I don't know," she replied, frowning. "He won't talk to me, either. I know I'm just his assistant…"

"You're more than that. He trusts you. We both need to keep trying, I guess."

"Yes, sir." Her dark eyes met Diego's. "I hate seeing him so unhappy."

"If you ever have any concerns, come to me, will you?"

"Of course."

That day, and every day since, he'd crammed his working hours into the morning and spent the afternoons with the children. The trip to Argentina had been very profitable for the stables and several deals were in progress that would see new additions to their polo stock as well as the sale of breeding rights. Being able to claim connection to the royal bloodline was a big thing for many breeders.

In the evenings he worked until dinner on business to do with his charities, and then after dinner he'd sometimes work until nearly midnight if something was pressing and couldn't wait. Each morning he had a to-do list for his assistant, Camila, to carry out while he was involved in his day.

But today he was playing hooky. The children had been fussing more and more about being bored and not getting out of the palace as they used to.

Ceci had been gone two months. As far as Diego knew, the kids hadn't left the palace grounds in all that time. Ceci had taken them places quite often. Of course they missed it.

So he'd arranged a car and proper security and they were going into the city for lunch and some shopping. Max wanted toys. Emilia wanted everything. The day was sunny and perfect for this sort of an outing.

They were dressed and waiting for him just past

noon when he came to get them at the nursery. Rose had dressed them appropriately, in casual but spotless and pressed clothing. She was looking very pretty too, he realized. Her dress was a floral print on an ivory background, with a wide belt at her small waist and ivory flats on her feet—sensible, he thought, for the walking they'd be doing. A wide-brimmed hat hung from her fingers, along the side of her thigh. There was an innocence about her that filled him with a sense of goodness.

"Are we ready?" he asked, clapping his hands together, and Max ran up and pulled on Diego's hand.

"Let's go! I'm hungry."

They were laughing as they piled into the waiting car, the driver shutting the door behind them. It wasn't until Rose was buckling them into their seats that the atmosphere suddenly got quiet. He looked at Max and saw the boy's eyes were wide. A glance at Emilia showed her blinking rather quickly. Rose noticed too, and when she turned to Diego for help, he gave a small shake of his head.

"Okay, what do you want to eat? I think we should eat as soon as we get there." Diego forced a note of cheerfulness, hoping to distract the children from what he suspected was a very bad memory.

Emilia shrugged.

"Come on, you two. You must have some favorites," Rose nudged.

Diego wasn't sure if she'd figured out why they were suddenly so silent, but she leaned forward and smiled at them, trying again. "I don't know what I'd like," she said. "The food here is very different. Perhaps the two of you will help me decide."

Max mumbled something.

"I'm sorry?" She peered into his face. "I didn't quite catch that, Max."

"He said churros," Emilia replied. "They're fried and have cinnamon on them."

"That's for dessert," Diego said, as the driver negotiated the way down the lane toward the gates and then the street.

"At school, we sometimes had 'Backwards Dinner'," Rose said, smiling a little. "Forks on the right. Knives on the left. And dessert first." She wiggled her eyebrows, coaxing a smile out of Max.

"May we really have dessert first, Miss Rose?" Emilia asked, her eyes lighting up.

"We'll see, shall we?"

The mood seemed to have lightened a bit, and on the way into the city Diego sat back and watched as she engaged in some subtle prodding to get the children to confess to their favorite activities.

It came as no surprise to Diego that Max's mostly consisted of food and outdoor activities, while Emilia liked shopping of all sorts. "I think we should visit the market in the square," Diego suggested. "We can have lunch at one of the tavernas nearby, visit a few shops, and then haggle with the vendors."

"Yes!" Max's face lit up. "It is so loud and bright. Last time I saw jugglers."

Rose nodded, and Diego was happy they'd decided to take the children on an outing today.

"Jugglers? That's exciting," she said, keeping the conversation going.

"Si," he answered. "It was just before…"

Max suddenly stopped, and the car was quiet.

Diego knew the moment she understood. She looked quickly at the children, then back at him. The funeral for their mother had been on the palace grounds, in the chapel. He suspected they hadn't been in the limousine since the night of the accident.

The moment passed, and Max and Emilia were talking to each other now in their excitement for the afternoon's events. Rose looked up at Diego once more and he gave a brief nod. "Now you understand," he said quietly.

"Is this why you haven't traveled lately?"

He spared a glance at the children and then looked back at her. "I thought it was time I focused on family."

"So the bad boy's reformed?" she asked.

"Maybe the bad boy needed a purpose," he answered, and her gaze of approval went straight to his heart. He didn't often feel as if his choices were appreciated, but this time he knew he was doing the right thing and for the right reasons. The time for playing around was over.

ROSE WAS STILL CONSIDERING DIEGO'S LAST STATEMENT when they entered the city. As flattering as it was to think she had captured his attention, it was far more gratifying to know that he was focused on the well-being of his family. She nearly asked him what he had planned, but her attention was diverted by the bright sights of tall houses, balconies made colorful by plants and flowers, and even lines of clothing strung between poles in some of the poorer areas. Pedestrians stopped and pointed at the car as they passed, not only because of the sleek black stretch but the royal flags adorning the hood.

"We're making a bit of a spectacle," Rose observed, peering out the tinted window.

"It's hard to go incognito," Diego said. "But really, there's not much to worry about. Besides, Father would hardly agree to us jumping in a plain old car for an afternoon in town."

She looked behind them. One of those "plain old cars" was behind them—black, expensive, new. Palace security.

"Don't worry. They won't intrude unless they're needed. You'll hardly know they're there."

"Do you always have security?" she asked.

He shook his head. "No. But then, I'm a big boy. I'm not the heir. And Marazur is pretty small, considering. Today it's just because…" The sentence trailed off and she knew he meant the children.

"I see." She did, or at least she thought she did.

They parked and headed into what she would call the equivalent of a pub. It was light and airy, though, with delicious smells wafting out the door, and gorgeous flowers spilling out of pots along the windows. No dark interior and heavy wood furniture here; instead there were colorful chairs and tables with bright tablecloths. They were led straight through to the back where they could have privacy, and Rose saw a number of heads follow their progress through the little restaurant.

The children sat together on one side, their backs to the door and the other patrons, while she and Diego faced forward, with everything and everyone in full view.

It dawned on her that this was on purpose. For protection. She didn't see any of their security, though. Wherever they were, they were doing a good job of being inconspicuous.

Rose was true to her word about dessert first, and they ordered churros to start. A basket of them came and Rose dutifully munched on one and found it delicious…and addictive. Max looked at her as if to say, "I told you so," while Emilia licked all the cinnamon off her crispy piece before eating the pastry.

They ordered lunch and talked about their plans for the afternoon while they were waiting. Once Rose saw, with some alarm, that a woman with a camera was angling along a wall for a picture. The man who'd shown them to their table, however, stepped forward and guided her back to her table. Diego acted as if nothing had happened, but Rose frowned. She'd never had to deal with any sort of celebrity attention before.

The food arrived and the rich, spicy scent of her paella—ordered on Diego's recommendation—made her stomach growl. Emilia giggled, Rose rolled her eyes, and everyone laughed. Max's eyes bulged at the size of his *bocadillo*, which Diego explained was a sandwich made with specially cured ham. Since Max tended to head straight for the meat at tea time or a meal, she wasn't surprised by his choice. Emilia, on the other hand, had what appeared to be an omelet made of potato and egg.

"*Tortilla Espaniola*, Miss Rose. My favorite." Her ponytail bobbed as she reached for her napkin and spread it gently on her lap. She was a six-year-old girl but also a princess. There was no forgetting it, even in a little taverna.

Diego's meal seemed somewhat lighter than she'd expected. It looked like some sort of vegetable combination, with a fried egg on the top of it. "What's that?"

"*Pisto*," he replied. "Roasted vegetables. Kind of like a, what's the dish…" He frowned. "Like the one that has eggplant in it."

"Ratatouille?"

He nodded. "That's it. Only no eggplant."

Next to it, her bowl of paella looked huge—and rich.

They dug in and she was delighted as flavors burst over her tongue. Rice, saffron, vegetables, gorgeous shrimp and spicy chorizo. There was no way she'd be able to finish it all. "Pardon my manners," she said lightly, "but would anyone like some? There's too much for just me."

The children stared at her for a moment. Clearly this was not a done thing at the dinner table.

"Max," she said, "Would you like to try a bite of the sausage?"

He nodded. Carnivore all the way, that one. In return, he offered her a sliver of the ham from his sandwich. She'd never tasted anything like it. Dry-cured was very different than what she was used to.

Then Emilia insisted she try some of her tortilla and a narrow slice of it made it across the table. By the time she'd tested everyone's choices, she was stuffed, but loving the different flavors. More than that, she'd enjoyed the whole meal, being with the three of them and knowing they were relaxed and happy.

"Dessert?" Diego asked, but she patted her belly and shook her head.

"That's what the churros were for," she said. "I couldn't eat another bite. That was delicious."

Diego nodded at someone and a few minutes later he leaned over. "We're fine to leave now."

They made their way back out into the sunshine. It wasn't far to the market; the taverna was just off the main square. "It's busy in here," Diego said, his voice firm. "Max, you need to take my hand, and Emilia, you take Miss Rose's. We don't want anyone getting separated, do we?"

Emilia slipped her hand into Rose's, then looked up and smiled. Rose smiled back, feeling her heart catch. Emilia was so trusting. Since the first day when she'd taken Rose through the gardens, she'd abandoned her resentful attitude. She'd been hurt, but Rose could see she simply wanted love and affection. Well, Rose had both of those in abundance. She squeezed Emilia's hand lightly, reassuring her.

Max, on the other hand, was tugging at Diego's arm. In no time flat he'd pulled them over to a clothing vendor where football shirts were for sale.

"How does he do that?" Rose leaned over and spoke in Diego's ear, quite loudly to be heard over the shopping bustle. "He's only three feet tall!"

"We've been here a time or two. He has a good memory, I guess." Already Max was pointing at a red and black jersey that was about six sizes too big.

The vendor clearly remembered them, too. "Ah, Your Highness," he said, bowing quickly. "And the young Prince Max. How may I help you today?"

They dithered over shirts, and Rose hid a smile as Max, in all his four-year-old authority, haggled with the vendor while having no idea about the numbers he was saying. But the vendor went along with him, frowning and thoughtfully bargaining until he threw up his hands at an agreed price. Diego took bills out of his wallet, and Rose noticed that it was for the original price listed on the sign. Diego winked at the vendor, took the shirt, and grinned widely as Max shook the vendor's hand at a bargain well struck.

Since they were at the clothing stalls, Emilia found a pretty skirt and then a little purse among the leather goods, as fine as Rose had ever seen. Rose looked longingly at a soft-as-butter handbag, but decided not to spend the money today. There would be other days. Today was for the children to enjoy.

But then there was a stall with the most stunning silver jewelry. Accented with gemstones and mother-of-pearl, the display glittered and she couldn't stop herself from going to look.

"Oh, this is gorgeous," she said, sparing a glance at Emilia. "Don't you think?"

Emilia nodded, and pointed at a particularly lovely bracelet. It was about half an inch wide, solid silver with little pale pink stones inlaid in a pretty leaf pattern. "How much?" Rose asked.

The vendor named a number of Euros that made Rose blink. "Oh."

Emilia, who'd been rather quiet during the purchase of her skirt, stepped up to the stall table. "No no no no no," she said, making it sound like all one word. She let go of Rose's hand and wagged a finger at him, and then let loose with a flurry of Spanish that had Rose gaping.

The vendor stood back, raised his eyebrows, and then to Rose's surprise, came back with what she thought was another offer. And back and forth they went, while Rose felt both abashed and fiercely proud that the girl was holding her own. Thank goodness the vendor didn't know who he was haggling with.

Emilia looked up at Rose with triumph in her dark eyes, and gave the vendor's final offer. There was no way Rose could turn it down now, not after all of Emilia's hard work. She began to reach for her pocketbook when a large hand came to rest on her shoulder.

"Allow me," Diego said, reaching for his wallet once again.

The look on the vendor's face was utterly priceless. Shock, embarrassment, confusion… Diego handed over the negotiated amount and the vendor handed her the bracelet. Then he plucked a small pair of earrings from the display and handed them to Emilia. He said something to her and she smiled and thanked him. Rose looked at Diego, and his face was full of pride.

Max was getting tired, so they only went a few steps from the vendor and then Diego hefted the boy on to his shoulders. "What did that man say to Emilia?" she asked, back to holding Emilia's hand again.

"He said she drove a hard bargain and she was going to make a great queen someday."

"Oh, that's lovely."

"I think so, too."

"You could have knocked him over with a feather when he realized who we were."

Diego laughed. "It's nice that he didn't at first. And by the way, you have great taste. The bracelet is beautiful."

"Em picked it out. And thank you for buying it for me."

"It's my pleasure. The children are very happy with you, Rose. It means a lot to know that."

She smiled up at him, and he smiled back.

They made a stop for a small ice cream, at Max's request. When they were done, they began making their way to the car. Rose had gotten accustomed to seeing their security now, and felt both secure and strange about being watched so closely. A little girl started straight toward them, and one of the guards stepped forward, but Diego shook his head. The girl couldn't be more than seven or eight, just a little older than Emilia. She carried a basket with red carnations.

Diego waved off the security.

When the girl was within a few feet, he squatted down so he was closer to her height. "*Hola, Chiquita.*"

She curtsied and then stood and greeted him in

return. Rose could barely hear what they said, but she caught him asking the girl's name. She missed the reply, but Diego immediately introduced Max and Emilia. The darling curtsied to both. Lord, she was adorable.

But it went beyond adorable into heartstrings territory when she took out two carnations and gave one to each of the children. She said something in Spanish—again, Rose was frustrated at not being fluent enough to keep up. Emilia answered back, and Max's face was dead-sober. They spoke for another few moments, and she did catch Emilia saying "Thank you very much."

Rose looked at Diego, questioning. But any words she might have said died on her lips. His eyes were full of tears. He looked away and cleared his throat, then turned back with a smile.

"Well, here we are, nearly to the car. What a day! Did everyone have fun?"

The children nodded, but their earlier exuberance was gone. Rose was perplexed.

Max fell asleep on the drive home, his carnation clutched in his hand. Emilia was exhausted as well, so she decided to spend the remainder of the afternoon on her bed with a pile of storybooks. Rose gave it fifteen, maybe twenty minutes before Emilia would snuggle down with one of her stuffed animals and be asleep, too.

Diego had helped her with the children, carrying Max upstairs, so she went to the little kitchenette in the suite that she used for snacks and tea time and heated a kettle for making coffee. "Would you like one?"

He shrugged. "I'd prefer a glass of wine."

She laughed. "None here, I'm afraid. I'm on duty."

"Right. Well, coffee will do."

She was fairly handy with the press and before long the fresh brew was in cups and she added her customary milk and sugar. Diego frowned. "Really? It's not even coffee after you do that."

She took a sip and smacked her lips, mocking, and finally coaxed a smile from him.

They sat down on the sofa, at either end as was appropriate. Rose let out a long breath, starting to wind down from the busy day. "So," she said quietly, "do you want to tell me what happened with the carnations?" The flowers were now trimmed and in a tiny vase one of the maids had brought up, and were sitting on the table where the children did their lessons.

"She was sweet, wasn't she?"

"I couldn't follow the conversation. It was too fast and there were too many other voices around."

He took a drink of his coffee before replying. "She gave each of them a flower, and said that she and her mother were very sorry about their mother. That was all. Just an expression of sympathy. But it was…I don't know. She was a stranger but it meant something to them, couldn't you tell?"

"Maybe because it was from someone their own age," Rose suggested. "Or because adults tend to give each other platitudes and don't know what to say to children."

"Sometimes I wonder if it's better to not bring it up." Diego slumped into the cushions. "It always upsets them."

Rose could understand his feelings, but she shook

her head. "Maybe, but if I were a child who'd lost a parent, I'd want to feel free to talk about them. So they wouldn't be forgotten. Expressing grief is important. Feeling like you can have happy memories without upsetting other people helps, too."

"How do you know so much?" he asked. She looked over at him and tried to stay detached, not get caught in his gaze. He was so completely open. It was a surprise, considering what she'd thought she knew of him.

"It's not from personal experience," she replied. "I just…I don't know. I've always tried to put myself in other people's shoes and empathize with them. How would I feel in their situation? It's served me well at times, but it can be a bit burdensome."

"I don't understand."

She swallowed against a lump forming in her throat. "When you put yourself in the position of someone else, even if it's just imagined, you take on their feelings, too. And their pain. And you'd do anything to make it better."

She looked down into her coffee cup and blinked. She'd never really admitted that to anyone before. Apparently they both tended to let down their guard with each other. And that tendency to want to fix things was the very reason why her relationship with her sister was strained. She helped, but she hadn't given Hayley what she'd really wanted. Rose had put her foot down and Hayley saw that as tantamount to a betrayal.

"I've always been an ostrich," Diego admitted. "I pretend it's not happening. I go on another trip or visit friends or whatever."

"Why, do you suppose?"

He thought for several seconds. "I suppose because someone's always looked after things for me so I haven't had to deal with them at all."

"Like when your mother died?"

Silence settled over the room, intimate and slightly uncomfortable. "Wow," he whispered.

"You're so attentive to the kids. Is it because you want to help them through what you already went through?"

"Of course it is." His voice was sharp and his brow furrowed. She'd struck a nerve.

"But Diego, you can't go through their grief for them. You should know that, especially if someone did that for you. Were you allowed to grieve for your mum?"

He looked away. "Damn, Rose…"

She put down her coffee and slid over on the sofa. It was probably not the best idea, but he was in pain. She could sense it and knew she should stop questioning him. He was a prince, for heaven's sake. And right now as much her boss as Raoul. But she slid over anyway. "You know what they're going through. And I think you're going through it again, maybe finally dealing with what you had to shutter away when you were little. I'm sorry, Diego. I'm sorry about Cecilia, Mariana, and I'm sorry about your mum. It's okay for you to feel loss too, you know."

His throat bobbed as he swallowed. He put his cup down too and put his hands on his knees. Rose simply waited. It had been a bold suggestion on her part. Very possibly treading into insubordinate territory. For some reason they were becoming friends, even though they shouldn't.

"I get frustrated," he admitted finally. "I was so small I couldn't see what Raoul and Father were doing. I know they were trying to protect me, but I ended up so spoiled. So…unequipped to deal with stuff. It got better when I went to England to study, you know. My best friend decked me my first day at polo club and it was something I needed desperately. Never upset an Irishman who's bigger than you."

She chuckled. She could picture it.

"Then I came back and I wanted to roll up my sleeves and help and I just…wasn't needed. I know what they say about me. I know what Raoul and Father think, but they don't help me change it. So I look after the stables and I run charities."

"Those are important things."

"I know they are. But put me anywhere near state business? I'm kept strictly hands off. They have no idea how capable I am, because they don't want to see it. Anytime I try to talk to them about it…"

He ran his hand through his hair. "It's like they just give me another toy. Send me on another public appearance. The same way they did anytime I asked about Mother or cried."

He looked over at her. "Okay, this is getting out of hand. I must sound like an idiot. Forget it."

She put her hand on his knee. "They tried to distract you," she said, "so they wouldn't have to deal with your grief, and theirs too. And you got cheated."

Diego laid his hand over hers. "I'm a prince. How can I possibly be cheated out of anything?"

"Because you're human, first and foremost. Maybe being a prince makes it even harder. Different rules apply."

She would not turn her hand over. She would not link her fingers with his, no matter how badly she wanted to.

But his thumb rubbed along the side of her hand, sending delicious tremors through her stomach. She needed to set boundaries like she had that night in the garden. She needed to remember that she was the nanny. They were not equals…

Except she'd just put them on a level playing field with her last sentence. They were both human, with feelings and needs and…

"Why," he murmured, "do I find it so easy to open up to you?"

"I don't know," she whispered back. "We shouldn't. It's not proper…"

"I have never been, nor am I likely ever to be, proper," he answered, and he did what she could not. He turned her hand over and twined his fingers with hers.

The tremors became full-on quaking as the tension shimmered between them. He was looking at her now, and she couldn't look away from the intensity in his eyes. She caught her lip in her teeth as her nervousness peaked, and his gaze dropped to her mouth.

Oh, she thought to herself. *Oh please. Don't… but please do.*

"Rosalie," he whispered, her full name sounding like music on his lips.

He leaned closer; she drifted in, unable to stop herself. *Just once*, she thought. *Just one kiss. Just so I know what it's like.*

His lips were warm, soft, beguiling. Rose's heart slammed against her ribs at the first contact, her breath squeezed in her lungs as she kissed him back, lightly, softly. As kisses went it was tentative, shy, sweet. And utterly, utterly devastating. Not what she would have expected from a playboy like Diego Navarro. It was better. Much, much better.

He shifted on the sofa, still holding her hand but moving closer. The kiss deepened, too, as anticipation waned and excitement took over. Gentle persuasion had her opening her lips and the kiss blossomed until their breath came faster and Rose's whole body felt sensitive to the smallest touch and sound.

"Rose," he whispered, kissing the corner of her mouth. "You're so sweet. So…"

He never finished the sentence. Their mouths fused again, more urgent now, and when his hand pressed to the back of her head, controlling and guiding, she acquiesced. At this moment, the world didn't exist outside this room.

Their lips parted, somewhat reluctantly, Rose thought, her heart still pounding. Diego moved his hand from her hair to her face, tracing his fingers down her cheek.

He was Diego Navarro, she realized, still dazed but aware enough to know that what had just happened was surreal at best and both unadvised and potentially jeopardizing to her employment.

He was a world-class playboy with loads of experience. She was a British nanny who'd had exactly one lover.

God, she was so outmatched.

"I'm sorry," she said softly. "That shouldn't have happened. We just… I just… got caught up in the emotion of the moment." She slid out of his embrace. She'd been in his arms, her mind shouted at her. Kissing him. Hearing him say her name…

"Don't back away," he replied, grabbing at her hand before she could get away. "Please. You're the only one who has ever understood. And don't point out our differences," he said, halting her contradiction before it even got out of her mouth.

"You have to know we can't do this," she said, slightly breathless. They absolutely couldn't. If she lost this job…if they ended up in the tabloids or something she'd never be hired again, and people depended on her for so much. "If anyone found out…"

"I know. It's a mess." He went from running his hand over his hair to rubbing his face. "Why couldn't you have been an heiress or aristocracy or something?"

She laughed a little. "Well, you can trace ancestors on my mum's side back as far as King Charles II. Of course, that doesn't say much for legitimacy…"

He rolled his eyes. "I know this is hard for you. And I don't want to make it more difficult. I really don't. And yet… being with you right now is the only thing that really makes sense. You see me, Rose."

But he didn't see *her*. Not really. He didn't understand what drove her, what her fears were, what her longings were. He was, she realized, focused on the children's needs, and focused on his own. But not hers. And it wasn't that he was wrong in those priorities. It just gave her a dollop of perspective and the realization that she had to protect herself as well.

"We can be friends," she said firmly. "I think we've gone beyond the 'strictly business' distinction, despite my best efforts. But no more kissing, Diego. I can't. Please don't put me in that position." No matter how desperately she'd like to be in that position—and more —with him. She couldn't be that selfish. "This can't be a palace affair." She emphasized it with the one point she knew would hit home. "I can't lose this job. Emilia and Max need stability and consistency."

"I wouldn't let that happen."

"Raoul has the final say in their care, Diego. You wouldn't be able to stop it."

He frowned. "I hate it when you're right. And I hate it even more when it goes against what I want."

She laughed. "That's because you're used to getting your own way. In some things, anyway," she added, in deference to his earlier confidence.

"I'm not sorry," he said, reaching over and squeezing her hand. "Not for the talk and not for the kiss."

"Me either," she admitted, though she knew she probably shouldn't.

Emilia came out of the bedroom, stretching and

yawning loudly enough that Diego immediately dropped Rose's hand.

"Tio Diego?"

"Si, Emilia?"

She came over and crawled up on his lap. She looked at Rose, then back at her uncle. "The girl today," she said, choosing English. "She was very nice. No one mentions Mama or Mariana. Sometimes I want to talk about them."

Diego met Rose's gaze and she smiled back at him. She was glad they'd talked. Maybe now he was better equipped to talk to Emilia about this. The distraction of the trip to the city was over, and real conversations had to happen.

"I miss them too, Chiquita," he answered, snuggling her close.

"Papa won't talk about Mama. But I don't want to forget about her. She…" Emilia's lip quivered and she started to cry a little.

"You will never forget her," Diego assured her. "Your Papa misses her a lot too. It hurts him to talk about her, but it won't always. And you can talk to me or Miss Rose whenever you like."

"But you always go away," she answered, picking at a fingernail and sniffling.

"Not now," he said firmly. "I'm doing everything I need to from here, so I can spend more time with you and Max."

"Really?"

"Yes, really."

She hesitated for a moment, as if deliberating if she

should speak or not. When she did, it was in Spanish, and Rose picked out Mariana's name, and her own, and *"amo"* – the Spanish word for love.

Whatever she'd said, Diego kissed the top of her head and smiled as he answered her back. To Rose's surprise, Emilia crawled off Diego's lap and stepped over to Rose and hugged her.

"*Gracias*, Emilia," Rose said, squeezing her in return.

"May I watch a movie?" Emilia asked, and Rose agreed.

"Tea will be here soon, too."

Emilia found a movie and, in the way of all young children, knew how to turn everything on and set it up to stream. Diego stood up, preparing to leave, and Max came tottering out of the bedroom at the sound of the movie.

"You don't want to stay for tea?" Rose asked Diego, following him to the door.

"I've got work to do tonight. I've had to start delegating with some of the charity duties. I can't put off travel indefinitely, but for now I'm managing."

Rose paused with her hand on the doorknob. "Do they know how hard you work? Or do they think you just play?"

He raised an eyebrow and grinned, and she knew the answer. Diego the playboy. She felt annoyed on his behalf, but this wasn't her battle to fight.

"Thank you for today. We all needed it. It was a lot of fun."

"Well, if there's one thing I know how to do it's have fun. Ask anybody."

"Diego," she chided softly.

She was gazing into his eyes again when a maid came down the hall bearing the tea tray. Rose backed off and Diego bid her a far more formal goodbye than he normally would. So he was worried about appearances, too, she thought.

Tea was served, and Rose sat on the sofa with two very mellow children, one on either side of her.

But what she was thinking about was the feel of Diego's lips on hers, his fingers on her face, and how it was completely impossible.

Any hope of not being in the news was demolished by six a.m. the next morning, when the paper was delivered to the palace offices as well as households and news outlets throughout Marazur.

Rose got a copy every day, using it to help reacquaint herself with the language. It was all in Spanish, but her stomach dropped to her feet and she didn't need a translator to explain the half-page photo of her, Diego, and the children that was splashed on the front page.

It had been taken when they were shopping in the market. Max was on Diego's shoulders, and Emilia held Rose's hand. To an outsider, they looked like a normal family doing some shopping, but there was nothing "normal" about it. They appeared far too familiar with each other. Maybe if she hadn't been smiling up at them it would have been dismissed more easily. But she doubted it. An appearance of the playboy prince was news. So was an appearance of the children. And her?

She scanned the words below the picture. Even in her limited Spanish, she knew that it had gone beyond news into speculation territory. Perhaps even scandal. Something about a young and pretty nanny, and Diego's reputation.

Thank God no one knew about that stupid kiss. The press would have had a field day with that sort of photo!

She reached for her coffee, appreciating the strong brew this morning. The children were chatting at the table, munching on fruit and pastries, oblivious to the turmoil now swirling through her. Raoul would see this. It might even go beyond Marazur... damn, damn, damn! This job wouldn't last forever, would it? And if she strayed from her official job description, it could hurt her future at the agency.

A knock at the door jerked her out of her thoughts and she dropped the paper on a chair and went to the door.

To her surprise, it was Raoul. On the few times he'd stopped by the nursery, he'd given a cursory knock and then come in with a "hello." Her stomach plummeted. Did his serious face have something to do with today's headline?

"Your Highness." She managed to get the proper address out of her mouth without stuttering.

"Miss Walters." He smiled, but she thought it looked rather grim.

"Please, come in. The children will be so happy to see you." She stood aside to let him pass.

"Papa!" Max scrambled down from the table first and came running. A little of the strain left Raoul's face as he knelt down and scooped the boy into his arms. Emilia, on the other hand, got up, put her napkin on her chair, and came over quietly. Rose frowned. Manners were one thing, but Emilia struggled so hard to be proper these days that she didn't smile very much. The most Rose had seen was yesterday at the market stall when she'd been haggling with the vendor.

Raoul spent a few minutes with the children and then told them to return to their breakfast. Once they'd gone back to the table, he looked down at Rose. He wasn't angry, she realized, with more than a little relief.

"You've seen the papers this morning?" he asked.

"Yes, Your Highness."

He nodded. "It's written all over your face. You look terrified. You're not in trouble, Miss Walters."

Miss Walters. He always called her that, as opposed to Diego, who only called her by her first name.

"I'm sorry that the children are in the paper, sir," she apologized. She was sorry for far more, but she was a grown-up. The children were innocent.

"They've been in the paper before," he said, shrugging. "When we're out in public, we expect the press will follow. It's how it is. But my late wife believed in taking them places and doing things with them." There was an edge of pain to his words. One such outing was the reason they'd been in the limousine that fateful night.

He picked up the paper from the chair and looked at it. "The children look happy," he remarked, then pinned his gaze on her. She had such a hard time reading his expressions, unlike his brother who seemed quite easy to figure out. "So does my brother."

She willed herself not to blush—or break eye contact.

"He has been spending a lot of time with the children. He loves them and they love him. You did know of the excursion yesterday?"

"Of course. Diego cleared it with me. And I made sure you had adequate security. These things happen. Particularly when Diego is involved." He shrugged. "He is a darling of the paparazzi."

She fought back the instinct to stick up for Diego. It really wasn't her place. But after yesterday, she was beginning to realize that Diego was often in that visible position because his family had put him there and didn't expect anything different.

"I wanted to be sure you were okay. I don't suppose you're used to handling publicity of this sort."

She wasn't, but now that she knew he wasn't angry, she was feeling slightly better, at least on the professional front. "I will be fine," she assured him.

He turned to leave. "Did you want to stay and spend some time with the children?" she asked, startled he was going so soon. He'd barely been around at all lately.

"I have a meeting in ten minutes. I will stop by later, though. Perhaps around tea time. I'll have Stephani check my schedule." He went into the room though and made sure to kiss the children and wish them a good day.

After he was gone Rose picked up the paper and stared at Diego, holding Max on his shoulders. It should be Raoul, she thought, with a little bit of bitterness and indignation. The fact that Diego saw the need and stepped in only made him more attractive in her eyes. A man who took on his own responsibilities and some that weren't his to bear. That his own family couldn't see his value had to be frustrating. Not that he ever showed it.

If the tabloids were to be believed, Diego Navarro was a man who didn't understand the meaning of the word "responsibility." But the papers were very wrong. He knew responsibility as well as several others, like loyalty, compassion, and family.

In the photo she was looking up at him and smiling. She could understand how it might be construed as something personal, because it was.

She liked him. She more than liked him. And that was starting to become a very real problem.

CHAPTER 7

Rose spent the day keeping to the regular schedule of meals, lessons, playtime, and naptime. When their tea arrived, she discovered a pot of blissfully hot English brew and a slice of orange cake for herself, and then the regular light snack for the children. Not one of the staff had mentioned the newspaper, but Rose had noticed a few sidelong glances and looks of sympathy sent her way. She assumed it was because she'd suddenly turned from nanny to a subject of romantic speculation. To anyone on the "outside" it probably seemed romantic and dreamy. But the reality was that any dalliance could ultimately get her fired. And even if it didn't, it could affect her credibility and ability to get work.

The cake tasted like comfort and solace. She wondered if Señora Ortiz had sent it as a pick-me-up. Or perhaps Diego had suggested it, as a peace offering of sorts. But how would she know? He'd also been conspicuously absent today, not stopping by even once, though he normally spent a part of his afternoon with the children and… well, and with her.

She frowned. That shouldn't matter in the least. So what if they'd become friends of a sort? It was only because of the children. And there was certainly no future in it. She'd do best to keep her feet firmly on the ground and her head out of the clouds. When Diego wasn't around, she could see things in a much clearer light. Blurring professional and personal lines was a big mistake, and one she needed to rectify right away.

Teatime came and went and no sign of Raoul, either. Rose seethed inside as she got the children ready for dinner. Granted, he hadn't actually promised to see them before dinner, but he'd still said he'd try. At this rate the only time they saw their father, or indeed their grandfather, was at the evening meal. That was not parenting. She'd seen it before on other jobs, and it had never sat quite right with her. Why have children if you were going to put them in a corner and pretend they didn't exist? Maybe her family had its fair share of dysfunction, but they at least knew each other and had memories to share over the contentious Christmas table each year.

She put a last touch on the bow of Emilia's dress, combed down a stubborn piece of Max's dark hair, and took their hands as she dutifully delivered them to the dining room.

Diego was in the salon off the dining room and stood as they approached. "Don't you look lovely," he said with a smile, "Emilia."

Rose's chest deflated. She should not have assumed

the compliment was for her. She'd chosen a plain black pencil skirt for today, but her customary white blouse was fitted and had a ruffle from collar to waist that she thought was exceedingly pretty. Of course he was talking to Emilia, who was quite cute in her flowered dress and delicate shoes. Besides, a compliment would be very inappropriate. Particularly today.

He stepped closer to Rose and smiled. "How was your day?"

She shrugged and offered a polite smile in return. "Fine, sir. The paper had some interesting reading."

She wasn't sure if the look of consternation was brought on by her use of "sir" or if it was the mention of the story in the paper. Diego's brows pulled together and his lips thinned. "I should have warned you. Pictures tend to happen."

"I particularly liked the part about me being the new palace plaything," she replied smoothly, watching Max and Emilia wander to the dining room door and peek inside. She'd taken some time later in the day to sit down with the article and work through anything that she didn't understand right away. *Palace Plaything* had definitely stood out.

"You're not a plaything."

She looked up at him. "But the women you're usually photographed with are, you see? I should have realized that it was a bad idea to go with you. I have my own reputation to worry about. The terms of my employment require me to be above reproach."

"And you are. We were," he insisted.

"Perception counts," she replied coolly. "I like you,

Diego, and I had fun. But I was right in the first place. I'm staff, you're royalty, and never the twain shall meet."

He frowned. "I'm not familiar with that expression."

Her throat tightened. "It means we each know our place."

Dinner was called and she straightened her shoulders. "And now you are called to dinner and I'll make my way down to the kitchen. Good night, sir."

"Good night," he echoed, but she felt his gaze on her back as she left the room and headed toward the stairs and the kitchen below. She'd drawn the invisible line, and it hadn't been that difficult.

Not putting a toe across it would be more of a challenge. The papers called him irresistible. She was just glad he still hadn't put together their previous, rather inauspicious meeting on the train. For him, a handful of pounds to pay for a few baskets of flowers was nothing. But it had been a very big something for her. And right now she certainly didn't need another reason to feel connected to him.

Diego sat through dinner wishing he could be anywhere else. While he appreciated Raoul's attempt to keep the children to a regular routine—Ceci had always insisted the children join them for the evening meal—it was depressing and colorless for Emilia and Max. He could see it on their faces. They picked at their food, and Diego saw Max swinging his legs beneath the table in absolute boredom. Ceci had always asked them about their day, and Raoul usually joined in. Now they ate, the men conversed a little, usually about state business, and then the children went back to the nursery.

His heart hurt. He remembered it being much the same for him and Raoul after Mother died. Mama Mariana had been their saving grace.

Just like Rose was now. And what he'd wanted to be a fun, pleasant outing had earned her the label of…what was it she said? Palace Plaything.

Ugh. No wonder she'd been cold with him. Even her speech in the salon earlier had been uptight and annoyingly proper, just like that first night by the fountain.

She was no plaything. She was a godsend to the children and a spark of life in a dreary household.

He looked over at his brother, at his father. They were discussing some upcoming function and dinner that the palace was hosting and paying very little attention to Emilia and Max. Indeed, Diego was the only one to notice that Max was stabbing his potato terrine over and over and over again, a look of supreme boredom on his face.

"Max," he said quietly, "don't play with your food."

Max looked up and Diego was startled to see tears in the boy's eyes. "What's the matter?"

"Nothing." Max blinked a few times and one tear slid over his little cheek. He wiped it away, sat up straight, and dipped his fork into his potatoes, taking a defiant bite.

Still Raoul didn't see.

Five minutes later, when their main course was taken away, Diego motioned for their footman and gave him a quick instruction. Then he smiled at Emilia and Max.

"The two of you are excused. You can have your dessert upstairs. One of the maids is going to deliver it to you."

The look of utter relief nearly made him laugh. Raoul and Alexander stopped talking long enough to stare in surprise, but Diego didn't care. He was going to say something and make them listen.

The children placed their napkins on the table and beat it for the door. While Rose was technically supposed to come to get them, they knew their way back upstairs.

"They have not had their dessert," Raoul said, staring at Diego. "We eat as a family. Ceci—"

"Ceci is not here," Diego replied, his heart pounding with apprehension. This was not a welcome topic, and he was likely to get slapped down for it. But it was important. "And sitting at this table and being miserable is not eating as a family."

Alexander cleared his throat. "Diego," he cautioned.

"No, *Padré*." Determined, he carried on. "In the offices you are Your Highnesses. Here at the table you are Padré or Abuelo. Those two little children are miserable. You didn't even notice that Max was on the verge of tears. They miss Ceci. They miss Mariana. And I understand the importance of duty and the hours you must work, but Raoul, you need to spend time with your children."

Raoul's eyebrows had lifted and his eyes lit with indignation. "Do you, Diego? Do you know the hours I must work?"

Diego had put up with being the younger son for many years, and he'd stayed quiet about his feelings. But not tonight. For a few months now he'd picked up the slack without anyone noticing or caring. "You don't think I put in work, too? Maybe it's not 'state' business but I've been running the stables and breeding program ever since Lucy married Brody. I sit on the board of several charities that are near and dear to my heart. And in the last month, with few exceptions, I've taken hours out of every day to kick around a soccer ball with Max or have tea with them both or watch a movie with Emilia."

"They have their nanny…"

"And she is not family." It pained him to say it, but he needed to get his point across. "Rose is a wonderful nanny, and thank God they have her. Otherwise they'd be totally alone."

He softened his voice. "Raoul, I know you're grieving. I can't imagine how painful it is. But your children need you. They have anything a child could want except for your time and your love. Don't deny them that."

Raoul's face paled.

"Yesterday, I took the three of them on an outing. We had a wonderful time. Did you know Emilia is a first-class negotiator? You should have seen her bargaining at one of the market stalls. We had lunch in a taverna. And we got our picture taken. As a result, your very proper British nanny got her picture in the paper and suffered a blow to her reputation because she was there with me and not you."

"It's not my fault you have a reputation of being a…playboy."

Diego picked up his wine glass, his fingers tightening

around the bowl, but he kept his voice smooth. "There are times that my reputation serves you very well, *hermano*. Remember that."

Alexander leaned forward. "Diego, enough."

But neither of them denied it. Diego put a human face on what could be construed as a stuffy, outdated institution. He also was a perfect distraction. While he'd been traveling, the press had followed him around, leaving the royal family in relative peace, to grieve. It hadn't been by accident.

"You're the crown prince," he finished softly, not wanting to cause further tension. "But Ceci brought out other wonderful qualities in you. She made you a better man. A husband and a father. Don't lose those qualities now, Raoul. That's all I'm asking."

Raoul nodded. "I'll clear my schedule for a few hours tomorrow. Maybe have lunch outside in the garden."

"That's all it takes," Diego agreed. "Now, if you'll excuse me, I'll go apologize to Rose for this awful position she's in."

He pushed out his chair and put his napkin on the table, leaving his tart untasted.

But before he went to see her, he went back to his rooms and changed out of his trousers and tie and put on a pair of jeans and a light cotton shirt, leaving the top two buttons undone. The evening was warm and he'd had enough of feeling stuffy today. His videoconference meeting had demanded a polished appearance, so he'd been in a suit since ten.

He wanted to talk to her alone, without the children

around. Emilia and Max tended to have big ears, and they had enough to deal with without trying to sort out adult problems.

He waited until half-past nine and then knocked on her door—hers, not the one to the nursery. She opened it half way.

"May I come in?"

She sighed. A big, heavy sigh. "I know," he added. "Boundaries and all that stuff. I won't order you to let me in. I just want to talk for a few minutes."

She opened it the rest of the way, and stepped back so he could enter.

Diego had always liked this room. It was less ostentatious than the family suites, and much smaller, and Mariana had always kept little keepsakes around. It was decorated differently now, though. He was shocked to realize that it had been redecorated since Mariana's death. Was there to be no trace of the maternal figures of this family left at all?

"You look surprised," she said quietly. "Surely you've been in the nanny's room before."

"It's been redecorated," he said roughly. "But this suits you." The green and pink decor was pretty, steady, calm. Just like her. He swallowed and let his gaze sweep over her. She, too, had changed. Instead of her official-looking pencil skirt and blouse, she wore soft flowy pants and a light pullover shirt. Her feet were bare and her toes were a dainty shade of pink.

When she wasn't in black and white, she did seem to love her pastels.

"What can I do for you, Diego? I just got the children to sleep."

He noticed a glass of wine on an end table, barely tasted. "I need to apologize. For the position I put you in and for not stopping by today. I had an unexpected conference call that I couldn't reschedule." Indeed, he was probably going to have to book some travel to Tanzania soon to oversee the implementation of a new program, which had hit an administrative snag.

Rose sighed. "I'm sorry too, for being so short with you earlier. It was more Raoul I was frustrated with, and myself." Her cheeks colored prettily. "I mean, Prince Raoul…"

He waved a hand, dismissing her consternation. "It's fine. I had a few words with him at dinner, too. Is Max okay? He seemed upset."

When Rose sighed again, he realized how tired she sounded.

"He was crying when he arrived back from dinner," she admitted. "Emilia was on the verge herself. I finally got it out of them that they miss their mother and also Mariana. Emilia is only a few years older, but she did say something I haven't been able to dismiss. That no one talks about her mother and that it seems as if she never existed."

Diego's heart hurt. "It's so hard to know," he murmured, putting his hands in his pockets. "If reminders are helpful or make things worse."

"I think right now they'd be helpful. At least in moderation. I think they'd like to talk about their mother without worrying about upsetting their father."

"Who isn't around much anyway," Diego added.

She nodded. "I don't want to overstep."

"You're not. God, you're not. I don't know what they'd do without you, Rose." He stepped closer to her. "Which is why I need to apologize for yesterday. I knew there would be photographers and I ignored it because I wanted to…" This was the tricky part. "I wanted to spend the day with you. Show you what our city has to offer. Instead I just opened things up to speculation and gossip."

Rose went to the table and retrieved her wine, then turned back. "You might as well come in and sit down." She gestured to the sofa in the sitting area of the suite. He tried to ignore the fact that a very plush bed was behind her. This was the whole problem. It wasn't just that she was good for the children or he liked her. There was attraction there, too.

She poured another glass of wine and handed it to him. "Thank you," he said quietly, and sat down on the far side of the sofa.

She took the chair next to him. "I did have a good time," she admitted, turning the glass in her fingers. "And so did the children. But we can't keep blurring the line. I like you, Diego." She looked up at him briefly, but looked away again. He wondered why she was avoiding eye contact. Was she lying? Or simply trying to avoid too much of a connection?

"I like you too much," she continued. "And when this job is over, I'm going to need another. No one wants to hire a nanny who's been *involved* with the family."

"But we haven't been involved," he protested, even

though he knew in his heart that was a lie. Nothing had been completely platonic between them. Not since that first night.

"What's true doesn't matter. Having us linked in the tabloids would be enough to guarantee I don't get work again. And I…" She looked away and took a drink of wine. "I have my own responsibilities."

It was an odd thing for her to say. Not on the surface, but paired with her body language, he got the feeling she was keeping a secret from him. Or at least, she thought she was. There really wasn't much about her life he didn't know about. Vetting had been thorough. She would do anything for her family, same as he would. It was a trait he admired.

"Rose," he said softly, "this job…the children need stability, and they already love you. It's a secure position until they are much, much older. Please don't worry about your employability."

Then he took a deep drink from his glass, because he realized that what he said was absolutely true, and the idea of having her here, in the palace, potentially for years, and being off-limits was a sobering and uncomfortable thought.

He couldn't do it. But he couldn't leave now, not when things were still so unstable within the family. Maybe his father and brother didn't see it, but for Diego it had always been family first. Even if he really wanted to strike out on his own, he wouldn't until he was sure things were okay here in Marazur.

Silence was thick between them, until Rose put down her glass and folded her hands in her lap, incredibly proper and every inch a British lady. Humble upbringing be damned, the woman had poise and presence.

"Was there something else you wanted to say?" she asked.

He downed the rest of the wine. "I spoke to my brother tonight after I excused the children. You are a wonderful nanny, Rose, but they also need their father. The atmosphere in the house is so different since Ceci died. Raoul doesn't laugh anymore or include them. He promised to make some time in his schedule tomorrow to be with them."

Relief crossed her face. "Oh, thank you. I mentioned it this morning and he said he was going to try, and then neither of you put in an appearance. That's why I was so short with you earlier. Well, that and the obvious."

"They really were upset, then."

"Max only ate half his tart before he started crying for his mother. Emilia got mad and snapped at him, but I think it was because she was also upset and if he kept it up, she was going to cry as well."

It was so unfair. "What did you do?" Diego asked.

"I wiped tears, calmed everyone down, got them in their pajamas, and we sat on Max's bed and read stories. It took a long time, but I finally got them both settled."

She looked up at him, her bluebell eyes wide. "And then I had a little cry myself, and poured a glass of wine."

"You care for them."

"Of course I do. I hate seeing them hurting. I love them."

And just like that, Diego knew he was in trouble. She'd said it so quickly, without thinking, that he knew it was true. Rosalie Walters with her sometimes prim ways, warm smile, and big heart, was sneaking past all his defenses. He loved it and hated it all at once. In this family, marriage meant loss. The king had lost his wife and Diego had lost his mother. Then his sister-in-law, and Mariana, too. He'd rather keep his heart safe and sound than go through that again. It would be ten times worse to lose the woman he loved.

And yet there was something wonderful about looking at Rose and feeling *seen*. Recognized. Appreciated.

"I should go," he said, standing and putting his empty glass on the table.

"Yes," she said softly, "you should. After today's newspaper, it wouldn't do for you to be caught coming out of my room late at night."

"The staff is discreet."

"They're also human, and I have to work among them."

"Right."

She walked him to the door, put her hand on the knob. Such small, delicate fingers, he noticed. And such a strong, caring woman.

He put his hand over hers. "Rosalie…"

He didn't know why he'd used her full name. She looked up at him, surprised, their hands still clasping the doorknob. He knew she couldn't possibly be aware of it, but her tongue snuck out to wet her lips and his gaze dropped and clung to her mouth. His head kept a steady chant of "It's a mistake," but instead he reached out with his free hand and pulled her close against his body.

He heard her sharp intake of breath, and then he dipped his head and kissed her, shutting out the voice in his head.

CHAPTER 8

Rose's head swam with the sensations coursing through her body— his hand, splayed against the small of her back, holding her tight against his hips; the breadth of his chest beneath her palm as she put a hand up for balance, and the hard, muscled wall her fingertips encountered through his thin cotton shirt. And oh, his taste, rich and dark and fruity like the wine they'd just drunk. His lips moved over hers, beguiling, seducing, sweeping her away into a fantasy such as she'd never encountered in her life.

She was in a palace and she was kissing a prince. A real prince, and for the second time in two days. And while she prided herself on her common sense, another part of her wasn't ready for it to be over yet. Because once it was it couldn't happen again and if this was all she could have she was going to let it be a moment to remember.

She expected him to end the kiss, but he didn't. Instead he seemed to settle into it, enjoying her mouth, adjusting his embrace until she melted into him. Briefly his lips left hers and he dropped kisses at the corner of her mouth, along her jaw, while his fingers traced a sensitive part of her neck. She gasped at the light touch, feeling rather unravelled as he kissed her again, deeper now. As if he were enjoying himself immensely. As if he liked kissing her. Her. A mousy little middle child from Guildford.

She found herself pressed against the door to her suite, sandwiched between the hard wood and Diego's body. He put his hands flat against the door, one on either side of her head, and kissed her in a way no man had ever kissed her before. Like she was the last bit of sweet icing on the cake.

She was in way over her head, outmatched both sexually and in rank. At this moment she could choose to be swept away and then wake up with a pile of trouble in the morning, or she could put on the brakes and halt the mistake before it got any worse.

She knew what she wanted, and she knew what the right course of action was. Reluctantly she put her hands on his chest and pushed lightly, and turned her head a little to the side, breaking away from the kiss.

Diego was breathing heavily, but he didn't push. Instead he rested his forehead against hers, and her heart stuttered a bit at the tender gesture.

"*Lo siento,*" he murmured. "Rose, I'm sorry."

"I know what it means," she replied. "And don't be. We've both been wondering. Wanting. But we can't, Diego." She closed her eyes tightly and wished it could be different. "We have never been equals. We never will be. Your family has been through enough. I won't be the cause of another scandal or source of speculation."

He backed away, but looked at her with tortured eyes. "You're a better woman than I deserve," he said, his voice low. "I know you are right. I just…" He stopped, frowned. "Never mind. It doesn't matter. I should leave you to your wine and quiet time."

As if she could possibly be calm and relaxed after what had just happened.

She slid to the side and he reached for the doorknob again. The door was half-open and he was taking a step into the hall when she stopped him.

"Diego?"

He turned to face her. He was so handsome, she realized. In photos, the adjectives most often used were "sexy" and "hot." But there was more depth to him than simply "sexy." Handsome required some sort of depth, a gravitas that the tabloids never seemed to capture. "Yes?" he asked.

"Thank you for speaking to your brother. And for caring for the children so much. You are a very good uncle. A good man."

He smiled, just a little. "And you like to look for the best in people, don't you? I'm not that good a man, Rose. But I'd like to be."

Before she could ask what he meant, he leaned forward and placed a little kiss on her forehead, then disappeared down the hall.

Rose shut the door and went back to her chair, picked up her wine glass, and took a long, restorative sip.

Here she thought the hardest thing about her new

assignment would be dealing with pomp and protocol. That was a cakewalk compared to having feelings for one of the royal family. Ugh, she thought, taking another drink. It was all so cliché, wasn't it? And of course it would be Diego, the resident playboy. She could just see the tabloids now: The Playboy and the Plaything. Her mother would have a fit.

The problem was that they were more than labels; they were people with real thoughts and feelings. Yes, he was a prince. And she was definitely the nanny. But they were also a man and a woman.

A man and a woman who seemed to understand each other more than they should. Who liked each other more than they should. Their kisses were really just a physical manifestation of a much larger problem: she cared about him, respected him, admired him. A lot. And a wise move would be to resign her post now and find another assignment through the agency.

"Miss Rose?"

A little voice came from the door connecting her suite with the nursery. Max stood in the doorway, his thumb in his mouth and his dark hair tousled.

She put her glass aside and patted her knee. "What is it, Max? Can't you sleep, darling?"

He came over and crawled up in her lap. She saw traces of tears on his face and he was still shaking a little. "Bad dream?" she asked, her heart melting as he snuggled in close.

He nodded.

"Want to tell me about it?"

He shook his head, and she wouldn't press. If he

didn't have dreams after the accident and all he'd been through, she would have been shocked. Instead she held him close and rubbed his back reassuringly. "You're safe now, Max. It's okay. I'm here."

He took his thumb out of his mouth for a moment; she knew he only sucked on it when he was particularly upset. To her surprise he sat up a bit and placed a kiss on her cheek before settling down in her lap again, his head resting in the curve of her neck.

Each time she took an assignment, she developed an attachment to the child. But this was different. Maybe it was *why* she was needed that made it so. They'd been through a lot, and under a microscope, too.

"*Te amo*, Miss Rose," Max whispered.

She cuddled him close. "I love you, too, Max."

Moments later he was asleep, his warm head sticky against her neck. She waited a while before gingerly rising from the chair, trying to keep him still as she made her way back to his bedroom. Once there, she tucked him back into bed and drew the soft sheets up to his shoulders.

Earlier she'd considered resigning. She couldn't do that, though. The children needed her; needed stability and affection and consistency. Her resigning would be one more person leaving them behind. No, she'd stay until they no longer needed her, or until someone told her to leave.

And she'd deal with her feelings with Diego.

For the better part of a week, Rose and Diego were polite when they crossed paths. There were no more picnics for four in the garden; Diego often took them out after their morning lessons and activities so they could expend some energy and get some fresh air, and Rose made the inevitable excuse as to why she couldn't go with them. Raoul, too, made more of an effort, and made time each day to have tea with the children in the nursery, hearing about their day and praising their reading or artwork. Their eyes lit up when their father came to see them, and Rose was gratified to see that they were happier than they'd been since her arrival. Diego must have had another chat with Raoul, too, because one day he brought a framed family photo that the children could put in the nursery. When he placed it on a little table, he said, "This way you can look at it and remember that your mama loved you more than anything in the world."

There were tears, but then they started sharing a few little memories. Rose slipped out of the room, then, wanting to give them their privacy to remember. And to heal.

The day following that particular nursery visit was a rare day off. Ernestina stepped in to watch the children and promised them a trip to the kitchen to help Señora Ortiz make *mantecados*—cinnamon crumble cakes—for tea time. Rose dressed in plain jeans and a light sleeveless blouse, put her hair up in a ponytail, and put a pair of sunglasses and a hat in her bag. She was going to go down to the city and do some exploring—no Diego along for the ride this time. Marco drove her down to the square in an unmarked car, and she made her way through the little streets and alleys with her senses wide open.

Boxes and stone walls cascaded with vibrant bougainvillea, oleander, and stephanotis, and the perfumed scent of hibiscus and jasmine mingled with salty air, fresh from the nearby coast. In the narrow streets she was shaded from the harsh sun, but once she entered the town square, there was less protection from the rays and she donned both sunglasses and hat. A café provided strong coffee and delicate pastry, and she smiled and tipped her server generously as she sat back and people-watched. More than once a sense of the unreal washed over her. She was drinking coffee in the Med on her day off from her job at the royal palace. It made her feel rather like Cinderella at the ball, except there were no horrible step-sisters waiting for her. And no Prince Charming to sweep her away.

Well, there was a prince. And he was definitely charming. But he wasn't for her. It didn't matter that he'd kissed her. They both knew it was impossible.

Still. It was rather romantic and dreamy. And it was a secret memory she'd carry with her forever. Maybe she'd tell her children and grandchildren about it someday.

If she ever had any children. Maybe her sister was right about that one thing. She spent her time looking after other people's children rather than thinking about having her own.

Once she'd eaten her pastry and watched passersby long enough, she wandered further into town to the market. Not the stalls in the square, where tourists gathered, but deeper into the area where the locals shopped for their produce and goods. One man with a magnificent mustache manned a cart featuring the bright colors and citrus scents of oranges, lemons, and limes. She bought three oranges and tucked them in her bag, intending to keep them for a snack with the children later. There were rows and rows of flowers and bunches of herbs, the heavy scent of basil and oregano blended with the slightly sharper aroma of rosemary and cilantro. Oils, vinegars, wine, cured meats, and cheeses with their overwhelming must drew her in, and she tried several before selecting some dry-cured sausage, smoked cheese, and bread for an impromptu lunch later.

There was the daily catch available, and her eyes widened at the mounds of oysters, slabs of tuna, and—she shuddered—whole eels. One ambitious vendor tried to sell her a cone of fresh baby shrimp, but she smiled and waved a hand before moving on. She'd always preferred her seafood to be properly battered, deep fried, and served with chips.

There were no children to worry about today, no Diego to distract her. It gave her time to think about her own family, and to miss them a little bit. In her other jobs, she could take a few days and catch a train and be home for a quick visit. Or pop up to London and see Hayley and Alice. Hayley usually gave Rose a hard time, and got in little digs about her job. Visiting Alice was the real bright light to those trips. The last time she'd splurged on tickets to take her niece to the ballet. Hayley had taken the opportunity to head to the clubs since she was usually "tied down."

Even Devon…he was a good sort, if a little staid. He still enjoyed a good game of cards and a cold beer now and again. Now she wasn't sure when she'd be home again.

But she could send presents home, couldn't she?

At a silversmith's she employed Emilia's haggling strategy and purchased a silver-and-rose quartz bracelet for Hayley and an intricate hair clip for Alice in the shape of one of the many hibiscus blossoms she'd seen this morning. Vivid fabric was draped over stands at another shop, and she bought a fine silk scarf for her mother and then paused at the sight of delicate white lace. It was absolutely exquisite, and she pressed her hand over her heart, gaining the attention of the merchant. So much for being coy.

"*Cuánto cuestas?*" she asked, touching the material with a finger. That was all, though. She was afraid of marring its perfection.

The woman looked at her shrewdly, then named a price that even Rose knew was exorbitant.

She stepped back and dropped her hand, then shook her head. Even with her fine wages, she couldn't justify spending so much on something she might never use. What would she ever do with a length of fine lace, anyway? It would more than likely sit packed away somewhere. Utterly impractical…and yet something about it called to her. Begged for her to buy it. She was not an impulse shopper, but she wasn't sure she wanted to walk away, either.

The woman shrugged, and turned back to her table, where she was tidying stacks of printed fabrics.

Rose turned away, then turned back again and named her price—half of what the woman had asked.

The light returned to the woman's eyes, and she tilted her head a bit and studied Rose. Rose left her sunglasses on. She had a horrible poker face, and this might give her the tiniest edge in bargaining.

The woman named a new price. Not much better than the first. Rose adjusted her bag on her shoulder and turned to walk away.

"Señorita! Wait." She said the word in English. Rose turned back around as the woman quoted a new price. A much better price.

Rose countered, and so it went on for a good five minutes. She started to enjoy herself as the woman pointed out the fine craftsmanship, the quality of the thread, the perfection of the design. Rose made a point of taking out her phone and doing the currency conversion into Euros, then turning the screen around so the woman could see. "That is the absolute most I can spend," Rose replied, her heart beating fast. Bargaining had been exhilarating!

The number was just over two-thirds of the original price. With a beaming smile the woman agreed, and wrapped the carefully-folded lace into tissue, and then another bag for safekeeping. Rose took it, paid her money, and carefully tucked it into her tote, away from the aromatic cheese and meat.

That only left her father and brother. She purchased a bottle of fine Marazurian brandy for her father, and found an old, worn copy of Don Quixote, in the original Spanish, at a book stall for Devon.

Her bag was getting quite heavy now, so Rose left the market behind and simply made her way out of the city by working her way downhill toward the harbor. It was by no means a short walk, and by the time she could see the vast blue of the ocean she was tired and her feet hurt. She flagged down a taxi instead, and gave halting instructions to be delivered to the closest beach. She wanted to dig her toes into the sand, feel the water lapping around her ankles, soothing her aching soles. She'd eat her lunch, wander for a bit more, and then call Marco to retrieve her.

The taxi driver spoke in rapid Spanish, and Rose struggled to keep up. She pieced together enough to know that the harbor was in town but any sort of beach was outside the city. She frowned a bit, wondering if it had been such a good idea to wander alone all day without so much as a map. The last time she had Diego with her, and a small but dedicated security detail. She didn't need that now, but she wasn't quite as confident as she'd been first thing this morning.

The beach was, indeed, outside the city and Rose paid the driver and shouldered her bag. The sand was dotted with umbrellas and people, and the waves looked deliciously refreshing. The breeze was brisk, and as she bent to slip off her shoes, a gust caught the brim of her hat and flipped it off her head, sending it reeling over the sand.

"Oh!" she cried, spinning around, but it tumbled like a wheel, turning over and over.

She sighed, and her eyes watered. She told herself it was from the wind and the sand blowing into her eyes, but it wasn't. As she retrieved her sunglasses from her bag, she admitted that she was tired. The walk had been long, the heat sapping, and the earlier peace she'd felt sitting at the café, calmly drinking coffee, was gone. She could call Marco right now and just go home. The beach wasn't going anywhere.

Maybe she was just hungry.

The plan for a picnic had been a good one, except there were no umbrellas free and no tables or places to sit unless she sat right on the sand, in full sunlight.

"Forget it," she muttered, and hooked her fingers into her shoes and headed for the water. "I'll dip my toes in the damned ocean and call for Marco." At this point, all she wanted was some shade and a cool drink and some peace and quiet. The water would ease her hot and sore feet and then she'd head back to the palace to enjoy the rest of her day off.

"*Pardon, señorita?*"

She'd just stepped to the edge of the breakers when a deep voice sounded behind her shoulder. She turned and saw a man, about thirty-five or so, holding out her hat.

"My hat!" She stepped back, her feet sinking a bit in the wet sand, and held out her hand. "Oh, *gracias*. Thank you."

"You are welcome." He looked around. "The sun is bright today. You should perhaps..." he frowned, as if searching for the right words. "Sit in the shade."

"I'd love to. But I don't have an umbrella."

He rattled something off in Spanish and her lips dropped open. All she could make out was something like "casa" and five minutes and walking…until she followed the path of his finger as he pointed east. "Your house? *Tu casa?*"

"*Sí!*" He smiled, showing her a perfect row of white teeth. He was somewhat attractive, though not quite her type. And she certainly didn't feel comfortable going to his house, shade or not.

"Thank you, but I'm fine. I'm just about to return to the…to home," she finished weakly. "I do appreciate you bringing me my hat."

"I insist," he continued, his smile widening as he moved closer. "You can sit on my patio, have a cold drink. Then I can take you where you need to go."

Hah. She could just imagine telling him to drop her off at the palace gates. Or sitting alone with him in a car, for that matter. The strange vibe strengthened, and once again she was aware of the mistake she'd made staying at the beach when she really was ready to be home. "No, thank you," she said, in her most priggish English tone. "Good day."

She turned to walk away, back up from the beach, hoping against hope that she could somehow flag a taxi, knowing full well that she might not be able to since she was now outside city limits. She didn't want to wait twenty minutes for Marco to arrive.

She'd gone three steps when his hand clamped around her arm.

CHAPTER 9

Diego stopped by the nursery around one thirty. He'd missed having lunch with the children, and he didn't really have time to stay long this afternoon, either. It looked increasingly like he was going to have to make a trip to Tanzania to meet with the board of directors for the women's education charity. The executive director had put in her notice and several projects were at critical points of development. Phone calls were taking up too much of his time. What he needed to do was go and spend about a week of serious focus and boots-on-the-ground work.

"Ernestina." He blinked in surprise as the maid opened the nursery door. "Is Rose sick today?"

"No, Your Highness. It's her day off."

To his recollection, she hadn't actually taken a personal day since she'd started working. She'd more than earned the time away.

"I've come to see Max and Emilia, but I can't stay long."

She opened the door wider. "They've been asking to go to the pool."

"I've been taking them most afternoons," he admitted, stepping inside. "And Rose has been taking them for a swim on the days I can't."

The maid's eyes widened and Diego laughed. "Don't worry. I won't suggest you take them, Ernestina. Thank you for watching them today."

She nodded. "They love Miss Rose. And so does the staff. She's..." Ernestina blushed and looked away.

"She's what?" Diego asked.

Ernestina hesitated, then lifted her chin. "She brought some happiness back to the palace. She smiles a lot."

Diego's chest tightened even as he nodded at the maid. That was exactly what Rose had done. She'd been a breath of fresh air. A ray of sunshine. A steady presence of stability and also...fun.

He'd never met anyone like her.

"I'll just pop in and say hello." Diego smiled and then went the rest of the way into the nursery.

He was listening to Emilia read him a story, showing off her skills, when his cell rang. The ringtone notified him that it was security, so he put his hand over Emilia's to get her to pause in her reading and then answered the call. When he hung up again, his easy mood had disappeared and concern sat like a stone behind his breast bone. Rose had gone into town, had done some shopping, but had then taken a taxi to one of the beaches. Which normally wouldn't be a big deal, but she was an employee of the palace and had gone without proper security. Not only that, but tourists were regularly targeted for all sorts of petty crime since it was a public beach and not a part of one of the seaside resorts with restricted access. Rose, with her fair skin and innocent smile, would be an easy target.

"I'm sorry, you two. I have to go take care of something." He kissed them both on the top of the head, but he was dialing Marco before he even got to the door.

"Marco? You drove Miss Rose to the city today?" He barely waited for the answer. "I need you to pick me up in two minutes."

The drive to the beach seemed to take forever, even though Marco made it in just under fifteen minutes. Diego didn't wait; he hopped out of the car and strode to the steps that led down a twenty-foot cliff to the sandy beach below.

There were tons of people here. Umbrellas dotted the sandy expanse and he hadn't even thought to ask what she was wearing.

But then he saw her. She was standing at the water's edge, holding onto her hat and talking to a man. Jealousy ripped through him without warning, and he clenched his jaw. This wasn't about being jealous. It was about safety. The man stepped closer to her, crowding her space.

Diego had just stepped forward when Rose smiled at the man, turned, and started to walk in his direction.

The man reached out and grabbed her arm, yanking her backward.

Diego ran forward, stopping to walk when he was several yards away. While he felt the urge to slam his fist into this guy's face, he wouldn't cause that kind of a scene. Because of Rose. Because she didn't need the trouble it would cause, and neither did the family.

He pasted a smile on his face, the one he saved for his most dreaded appearances, and put his sunglasses on.

"Rose, darling!" After years at Cambridge and abroad, he could do a pretty good posh accent. It might make him less recognizable, between that and the sunglasses.

She looked up and relief rushed across her features when she saw him. "Oh, hello…darling," she answered, and he watched as the man let go of her arm.

"Everything all right? I'm so sorry I'm late. I was detained with the children. The nanny took the day off."

The man took a step backward, and Diego moved in and took Rose's hand in hers.

"This nice man captured my hat," she said, affecting a laugh. "The wind blew it right off! Down the beach it went."

Diego slid his arm around her waist. "Well, thank God. We wouldn't want your delicate English skin to burn, would we?" He smiled down at her secretly, and added, "Though I do think there's an aloe plant at the villa. I could help soothe any tender bits."

Her already pink skin turned pinker.

"Good day, Miss," the man said, backing away quickly.

"Thank you for finding my hat!" she called after him, but once he turned around, she wilted against Diego. "Just in time," she murmured.

"Come." He dropped the English accent and the affected light mood, but still held her hand. "Let's get you home."

He led the way back up the beach to the steps, and then the waiting car. Marco didn't even make eye contact with them as they got in the back seat. As soon as they were inside with the doors closed, Diego let go of her hand and turned toward her, the anger he'd held back rising up.

"What were you thinking? A single pretty woman on a beach alone, wandering around? You might as well have printed a target on your back!"

She spun toward him, her eyes wide and her mouth open in surprise. Then her brows pulled together. "It was my day off! I can do what I choose, Diego. I don't have to ask your permission, you know!"

Marco, to his credit, never even blinked or peeked at the rear view mirror. He just drove steadily, away from the ocean and up toward the city again.

"Yes, you can do as you please. We *are* a free country, after all. But you aren't familiar with the area, and you're not fluent, and you are an important member of the staff. You should have...cleared an itinerary and taken security!"

Rose lifted an eyebrow. "I'm staff. Not part of the royal family, *Your Highness*. I hardly rate personal security." She turned her head and stared out the window.

He hated when she said "Your Highness" in just that way.

"Regardless, you were careless. Thank God I arrived when I did."

"Thank God…" Her lips thinned and her eyes flashed as she turned back to face him. "I didn't need rescuing, you know!"

"That's not what it looked like. Or what it felt like when you wilted against me."

Her pink cheeks turned a deeper shade of red. "I was going along with your stupid plan. It's not like I was going to shout 'oh look! It's the prince!' to the entire beach."

"He grabbed your arm." Thinking about it still made Diego's gut clench.

"And I would have pulled away and left. Or screamed. It was a public beach, you know."

"And your bag. Is everything still inside it?"

She looked confused. "What?"

"Check your bag. Are you missing anything?"

He watched as she rooted through her bag and her face whitened. "My wallet. Are you saying…"

Diego sighed. "Tourists are targets in certain areas. What was in it?"

She sat back against the cushions of the seat. "Just some money. A credit card."

"No ID?"

"I didn't think I'd need my passport at a café and market."

He appreciated the snap in her tone. He preferred a little heat to crying or dramatics. For all her sweetness, there was a toughness to his little English Rose.

And she'd probably cuff his ears if he ever called her that out loud.

"What are you smiling at?" she demanded.

"Nothing. Sorry. Anyway, we can cancel your credit card. How much cash did you have?"

She raised an eyebrow. "Certainly not as much as I left the palace with."

"Good shopping?"

"Very." She turned her head to look at him as the level of antagonism in the back seat went from a boil down to a simmer. "How did you even know where I was?"

Diego knew she was probably going to be furious at his next words, but he wouldn't apologize for taking what he considered necessary precautions. "When you called for Marco to take you to the city, a security detail was sent as well. They heard you give the taxi driver instructions for the beach and called me."

Her mouth had dropped open and *poof!* They were up to the boil again. "You had me followed?" Without waiting for an answer, she leaned forward so she could see Marco's profile. "And you. You didn't think to tell me?" she accused.

"Leave Marco out of it. He was just following my orders. And the security was really just one woman, who would have stepped in and got you out of any sticky situation. Until you got into the cab."

"I can't believe you did that." She scowled at him. "How do you people even live like this?"

He sent her a long, hard look. Was it really so bad that he'd wanted to be sure she was safe? Particularly if she went anywhere alone. The fact that the man at the beach had even touched her sent an uncommon jolt of rage through his veins. What if someone had recognized her? She'd had her picture taken once before, and she hadn't like the headline that had accompanied it. The security had been set up to be unobtrusive, and to merely step in if needed.

It had been a part of his life for so long he hardly thought about it anymore, but that didn't mean he couldn't understand her frustration. She wasn't accustomed to this sort of intrusion. But she could have been a little more grateful for the help.

"You work," he said stiffly, "for the Navarro household, and for the Crown Prince of Marazur. You are in charge of the heirs to the throne. Did you really think you wouldn't have your own security?" He let out an exasperated breath. "Did you even read your contract?"

"I thought I'd have the freedom of a day off to myself," she snapped.

Marco looked in the rear view mirror then. Diego shook his head. Not many people got away with speaking to him in such a familiar and antagonistic way. He might not be the stern man that his brother was, but he wasn't a pushover, either.

They turned up the drive to the palace.

Marco pulled around to the back and the servant entrance by the kitchen. Rose didn't speak and neither did Diego. When Marco opened her door, she scooted out and took her bag with her.

Marco shut the door and got back in behind the wheel. Any other day, Diego might have gotten out with her. Walked her inside. Stopped in the kitchen for a piece of cake or a taste of whatever Señora Ortiz was cooking. But not today. He was annoyed. Supremely annoyed. At her for being so…incorrigible, and at himself for caring so damned much.

It was more than inconvenient. It was becoming a problem.

Marco drove around to the front of the house again, put the car in park, and opened Diego's door. "Sir," he said quietly.

"Thank you, Marco," Diego said quietly. "For all you did today."

"It's my job, Your Highness."

Diego smiled then. "And you do it well. You look after us all."

"Not all of us," Marco said quietly.

Marco had come out of the limo accident with only scratches and bruises. But he had to live with the scene for the rest of his life, and Diego had temporarily forgotten.

"All of us," Diego affirmed, and put his hand on the man's shoulder.

He went inside and went straight to his office. Not to the nursery, not to her room, not to the kitchens. He needed to calm down and figure out exactly what he was feeling. Thinking. And to do that, he needed to focus on something else for a little while.

Anything else.

ROSE SLAMMED HER BAG DOWN ON THE CHAIR IN HER suite and put her hands on her hips. He'd had her followed. Followed! She'd thought she'd been enjoying a quiet day alone and the whole time she'd been watched.

It made her feel odd. And a little creeped out.

And now her wallet was missing. She'd only had twenty or thirty Euros left anyway, so that was no big loss. She retrieved the rest of her cards and called the number on the back of one, in order to cancel the stolen one before a charge could be made on it.

When she hung up, she was slightly calmer, but not much. It wasn't so much that he'd made sure she had security but that he hadn't told her about it. To make matters worse, she'd looked up and saw him crossing the sand and she'd felt…rescued.

For God's sake. Rescued. How pathetic was that? She was fully capable of looking after herself. She'd already realized she should leave the beach and would have done so if he hadn't rushed in to save the day.

Rose went into her bathroom and the face that stared back at her in the mirror gave her a start. Her hair was a mess of tangles, and her skin…oh, her skin. It was pink, all except for around her eyes, where she'd worn her sunglasses. Her arms, too. Diego hadn't been kidding about her pale English skin. It hadn't been ready for the brashness of the Mediterranean sun. She put her palm against her upper arm; it was hot to the touch.

She stared in the mirror again and saw her lip wobble. What the heck?

She had nothing to cry about. She had a great job with wonderful children, and for the most part it was enjoyable and not difficult. So she'd had a not-so-great ending to an otherwise great day…big deal. Except…

She sniffed. Except she'd been delivered to the servant's entrance and Diego hadn't even said goodbye. He'd driven away, leaving her standing there, angry and unsure. It had been a very deliberate snub. And she had no reason to be mad about it, because she'd been the one to point out that simple nannies didn't require personal security. She was the one who kept pointing out the difference in their stations.

As she stared at her disheveled reflection, she was at least honest with herself: she kept pointing it out so she didn't have to deal with the real issue. She was falling for Diego. Not in an "I've got a crush" sort of way, but a deep affection and respect. And longing. When she'd seen him striding through the sand this afternoon, her heart had leapt, so glad to see him in a time of trouble. He'd brought with him a surety that everything would be all right.

That he'd take care of her.

Her, who'd never really needed taking care of before. Who usually ended up taking care of everyone else.

She could love him very easily.

And he was not for her. Not in a million years.

She bit down on her lip to stop the tremble and turned on her shower. Some cool water and perspective was needed here.

When she got out, she pulled on a pair of boxer shorts and a tank top, then went searching through her cosmetic bag for some decent lotion to apply to her burned skin. The gentlest thing she found was a small pot of her eye cream, guaranteed to soothe. She wasn't about to use it all on her shoulders and arms. Maybe one of the maids would have something. Ernestina was right next door, with the children.

Rose checked the clock on her phone. It was tea time, so perhaps she could sneak in and out again without causing a ruckus. She left her room and entered the nursery quietly, and paused for a moment, listening to the happy chatter and the sound of cutlery on plates and Ernestina's cheerful voice. The maid really was much happier now that she was back to her usual job. She'd practically volunteered to watch Emilia and Max for the day. There was a difference between a job for a few hours and a job day in and day out, it seemed.

She stepped through to the sitting room and caught Ernestina's eye. The maid's gaze widened as she took in Rose's burned skin. "Oh, Miss Rose! You didn't take your sunscreen today. *Dios mio!* You are red."

So much for being unobtrusive.

"Miss Rose!" Max came hurtling toward her, nearly knocking over his drink the process. "We got to make *mantecados* with Señora Ortiz today! And we are having them with our tea!"

Emilia held out a plate. "Would you like one, Miss Rose?"

"Of course I would." She realized she'd forgotten all about lunch today and that her wares were still in her bag, overheated and no longer fresh. She bit into the little cake and held out her other hand to catch the crumbs. "It's delicious." Indeed. She was pretty sure the main ingredient was butter.

"Did someone say *mantecados*?"

Her heart stuttered.

Diego stood in the doorway, beaming, but his smile slipped when he saw her. She realized she was utterly underdressed and her burn was on full display.

"*Dios mio.*" He echoed Ernestina's previous sentiment. "I knew you had burned a little, but not this."

"I actually came to see if Ernestina had something I could use for it. I seem to be strangely low on aloe." She lifted an eyebrow. He had made that silly statement on the beach about having an aloe plant to assist in her "tender bits."

Ernestina clucked. "I don't, but Maria is sure to." She named one of the other maids. "She has more creams and potions than a girl her age needs." Ernestina blushed then. "Begging your pardon, Your Highness. I forgot myself…"

Diego just laughed. "I don't care about stuff like that." He shrugged. "I could have my assistant find you something, Rose. Or Stephani. You know, Raoul's assistant. She's the most resourceful person I know. Prepared for any emergency."

"Anything would be a help." She spared a glance at Diego, relieved that the earlier hostility appeared to have waned. "I thought Raoul was coming for tea?"

"He got held up on the phone. He sent me with a message to tell the children that he will tuck them in and read stories tonight instead."

Rose gave him a small nod. "Thank you, Diego."

Understanding softened his eyes. "You're welcome." They both knew that he'd spoken to Raoul and that Raoul had been more present in the children's lives ever since.

"I'm going to go back to my room to lie down. I really did get too much sun today," Rose said, sending a wave to the children. "The cakes are delicious, Diego. I'm sure you'll enjoy them. Emilia? Max? I'll see you in the morning."

With a small smile she scooted back out of the nursery and returned to her room.

Whether it was the lack of food, too much sun, or just exhaustion, a headache took up residence behind Rose's eyes. She drank some water, but her stomach didn't feel quite right, either. The air-conditioned room was a blessing, though, and she decided to crawl beneath her crisp, cool sheets to have a nap.

When she woke, much later, the light in the room had dimmed and her headache was more of a dull ache than a full-on throb. She squinted and looked up to see Stephani, Raoul's assistant, depositing a small tray on a table.

"Oh, goodness."

Stephani straightened abruptly. "Oh. I'm sorry if I woke you. Diego mentioned you had a touch of heat stroke and a nasty sunburn. I thought I'd leave you a few things."

Rose sat up. "That's sweet of you. Thank you, Stephani."

"It's no trouble." She smiled and Rose thought perhaps it looked a little sad. "You know, I've worked for the family for a number of years. Close to a decade, I think. Raoul used to get me to do little errands for Cecilia all the time. I miss her. She was my cousin, you know, and we used to…" She frowned. "Oh, this is silly. I shouldn't be talking about it."

"No, please," Rose said, patting the edge of the bed. "Come, sit. I've been here a month and while I am very happy and love the staff, I miss talking about…things. Only if you're comfortable, of course. It's not your job to look after my loneliness."

Stephani gave her an assessing look. "Begging your pardon, but Diego seems to help in that regard."

The honest statement took Rose aback. "I…I mean, it's…"

"He's the loneliest person I know," Stephani said. "And that includes Raoul. Diego just hides it better." She perched on the edge of the bed. "It's difficult when you care about someone and they're on the opposite line of what propriety allows."

Rose wondered if she was speaking from personal experience. And Raoul had been married to Ceci…did that mean Stephani had a thing for Diego?

"Am I…intruding on a friendship, Stephani? Is it all right to ask that?"

Stephani's face relaxed. "Oh, you're thinking me and Diego? Not at all." She laughed lightly. "I just mean I've seen it often enough. Propriety makes things difficult. In the end we're all human. We all want friends. Connections don't really take class and status into consideration."

She patted Rose's hand. "I should go now. There's a

bottle of aloe gel for your burn. And some water and pills for your headache, if you still have one."

"Thank you. You're very kind."

"I like looking after people. I don't get a chance very often, now." She frowned. "Raoul is very stubborn about admitting weakness or accepting help. I've been his assistant long enough I try to anticipate his needs."

"I think both brothers are stubborn," Rose said darkly, and Stephani laughed.

"Well, between you, me, and Señora Ortiz, it's up to us to take care of the family. It's up to me to keep Raoul on task. You're in charge of the children, who rave about you, by the way. And Señora Ortiz? She keeps everyone fed and happy."

Food. The mention of it made Rose's stomach gurgle. A pastry in the late morning and a small cake at tea was not enough to eat in the run of a day.

"Put lots of aloe on the burn and reapply as often as you can," Stephani advised. "Hopefully it'll calm quickly."

She left then, leaving Rose alone with her aloe and aspirin.

Her stomach growled again and she popped the pills and then chased them with the cold water. Maybe she could put decent clothes on and sneak down to the kitchen for a snack? Something to hold her over until breakfast? She eyed the aloe. If she applied it now, whatever she put on would get sticky from the gel. She'd get some food, and then come back, put the tank back on, and slather it on. The burn was so hot that she could feel the heat coming off her skin.

Getting caught roaming the palace in pajamas wasn't really an option, so Rose slipped on a pair of loose linen trousers and a feather-light sweater that draped rather than clung to her skin, particularly her arms. With her hair anchored up in a top knot, she headed for her door and the hallways that would lead to the kitchen and comfort.

She opened the door and nearly ran into Diego.

CHAPTER 10

He carried a tray in his hand, and the smell coming from the covered dish was delectable. Her stomach growled but she ignored it.

Stephani had just told her she thought Diego was really lonely. Hadn't he said something similar, that first night he'd found her by the fountain? It seemed so long ago now, instead of just a matter of weeks.

He'd been angry with her this afternoon. And yet here he was, at her door, bearing what appeared to be a late dinner.

"May I come in?" he said quietly.

"Of course you can." She stepped aside. She wished she could still be angry at him for what he'd done today, but she couldn't. Time and a nap had cleared her mind a bit. And while she might not say it out loud, she was very aware that her annoyance had been partly at herself for feeling such a weakness for him, and part humiliation for getting herself in an awkward position in the first place.

This was not her world. And yet Diego made sure she was looked after. Protected.

Fed.

"What's in the dish?" she asked, following him into the suite.

"Oh, Humble Pie, I would imagine," he said dryly, then smiled at her. "I asked in the kitchen. You didn't go down for dinner."

She shook her head. "I think I had some heat stroke. I didn't feel well, so I took a nap. And Stephani came by with some water and pills for my headache, and aloe for the burn."

His gaze ran over her arms, cheeks, and chest. "Have you put any on yet?"

"No. And I will, but honest to God, you've got to let me at that food. I'm starving. I haven't eaten all day. Not since a pastry and coffee this morning."

He whipped off the lid and revealed a steaming bowl of some sort of stew.

She sat at the table and gestured to the chair beside her. "Have a seat. I take it you're going to join me in the wine?"

"If you want. I can leave you, if you like. I know you're not happy with me."

She'd taken a large, succulent bite of spicy shrimp, and she savored it before she answered. "I'm not mad anymore. Not at you, anyway."

"I should have told you," he admitted. "I set it up with the security team the day after our picture got into the paper. I didn't want you to get caught off guard by the press or anyone else. But not telling you was wrong."

"It was, but I can forgive it. I know you were just trying to protect me. This is all new to me, that's all. And you came striding across the sand when I was feeling tired, and cranky, and then foolish." It was all she was willing to admit, but it was the truth.

"Maybe next time you can take a friend."

Rose laughed. "A friend? I'm friendly with the staff, I suppose. But I don't have friends, not… not a girlfriend." Not like she'd had back in England. She was suddenly very homesick.

"Are you lonely, Rose?"

She met his gaze. He was opening the wine, his strong wrist turning the corkscrew as he watched her. She put down her fork. "Sometimes. Not often. I'm busy here, and everyone is lovely. They really are. The children keep me occupied and entertained, and I have anything a woman could want. My own suite, the gardens, even the camaraderie in the kitchen at night, for a cup of tea and a sneaky piece of cake."

"But it's not family."

"I'm used to being away from them."

"And used to not being a burden on anyone? Being the one to take care of others instead of letting others take care of you?"

She speared a chunk of chorizo. "That's not a bad thing." And she sent him a grateful smile. "And just tonight, both you and Stephani have made sure I'm cared for. So there."

He chuckled and handed her a glass of wine. "Nice try. It might have worked if you hadn't added the 'so there.'"

She chuckled in return and ate some more, then took a restorative drink of wine and sighed. This was better. Señora Ortiz's excellent cooking and a fine wine, while sitting across from a real-life prince… She laughed again, staring into her bowl.

"What's so funny?" He looked amused as he waited for her reply.

"This is just so surreal. I'm in a bloody castle, you see? And I'm entertaining a prince in my room. *El príncipe, Diego*," she said, the accent rolling smoothly off her tongue. "I'm pretty sure that no one in my family would quite believe it."

Except Hayley, of course. Hayley was already pumping her for information in her emails. Rose loved her sister, but she would never betray the Navarro family. With or without the confidentiality agreement she'd been asked to sign.

"I'm just a man, Rose. The title…that's an accident of birth. And yes, as you said today, I live a certain way. It comes with the title. But underneath all this…" he waved his hand around the room, then placed it on his chest, "I'm just flesh and blood, same as you. I have needs and wants, just like you. I have feelings that have nothing to do with me being a prince or you being the nanny, and everything to do with you being an incredibly compassionate, strong, beautiful woman."

"Diego." Her heart pounded now, thumping against her ribs as his words sounded in her ears and went straight to her soul. This would be such a mistake.

"I know, I know. And I don't have the answers, Rose. I should and I don't. All I know is that I have these feelings and they're not going away." He put down his glass and focused his gaze steadily on her face. "You make me want to be a better man, Rose. And that is something I have never felt before."

It was unimaginable that he was saying these things to her. And yet she knew he was, because he was sitting right across from her, as earnest as she'd ever seen him.

"What would you have me do, Diego?" Simply asking the question scared her, because she hadn't come right out and said no. That she was entertaining the idea was insane. "What if Raoul found out? What about the children?"

He got up from the table and spun away. "So neither of us should be free to have a personal life away from obligation? That's cruel. And if and when the time comes, I'll deal with Raoul and our father." He sounded so sure of himself. Confident and strong.

"Your father is the king," she reminded him.

"And a man," Diego persisted, coming over beside her and kneeling by her chair. "A man who once loved a woman no one approved of. He's not heartless."

He put his hand over hers.

"Don't use that word," she whispered. "It's…precipitous."

Too soon. This was all too soon.

Instead he lifted her hand and kissed the base of it, by the pad of her thumb. She bit down on her lip, bracing herself for what she was sure was going to be seduction. With each passing moment, she was less inclined to fight it.

She wanted him, too.

The man. Not the prince.

He tugged on her hand and she got up from her chair and followed him to the sofa, where he sat beside her and trailed his fingers lightly over her forearm.

She was afraid. Afraid of starting something that could never end well. Afraid of losing her heart. Of losing everything.

And yet she was helpless to do anything but close her eyes as he leaned closer and touched his lips to hers.

He kissed her with such tenderness. With such… care. He wasn't anything like the papers said. He loved, deeply. He looked after his family behind the scenes, asking for nothing in return. All he wanted from her was this moment. She cared for him too much to deny him.

So she slipped her hand up over his collar and along the back of his neck, drawing his lips harder against her own.

And oh, could he kiss. Soft, yet sure. Slow, but with a pulse-accelerating seduction that stole her breath. He wrapped her in his arms and they fell back against the cushions, lips and tongues tangling as their bodies pressed together. Rose's tender skin tingled uncomfortably, but she ignored it in favor of the bliss of being held firmly yet carefully, as if she were something delicate and special.

His hand spanned her ribs, then slid beneath her sweater to cup her small breast. She'd only put on a bralette when she'd changed, and his hand was warm through the thin cotton barrier. She pressed against his palm.

He slid his mouth away from hers. "Your face is so

hot," he murmured, kissing the tip of her nose. "And I can't promise I'll have much more willpower. Let me help you with the aloe." He removed his hand from beneath her shirt.

It was like being doused in cold water, or stepping outside on a raw January evening in Surrey. She'd been prepared for…everything, she realized. She'd moved into his embrace, sure that they were going to end up in her bed. Now he was putting on the brakes, and rather sharply.

"Did I do something wrong?" she asked, braving a look at him.

"No," he answered, his voice low. "You did everything right. But I don't want to rush. I want us to take our time. Be really, really sure. This is…" He looked down for a moment, and then back up. "This is too important to take lightly, Rose. I want to see where it leads, but I want to be careful. For all our sakes." He held her hand as he spoke, a token of his sincerity.

She'd expected seduction, but not this sweet, serious consideration. She appreciated it, more than he probably understood. She knew all about wanting to do the right thing for everyone. Most of her life choices had been made according to that philosophy.

"Wait. See where it goes?" She bit down on her lip, both excited by the prospect and terrified, too. It was different when she was just thinking about this one night. This one moment. But was he talking about…dating?

He sighed. "I'm not in the habit of kissing nannies, or confiding in them. I don't want to treat you cavalierly, either. You're too important to my family." He hesitated. "To me. Caution seems like the right approach."

"You're worried," she said, squeezing his fingers.

"A little. And I want us to get to know each other without a lot of input from my family or the press or anyone else. Can we do that? What you said today was so right. Privacy is a rare commodity. Can we at least cling to what little bit we might have until we figure things out a little more?"

"It'll feel like sneaking around," she replied, sitting back against the cushions.

"I know. But don't we deserve to get to know each other without an audience?" He frowned. "That's all I'm asking. Just a chance for us to sit like this. Talk. Kiss a little." The impish grin flitted across his mouth once more. "Be normal."

It did sound lovely. And despite her misgivings, she saw his point. If they were really going to explore what was happening between them, it made sense to do it privately before creating a stir in the household. It might give them a chance to decide if it was really worth fighting for, or if it was going to burn out as quickly as it had flared to life.

He kissed her, and it was several minutes before they sat up straight again. Rose's head spun, both from the kisses and from the heavy beating of her heart.

"Go put that shirt on again," Diego said. "It's been hours since you got back. You really need to take care of your sunburn."

She did as he asked, slipping into her bathroom to change her sweater back to the sleeveless tank. When she came back out, he was squeezing some of the gel onto his hands.

"Sit," he commanded, pulling out one of the chairs next to her table.

She did as he said. The light scent of the aloe filled the air and the first touch of gel to skin was a cold jolt. She gasped and then laughed, and then closed her eyes and simply enjoyed the cool sensation as he carefully smeared the gel over the back of her neck, the crests of her shoulders and down her arms. He rubbed some on his hands and placed them on her cheeks, then dropped a soft kiss on her lips before adding more to his palm and placing it on her chest.

Another few moments, a shift of his hand, and they'd be back in seduction land again. But he didn't. He stayed a perfect gentleman, to Rose's disappointment. His fingertips gently rubbed the cool gel into her skin, easing the heat and tight feeling the sunburn had caused.

"Thank you," she murmured, her voice strained.

"*De nada*," he murmured back, placing a kiss on the top of her head. "I don't want to fight any more like we did today, Rose. I will be honest with you from now on. May I see you tomorrow?"

"Of course."

"It's a date, then."

She laughed a little, her chest cramping with delicious anticipation and a hint of apprehension about what they were agreeing to. "A date? Here at the palace?"

"Don't underestimate me." He flashed her a grin. "I do love a challenge."

The smile slid from her face. "That's not what I am, is it? A challenge?" She really hoped not. There was too much at stake, and more for her than for him. She wanted to believe him. Believe *in* him, the way no one really had before.

"No, Rosalie, you are not." He turned her to face him. "This is not a game for me. I know it's fraught with complications. But for once in my life, I don't want to rush into anything impulsively. I want to take care."

Her heart melted. "Okay, then," she whispered, touching the hair just above his ear. "A date for tomorrow."

"I'll meet you here around ten? After the children go to sleep?"

"That sounds perfect."

"Sleep well, Rose." He leaned forward and kissed her lips again, and she walked him to the door as he carried the dinner tray. She opened the door first and peeked outside. When she saw the coast was clear, she stood back and let him leave.

Once he was gone, she shut the door and rested against it for a moment. Was she out of her mind? This could make a mess of everything. And yet…they cared for each other. She certainly cared for him, and for the first time since she'd started calling herself an adult, she felt like she deserved to have something for herself. Not so she could send money to her sister to help with Alice's upbringing. And not for her parents, either, who had never overtly pressured her but who were so happy that she was able to "travel" a bit as they'd never been able to afford. She was, she realized, a people pleaser.

For a few moments today, while she'd been at the market and at the café, she'd started to feel what it was to please only herself. Was she not entitled to what she wanted once in a while?

Of course wanting to snog a prince of Marazur might be aiming a bit high for her first time out, but when opportunity knocked…

Who was she to refuse to answer?

DIEGO PAUSED OUTSIDE HER DOOR AND LET OUT A DEEP breath. He was nervous. Nervous! Him! Wouldn't the tabloids get a kick out of that?

He'd left the suit jacket back in his suite, and the tie, too, but wore charcoal gray, finely tailored trousers and a dress shirt, open at the collar. He ran his hand over his hair one last time, then knocked softly on the door.

She answered it, a little smile on her face. "Hi," she whispered.

He grinned. "Hi. Come on."

She was wearing a dress. Nothing fancy, just a light, flowy thing that drifted around her thighs and made her legs look very long. She had some sort of a wrap in her hand, but she took his other hand in hers and let him tug her along. He checked the halls both ways, then gave her a peck on the cheek.

"Where are we going?"

"You'll see."

He'd wanted privacy, so he'd gone up to the roof earlier and set everything up himself. The only person in on it was Señora Ortiz, who was his keeper of secrets. She'd given him a disapproving look, sighed, and then did what he'd requested.

Rose's sandals tapped on the stone steps, slightly behind him, as he led her through a long stairway to the roof and the parapets. While the weather was still warm and balmy, it was past ten o'clock, and there was a slight chill to the air as they stepped through the door and onto the flat expanse of stone.

Then he turned and watched her face.

"Ohhh." She drew out the word, a note of awe trailing on the breeze.

He followed her gaze, taking in the effect of his earlier handiwork.

Lights twinkled in potted shrubs and trees, and hurricane-type lanterns were placed around the square space, casting a cozy, intimate glow. A thick candle sat on a café table, surrounded by a glass globe to keep the wind from blowing it out. Beside the table was a stand and an ice bucket with a bottle of champagne inside it. And on the table's surface was a single rose, which he'd cut from the gardens himself. An assortment of strawberries, figs, grapes, and cheeses sat in crystal dishes.

"You did this?"

He shrugged. "I couldn't take you out somewhere fancy, so I brought it to you. I've lived in this castle since I was a boy. I know where things are kept. I just had to convince Señora Ortiz to let me sneak some food out of the kitchen, and dishes out of the crystal cabinet. She told me she's going to count it all in the morning." He grinned at Rose, who smiled back. Señora Ortiz was stern, but a softie underneath. She wouldn't bother counting anything. She would, however, worry.

"Does she know who it is for?" Rose asked, and he heard the hesitation in her tone.

"Probably. Maybe not. She won't talk, though, Rose. You can be sure of that."

Rose took a step forward, then spun around in a circle. "This is beautiful, Diego. And I'm not afraid of her talking." She smiled a little, one corner of her mouth turning up as her eyes twinkled. "I'm more worried about her disapproval. I don't think anyone would want to be on her wrong side." Her gaze softened. "She's been more than kind to me since my arrival."

"Everyone loves you," he said, stepping forward to take her hands. "Ernestina told me as much yesterday. If anything goes wrong, they won't place the blame on you."

She lifted her chin, like she was about to protest, but he shook his head. "No, enough of that sort of talk. Come over here and have a glass of champagne. I'm going to show you the kingdom."

He poured her a glass of bubbly and then one for himself, touched his rim to hers, and then drank. Damn, she was beautiful. When she shivered, he put down his glass and took her wrap from her hand, then spread it over her shoulders. Together they walked to the edge of the wall, and he showed her the shadowy view; the faint lights blinking as a plane took off from the island airport, the sky where the streetlights from the city cast a rosy glow on the horizon. On the other side, they could see past the black line of the trees to the fields and undulating hills beyond, the countryside where farmers grew their lemons, grapes, olives, and more. He explained how there was another city on the island, further inland, that was more industrial in nature. And that most of their trade was done with Spain and Italy, and that tourism played an important part of their economy. "We're a small principality," Diego explained, "and we have challenges to meet to stay vital. To stay independent. A lot of people say that monarchies are outdated, but they still like the idea of castles and kings and queens. Now, though, we have to prove our usefulness. It's not enough to be a figurehead."

She tilted her head up so she could look at him. "Your insight and talents are underrated, you know."

He sighed. "I know. And I did that to myself. I'm the spare heir. I didn't have responsibilities the same as Raoul. I went away to school. Played polo. Partied. Showed up in the tabloids too much. For a few years now, I've been trying show Raoul and my father that I'm more capable than they give me credit for. But living down my reputation has proven harder than I expected." He rolled his shoulders and cleared his throat. "More champagne?"

"Of course." She held out her glass, and they went to the table for a refill.

"Diego, have you asked Raoul if you could assume some of his duties? Maybe if he knew you wanted to help…"

Diego laughed. "I've offered. Raoul's not good at delegating. And besides, he spent the better part of his life trying to shelter me from the burden of the crown, ever since our mother's death. I was spoiled. I acted like it. I can't expect his attitude go to away overnight."

"So you what? Manage the polo ponies?"

He nodded. "Lucy did it for a while, when I was still in England and Ireland most of the time. She comes from a racetrack background, you know." He held out the bowl of strawberries and watched as she selected one. "That was how my father met her mother. And when Father sent Lucy to Canada to negotiate some breeding stock…well, she ended up staying. I had come home and needed something to do, and I knew horses."

He loved it, even though it was one of the more frivolous concerns of the monarchy. "Our reputation remains strong. A pony from Marazurian stock commands big dollars."

He held out her chair so she could sit. "But enough about me. What about you?"

She laughed. "What about me?"

"Tell me everything." He grinned, but he wasn't exactly teasing. He did want to know everything. "You grew up in Guildford. You have a brother and sister."

"And a niece, and two parents, and some old friends I haven't seen in a very long time. My upbringing was pretty boring, really. I did all right on my A levels. Went to church every Sunday—I notice your palace doesn't have a chapel, incidentally. I'm Church of England, which must make the Catholic in you shudder." She winked at him and he laughed. She could do that so easily, he realized. Make him laugh. Smile. She was just easy to be with. She had no expectations of what he should be like, no false glamour. She was simply Rose, no matter where they were or who they were with. He loved that about her.

There was that word again. It was sneaking into his vocabulary more and more.

A gust of wind skimmed over the top of the candle globe, and the flame bobbed and flickered for a minute before settling back again. Diego looked at Rose in the candlelight and felt his chest constrict. Her hair fluttered in the breeze and she tucked it behind her ear to get it out of the way. For the first time in his life, he didn't want the evening to end. He wanted to stay right here, looking at her.

"You're looking at me funny," she observed, taking a drink of champagne.

"I was just thinking how lovely you are," he replied. "And how this might be the nicest date I've ever had."

"Now I know you're talking nonsense." She popped a grape into her mouth and smiled wickedly. "I bet you say that to all the girls."

"Yes, but this is the first time I've meant it."

"And you probably say that, too," she laughed.

He looked into her eyes. "No," he answered, his heart thumping madly, anticipating his next words. "Rose, this date with you makes me not want to have any dates with anyone else."

CHAPTER 11

Rose stared at him, unsure of what to say. The last hour had been utterly perfect. Candles, twinkle lights, champagne under the stars…what more could a girl ever ask for? And Diego, sitting across from her, being so devastatingly gorgeous and sexy that she felt like an awkward, naïve schoolgirl. She didn't belong here…and yet he insisted she did.

And now he was saying things that made her hope for the fairy tale. And fairy tales were the one thing she didn't believe in. It wasn't that she was bitter. It was more a case of knowing how the world worked, and knowing that happiness had to be earned. Girls like her didn't have a prince fall into their lap.

"You don't believe me," he said gently. "Why?"

"I don't know," she answered. "It's not you. It's that…I don't believe something like this could happen to someone like me. I don't trust it. It's too surreal."

"And yet here we are. And you don't have to trust it. You just have to trust me. Can you?"

Her heart stuttered. "I want to," she admitted, "and that scares me."

"Because of our differences."

"Because I'm not princess material. I'm the help. Even Cecilia…she was from a wealthy family, was she not? She fit into this world nicely. I'd simply be awkward and always worried about doing the wrong thing. Saying the wrong thing."

"Don't be silly. You've been working for aristos for years and have more class in your little finger than most women do in their whole body. This almost sounds like reverse snobbery, Rosalie Walters." He lifted his brows, challenging her.

She held out her glass and he drained the last few drops of the champagne into it. If she were going to confide in him at all, she wanted a touch more liquid courage.

"And what would people say if they knew my background?" She drank deeply, ran her tongue over her lips, and savored the last taste. "I'm from a working class family. My address isn't in the swanky part of town. My brother is a vicar and he and his wife barely make ends meet. Then there's my sister…"

"What about her?" Diego leaned back in his chair and crossed his ankle over his knee.

"She had a baby when she was still in school. The father took off and left her alone, and she thought that I should be her nanny, considering I had all the training. When I said no, that I was signing on with an agency, she was furious." More than furious, Rose remembered. She'd said all kinds of hurtful things. "She said that I'd never find a man of my own to give me babies so I was going to look after someone else's. And that I wouldn't look after hers because I was jealous because at least someone had wanted *her*. The press could easily dig that up and make a case about Hayley's sour grapes. It's better for everyone if I stay in the background." It hurt her deeply to say it, but it was the truth.

She swallowed against the bitter taste in her mouth. Hayley knew how to be vicious. Rose had always been a bit of a wallflower. She'd had a few brief relationships in university but no one, ever, had fallen head-over-heels in love with her. Hayley's words hit a sore spot because they'd felt true.

All the same, Rose loved her work. It was incredibly fulfilling.

"So you don't have a good relationship," Diego said, frowning a little. "Is that really a problem?"

"We get along better now. But she's young, and trying to make ends meet in London. I send what I can so that they…so they have enough. And I try to spend some quality time with Alice when I'm in the city. But Diego, don't you see? If you want to stay out of the rags, dating someone like me isn't the way to do it. The press is sure to dig up stuff on my family and our working class roots." Her heart sank as she realized her faith in her sister wasn't that strong. "And despite getting along better, I wouldn't put it past Hayley to make the most of it, either. I have a freedom that she doesn't. Even though she loves me, she resents it. As much as I hate to say it, she could be bought."

Diego reached over and took her hand in his. His

fingers were strong and warm, and he rubbed his thumb over her wrist.

"The thing about the tabloids is that they'll write stories anyway, whether they have a basis in fact or not. So no matter who I date, there's a certain level of damage control to be done. And Rose? I'm finished letting the paparazzi dictate my life. I decided that the moment I saw the news of the car wreck on the pub TV screen. There were camera flashes going the whole time, like our tragedy was for their profit. My life decisions are not going to be made based on what the press might say. And they certainly won't keep me from being happy. Life is too short." He held her gaze. "Too precious."

Nothing he'd said was as comforting as his last words. There was a strength and integrity to them that she appreciated, and showed her once more who the real Diego was. He was a strong, behind-the-scenes man who put his family first, with a definite romantic side. How could she be immune to that, particularly when he didn't seem to care a bit about her background?

"I'm glad to hear it," she answered, relaxing a little.

"Rose, I want to be with you. Is that so bad?"

"Of course not."

"Then let's see how it goes, shall we?"

"And what if it doesn't work out, Diego? What then?" She wasn't sure how she'd feel about working at the palace, having Diego coming and going, and not hers. Not…friends.

He twined his fingers with hers. "Then I will do what I've been threatening to do for a long time, and set up my office elsewhere. Outside the palace." His gaze searched hers. "Before you arrived, I was hardly ever here. I never had a reason to stay."

"The children…"

"They had Ceci and Mariana, and their father. And once you arrived, I didn't need to be here anymore, either. But I am. And it's because of you, Rose."

He was very good at giving speeches, and making her all mushy and sappy. "It strikes me as surreal every day. Like I'm going to wake up and have imagined that you really care for me. That this is really happening. But it is. And I'm scared, Diego. The idea of this working out is too huge to comprehend. And the idea that it won't hurts my heart."

"Then don't think about that. Just think about this."

He stood and tugged at her hand, pulling her into his arms. She expected him to kiss her, but he didn't. He just folded her into his arms and held her close.

And in that moment, with her face against the crisp fabric of his shirt, the scent of him filling her nostrils, and the warmth of his arms around her body, she felt herself fall into love for the first time in her life.

FOR TWO WEEKS, ROSE AND DIEGO CAUGHT STOLEN moments alone. Once he brought her coffee while the children were napping after a vigorous swim in the pool, and fed her little almond cookies and kissed the crumbs off her face. Another afternoon he took her on a proper tour of the palace, pointing out the works of art lining the hallways and the impressive ballroom that was used for parties. His sister had been presented at a state ball, he told her, and accepted as a princess even though she was the illegitimate daughter of Alexander. He squeezed her hand when he told her that story, as if to say she wouldn't be the first to challenge the royal status quo.

There were long talks over glasses of red wine in the evenings, but after a while Rose knew that eventually the sneaking around would have to stop. She had mixed feelings about it. On one hand, she felt guilty about hiding their relationship and it was difficult to steal time together. On the other hand, she knew that once they went public, everything would change.

Diego came to her one evening and sat across from her in her suite. "So, next week is Raoul's birthday, and we've decided to throw a party. Nothing too fancy."

"What's your definition of too fancy?" she asked, crossing her leg over her knee and taking a sip of a particularly nice *tempranillo*.

He grinned. "Well, there will be…people. Probably a hundred or so. But not official like a state dinner or anything. We'll have food. A giant cake. Some dancing. The children are requested to attend through the dinner, but then they can go to bed after that."

"And Raoul isn't telling me this why?" She wondered why Diego was the one letting her know the plans for the children instead of their father. Most communication regarding specific requests came from him or through Stephani.

"Oh, he will. Tomorrow. We've been discussing it for a few weeks now. Invitations have gone out. The menu's been decided."

"I see. I'll be sure to have the children ready. Will they be needing new outfits?" She smiled softly. "Emilia would probably love a new dress. Maybe we could go shopping."

"You should get one for you, too," he suggested. "You'll be accompanying the children."

"I will?" Her brows pulled together. "But surely I'll just deliver them to the party, as I always do, and retrieve them after dinner?"

"Not this time." He sat back against the sofa cushions. "Before, they always had Cecilia to keep them in line at a big function. Not three bachelors. They need a steadying hand."

She imagined going to such a party and instantly felt overwhelmed. "You want me to sit with the children?"

"Yes. At the head table, to keep an eye on them."

To keep an eye on the children. Not as his date. Strictly as the nanny. Which was as it should be, so why was she disappointed?

This together/not together thing was more difficult than she'd expected. What were they even doing? Playing at a relationship? The kind where he put on his tuxedo, sash, and medals and sat to the left of the king, and she sat at the end of the table, making sure children used their napkins and otherwise being invisible? And then getting together behind closed doors and talking about how much they cared about each other? It was no way to run anything.

"You don't look happy," he observed, leaning forward again. "What's wrong?"

She looked up and met his gaze. "Diego, what are

we doing?" she whispered, unable to keep the note of longing out of her voice. "We can't be in public, we can't keep going on like this. It sounded all right in the beginning, but weren't we just fooling ourselves?"

He reached out for her hand. "Don't say that. You know I care about you. You're not just the nanny, you *know* that." He turned her hand over and kissed the base of her palm. "There's something special between us. And going to the party makes you visible, yes? Why not ease you into the spotlight? We already have the pictures from the market that day. A few more family appearances, make it seem like you're one of the family more and more… To everyone."

"You mean, to Raoul and your father. To ease them into the idea."

He smiled. "Yes, now you're getting it."

Her heart trembled. She should have listened to her gut all along. It wasn't even that Diego was a bad guy—he wasn't. But she'd been in lukewarm relationships before. Easing into anything sounded lackluster at best, and certainly not the action of a man who was ready to stand up and make her his.

At first she'd thought propriety was her biggest concern. But she realized, quite suddenly, that there was something bigger at play. Maybe there was something to what Hayley had said after all, about how she looked after other people's children because she didn't think she'd have any of her own. Unintentional or not, she wondered if perhaps she considered herself such a wallflower that no one would ever take notice. Would ever give her the fairy tale.

Fairy tales, she realized, were horribly overrated. The reality was very different than being whisked away into a perfect fantasy. Instead it felt like navigating a professional and personal minefield.

She kept her gaze even as she looked at Diego. "You know, you could just tell them that we've been seeing each other. See what they say." Her heart clenched a bit. There was always the chance that she'd be sacked, but if they found out by accident, that would probably happen anyway.

He frowned. "I just think the party isn't the time, you know?" He stood from the sofa and paced a bit. "The timing's a bit tricky. Remember how I talked about damage control a few weeks ago? There are so many things to consider about the party. And guests from around Marazur and other countries. When we talk to Raoul and my father, it should be something we can discuss and make a plan forward."

He put his hands on his hips and looked down at her.

"You have always struck me as spontaneous. Impulsive," she replied, folding her hands in her lap. He didn't need to see them shaking.

He came and sat by her side. "Darling, I am. But my family has to be handled with care. I don't want to start a paparazzi firestorm. I want to show them I care for you but that I want to work with them to make this the easiest it can be for the monarchy."

She stiffened. "I didn't realize I was a problem to be solved."

"You're not!"

"Of course I am," she replied. "I am an issue that needs to be handled. Strategized."

"That sounds cold." He touched her knee. "Just come to the party. Enjoy yourself." His gaze was so warm and intense that she didn't want to look away. Felt herself being convinced by those dark depths and his honeyed voice. "Please, *querida*. Be a part of our family for the evening."

"But I wouldn't be a part of your family. That's what you don't seem to understand." If Raoul dictated it, she'd have no choice. But for right now, she did.

She removed his hand from her leg. "Diego, for the past two weeks, we've had some amazing stolen moments together. But for me to go to this dinner… I wouldn't be able to pretend I wasn't the nanny. And I would feel like…well, like I really am the plaything that the papers called me."

She got up from the sofa. "I think I need to think about us for a bit, Diego. Maybe it would be better if we didn't see each other for a few days. This is so confusing."

"That's what you want?"

"Yes, it is."

He nodded. "I know this situation is a lot to handle and it can be overwhelming. If you need some time to think, I'll respect that. I would never want to hurt you, Rose. Just know that I want you to be there." His voice softened. "I want you to feel you belong there."

Her throat tightened and a stinging took up residence just behind her nose. "I know that," she answered, and it was true. He didn't want to hurt her, but he also didn't know how to fight for her, either. It didn't have to be a grand gesture to the whole world, but perhaps, if this party was truly a big thing, he could have an honest chat with Raoul about his feelings. Their feelings.

That he was backing away felt like a let-down, even if it was cushioned by respect.

She cleared her throat. "I'll speak to Stephani about a dress for Emilia tomorrow, and anything else the children might need." And for arrangements, too, that didn't include her sitting with the family at dinner. The Prince's Plaything. Palace Plaything. Playboy's Plaything. There were any number of variations but all of them were the same. Maybe their feelings for each other were genuine, but in the eyes of the world, she would always be *the help*. The gold digger. Perhaps an opportunist. And she was starting to realize that the potential labels really did bother her. She and Diego had been self-indulgent these last few weeks, and it had to stop.

They either had to go into this all the way or not at all. There was no "easing" in. If she were worth it, if *they* were worth it, Diego had to stop worrying about fighting *with* her and start fighting *for* her. Until he was willing to do that, it would be better if things cooled off.

"I need to get some sleep now, Diego. Maybe we should call it a night."

He put his wine glass down next to the bottle and put his hands in his pockets. "I don't want to leave you this way," he said quietly. "I promise, Rose, I didn't come here to upset you. I'm trying to do the right thing and in the right way. This is all new territory for me, too."

The confession softened her resolve just a little bit. "I'm not upset," she said, which was only a half-lie. "I mean, I really do need to think. We always knew this was going to be complicated." Though she hadn't thought it would be *this* complicated. Still, if Diego couldn't tell his family about her, how could he expect her to face the world, who wouldn't be nearly as understanding or kind?

A flash of hurt crossed his face before he sighed. "Then I guess all I can say for now is *Buenas noches*," he whispered, and kissed her forehead. "If you need anything—and I mean anything—over the next few days, I'll either be down at the stables or in my office. I'm still working on that education program snag."

He was a good man; she knew that.

But being a good man wasn't the issue. Navigating the ins and outs of a complicated relationship was. They had to be completely united in their approach, and Rose wasn't convinced he really understood her perspective—or if he ever would.

CHAPTER 12

The days leading up to Raoul's special day were a flurry of activity around the palace. Rooms were prepared for guests, menus finalized and tweaked, silver polished and linens pressed. A secret celebrity and his band were being flown in to perform after the cutting of the birthday cake, and extra security arrangements were put in place.

And this was a *small* party. Rose had skirted around her share of drawing rooms and cocktail parties, but this was something utterly different.

The day before the big event, Stephani stopped by Rose's room while the children were at dinner with their father. She breezed into the room with a garment bag in her hand and a determined set to her full mouth.

"Did we forget something for tomorrow?" Rose asked, shutting the door behind her. "Emilia's dress came from the shop this afternoon."

"Yes. *Your* dress." She held out the bag and shook the hanger.

Rose took a step back. "Oh no. We already discussed this. I'm going to deliver the children to the party and pick them up after cake."

"No, you're going to be sitting with them. In this." She shook the hanger again.

Rose sighed. "Stephani…this is too awkward."

"Because of Diego?"

Rose frowned and pinned Stephani with a look. "What do you mean?"

Stephani took the bag and hung it on the closet doorknob, then came back, took Rose's hand, and led her to the bed, where they sat side by side. "It's no secret that you and Diego are…friends."

The way she said friends let Rose know they hadn't been fooling anyone.

"Which is exactly why I shouldn't go." She pulled her hand away and sighed. "It's so inappropriate. And I wanted to believe in the…in the fairy tale. When we're together, it's so easy to think it's just the two of us. But it's not. The nanny cannot be the prince's girlfriend. We all know it."

"Why not?" Stephani scowled. "Don't you deserve happiness?"

"It's not about that."

"Of course it is. And doesn't Diego? The office staff talks too, you know. He's in the office every day, on top of things. Smiling, happy. With a purpose. You didn't know him before, but Rose, you've been so good for him." Stephani halted, then met Rose's eyes. "I've worked for Raoul for a long time. He underestimates his little brother. But you don't. You've given Diego a sense of pride in himself."

Heat crept up Rose's cheeks. "Surely not."

"People in the palace see more than many think. If you care about each other, why shouldn't you be happy? Diego's broken rules before, and for less exalted reasons."

Stephani patted her hand. "Rose. Everyone worried about the children after Ceci and Mariana died. This beautiful castle was like a tomb. And then you came. And they stopped crying. And people started smiling. And we heard laughter again, and Raoul stopped tiptoeing around, and Diego…he asked Raoul personally for you to come to the party with the family. You should have heard him speak of you, Rose, telling his father and brother how important you are. He admires you very much."

Not just kissing and flirting, then. Butterflies took wing in her stomach as she remembered the long talks and glasses of wine they'd shared, the romantic night on the battlements, the touch of his lips on hers. And if what Stephani said was true, maybe he hadn't told his father and brother they were seeing each other, but he spoke of her as if she were…special.

"I don't like to hope," she murmured, staring at her hands. "It's always led to disappointment. Besides, we both agreed the other night. This can't be a…a thing. He's not ready for us to be a real thing. I said I wasn't comfortable keeping this from the king and from Raoul, but he wants to 'ease' our way forward. It's impossible."

Stephani was quiet a moment, and when Rose

looked up, she saw the other woman with a strange, wistful look in her eyes. "But what do we have without hopes?" Stephani asked. "Without dreams? Not everyone has theirs offered to them. You have an obligation to grab at your chance of happiness, don't you think?"

That sounded rather like the voice of experience, and Rose wondered what lay beneath Stephani's perfectly polished and professional exterior.

"I still don't want to be his secret. His…girl on the side." It sounded awful but honestly, that was how she felt. "If he were really sure, he'd say something, don't you think? I mean, not publicly, but to his family?"

Stephani hesitated. "Rose, this is the first event to be held at the palace since Ceci died. It's in Raoul's honor. Over the years, Diego's frequently made himself the center of attention. If he's staying quiet, perhaps it's because he wants Raoul to have this one day without Diego…what's the saying? Stealing his thunder? Maybe he wants you there but wants to find a better moment to talk to them."

Rose hadn't considered that this was Raoul's night. Stephani's words also echoed Diego's from the other evening, saying he wanted to find the right time. She wondered if she was asking for too much; after all, Diego had navigated these waters before and probably knew what he was doing. "Are you going to be there?" she asked, hesitantly letting herself dream just a little bit.

"Of course. I'm planning it and have make sure everything runs like clockwork." She smiled. "So you'll have a friend there. And another member of the working class, so to speak."

Rose was so tempted. She looked over at the white bag hanging on the closet door. How long had it been since she'd really dressed up for a fancy dinner? Would she look back on this and kick herself for not going when she had the chance? Not everyone got an invitation to the Crown Prince of Marazur's birthday party. "I'll try the dress on. No guarantees, though."

Stephani's face brightened. "Go do it now. I want to see if it fits. I picked it out myself."

Excitement prickled a bit as Rose got up from the bed and went to the closet. The bag was heavier than she expected, and she hurried to her bathroom to try it on. When she unzipped the bag, her breath caught. It was stunning—a 20s-style rose pink dress with silver beading and fringe along the hem. She'd been expecting a little black dress. Something understated and elegant. Not this. It was too…obvious. But beautiful enough that she couldn't resist slipping it off the hanger and onto her body.

But not before she saw the designer label. There was a distinct moment, as she did up the side zipper, that she had the feeling that she was Cinderella and Stephani was her fairy godmother.

She stepped out of the bathroom and Stephani's eyes lit up. "*Preciosa*," she whispered, putting a hand to her chest. "Oh, Rose. It's perfect. Do you like it?"

Rose nodded. "I shouldn't. It's from Italy, isn't it? It's too much."

"No, it's not. Besides, I'm wearing a Versace. It's

expected. It's not like you can go shop off the rack for the crown prince's birthday party."

"Oh, this feels like such a mistake." She reached for the top of the zip, starting to panic all over again.

But Stephani rushed forward. "It's not. And besides, this is the first event since Ceci's death for the children, too. They'll be more comfortable with you there. Emilia especially. I think that sweet little girl will like having you by her side." She smiled. "And Max is all boy. He'll need watching or he'll sneak too much cake."

Rose might have refused, despite the dress, except Stephani brought up the one reason she would do anything: the children. It was her job to watch them, but even if it wasn't, she'd want to make sure they not only got through the evening but enjoyed themselves, too. They shouldn't suffer because of her confusing personal life. She would do it for them and deal with the rest like a grown-up.

Stephani sighed. "Please accept it and come. I have shoes for you, too, arriving tomorrow. Silver ones, to match the beading. Tell me you can be bribed by Manolos."

Rose wasn't able to refuse Stephani. Diego had been easier, but now, with the dress, and everything Stephani had said…surely Rose could enjoy being dressed up, eat a delightful dinner, have a piece of whatever delectable cake Señora Ortiz was planning, and then call it an evening when the children had to leave for bed.

Surely she could do her job and put her relationship with Diego to the side for a few hours.

"Would I be sitting close to Diego?"

Stephani shook her head. "No. Raoul will be in the middle, with his father on his right, and Diego beside him. The children will be on his left, and you at the end. Opposite sides of the table. There doesn't have to be any tension. Just come. Raoul is so grateful for how you've been with the children. He wants you to be there, Rose."

"He sent you? Not Diego?"

"Raoul did. I promise."

That was the clincher, then. "You could have said so before," Rose replied, lifting her chin. "Raoul is my boss."

"But then I wouldn't have known how you feel about Diego." Stephani grinned. "Someone around here should have a shot at the fairy tale."

Rose looked at Stephani closely. "What about you, then? No husband? No boyfriend?" She grinned. "No Prince Charming?"

Stephani smiled, but Rose saw sadness behind it. "Oh, not for me," she replied. "I gave my heart away quite a while ago. It hasn't come back to me yet."

Rose wanted to ask her about it, but she needed to get the dress off and figure out what she was going to wear for jewelry and how she was going to do her hair. With a quick hug of gratitude, she sent Stephani on her way and then stood in front of the full-length mirror, her eyes and cheeks bright with anticipation.

She was going to the ball. There was no carriage, nor any glass slippers or clock chiming at midnight, but this was her first—perhaps her only—chance at a royal party.

Diego looked in the mirror outside the drawing room and straightened his bowtie one last time. He was used to wearing a tux, but preferred to be more casual. Right now the tie was squeezing his neck and sitting a bit to one side. Frowning, he tried adjusting it again.

"Here, let me fix that. You're going to mash it to bits."

Stephani stepped up to him and reached for the silk edges of the tie. "You're late. Your father and brother are already inside at the cocktail hour."

"Sorry. I got tied up on the phone."

"On your brother's birthday?"

"Still having issues with the Tanzania group." He chanced a look down at her. She was frowning, her tongue between her teeth, and gave his tie one last tug. Then she stepped back and smiled.

"Camila said you've been dealing with some issues there. Anything our office can help with?"

Diego shook his head. No way did he want Raoul's help. If anything, he needed to prove he could do something of value all on his own. "I can handle it. But I'll let you know if I get stuck and need a hand."

She patted his arm. "Well, don't let pride hold you back. And someday Raoul will appreciate you, Diego. It'll come."

"Thanks?" He gave her a sideways smile. "Okay, so who do I need to charm? Camila gave me the guest list but I put it in my desk and didn't have a chance to look at it."

She gave him the final rundown of the guest list, and he made his way into the drawing room, accepted a glass of white wine, and wished he could have something stronger. He knew Stephani had convinced Rose to come and he was nervous about seeing her again.

He scanned the room, looking for no one in particular, and took another drink of wine. Being without her for the last few days had been hell. He'd got used to seeing her at the end of the day. Seeing her smile, hearing her voice, kissing her lips. Watching her with the children. She was everything he'd always wanted, even though he wasn't looking for it. She was running scared and he was…

He was falling in love. It should be scaring him to death but all he could think about was how he was going to convince her to stick with him. How was he going to break it to his father and brother that he'd fallen in love with the new nanny? What was he prepared to do to keep her by his side? He'd been thinking about it nonstop. He was the go-with-the-flow prince, but he'd never truly had anything worth fighting for before. The first step was being honest. But he hadn't wanted to do it tonight. Tonight was too important, and Raoul needed support, not another complication on his plate.

Diego mingled for a good half hour, until everyone was called in to dinner. And at that moment Rose stepped to the door with Emilia and Max and his heart stopped.

Good God, they made a sight. Emilia in her pretty white dress with the blue sash, and Max in a little suit with a black tie and polished shoes. But Rose…she was a vision, in a color that was the same as her name but glittering with silver beads and crystals. She'd done something soft and romantic looking with her hair, and she had the sexiest silver heels on her feet.

Raoul stepped to his side. "Roll your tongue back into your mouth, *hermano*."

Diego gave his head a shake. "Sorry. I just…" He looked over at his brother. "I didn't realize it was that obvious."

"Very. Has been for a few weeks, if one is inclined to look," Raoul said. He frowned. "It's not a good idea, Diego."

Diego immediately felt the urge to come to her defense. To *their* defense, but he took a careful breath and smiled at someone passing by. "I can't seem to shake it. She's amazing. Sweet and kind and loving and infuriating."

Raoul's features softened just a bit, and Diego thought he looked rather sad. He wondered if Raoul was thinking of Ceci. Of course he must still be grieving. "She's the nanny," Raoul cautioned. "You've always kept your…indiscretions away from the palace."

Diego's gaze snapped to his brother. "There haven't been any indiscretions," he bit out, trying hard to keep his cool. Rose was different. She was important.

"I'm glad to hear it." Raoul gave a small smile and Diego noticed the lines of strain around his brother's eyes.

"Let's leave it for tonight," Diego suggested. "It's your birthday. Let's enjoy the evening. I hear the cake is a work of art."

Raoul put his hand on Diego's shoulder. "Just be careful. I don't want Rose to be hurt, or you either. And the children need stability."

"Neither of us would do anything to hurt the children," he replied, his previous resolution to keep his cool disintegrating. He would not create a scene, but he saw now what Rose had wanted from him. To own their relationship and not act as if it was something to hide. He glanced up at Raoul. "It's not because of her class, is it? Because she's got more class in her baby finger than most of the women here tonight."

Raoul laughed, easing the tension. "Of course it's not. She's lovely. But perhaps too lovely. Being a part of this family has its challenges. We'll talk later."

Raoul left his side to greet Rose and the children, exclaiming over their new clothes and squatting down for a hug. Rose met Diego's gaze over Raoul's shoulder and smiled timidly, her cheeks coloring prettily.

His heart thudded, and he smiled back.

He went over to greet her, hoping he didn't stammer or look foolish.

"You look dashing," she said quietly, touching his lapel lightly before dropping her hand.

"And you really came." He smiled down at her. "Rose, that dress…"

"Thank Stephani. She wouldn't take no for an answer and insisted I be dressed appropriately. She's a force to be reckoned with."

Once her first blush had faded, he realized she was more distant than he liked. Her reply lacked her usual warmth. Was she still mad at him? Nervous? He tried to lighten the mood. "Which is why Raoul is determined he'll never have another assistant. She knows his routines and moods better than anyone." He looked into her eyes. "Rose, about the other night—"

"I really must get the children. I'm on duty tonight."

Her feelings couldn't be clearer, and he wished he could really talk to her but the crowd was making its way into the massive dining room. Diego gestured with his hand. "Shall we go?"

Raoul approached with Emilia and Max holding on to each of his hands. "Shall we go in?" he asked, motioning for the children to take Rose's hands instead. The king joined them, nodding at Diego and then smiling at Rose. "Miss Walters," he said, smiling. "I'm pleased you could join us. The children look wonderful —and happy."

She dropped a curtsy. "Thank you, Your Highness," she replied, looking down demurely. Diego saw his father's eyes light with approval. Maybe there was a hope. After tonight he'd have a frank conversation with his father and brother about his feelings and intentions, and how it should best be handled both in and outside the palace.

He was willing to work with them, but he wasn't giving up. He wanted her in his life and he'd prove to her she belonged there.

CHAPTER 13

Rose entered first, holding the children's hands and walking to the far end of the dais, where seats were arranged for the three of them. Emilia was tall enough to manage without any sort of bolster, but Max needed the extra height. She helped him clamber up as Diego, Alexander, and finally, Raoul, the guest of honor, entered the room to a round of applause.

As soon as everyone was seated, a flurry of activity came through the doors as servers appeared, whisking covers off plates and placing the starters gently in front of the guests. The first course was prawns in a béarnaise sauce, though a more child-friendly variation was presented to the children. Rose assisted them through the proper flatware and etiquette, but they'd eaten *en famille* so many times that it took only a few words and they had their napkins properly on their laps and were delicately tasting the succulent prawns. Rose tried them as well, and the course was paired with a spectacular white wine, crisp and smooth.

Several minutes later, the plates were taken away and a new course was placed in front of her. This, when she asked, was sea bream with chanterelles and truffles, and the flavors melted in her mouth. While she'd eaten well in the kitchen, this was elevated to a whole other level. She closed her eyes and simply savored, and regrettably left a third of it on her plate, and about half of her wine pairing as well. How was she to get through a main course and dessert without her dress becoming suddenly too small, or her head too light?

The children picked at the fish, which was clearly not their favorite. But when their mains came, they ate with gusto. The veal was tender and mild, the fava beans done to perfection. While Rose knew she shouldn't, she ate every morsel, and the Pinot Noir pairing was amazing. Emilia and Max cleaned their plates, though she reached over once and dabbed Max's mouth with his napkin. He grinned up at her, his little bowtie bobbing, and she nearly laughed.

"Miss Rose?"

"Yes, sweetheart?"

"You look very pretty." He batted his dark eyelashes and she wasn't sure if she should melt or roll her eyes at his obvious charm.

"You sound like your *Tio Diego*," she cautioned, placing his napkin back in his lap.

"That's because *Tio Diego* loves you."

Her heart stopped for a second. "Oh Max, don't be silly," she said.

"He does." He'd switched to Spanish, but she was able to translate easily. "He loves you like my father loves my mother."

She had to blink rapidly as she smiled at him, at a loss as to how to respond. Finally she patted his knee. "So what kind of cake do you think we will have tonight?" she asked him.

Cake was a good diversion. He chattered for a few minutes about his favorite kinds, but Rose couldn't get his words out of her head.

And then the cheese course arrived, a signature Navarro *Cabra al Vino* and figs, along with a spectacular Rioja. Even though she only had a few sips, her head was a little fuzzy, and she drank deeply from her water glass. Music played in the background, and when she looked over, Diego caught her eye and smiled. She nodded back, determined that she keep things polite, if distant. Things were just so complicated, and the longer the evening went on, the more out of place she felt.

When she looked over at the children, she discovered that they'd eaten the middle of their cheese but left the wine-soaked rind, which was likely a bit strong for their tastes. Emilia's legs began swinging beneath the table, a sure sign she was getting tired, and Max started playing with his figs.

She really hoped there was cake soon, so she could take the children off to bed. While the opulent setting and incredible food had weaved a spell, she couldn't totally escape the reality of the situation. She picked at her figs and looked around the room. These were not her people. They were either rich or aristocratic or both, and she was neither. She could practice etiquette and say the right things without much difficulty, but that was a far cry from belonging.

Maybe Diego had wanted her to attend tonight to show her she could hold her own, but instead she was just more aware than ever that she was out of place. And because of their "secret," she didn't feel as if she had any support. The sooner the dinner was over, the better.

She touched Max's knee when he fidgeted through Diego's toast to his brother, and sent him a look of warning to sit still as Raoul responded. As he sat through yet another round of applause, she leaned forward. "There will be cake now, and then we can go back to the nursery. If I know Señora Ortiz, the cake will be worth the wait." She winked at them, but she'd spoken the truth. The cook was fabulous at everything, but she was particularly talented at cakes and pastries.

A cart was wheeled in, with a tiered cake adorned with edible flowers at its center. Raoul stood and motioned the children forward, and together they blew out the candles on the top layer. Raoul, as the guest of honor, cut the cake and tasted the first corner from his fingers, then laughed and cut pieces for Max and Emilia. After that, plates of pre-cut slices were delivered to everyone, along with strong coffee and a dessert wine that Rose declined.

The cake, though…it was scrumptious, with the flavors of almonds, oranges, and lemons. She'd never had anything like it. The menu card at her place said it was *Tarta de Santiago*.

"Will Papa open his presents?" Emilia asked, tasting a tiny bite of the cake and getting powdered sugar on her lips.

"Not now," Rose said. "He'll open them later. Once dessert is done, we can go back upstairs. I'll tuck you into bed and your father will visit tomorrow and will open your very special presents. Okay?"

"*Sì*, Miss Rose," Emilia answered.

She was such a precious girl, Rose realized. Her dark curls and big eyes were so like the pictures Rose had seen of Ceci, and she was sweet and polite. Rose hoped, though, that she was able to have fun and just be…a kid. Max seemed to accomplish that a bit more easily.

After cake, guests began moving freely about the room, and soon they would go en masse to the ballroom, where music and dancing awaited. Rose made sure faces and fingers were clean and unsticky, then took the children to say goodnight to their father before taking them to bed.

Raoul was sitting in his chair with a child on each lap when Diego slid up behind her.

"You're coming back down to the party, right?" he asked, his breath tickling her ear.

She shivered. "I hadn't really planned on it. My job for the evening is done."

He came around to face her and she knew she'd have a hard time resisting his handsome face and charming eyes.

"It would be a shame to waste that dress. It will catch the light of the chandeliers, you know. Just…come down for a few minutes at least. Have a glass of champagne and listen to the music. It's not every day you get to hear him live."

It was tempting, and Diego had said nothing of dancing. Just champagne and music. "I don't think so. It's been a long day."

Raoul stepped to Diego's side. "Miss Walters, you look lovely. And the children were perfect tonight. Thank you. Seeing them happy again is the only gift I really need."

She smiled up at him. "I would say it is my job, sir, but I'm very fond of them."

"They feel safe with you." He reached out and took her hand in his, not quite a handshake but not quite anything more, either. "Diego made a wonderful choice when he picked you as our nanny."

Her heart warmed and her eyes stung a little. "Thank you," she whispered. Diego still stood close to her, and he put his hand on her shoulder in support. In that moment Rose's feelings were overwhelmingly surreal. The crown prince was saying incredibly kind things and his younger brother was touching her rather intimately…in public. She felt appreciated…and she felt loved. What an extraordinary family. Earlier she hadn't felt supported, but now…

"You'll come down and join the party, won't you? After the children are in bed?" Raoul looked at her earnestly.

"I hadn't planned on it, sir."

"I insist. You deserve a little fun, too. Have a glass of champagne."

Now she was in a tight spot. She couldn't very well

refuse, could she? "I suppose I could pop down for a few minutes."

"Good." He gave her a nod and a smile.

She cleared her throat. "All right, let's get these two packed off to bed, shall we? Come on Emilia, Max. Special stories tonight. And extra time with the toothbrush thanks to all that cake."

Max made a face and they all laughed, and then Rose took them by the hand and left the room. But she felt Diego's gaze on her back, and heard her promise to return echo in her head.

THE DANCING WAS IN FULL SWING BY THE TIME ROSE entered the ballroom. She stayed to the perimeter, trying to remain inconspicuous, and found a place close to the wall where she could hear the music and watch the dancers beneath the chandeliers. She smiled a bit as she realized that the setting didn't actually resemble what she'd imagined. No one was spinning around in a swirl of skirts to a waltz or anything so staid. Instead hips and feet were moving and shoulders shaking as they kept up with the band. The lights were dimmed and created a more intimate glow than there'd been at dinner, and the stage lights reflected off the crystals. Raoul was in his thirties; many of the guests were just on either side of that number. The atmosphere was more like an exclusive club than a palace ballroom.

A footman she didn't recognize came past with a tray of champagne. She selected one, took a sip, and sighed. One glass, a couple of songs, and she'd disappear. Still, this was one for the memory banks. Her friends back home wouldn't believe it, would they? She smiled to herself. If nothing else, the last few months had been an adventure.

"You did come."

Diego appeared at her side, his hair slightly damp from dancing, presumably. He'd taken off his tuxedo jacket, his bowtie was gone, and the top button of his blindingly white shirt was undone. He'd never looked so delicious, and the wicked glint of his eyes only fanned the flames. Why could she not resist him? Why did she react to every look, touch, sound of his voice?

"I said I would." She ignored the flutterings and lifted her glass. "Champagne. And the music is fabulous."

"Look," he said, pointing. "Even Raoul is dancing."

Indeed he was. He was on the floor, dancing smoothly though still with a certain amount of reserve, Rose thought. And Stephani was his partner, looking thoroughly elegant in her Versace little black dress and her dark hair swept back in a neat updo.

"My goodness," she said, laughing. "Now there's something I didn't expect to see."

The song ended and the tempo slowed a bit. "Put your glass down and come on. You're going to dance with me." He reached for her free hand and gave it a tug.

She pulled back a little. "Oh, is that such a good idea?"

"Raoul's dancing with Steph."

"Yes, but there's a difference in an executive assistant and the nanny, Diego. And I'm pretty sure they haven't been carrying on in secret."

"One dance." His dark eyes pleaded with her. "Please." He lowered his voice. "*Por favor, corazón.*"

Ah, yes. The language and accent that would make any woman swoon, and she was no exception. She couldn't refuse when he spoke that way and looked at her with what she could only describe as bedroom eyes. She drank the rest of her champagne, put her glass on a table, and took his hand. "One," she said firmly.

Tremors rippled through her stomach as she stepped onto the floor with him and he took her in his arms. It felt as if everyone was looking at them, but when she looked around it seemed no one was even paying attention. Her gaze darted up to his face and he smiled at her, tightening his fingers around her hand while is other palm rested firmly against the small of her back. "Relax," he murmured, as he started to move his feet. "Just dance with me, Rosalie."

She swallowed nervously, but managed to shuffle her feet a bit, until bit by bit she let go of the tension in her limbs and melted into the embrace. He guided her easily, expertly, his shoulder warm beneath her hand, the scent of his cologne magnified by the heat of his body.

"You are so beautiful," he said, leaning close to her ear. With the music and crowd, she knew it was the only way she'd be able to hear him, but the close proximity of him added to the crazy awareness happening right now. "I'm crazy about you, Rose."

"Oh, Diego." She leaned back a little and looked into his face. "You shouldn't say things like that."

"It's the truth. Since you came here, you've turned everything upside down. And in a good way, you see? I never thought I could feel like this. That I'd want to. But I do."

The air she gulped into her lungs strained against her ribs. "Just dance with me, Diego. One dance. Then I have to go…"

He squeezed her hand. "Everything's changed, can't you feel it?"

Her heartbeat thudded with fear and anticipation. "Has it?" she asked, shaking her head. "I can't keep sneaking around, and you heard Raoul tonight. The children…they need me. They have to come first."

"And why can't they still? We can make this work." He straightened a bit, and Rose saw the stubborn tilt to his jaw. "I'll make it happen."

And just then Rose was reminded of her first night at the palace, where they'd met at the fountain and she'd felt so outmatched. Palace playboy or not, Diego was a Navarro, and he was confident and used to getting his own way. The stakes were far higher now. Real feelings were involved, and she didn't want to be either manipulated or hurt.

"What are you going to do, issue a royal decree?" She lifted an eyebrow. "This is what I want, so deal with it?"

"If I have to." He wasn't smiling anymore.

"Don't be ridiculous." She moved to pull out of his arms, but he held her fast.

"Don't run."

"Is that an order, too?"

He frowned. "Rose, what's got into you? I'm trying to tell you how I feel! That I'm willing to do whatever it takes to make this work."

She knew what had got into her. More than a romantic date on the rooftop, or a kiss in the intimate confines of her room, or even holding hands ever so briefly walking down a hall. It was this setting, tonight. When she was next to him, she tended to forget. But it was just like that day in the city. Someone would always point out that she didn't measure up. That she didn't *matter.*

What had got into her was fear, plain and simple. Because she wanted to say yes. She wanted to say yes so badly that she was nearly willing to throw caution to the wind.

The song ended and Rose stepped back. "I have to go," she said, trying hard not to stutter.

"Don't," Diego said, reaching for her hand, but she stepped back, then pasted on a smile and affected a little curtsy in case anyone was watching. Of course they were watching…how could they not?

"I said one glass and one dance. I have to get back. Goodnight…"

She turned and wanted to run but didn't. Instead she walked carefully, deliberately, to the edge of the room again, then skirted the perimeter until she got to the doors. Her heart pounded as she hoped he wasn't going to follow her, but she was too afraid to look back. Instead she smiled at people along the way, nodding politely, then once she got outside the room, she let out a breath and picked up her pace.

When she got to the stairs her feet were aching so much from her shoes that she slipped them off and hooked them in a finger as she climbed to the next story and then headed down the long hall toward the nursery and her room just beyond it.

Once inside she shut the door, dropped her shoes, and leaned back against the cool wood.

This wasn't just caring anymore. She was utterly, totally, in love with him. How could they possibly live here together? She certainly couldn't continue sneaking around with him, couldn't bear the thought of being only his mistress, absolutely couldn't be his wife…good heavens, what a scandal. And this was his home. She could leave…

But she thought of the children and knew she couldn't leave them. Not after they'd already had so much upheaval.

What in the world was she going to do?

CHAPTER 14

He couldn't believe she'd walked away like that.

Diego stared through the crowd at the rear door of the ballroom and saw her pink dress slip through the gap. He'd been trying to explain his feelings. To show her that they could be together, that it would be all right. And instead she'd run. Run! Rose didn't run from anything. Nothing scared her…except, apparently, this.

He could just let her go. Let the affair die a quiet death, move on, focus on other things. Only he couldn't, because he suspected rather strongly that he could go just about anywhere and she'd be there. In his head and in his heart. That meant the only thing to do was go after her. His heart clubbed against his ribs as he threaded his way through the crowd to Raoul.

He pulled his brother aside and met his startled gaze. "I've got to go. I just didn't want to leave without making my apologies."

Raoul frowned. "What's going on?"

Diego took a deep breath and squared his shoulders. "I love her, Raoul. I don't know if she'll have me or not, but I have to at least tell her how I feel."

"This is the real thing?" Raoul maintained his stern face. "Because she's not a girl to be toyed with, Diego. Nanny or not. Rose is a sweet, kind woman."

"Don't you think I know that? And I wish it wasn't complicated. I swear I do. I didn't set out for this to happen. I certainly wasn't looking to fall in love. It found me."

Raoul smiled a little, the curve of his lips breaking his icy features. "Well, you'd better tell her, then," he answered. "Go."

"You're sure?"

"I didn't know it was like *that*. Love is love, *hermano*."

"Thank you. And happy birthday."

Diego left through the main ballroom doors, paused to pluck a single white rose from an arrangement, and took the curving stairs two at a time.

He slowed when he approached her door and ran his free hand over his trouser leg, nervous about knocking. He'd never been in this position before. Never cared enough about a woman to lay it all on the line, but this was different. They would figure it out—how to be together, how to make it work for the children's sake. Even if he had to move out of the palace while she was here, to give a better impression of propriety…he'd do it.

He took a deep breath, let it out, and tapped on the door.

She didn't open it. "Go away, Diego." Even muffled by the thick wood, he could hear the frustration and longing in her voice.

"No. There's something I need to tell you, Rose. And this isn't going to go away."

Through the closed door he heard, "So tell me. And *then* go away."

He swallowed against the lump in his throat. This wasn't how he'd ever pictured saying these words to a woman. He rested his forehead against the door. "I love you."

The knob rattled as she opened the door a crack. "If you're just saying that to get me to let you in…" Most of her face was hidden, but he could see the strained look in her eyes as she peered out at him.

"I've never said those words to another woman." He held up the rose. "And I'm certainly not going to use them as a ploy. I love you, Rose. And my determination to make this work is because I believe we belong together, not because I'm used to getting my way."

She stood back and opened the door. "Get out of the hallway," she said with a sigh. "Before someone hears you."

He stepped into her suite and held out the rose. "I could send you bouquets of flowers and fill this room," he said, "but sometimes a single bloom says enough, don't you think?"

She took it in her hands, an odd look on her face. "And why white?"

He considered telling her he'd plucked it on the run, but instead scoured his brain for meanings. "White roses. They're wedding roses, did you know that? And new beginnings." He stepped forward and clasped her hand. "Let's make tonight a new beginning for us."

Her eyes glistened as she met his gaze. "Do you realize that once, many years ago, I handed *you* a white rose?"

He frowned, wondering what on earth she was talking about, when she continued.

"I was selling flowers on a train platform, trying to make money for school. I was so poor in those days… my family didn't even know how tight my budget was, and that some days I hardly had anything for food. I lived on day old buns, peanut butter, and porridge. You bought a rose from me, and then you bought all my flowers and told me to brighten someone's day by giving them away."

He stood back and stared at her. He vaguely remembered the day…he'd been…where? Somewhere with Ryan, and they'd gone out, and he'd had a very nice evening. Woke in the morning feeling like a million dollars and generous. And he'd seen the skinny girl with the flowers and had impulsively given her a wad of cash.

"That was you?"

She nodded. "I was going to school to learn childhood education. The degree that took me to the agency and led me here. And that one day of sales got me through the month."

He couldn't believe it. She'd been here months already and had never breathed a word. "Did you know who I was?"

She nodded, still holding the stem of the rose in her

fingertips. "Of course I did. My roommate was a big polo fan. The 'sport of kings' and all that. She was always very excited when there'd be word that you were playing. A real prince." She smiled a little, a sweet little curve of her lips. "I never told her about the flowers, though. I wanted to keep that little bit of you to myself. That day I saw a Diego Navarro who was different from what I read in the rags. And I've seen that generous, caring man time and time again since I arrived here."

"I still can't believe it," he whispered. "If that's true, why do you keep fighting it? Us? Because that sounds an awful lot like fate to me."

"Don't you see? If we're together, I won't get to have you to myself. Our relationship will be in the spotlight. And I know it's not fair of me to blame you…you didn't choose this, you were born to it. But it'll bring attention to the children, and a possible scandal to your family…" She blinked and a single tear fluttered on her lashes. "It's not that I don't care about you. This is just so different from what I thought I wanted. And I'm… afraid." She looked up at him and her lip quivered. "Look at you. You're the playboy prince. I'm just some plain English girl. I'm scared I won't be enough for you. That you'll figure out that I'm dull and ordinary and it'll be too late. And I'll be the one left hurting and broken."

"Don't say that. If anything, you're too good for me. You're sweet and generous and lovely and you go through your day trying to make everyone else's a little bit better." He stepped closer and put his hand along her cheek. "I don't care what people say, Rose. I'll never inherit the throne, but I still want to have a purpose.

These last weeks…with you…I've felt more vital than ever before in my life." He lifted his other hand and put it along her jaw so he was cupping her face, and then he dropped a soft, sweet kiss on her lips.

Lips that trembled beneath his.

"What is it?" he asked.

She bit down on her lip. "It's your father. It's Raoul. They don't know and when they find out they'll never approve. I can't sneak around anymore, and I'm not sure I'm up to all the barriers we'll face. You're the prince. I'll be labeled an opportunist, a gold digger…"

"Raoul already knows."

"He does?" Her eyes opened wide at the knowledge.

"I told him I was in love with you. And he told me to be careful, but don't underestimate him or my father. We accepted Lucy into the family, even though she is only our half-sister. And we did it publicly, despite the scandal. The best way to meet criticism is head on. Lucy came to Marazur, and had her own ball to announce her to the public as a Navarro. Do you think we think less of her because she married a rancher from Canada? Of course not. We love her and want her to be loved. When it counts, family is everything and we stick together. They'll want nothing less for me. And for you, too. You'll see. You just need…" He nodded, smiling a bit as the answer seemed suddenly so clear. "You just need to have some faith. In my family. In me. In love."

He looked into her eyes and said it once more, just so she knew for sure. "I love you, Rose. *Ti amo.*" She trembled beneath his hand. "Say you love me, too," he pleaded.

She nodded slightly. "I do. Oh, I do, Diego. I'm sorry I pushed you away. That I'm so afraid…"

"You don't have to be afraid. Not anymore."

"I do love you." Their gazes locked, and as she said the words, the air seemed to spark between them.

"Tonight, then?" he asked.

She nodded. "Tonight."

And he stepped forward and kissed her until he ran out of breath. Then he reached for the zip on her gown with shaking fingers.

For the first time in his life, he was going to make love to the woman he'd fallen in love with.

CHAPTER 15

Rose slipped out of the bed and tiptoed to the walk-in closet. Diego was sound asleep, the remnants of his tuxedo draped haphazardly over a chair, and her elegant dress was in a heap on the floor. But she couldn't worry about that now. Right now she needed to get some air. To think. To stop panicking.

Being with Diego had been so much more than she'd imagined, and that was saying a lot. And when he'd fallen asleep, she stared at the ceiling, trying to bridge the disconnect between what she was feeling and what would happen next. Tried to imagine herself as a…a princess. She couldn't. And yet she could easily see herself on Diego's arm, in his life. And the possibility of being an aunt to Emilia and Max…there could be nothing sweeter.

She slipped on a pair of yoga pants and a simple T-shirt, then put her hair up in a ponytail. What she wanted right now was a walk in the gardens. The soothing beauty of the flowers and the open air would calm her and help her think clearly. She hooked a pair of plain sandals on her finger, then tiptoed out of the room and down the back servant's hall until she reached the side entrance to the grounds.

The guests had either departed or had gone to bed. There was a distant clink—probably staff up late, putting everything away. A low rumble caught her ears and she saw a couple of trucks crawling away from the castle. She figured it was probably the band and their equipment. Tomorrow it would all be back to normal. Except…

The garden was quiet and dark, and she took a deep breath and let it out slowly while the perfumed scent of the flowers drifted around her. She slipped on her sandals and began winding her way through the paths, her feet crunching on the fine crushed rock. Maybe she'd go sit on the bench by the fountain for a while. Clear her head. Get rid of this pit of uncertainty that sat in her stomach, which was in direct opposition to the elation she felt at having made love to Diego.

But when she got to the bench, it was occupied. By Raoul.

She paused, but he must have heard her feet on the rock because he looked up, startled. She was surprised, too, because his eyes were red-rimmed and unbearably sad.

"I'm sorry," she said quietly, taking a step back. "I didn't mean to intrude."

"You're not," he replied, and slid over on the bench. "I'm s…s…sitting out here feeling sorry for myself." His words were slightly slurred.

She should turn around and go and leave him in peace. But it was hard to turn away from someone who was so obviously hurting. And inebriated.

"Shall I get someone for you, Your Highness?"

He laughed, a bitter sound. "No. Besides, who would you call? My father? He's had enough of his own grief. Diego?" His gaze narrowed. "Actually, I rather thought he'd be with you."

Her cheeks heated.

"I see," he said knowingly, a little sad smile on his lips. "He's in love with you, you know."

A knot of nerves tangled in her stomach and she quickly changed the subject. "Perhaps Stephani, Your Highness?"

His gaze pierced her, and she wondered if she'd somehow touched a nerve. "She's gone home," he said sharply. "Where she belongs."

"I see." She didn't, but Raoul was edgy and she wanted to help him. She went to the bench and perched beside him. "Was today the first party without your wife, Your—"

"Raoul," he interrupted. "No more Your Highness, please. Not now. Not when I've had far too much brandy to be sensible."

"Raoul," she said softly, waiting.

"And yes," he admitted. "It was."

"I'm sorry."

"Me, too."

He reached into the inside pocket of his jacket and withdrew a silver flask. Spun off the cap and took a long drink of whatever was inside—most likely the brandy he'd mentioned before. He grimaced and replaced the cap, but then belatedly handed it over to her, offering her a drink.

"No, thank you," she said quietly.

He leaned back on the bench. "So you and Diego. Interesting match."

"He told me you are aware of our…relationship." Her heart pounded with something that wasn't quite fear but definitely anxiety.

"Do you love him, Miss Walters?"

It was a complicated question, but she answered simply. "Yes, I do." At Raoul's silence, she swallowed and added, "But I haven't been comfortable with it. I am here to care for Emilia and Max. It wasn't anything I intended to happen."

"I know that." He swivelled his head in her direction, his chin dropping as if his head were heavy on his neck. "I have never seen my brother like this. It is good for him, I think. He's happy."

"But I'm…nobody."

"And you think that will create problems?"

"And the children have to come first. Oh, Your… Raoul," she corrected, "they are such sweet children, and they still miss their mother. I would not sacrifice their well-being for my own selfish fancies."

His gaze hardened. "Is that what Diego is to you? A selfish fancy?"

The knot of nerves hardened into a heavy ball, settling right in the pit of her stomach. "Oh, no, of course not. He is…"

She hesitated. Thought of how he smiled at her.

Held her as they danced. Sat with his arm around her as they talked in the dark.

The way he'd made her feel like the only woman in the world only an hour ago.

"He's everything," she admitted quietly.

When she looked at Raoul again, his jaw was clenched tightly. At first she thought he was angry, but one look in his eyes told her he was simply trying to hold back his emotions.

Raoul, it seemed, was a sad drunk. And it wouldn't do for him to be seen in this condition.

"Sir," she said softly, reaching out and putting her hand on his arm. "We can discuss all this at another time, can't we? Let me help you inside. You need a chance to rest. Rehydrate." She tried a small smile. "The children will want to see you tomorrow, without the smell of brandy, don't you think?"

He nodded. "I'm sorry I got maudlin."

"Entirely understandable," she answered briskly. She stood and held out her hand. "How steady are you? How long have you been sitting out here, sipping from your flask?"

He grinned up at her, looking as goofy as it was possible for the very proper prince to look. "Long enough."

Raoul put his hand on the arm of the bench and pushed himself upright, but she saw him reel unsteadily as he found his feet. The last thing he needed was to be seen staggering into the palace, or wandering through the gardens and taking a wrong turn on the paths. She slid up beside him and linked her arm with his. "Okay," she said cheerfully. "Oopsie daisy and on we go."

He laughed, took a misstep, and stumbled on the path. Rose smiled secretly, and put her arm around his waist, for once not worrying about protocol around him. With Diego she forgot about it all the time. But not with Raoul or his father.

"I apologize," he said soberly. "This isn't like me at all."

"I certainly didn't have you pegged as a drinker," she replied easily. "But everyone is entitled to a weak moment or two, Raoul. You've earned yours. And there's no one to see but me, and I won't breathe a word."

He nodded and staggered a bit, but she kept her arm around him to help him stay on his feet.

"It's just that I miss her," he said, the 's' sound drawn out just the slightest bit in each word. Worse than the slur was the melancholy behind the words.

"Of course you do. But I do hope you'll be happy again someday. You're too young to be alone forever." She gave him a little nudge. "Granted, you don't have much to offer a lady, but you might be able to scratch up some woman willing to take you on."

He stopped, stared at her a moment, and then chuckled. And the chuckle turned into a laugh, and she smiled widely. Teasing him had been a bit of a gamble, but it was good to see him smile.

"Thank you, Rose," he said, sighing at the end of his laughter. He clumsily folded her into a hug. "I can see why Diego cares for you so much. Don't worry about

Father and me. It won't be our first scandal and it certainly won't be our last. It will just require a plan to ease things in, yes?" He stood back. "We should have a family meeting and decide how to proceed."

Rose bit down on her lip, suddenly feeling overwhelmed again, particularly since Raoul was echoing Diego's earlier thoughts. "Easing things in sounds okay," she admitted. "It might save me from a panic attack or two."

He smiled again and then leaned down and kissed her cheek. "And we will sort out the children, too. They'll be delighted. They love their *Tío Diego*."

She linked her arm with his again. "Come, let's get you inside. We both need our beauty rest."

It didn't take too long for them to reach the doors. "Are you all right now?" she asked, wanting to avoid being seen helping Raoul anywhere. Far better to be discreet.

"I can manage. You?"

"Oh, I'm right as rain, sir."

She turned to leave when his voice stopped her. "Rose?"

"Yes, sir?"

"Thank you. For what you said. For being so good for our family."

Happiness warmed her from head to toe. "It's my pleasure. Truly."

She left him there, knowing he'd be fine to make it back to his chambers.

And upstairs Diego waited for her. She wasn't sure what she would say or do when she got there, but talking to Raoul had at least allayed her fears a little. The family would help them, and it would all be okay.

DIEGO SLIPPED OUT OF BED AND LET ROSE SLEEP. IT WAS only just after five; he could make it back to his room without being seen. They didn't need to invite unnecessary gossip. But today, once the dust had settled, he would sit down with his father and brother and they'd come up with a plan. For now, she deserved some extra sleep.

As quietly as he could, he slipped on his trousers and white shirt, and grabbed his abandoned shoes and socks. He gave one last, tender look at the form sleeping beneath the cozy duvet. Her casual, black clothes were in a small heap on the floor. He'd awakened when she'd come back into the room, not realizing she'd ever left. And she'd quietly stripped and climbed back into bed with him, curling her soft, strong body next to his back, spoon-fashion. Her contented sigh had told him everything was all right, so he'd closed his eyes and they'd gone back to sleep.

The hall was dim and quiet as he pulled the door gently closed with a soft click of the latch. He met no one as he went back to his suite, and once inside he stripped and took a hot shower. The agenda for the day was a light one after the ball, and he dressed semi-casually—no jeans or T-shirts, but in pressed trousers and a collared shirt rolled up at the elbows. His hair was still damp when there was a knock at his door.

Smiling, he wondered if Rose had heard him leave and come after him. He swung open the door and saw…

Stephani. With a very grim set to her lips and a frazzled look about her eyes.

"What's going on? It's not even six."

"I got a call about an hour ago. Today's paper. You can bet it'll be in the tabloids as well."

He stared down at the black and white image at the center of the newspaper she held out. *A New Mother for the Prince and Princess?* shouted the headline, and the photo showed Raoul, locked in an embrace with a woman wearing dark clothes and sporting a blond ponytail. In smaller print, beneath the picture, was a line that was even worse. *Crown Prince shakes off mourning during birthday celebrations with unknown guest at the palace.*

"It's Rose," he said numbly.

"It is?"

He nodded. "I'll explain more when we're all together. I take it Father and Raoul have been shown this as well?"

"Your father has, and is going to be in his office in ten minutes. Raoul was harder to wake, and for the first time in my memory, he cursed at me." Diego frowned and she amended, "Not at me, in particular. Just at the picture. Then he held his head as if it might fall off."

"He was drinking?"

"Apparently. Can you meet with us as well? Damage control is going to be front and center today, I'm afraid."

"I'll be right there." He gave a grim smile. "And

make sure there's lots of coffee. Though I expect Raoul has sobered up rather quickly."

After Stephani's departure, Diego grabbed his phone and did a quick internet search. The gossip sites were picking up the picture already. The headlines were horrendous, too. Raoul hadn't been a widower that long. The vultures were circling and they were going to be merciless. *What about the children?* appeared more than once, and Diego winced.

He slid his phone into his pocket and made the walk to the office wing of the castle. A plan had already started to form in his mind, and time was of the essence. Before entering his father's domain, he made a quick phone call to Camila and asked her to come to the office as soon as possible. Then he took a deep breath, let it out, and opened the door to his father's inner sanctum. His whole life he'd dreaded coming through this door; it usually meant he'd done something wrong. But today that would change. Today he'd do something right... because he was finally needed.

CHAPTER 16

Rose woke and stretched, then looked over at the space beside her. Diego was gone. She wasn't sure if she should be upset that he hadn't woken her first, or touched that he'd let her sleep after their long night.

She stared at the ceiling and smiled. First Diego, then the support of his brother…for the first time, she felt as if things might actually fall into place.

That she might actually be able to be with Diego. A bloody prince, for God's sake! She giggled a little and rolled herself up in the covers, indulging in a few moments of girlish triumph. But the truth was, the prince thing just *felt* weird. She'd discovered the Navarro family to be kind, generous, and hardworking. Certainly they lived according to their status, but there was no extravagance simply for showing off. The qualities of honor, duty, and loyalty to the family were threads that kept everything together.

It was a privilege to work here. And a dream come

true to be loved by a man like Diego. That they might have a future…

She couldn't wait to see him later, but first she had the children to tend to. She got out of bed and hit the shower, then dressed and prepared to take the children downstairs for breakfast. Rose thought she noticed some strange looks headed her way from some of the staff, but she ignored them for the moment. It had probably got around that she'd danced with Diego last night. Sitting with the children at a banquet was different than dancing with a prince, after the children had gone to bed. As Raoul had assured her, they'd come up with a plan.

It wasn't until mid-afternoon that she wondered if something was wrong. Clouds had swept in during the late morning, and now a low rumble of thunder and the threat of rain kept them indoors. Normally Diego would pop by to see Emilia and Max shortly before two o'clock, but as the minutes ticked by and he didn't arrive, a sense of unease put her nerves on edge. At three Max fell asleep watching a movie and Emilia looked to be right behind him, as they'd had a later night than usual at their father's party. Their tea arrived, carried by Ernestina. The maid smiled tightly and put the tray on the table, but Rose reached out and touched her wrist.

"Ernestina, is there something going on? We've hardly seen a soul all day." She swallowed and met the maid's eyes bravely. "Is there…any gossip I should be aware of?"

That the maid hesitated spoke volumes.

"What is it?" She looked over at the children. They had both nodded off and wouldn't hear any details.

"This morning's paper. You haven't seen it?"

Rose shook her head, wishing she didn't have such a heavy sense of dread. "We went to breakfast but I didn't see a paper, and we've stayed inside most of the day because of the weather."

"It…oh, Miss." Ernestina looked genuinely distressed. "None of the staff believes any of it. Just remember that when you see it."

"When I see what, Ernestina." She didn't bother to phrase it as a question; instead the words came out forceful and frustrated.

When the maid didn't answer, Rose let out a huge sigh. "Please stay with the children for a few minutes," she instructed. "I'll explain to the Señora Romero so you don't get into trouble, and be back as soon as I can."

"But Miss Rose—"

She didn't wait to hear Ernestina's protests. The atmosphere had been oddly strained and clearly she wasn't imagining things. The first thing she needed was a newspaper to see what all the fuss was about. Then she'd figure out why Diego had avoided her all day. Her heart chilled for a moment. He'd said he loved her last night. She'd believed him. She'd been right to, hadn't she?

The office area was quiet, and Rose went to Camila's office first, searching for Diego. But the assistant was on the phone, and she looked alarmed when she saw Rose standing in the doorway. She held up one finger, but Rose waved her off and headed to Stephani's desk.

Stephani was focusing on her computer monitor when Rose approached, and the same look of alarm crossed her features before she consciously smoothed it away. More worrisome to Rose was the flash of sympathy on the other woman's face.

"Stephani," Rose said carefully. "Camila is on the phone. Is Diego in?"

"I'm sorry, no."

The dread tightened into a painful ball in the center of her chest. "And Raoul?"

"With the king, in Alexander's office."

"Steph, what's going on? Everyone's looking at me sideways today. Diego hasn't been to visit the children, and I know something's wrong. What could have happened between last night and this morning?"

The look of pity was back, and Stephani handed over a copy of the newspaper.

The ball of dread, along with all the feeling in her body, seemed to drop right to her feet. She knew right away the moment the photo had been taken. When Raoul had hugged her in the garden, and then kissed her cheek. Her face wasn't visible, but his was, if a bit grainy. And there was her stupid ponytail that she'd put in before going out to the gardens.

She read the headline and wasn't sure if she wanted to weep or ball up the paper and heave it into the trash where it belonged.

"Everyone's seen it?" Her voice came out sort of strangled, and she cleared her throat.

"Yes."

"And they think that I..." Oh Lord. Did the staff

really believe she was fooling around with Raoul? It was Diego who'd captured her heart. Ernestina had said not, but…

"You need to speak with Raoul and the king," Stephani advised in a low voice.

"But Diego…"

"Diego isn't here, Rose. He's gone."

The cold feeling rushed back, and she actually felt herself weave a little bit. She put her hand on the side of the desk for support.

Stephani got her a chair and sat her in it, then brought her a glass of water. "Don't say anything more here," she said quietly.

"Why not?"

"Take a look at that picture again, Rose. Then maybe you'll understand. I'll let them know you're here."

Rose looked at the photo again. It wasn't a great picture, and enlarged it was indeed quite grainy. With her back to the lens, her identity was shielded to anyone who didn't know her.

With her back to the lens. But her back had been toward the castle wall…

She looked up at Stephani. "Oh. I see."

"I thought you might. Come with me, please."

She led Rose to the king's office, and it was even grander than Raoul's. Intimidated and unsure of herself, Rose stepped inside and dropped into a curtsy.

"Good afternoon, Rosalie. Please, come in and sit down." Alexander swept a hand out and gestured toward a tufted chair to the side of the massive desk.

It was like being called to the headmaster's office.

"Don't be afraid," Raoul said gently, and she belatedly noticed him standing beside a bookcase. "None of this is your fault. You were caught in the crossfire, and we'll make sure you come out of it unscathed."

Slightly reassured, she perched on the edge of the velvet upholstery. "I am so sorry," she breathed, looking first at Alexander and then at Raoul. "Last night—"

"Last night you were a friend when I needed one. I don't usually have that much to drink, and you listened to me and helped me inside. I'm indebted to you, Rose, not angry."

He was using her first name. That, too, was reassuring.

"The photo," she said carefully. "It was taken from inside the castle, wasn't it? Not with some huge tele-photo lens from the paps."

Alexander nodded gravely. "Yes. We're not sure if it was one of the staff or someone hired for the event who hadn't left yet." He frowned. "If it was someone here, within our household, this might not be the end of it. There's more story to sell, you see."

"More?" She tilted her head. "You don't think the insinuation and photo was enough?"

Raoul came over and took the seat next to her. "They would have seen your face, Rose."

And her identity, so they could feed the tabloids more and more. That she was the children's nanny. Perhaps even her relationship with Diego. They'd been discreet but not invisible. "I should resign," she said quickly. "Then the story will go away."

"You'll do no such thing," Alexander said.

She looked into the older man's face. It was clear where his sons got their good looks, and the determined set of his jaw was very much like Diego's when he got something in his mind and wouldn't let go. "I appreciate that, sir, but for Emilia and Max's sakes, maybe it would be for the best."

"And take away another person they've come to love? I think not. We'll handle this the way we always handle things in our family. Head on."

Raoul nodded. "We're looking at all the time stamps for vehicles leaving the grounds after two a.m. There aren't many. Stephani is also checking logs with Marco, as he and his staff did stay on duty until the last guest had gone."

"But it doesn't make the story disappear. And it doesn't explain why Diego isn't here, either." She checked herself and met the king's gaze. "I apologize, sir. I seem to have abandoned the proper protocol."

His gaze softened and she would swear he got the same sympathetic look in them that Stephani had given her only a few minutes earlier. "Rose, it's no secret to either of us that you and Diego have formed an attachment."

Her cheeks flamed.

"None of us can control who we love. No one knows that better than I. Even when it makes life ten times more complicated."

"I see."

"Diego has left for Africa. There's been an ongoing

issue with one of his charities that needs his attention, and he also has a friend meeting him there. Ryan."

She scrambled through her memories of their chats. Ryan—his mate from uni who got him in and out of scrapes. "I know who you mean. But why Ryan?"

"To bury the story," Raoul said. "Didn't he explain before he left?"

"I haven't seen or spoken to him all day. Not since..." She swallowed, realizing she was speaking to the king and crown prince and not just brother and father. "Not since before I saw you in the garden."

Alexander and Raoul shared a look.

Then Raoul turned to her with that same pitying expression and the ball of dread bounced back.

"To bury the story, he'll create a new story, Rose. He'll put himself front and center and take the focus off of me and Marazur."

"With...Ryan."

"With Ryan, and very likely a few lovely ladies in a very public place."

She pictured it and felt a little sick to her stomach. Just last night he'd said he loved her. Over the last few weeks, he'd convinced her that she made him a better man. That his reckless days were behind him and he wanted to be taken seriously. Now he was going to flaunt himself around on a whole other continent as if she meant nothing.

"He'll hide your scandal by creating one of his own."

"Exactly." Raoul leaned forward, looking into her eyes. "It's just for show, you know. I don't know why he didn't tell you before he left, but I know he loves you very much."

She sat quietly for a few minutes. First of all, the image in her brain of him living it up at some exotic club with an exotic woman was like taking her biggest insecurity and stabbing her in the heart with it. And even if it was for "show," as Raoul put it, she knew that he'd be back to square one, at least publicly, in shedding his bad-boy-prince image. It would be a hit to their relationship...if they even truly had one.

Because what hurt the most was that he'd gone without saying a word to her. Without letting her in on the plan, without consulting with her, without saying goodbye.

As if she weren't important enough to say goodbye to.

"I should get back to the children," she said quietly. "I ordered one of the maids to stay with them until I returned. She'll probably get in trouble with the housekeeper."

"I'll make sure she doesn't," Raoul assured her.

"Rose," Alexander said, "Let's keep this meeting between us, shall we? Until we find out where the picture came from? Our entire household staff signs a confidentiality agreement, as you know. It's possible someone has violated those terms. Keep it between Raoul and Stephani and myself, if you don't mind."

"I don't mind at all." She looked at Raoul and felt her temper rise a bit. "I can't imagine who would want to hurt you or the children after all you've been through. It's despicable."

"I agree. That's why they need you, Rose. And I'm truly, truly sorry that you've been put in the middle of our family drama."

She lifted her chin, indignation a welcome reprieve from the self-pity that had threatened her moments before. "I was already in the middle, sir, when I… when we… well, you know what I'm trying to say, I'm sure. Please excuse me. I'll have the children ready for dinner shortly."

"Thank you, Rose."

She left the office and shut the door behind her, then let out a long, slow breath. Stephani came around the corner and they shared a look that Rose translated as "what an ungodly mess."

"You're okay?" Stephani asked.

She wasn't, not really. Not when she thought about Diego leaving without a word. There had to have been a better way to deal with the situation than to go to another continent and then head off to the nearest club and party it up.

Maybe he did find her dull. Maybe he missed the freedom he'd always enjoyed. Maybe she'd known better all along and had ignored those little voices because she'd so desperately wanted him to mean what he said.

"I'll be fine," she replied, straightening her spine. "I've got to get back to the children." She was halfway to the exit when she turned back. "Oh, Stephani, about the dress last night. What should I do with it?"

"Keep it." Stephani smiled at her. "You looked lovely."

But she didn't want to keep it or look at it again. It

was a reminder of too many things. "I don't have any use for it again," she said quietly. "Perhaps you could…I don't know. I don't know what people usually do with these things."

"Just put it in the garment bag for now and we'll worry about it later," she advised.

"All right."

And then she made the long walk back to the nursery, relieved Ernestina, and got the children ready for the family dinner. Once they were delivered to the dining room, she went to the kitchen and got her own supper but took it to her room to eat privately. Went through the motions of retrieving the children and getting them ready for bed.

And still no word from Diego. No call, no text, no…nothing.

She crawled beneath her covers and closed her eyes. She wouldn't cry. She would simply get on with things, as she always did. The way she should have from the beginning. She'd put money in Hayley's account for Alice. She'd write charming letters to her parents about how wonderful her life was. She'd send birthday and anniversary cards and presents because she never forgot anyone's special occasion.

But she would not cry for herself. And she certainly wouldn't cry over Diego Navarro.

CHAPTER 17

Thirty-six hours later, the first story appeared. Diego hadn't wasted any time; the photo looked to be in some sort of club, and he was holding a drink in one hand with his arm around a woman's waist.

Rose angled her head and studied the red-haired beauty. There was no denying she was gorgeous, and she was leaning into him with what Rose could only interpret as familiarity. The desire to know who she was was overwhelming, and Rose tossed the paper aside as soon as she read the first line: *Not to be outdone by his brother, Prince Diego appears in a Dar es Salaam club, partying with an unidentified beauty.* That was the only mention of Raoul. The plan to deflect attention was already working, but she felt like a casualty in all of it. The worst of it was she was partly to blame. She'd been the one to sit with Raoul and to help him inside.

Her mother always used to say, "No good deed goes unpunished." Boy, had she been right. She never should have gone back down to the ball, or danced with Diego, or slept with him, or freaked out and gone walking in the gardens. If she hadn't been there, none of this would have happened.

For the next two weeks, photos appeared online and in the tabloids. One night it was the redhead, another it was a stunning woman with flawless dark skin and the best set of cheekbones Rose had ever seen. Then there was the pic of him doing shots with a man identified as his friend Ryan, fellow college mate and polo team member.

As almost an afterthought, his charity for women's education was mentioned at the end of the articles. One questioned how much work he could possibly be doing if he was partying every night.

Nothing was mentioned about the source of the initial picture, but then another article appeared, this one on a prominent celebrity website. There was a picture of Diego, looking rather melancholy and sipping on something from a highball glass, and next to it the original picture of her and Raoul in their badly lit embrace. *Getting over a broken heart: brothers torn over the nanny* was printed in big font just below the photos.

This time she couldn't look away. She read every single, salacious word. How the woman in the photo was the palace nanny, how she'd led on Diego only to betray him with his brother, and so on.

When she was done, she went to the bathroom and threw up.

Her sister would see this. And so would her mother, because someone wouldn't be able to resist the temptation to show her. And Raoul and the children… She wiped her mouth and ran herself a glass of water, the tumbler shaking in her hand. Her professional reputation was in tatters. There was no way she could stay on at the palace, and no one would hire her now, either.

Who in the household hated her so much? She couldn't think of a single person who hadn't been pleasant. Perhaps their motivation was money; gossip was a high-paying business. But to be so heartless…

She went back to her laptop and looked at the site again, studying Diego's picture. He looked unhappy, with his arm resting on what appeared to be the bar, and a few empty glasses and an abandoned rose littered the top.

A white rose. Her chest cramped. This was too hard. And now she was frozen, unsure of what to do or where to go next. Crawl home with her tail between her legs, nursing what remained of her broken heart?

Her life had often been lonely, and it had never been particularly easy, but she'd never really felt hopeless. Until now.

There was a knock at the door, and she didn't want to answer, but she figured she'd better in case it had to do with this latest development. When she opened it, she was surprised to see Señora Ortiz on the other side, holding a tray.

"May I come in, Rose?"

"Of course." She wasn't in the mood for food, but Señora Ortiz had been the first friendly face here and there was something comforting and motherly about her that Rose needed very badly. She stepped aside and closed the door behind the cook.

"You've been avoiding the kitchen," Señora Ortiz said plainly.

"I've been avoiding everyone," Rose admitted. "It's been a strange few weeks."

"I brought you a few things." Señora Ortiz took the cover off the little dish. "The orange cake you love so much. Some very English tea. A flower to brighten your day."

Rose's throat clogged at the thoughtfulness. "Gracias, Señora Ortiz." She sniffed a little.

"Oh now, *pequena*," she murmured, coming over and giving her a hug. "It will all work out, I promise. And you should know that this wasn't my idea. Someone suggested it."

"Who?"

"Someone who knows you love my orange cake. And who specifically said I should put a white rose on the tray."

Rose looked at the blossom and back at Señora Ortiz. Maybe it should make her feel better, but it didn't. It just served as a reminder of painful feelings, and how Diego had left without a word. Why would he send this kind of message now? She found it hard to believe that he'd be that cruel, but she also didn't trust any of her instincts and feelings anymore.

"Rose," the older woman whispered, "Don't cry. It will all work out, you'll see. He loves you."

"I don't think so," she replied. She hadn't realized

she'd started crying, but a touch of her fingers to her cheek confirmed it.

"Have some faith. And don't give up yet." She patted her hand. "I need to get back."

"Thank you for trying," Rose said softly. "I do appreciate it."

"You're welcome. Eat the cake. You've barely eaten enough to feed a bird these last days."

When Señora Ortiz was gone, Rose poured herself a little tea. Then the aroma of the cake hit her nostrils and she tried a tiny bite. Before long the whole piece was gone and Rose was crying, the stress of it all finally coming out. Desolate, she opened a bottle of wine and poured a large glass. If she were going to resign her post, she might as well enjoy a fine vintage before giving her notice.

And if she managed to drown her sorrows in the process, all the better.

DIEGO SAT AT THE PLAIN, MAKESHIFT DESK AND RAN HIS hand through his hair again, staring at the papers before him. This nearly made sense now, and the proper permits had all been filed. Two weeks of being visible at night and working all day had taken their toll.

"Diego. For God's sake, man, shave or something." Ryan stepped into the office, looking clean and trim and not at all like he'd polished off the remainder of the whiskey last night.

"I will. As soon as I'm done here. I can't go out

tonight. I need to get one night of decent sleep."

"Then maybe you can do it on the plane, eh? I have a message for you. Your brother says you're to go home."

Diego lifted his head at the surprising news. "Really?"

"He didn't say much, but he did say that he's got all the information you need and that you should be there." Ryan raised his eyebrows. "And he also said that I was to tell you thank you. Seemed a bit odd to me."

"It is." Diego sighed as relief flooded him. "Raoul hasn't always appreciated my…efforts on behalf of the family."

"Maybe he knows this time there was a personal cost. You still haven't heard from her?"

That was the one thing that kept bothering him. He'd left his private number for Rose in the letter that explained everything. Her silence had troubled him for days. When Señora Ortiz had said she was barely eating, he'd sent her a message in the best way he knew how. Señora Ortiz, at least, he trusted.

"So go back." Ryan came over and put his hand on his shoulder. "Brenna and I will stay here and oversee things for a week or so if you want. It's so close to going forward that things will be fine."

Diego looked up at his friend and felt a wave of affection and gratitude. "You and Bren have been amaz-ing," he said. "Through everything." The fact that Ryan's little sister had agreed to come along and be a romantic decoy was friendship above and beyond. That she'd proved an incredible asset working with the authorities to finalize all the legalities was a pleasant surprise. Diego was considering putting her on his staff, if she could be enticed away from her job in Dublin.

Ryan handed over a paper. "The assistant—Steph, I think she said—gave me these details for your travel."

Diego frowned. "Hmmm. She's Raoul's assistant, not mine."

"Don't ask me, mate. Just get packed and in the air. You know you're dying to get back to her."

He was. He and Rose had a lot to discuss, that had been postponed for over two weeks while he put out fires and played the part of the playboy.

"Call me at any time," he said to Ryan, signing the last piece of documentation that was needed today. "And if you and Brenna can stay a bit longer, and liaise with the office staff here, that'd be fantastic."

"Gives me something useful to do." Not to mention Ryan had taken on the responsibility of security for the school as well as acting as Diego's personal bodyguard.

Diego got up and gave Ryan a quick man-hug. "Thank you," he said gruffly.

"What are friends for?" Ryan asked, and then chuckled. "Besides spending your money, that is…"

Diego was still laughing when he left the office, but his laugh settled into an apprehensive frown as he packed, headed to the airport, and settled on the jet headed back to Marazur.

If he was free to go back, it meant they'd found the source of the leak. And since he'd been provided with no details whatsoever, he could only assume it wasn't good news.

Despite Stephani's directive to report to Raoul's office on his arrival, Diego got Marco to deliver him to the back of the castle and the staff entrance. It was still early—just past seven—and he snuck in the kitchen, knowing Señora Ortiz would already be at the day's baking.

She was just taking a pan of hot rolls out of the oven. Diego leaned casually against the door frame and waited for her to notice him. When she did, she put her hand to her heart. "You are just as sneaky now as you were as a boy!" she chided, then laughed. "Welcome home, Diego."

"It's good to be home." He went forward and kissed her cheek, and she flapped her hand at him as she blushed. He grinned. The last two weeks had been so exhausting. Normally he came and went as he pleased, but now he was thrilled to be home. It felt right.

"I'm starving."

"You're always starving," she observed, but then

took a few rolls and put them on a plate. "Here. And there's coffee if you want it."

He buttered the rolls, watching the yellow goodness melt into the bread instantly. The first bite was pure, airy heaven.

"You flew all night?"

He nodded. "Most of it, yes. I was summoned." He wiggled his eyebrows. Being summoned wasn't the annoyance it used to be, either.

And then he let his smile fade. "How is Rose?"

"Quiet. She doesn't come to the kitchen as much and takes her meals upstairs."

"You took her the cake?"

"I did. I think she understood, but she's upset, Diego. Seeing the pictures of you in the papers…and she feels responsible for everything. I can tell."

"I'm going to see her first."

"Better hurry, before she has to be up with the children."

He crammed the last of the roll in his mouth, passed on the coffee, and headed to the stairwell. He couldn't wait to see her. Hold her and kiss her and assure her it was all going to be okay now.

She answered his knock, but her face blanked in surprise when she saw him there. "Good morning," he said, and smiled. She looked so beautiful. Nothing fancy or different than usual. But after two weeks of clubs and women—other than Brenna—who were anxious to get their five minutes of fame with the prince, Rose's simple trousers, blouse, and top knot were pretty and refreshing.

"You're back."

His brows pulled together at her flat, unenthusiastic tone. "No one told you I was coming? Raoul sent for me yesterday. I'm just arrived from the airport."

"You must be tired. You had a busy few weeks."

Alarm settled in the middle of his chest at the inflection of "busy." "I did. But apparently the mystery of the photograph's been solved. I don't need to be away anymore."

Rose smiled wanly. "You must be relieved. Is there anything else? I need to attend to the children soon."

He went into her room and shut the door behind him. "What's going on? I know it was rough, but are you…angry with me?"

"Really? You're going to ask me that?" Her voice lifted and she let out a breath and rolled her shoulders, as if trying to regain her composure.

"Is it the news stories? Those were all calculated, you know that. All on purpose, to form a diversion."

"Oh, I'm aware. After the first day, the mystery woman in the garden was forgotten, replaced with the game of 'who's Diego out with tonight?'"

She was angry. Very. He hesitated a moment, trying to decide the best tack to proceed. "Nothing happened," he assured her quietly. "I promise, Rose. It was all for show. Surely you believe me. I value our relationship more than that."

The sound that came out of her mouth was surprising, considering he'd just been incredibly honest. It was a half-laugh, half-scoff suffused with incredulity, and he knew women well enough to know he'd somehow managed to step on a landmine.

"You value our relationship? That is seriously what you're going to say to me, when you didn't even value it enough to say goodbye?"

"I know I left in a rush, but you'd been up late, out walking…I wanted to let you sleep. You looked so lovely in the morning. I explained it all in the letter I left. I know it's not the same as in person—"

"Letter? What letter? The last words you said to me were in my bed, after the ball. Yes, I went out walking, and yes, I bumped into Raoul and we talked and I helped him back inside because he was drunk. You were asleep when I got back, and when I woke up in the morning, you were gone. Full stop. Not once single communication since then, Diego. *Not one.*"

The unease in his chest grew. "I swear to you, Rose, that I left you a letter. Camila was to look after everything, and deliver it to you later that day."

"Hmph," she scoffed again. "I haven't spoken two words to your assistant since you left. The one time I stopped by her office, she was on the phone and I went to see Stephani instead."

Camila hadn't given her the letter. Goddamn it all.

"Rose," he said carefully, "I swear on my mother's grave that I wrote you a letter. It wasn't long, but I did explain why I was leaving, and that our night meant everything to me…and that I love you."

A flash of vulnerability crumpled her face, but only for a split second. "Please don't," she said, turning away. "It's not fair, Diego. I can't do this anymore."

. . .

Rose couldn't look him in the eyes; it made her too vulnerable. Too needy. He'd knocked on her door and she hadn't had any time to prepare. Just *boom*, Diego —and all the emotions that went with his sudden appearance.

The sad, horrible truth was that she wanted to believe him.

"Don't say that," he said, coming to her side and reaching for her hand.

She pulled it away, trying desperately to be strong. "It's already done," she replied, hating the quaver in her voice. "I handed in my notice yesterday." She'd remain for another two weeks, and then she'd be gone. Off somewhere… certainly not another nanny job. No one would hire her now, and the agency would be sure to cut her loose.

"What do you mean? This is ridiculous!" Diego's voice lifted. "You belong here! The children need you."

She stared at him now, a hole opening up in her chest. "Did you see the latest story, Diego? It had *my name*. Accused me of coming between two brothers. I don't know why *you* had to leave the morning after the ball. It should have been me. Without me, there *was* no scandal. No story! I should have been the one to go!"

"I went because for the first time my family needed me, and I could do something to help beyond looking after some ponies or playing in the garden with my niece and nephew. Don't you get that? This was finally my chance to prove myself. To have some value."

Silence fell over the room.

"Well," she finally said, her voice clear and quiet, "your need to be needed came at a cost. I could have resigned, found another position, and kept this all under wraps. But you had to play the family savior, and now I'm without a job, without a reputation, and…" She tried to swallow against the lump in her throat to keep her tears away, but she didn't quite succeed. "And I don't know how I'm going to face my family. Maybe you needed to prove yourself, but I've always been the one who held our family together. Who fixed things. Kept the peace. Never made trouble. Now I'm an embarrassment."

"That's not true! None of it's true."

"It doesn't have to be true," she replied. "I've learned very painfully that it just has to appear to be true."

"I left you a letter," he pleaded, coming closer. "Rose…"

"I can't, Diego. This has cost me too much already." Her lip wobbled. She did love him, she did. More than she'd ever thought possible. She even understood his need to prove himself to his family. It was one of the things she admired about him most. But it had also made her a casualty. From the first time he'd kissed her, she'd known she was over her head. Now she had to pick up what pieces remained and find a way to start over.

"If you could go, please, I need to compose myself before seeing Max and Emilia. They don't know anything about this yet."

"They're going to be crushed," Diego said, shaking his head. "Don't do this to them."

The children were her weak spot. She would do anything for them, but she also knew that to stay would mean it being more difficult in the long run. This wouldn't be forgotten, and they were too innocent to be caught in the middle.

"I'm sorry, Diego." She went to the door and opened it, waited for him to leave.

"I'll go—for now. But we'll talk later, Rose. This isn't over. I've waited too long for you to let you go now."

She closed the door behind him, then rested her head on it briefly.

She didn't want to leave. She didn't want to resign and go home with her tail between her legs. What she wanted, deep down, was the fairy tale. She wanted what had been just within her grasp the night of the ball. A future with Diego. To be a part of his family, and see the children every day, and perhaps…oh, perhaps, to have a few of her own someday. For approximately an hour and a half, she'd allowed herself the luxury of dreams. And perhaps that was what no one understood. She had never been a dreamer, and this was why. The inevitable, horrible thud when the dreams came crashing down.

But for now, for this moment, there was a boy and a girl next door, waiting to play, and read, and have messy snacks and faces washed and all the regular routine they were used to. Ceci would want her to shield them from all of this. And so she would. The only way she knew how. By doing her job.

~

DIEGO MARCHED INTO RAOUL'S OFFICE, NOT EVEN pausing to say hello to Stephani. Raoul looked up, startled, as Diego shut the door and strode forward to the desk.

"What in the hell?"

Raoul's eyebrow instantly shot up into the air. "Calm down and tell me what the problem is. And welcome home."

Diego sat on the edge of the chair and fidgeted, his knee bouncing up and down at a rapid pace. "I went to see Rose this morning. She resigned? And you let her?"

"The second news story affected her deeply. It also allowed us to figure out who was feeding the press. We called you back from Africa because we thought you'd like to deal with it personally."

Diego heard the last part but pushed it aside for a moment. "Are you saying you used Rose as bait? That you used her to set a trap, and the hell with the consequences?" The very idea made him feel sick to his stomach.

"The person had to have known her identity. Though there weren't any guarantees, we suspected whoever took the photo would send another, or leak other information. The second time she was a bit careless, and we got her."

Diego's knee had been bouncing nervously, but he halted its movement and stared at Raoul. "She?"

"It was Camila, Diego."

His assistant. His damned assistant, who had access

to all his files, personal information…his own staff that he trusted implicitly. He'd given her the letter for Rose the morning he'd left for Tanzania. He pushed past the stinging betrayal. "Oh, that explains so much," he growled. "You haven't confronted her yet?"

Raoul shook his head. "We've kept everything very discreet here. Stephani is the only other one who knows, besides me and Father. Camila took the photo and sent it that first night. After you left, we started going through the event staff, looking for a leak. Then we had to look at household staff. Stephani was the first one to suspect. She called a friend of a friend, who knew how to, shall we say, access certain things. Between a lovely deposit in Camila's bank account and phone records…"

His own assistant. Camila had been here for three years now. Quiet, good worker, reliable. Why would she do such a thing? If it were just for the money… but to hurt the family in such a manner…

"Is she in yet?"

"I don't know. Don't fly off the handle, Diego."

"Don't fly off the handle? Are you serious?" He got up from the chair and paced for a moment. "I just left Rose. She said she resigned and that it's over between us. Do you know why? Because I left a damned letter explaining everything with Camila, and it never got delivered. Now I find out that you basically…what is the saying Ryan uses? Threw her under the bus? And you accepted her resignation? What were you thinking?"

Raoul showed no sign of being upset. He merely met Diego's gaze evenly. "I was thinking we'd better call you back here so you could have the honor of firing your assistant and start winning back the woman you love. Nothing's been done that can't be fixed."

Diego stopped pacing and stared at his brother. "What?"

"You and Rose have done nothing wrong, except maybe fall in love, and that's not wrong, it's just troublesome. And you didn't hesitate before coming up with your diversion plan, which, let's face it, took the spotlight off of what was happening here. It also took your efforts to legitimize yourself and flushed them down the proverbial toilet. You took one for the family, Diego. For me. The least I could do was give you the pleasure of taking out the trash and winning back the girl."

The speech was so unexpected that Diego realized his mouth was hanging open. Then a smile began to blossom on his face. "You think I can win her back?"

"Are you kidding? She was heartbroken while you were gone. Oh, she tried to hide it, but it was easy to see. You explain what happened, and find that letter? She'll come around. If you want her to," he added.

"Of course I want her to. I want to marry her."

Raoul's face split with the breadth of his grin. "That's wonderful news. We all love her. And she's very good for you."

Diego sat again, feeling like the wind had been sucked from his sails. "I want to marry her," he murmured, and wondered why he was suddenly so shaky.

Raoul came over and put his hand on Diego's shoulder. "It's a big thing, isn't it? When you find the woman you want to spend your life with?"

Diego didn't answer, but put his hand over top of his brother's. They were both thinking of Ceci.

"I'll come find you when it's done," Diego said, standing again.

"Please do. And if you manage to smooth things over with Rose, we'll have a champagne toast in the library."

CHAPTER 19

Rose sat in the garden, deep among the roses, trying to sort out her feelings. Raoul had taken the children off to some festival event in town for an hour or two, with Marco and private security in tow. He'd suggested, in that quiet but firm way of his, that she take a few hours off for herself.

She rather suspected he thought she and Diego would take advantage of the privacy. But she wasn't ready to speak to him yet. Trying to separate logic from her emotions was proving too much of a challenge today.

So it was rather unfortunate when he came down the stone path, whistling lightly through his teeth, looking as if he hadn't a care in the world.

Maybe he wouldn't see her among the bushes.

"I was told I could find you here," he said easily, coming to sit with her on the iron bench.

"I'm sure you were," she replied, folding her hands in her lap. "Diego, this morning…"

"This morning neither of us were in possession of all the facts," he interrupted, and he reached into his back pocket and took out a folded envelope.

"What's that?"

"The letter I wrote you the morning I left for Dar es Salaam. I gave it to Camila. She never gave it to you. Instead she betrayed me, you, my family…"

Rose gaped at him. "Camila? She's the one?"

He nodded, and Rose could see he was upset. "I trusted her. But I shouldn't have, I guess. When you and I…well, jealousy is a powerful motivator. And when opportunities can pad a bank balance nicely, apparently it's easy to be persuaded."

Rose didn't know what to say. "But she hardly ever spoke to me."

"Nor will she. She's gone. Been gone for a few hours now." He reached into his pocket and took out a tiny electronic card. "Minus the SIM card for her phone. Security is going to go through it and scrub all the photos or anything else she might have on there. Her computer, too."

"So much for the confidentiality agreement we all had to sign," Rose muttered, but in her heart she was glad. Glad that whoever had betrayed the family had been discovered. Glad she was gone. "Are you going to take any legal action?"

"As long as she keeps her silence, there's no issue. We can repair the damage done. At least I hope we can."

Except Rose had been compromised so unfairly. She wasn't sure it was fixable.

"Read the letter, Rose."

"Diego…"

"Please. I have things to say but I want you to read it first."

She tore open the envelope and took out the single sheaf of paper, then skimmed the words. Half way down the page her eyes blurred with tears, and she had to blink them away in order to keep reading. For Diego to say he loved her was one thing. But for him to put his feelings into a letter, with ink and paper…there was something intimate and special about it.

"Rose, everything's changed for me these past few months. When I went into the kitchen and saw you sitting at that table, with your china cup of tea and slice of cake, the world shifted. Everything started falling into place. Being with you, and Emilia and Max, and focusing on the family, and my projects…it seemed as if I finally knew where I was supposed to be. Who I was supposed to be."

He turned on the bench and put his hand on her knee. It was warm and reassuring and she wanted so badly to turn into his arms. But this was too big, too important to not sort out everything, so she let him go on.

"When I was away…" He frowned, started over. "In the past, sometimes I'd deflect attention from the palace by acting out. Not that I needed much encouragement, but it's not an isolated strategy. And I held it over Raoul's head more than once. This time, though… he's been through too much. He's still grieving, for God's sake. And the children…it angered me to think of anyone using them as pawns in whatever game they were playing. The headline wasn't just that about the grieving widower. It was about a mother for the children and it was just so…low."

"Children are not pawns. Not…leverage." She nodded at him. They could definitely agree on that.

"No," he replied soberly, "they are not. And so I came up with the idea of going to Tanzania and pulling my party act one last time. I was going to have to go there anyway, to sort out the school situation, so I bumped up the trip, got Ryan and Brenna to meet me there, and made sure I was seen. Every night."

"Oh, I know," she said ruefully.

"Camila didn't just want to create a scandal, she wanted rid of you," Diego admitted. "She said so when I told her to get her things and she'd be escorted off the grounds. She was jealous. Turns out my brilliant strategy actually made things worse. I'm so sorry for that."

Rose couldn't help but smile a little bit. "Of course she was jealous. You *are* the most eligible bachelor in the country."

"She didn't count on me going away. She thought we'd send you away instead, and she'd have her chance." He smiled and shook his head. "She didn't count on getting caught, either."

Rose shook her head. "People will do some crazy things in the name of love."

He laughed a little. "It's not the first time. But I'm not going to tell you those stories today. Today I'm trying to convince you to stay. Stay with the children. Stay with me. Marry me. We'll hire a new nanny for Max and Emilia—I'm sure you can recommend someone lovely." He squeezed her knee and gazed into her eyes. "I love you, Rose. That's all that matters. I told you once that I wasn't about to let the press dictate my life anymore. Two weeks ago we decided to control the story. Today I want to start writing a new one."

And oh, she wanted to. So badly. But she was still afraid. "But what will they say about me?" she asked, looking down at her lap. "That I'm the gold digger who took advantage of her position in the royal household? I don't want to be the cause of more gossip."

"So we give them an exclusive and the story we want to tell." He took her hand. "We give them the truth. We give them the love story."

She looked into his eyes. From the very beginning, the reality of this man defied the persona in the press. He was kind, generous, focused on family, funny, warm, loving. He was willing to sacrifice for those he loved… and stand up to them when he needed to.

And right now he was standing up for her.

She'd been wrong. Misled, certainly, by Camila's manipulations. But wrong not to believe in him when he'd always told her the truth. Wrong to put more weight on her own insecurities than the truth before her eyes.

"You really want to marry me?"

"I do. My world makes sense when you're in it."

"And your family? They really don't disapprove?"

He smiled. "Raoul brought me back because he said I'd earned the right to deal with Camila and also to win you back. We all love you, Rose. And our family, for all its old-world traditions, is good at one thing. Following our hearts."

The dread in the pit of her stomach had disappeared, replaced instead by a delicious swirl of nervous anticipation. He loved her. She loved him. More than that, she trusted him.

"Then my answer is yes," she replied, letting the smile that was filling her heart be revealed on her lips. "Yes, Diego, *el principe, mi amor*… I will marry you."

He gathered her into an embrace, holding her close against his chest and she let out a happy, contented breath as she wrapped her arms around his waist.

"Did she say yes?" came the call from the corner of the garden.

Rose burst out laughing as Diego called back. "She did! She said yes!"

"Miss Rose! Miss Rose!" Max and Emilia left Raoul's side and came running, pell-mell, down the path. "Is it true? Are you going to marry *Tio* Diego and be *Tia* Rose?"

Rose gathered them into a happy hug. "I am. If that's all right with you, of course."

"Of course it is!" Emilia's dark eyes sparkled. "Miss Rose, if we can't have our mama, at least we have you. I love you, Miss Rose."

Rose's eyes watered as she held the girl close. Raoul followed behind at a more respectable pace, and to Rose's surprise, Alexander was by his side. Oh my. This was just so…unbelievably overwhelming.

"It's nearly tea time," Raoul announced. "So we've

ordered champagne and cake in the garden. It's about time we had something to celebrate."

Rose stood and went to stand before Raoul. "Thank you, sir. For all your support. It means the world to me."

"No more sir," Raoul decreed, giving her a quick hug. "I'm gaining a sister, aren't I?"

"And I another daughter," Alexander said, stepping forward. "Congratulations to you both."

The champagne arrived and they all had a glass, with sparkling water for the children. Once they'd toasted and sipped briefly, Diego pulled Rose to his side. And as they chatted and laughed, Rose felt a contentment that was so deep and so pure it made her blink a little faster to clear the moisture in the corner of her eye.

It really was the fairy tale. Not because she was marrying the prince and going to live in the castle. But because it was love, real and yet somehow magical, and it was all she'd ever really needed.

THE CROWN PRINCE'S BRIDE

Donna Alward

ABOUT THE CROWN PRINCE'S BRIDE

The kingdom or his heart?

After losing his wife and future queen in an accident, Crown Prince Raoul Navarro knows he'll never find that kind of love again. Now he must focus on running the kingdom and raising his two children. The idea of falling in love again feels impossible. And yet his future stretches out before him, bleak and lonely…

Smart, loyal, and discreet, Stephani is Raoul's assistant and his wife's cousin. She adores her job, except for the teensy complication that she's been in love with her boss since her first week of employment. She'd never act on it, though. Raoul is first in line to the throne and she's his assistant. Raoul is nursing a broken heart, and a woman like Stephani isn't the kind to be a future queen.

When Stephani steps in as his plus one at a state dinner, Raoul suddenly takes notice. She knows all the players and protocol, but this is something more. Is this captivating woman the same one who's run his office for years? And will one impetuous midnight kiss change the course of the kingdom forever?

CHAPTER 1

L*ate August*

Stephani surveyed the ballroom, ensuring everything was running smoothly and to her satisfaction. As the executive assistant to Raoul Navarro, Crown Prince of Marazur, it was her job to make sure that his birthday party went off without a hitch.

So far, the dinner had been delicious, the traditional almond cake devoured, and the music and dancing had begun. She started to breathe a bit easier now.

"Señorita Savalas? Champagne?"

She turned to the footman who carried several full glasses on his silver tray. "*Sí, gracias.*" She smiled and took a flute from the tray, then sipped gratefully. The dry, fizzy liquid delighted her tongue. By royal standards, the party was small, but no expense had been spared. Including this particularly fine vintage.

Raoul deserved a wonderful party after the year he'd had. Considering this was the first real event at the palace since his wife, Princess Cecilia, had tragically died, Stephani had pulled out all the stops.

It was her job. And it was more than just a job, too. Because for the last seven years, she'd been in love with her boss.

Her boss, who had been married to her cousin.

Her boss, who was now a widower with two small children.

Right now, Raoul was mingling with a group that included the finance minister and the gentleman's twenty-something daughter. The girl looked up at Raoul with something like hero worship, and Stephani smiled to herself. He was at least ten years too old for her, but he was extraordinarily handsome with his black hair and dark, soulful eyes. New lines had appeared at either side of his lips, but Stephani thought they only added to his allure.

She joined the group and smiled at everyone, then spoke briefly before turning her attention to the Italian attaché. There was also a representative from the French tourism ministry, and she switched languages effortlessly.

"You're exceptionally good at that."

Raoul's deep voice vibrated at her ear and she suppressed a delighted shiver. She pasted a platonic smile on her face and turned around. "Oh, hello. Having a good time?"

"More than I expected. And what about you? Are you enjoying yourself? Or just working the room?" He lifted an eyebrow.

"Just making everyone feel welcome."

"And showing off the fact you can speak..." He counted silently on his fingers. "Five languages? Six?"

"Five," she confirmed. "My Russian and German are more of a danger than an asset. I could ruin diplomatic relations in two sentences."

He chuckled, and she let herself enjoy the sound. Raoul didn't laugh much at all recently, but the wine pairings at dinner and the open bar had loosened him up considerably.

She hadn't seen him this relaxed since...

A confusing wave of grief swept over her. Maybe she'd had a secret thing for Raoul for ages, but she'd also loved her cousin deeply. Everyone had loved Ceci. And Stephani missed her. Ceci would have loved a party like this. She would have sparkled like the diamond she was. Stephani was far better behind the scenes. It had always been that way, even when they were kids.

"It's good to hear you laugh, Raoul."

His eyes met hers. "It's good to laugh again. It's been a while."

"Of course." She didn't want to dampen the mood of the evening, so she smiled instead and nodded toward a woman skirting the dance floor. "Look. Rose has come back. The children were lovely at dinner, don't you think?"

His gaze followed the new nanny. "You helped with her dress for the evening?"

"I did."

"My brother can't take his eyes off of her."

"I think Diego has finally met his match. Do you approve?"

"Yes and no?" He shrugged. "My first priority is the children, and they seem to adore her."

"Of course."

"But she is also a lovely person." He sent her a sideways smile. "Better than Diego deserves."

She laughed a little. "You don't really believe that."

"No, I don't. He's been...different. Especially the last few months. Since..."

His voice trailed off, but she knew what he'd meant. Since Ceci died.

Everything was different since Ceci had died.

He nudged her elbow. "I don't want to drag down the party. Do you want to dance, Steph?"

Did she? She'd only imagined it a million times. Particularly at every palace function when she'd stood on the sidelines with her clipboard while Ceci held Raoul in her arms. The perfect couple, a prince and princess, utterly in love.

She hesitated long enough that he stepped back. "*Lo siento*. I didn't mean to make you uncomfortable."

"You didn't," she hurried to assure him. "I'd love to dance." It might be her one and only chance. She put her champagne down on a nearby table and smiled up at him. "Shall we?"

The band had switched to a slower song, and he led her to the polished parquet and took her in his arms. She swallowed tightly...oh my. He was smooth, effortless, and his hand was warm against the hollow of her back. His fingers tightened over hers and she bit down on her lip. Raoul, she thought, wondering why on earth she insisted on torturing herself day in and day out. Why couldn't she manage to shake this silly attraction? Besides, he only ever saw her as his assistant. If he had any idea of her feelings...Ugh. Work would be unbearably awkward.

"You look lovely tonight," he said, his lips only inches from her ear. "The little black dress was a good choice."

"It's Versace." She strangled out the words.

Their feet kept moving, and their bodies seemed to drift closer, until the lapels of his jacket brushed against her breasts. She could feel his heat, smell his cologne.

She should resign. Find another position somewhere, away from the longing for what she could never have. Except this was the perfect job. Wonderful pay, wonderful perks, and...well, the family relied on her. She knew that. It was more than a job, and more than just Raoul. She cared about them all. King Alexander, Diego, the children...they were her family now that Ceci was gone. She had no immediate family of her own. What remained of the Savalas family was spread out over Greece and Spain. She didn't even know half of them. Ceci had been her anchor, and in her absence, the Navarros had become her surrogate family.

The song ended and Raoul stood back, but his face had lost the relaxed easiness of before, and a small furrow had appeared between his brows. "Is everything okay?" she asked, suddenly panicked that maybe she'd been the one to drift closer and inadvertently created an awkward moment between them.

"Diego danced with Rose, and she's just left him

standing in the middle of the floor," he said quietly. "Maybe there's trouble in paradise."

"You should talk to him."

"I know. It's never been easy, though. We're so different. We always seem to cross swords."

"That's because you're more alike than you think. You have to start giving him a chance. He's more reliable than you think."

Back to business. She felt on solid ground when she could focus on business.

She patted his arm. "I'm going to check on the kitchen staff. Señora Ortiz is planning a smaller buffet close to midnight."

She went to leave, and he reached for her hand. "Stephani?"

She focused on his face, because the fact that he was holding her hand was doing funny things to her insides. "Yes?"

"Thank you for all this. I know I've been difficult the last few months. Tonight, having people and music in the house again..."

The butterflies in her belly grew heavy. "It must be difficult."

"Yes. No. I mean, it's been good. I can't live my life being gloomy and unhappy all the time. This wouldn't have happened without you."

She smiled. "The people need to see that you're still okay."

He squeezed her fingers. "I need to know I'm okay. This helped. Thank you."

And he leaned forward and kissed her cheek.

His breath was warm against her skin, and she might be mistaken but she would swear his mouth lingered there just a moment longer than necessary. Heat rushed to her face and she muttered a hasty "you're welcome" before darting away. She didn't want him to see her blush. Or the fact that his casual touch had the power to make her normal unflappable reserve desert her completely.

Raoul downed his fourth—or was it fifth—Scotch and put the cut crystal glass down on a table. The midnight buffet had been set out, a light meal for those partygoers working up an appetite on the dance floor. Diego had disappeared ages ago, chasing after Rose.

His brother was in love. The real thing. And Raoul had congratulated him and wished him well, when all he could think of was how horrible it felt to have his heart ripped out of his chest in the actions of a moment. That perhaps love wasn't worth it. He might actually believe that if it weren't for Emilia and Max. The children were all he had left of Ceci, and he wouldn't trade his marriage with her for anything.

Not even the pain of losing her.

They hadn't let him go to the scene of the accident, but he didn't have to. The news had shown the mangled wreck in full detail. A leaked phone video had shown the paramedics taking Emilia and Max from the car, and their driver, Marco, sitting with a white bandage on his uncommonly pale face. And there'd been a glimpse of the body bags, too—Ceci's, and Mariana's, the royal family's nanny.

He went to the bar and got another Scotch. He was a year older, and life did go on. He even had moments of happiness. Tonight had been fun, but now that the evening was winding down, he was missing Ceci more than ever.

Would it be very bad form for him to leave the party before his guests? He suspected it would.

As he took a drink of his Scotch, he spotted Stephani across the room. She didn't look tired at all, even though he knew she'd been here since about seven this morning and hadn't stopped all day. He wasn't sure where she got her stamina, but she was the best assistant he'd ever had. She'd been working for him long enough that she anticipated his needs. Hiring Ceci's cousin had started out as a favor to his wife. Stephani had graduated from university but was working as an event server at a resort in Barcelona to make ends meet. She hadn't had the resources Ceci did—she'd been the poor cousin who'd had to work her way through. Ceci had known Stephani wouldn't take a handout, and Raoul had reluctantly agreed to give her a chance. It turned out to be a brilliant business decision.

He sipped again. Didn't hurt that she was gorgeous, either. Her silky hair was the same inky color as her black dress, and she wore heels that showed off her very fine legs. Stephani worked the room like the greatest of ambassadors and hostesses rolled into one. She was so like Ceci in that regard, warm and generous. But different, too. Focused, sharp.

Ceci's biggest quality had been her capacity for love and kindness. Stephani's was to take that warmth and use it to its best advantage—while staying out of the spotlight.

She laughed and he swore he heard it across the room, above the music and the chatter. His body tightened in response, an uncomfortable and yet somehow welcome experience. He was thirty-seven, for God's sake, and heir to the throne. Unlike his brother, he didn't have the luxury—or the inclination—to play the field. But he was still a man. A young man, really. What was he going to do, stay a widower for the rest of his life? Stay celibate? It was utterly unrealistic.

Maybe he shouldn't have had so much Scotch. He should go. No one would miss him now, would they? Particularly not Steph. He'd thanked her and kissed her cheek, and she'd literally run off. What had he been thinking?

He left the ballroom and headed for the stairs, then reconsidered. He'd rather get some fresh air and clear his head after all the alcohol.

The hall to the back entrance of the castle was narrow and once he descended the steps, he reached a stone-encased alcove. Fresh air filtered in, moist and balmy in the summer heat, and he shrugged off his jacket and dropped it in a corner. It would be dusty, but he didn't care. Instead he leaned back against the cool stone and closed his eyes. His head swam instantly, and he opened them again, seeking equilibrium.

And there she was.

"I brought you a bottle of water," Stephani said

softly. She uncapped it and held it out. "You need to rehydrate."

He took it and drank deeply. "How did you know I was here?"

She met his gaze evenly. "Your Highness, it's my job to know where you are at all times. Even more than your security."

"Thass right. You're my right hand." He heard the slur and was mortified. He never got drunk. Never. But he had tonight. It was definitely a good thing he'd left the party.

She smiled at him. "Oh my. You did hit the Scotch rather hard, didn't you?"

He didn't answer. Didn't know how to answer.

"Slurring in front of the finance minister wouldn't be a smart move."

He looked over at her. "Really? I doubt he'd notice."

"Oh, he'd notice. Rumor has it he addressed his own alcohol issues a few months ago and has been dry ever since. I watched. He didn't take any wine at dinner."

And this was one of the reasons Steph was so valuable. She always had her ear to the ground. Always seemed to know what was going on and with whom.

Which made him look at her a little more closely. "So, Miss Observant, how long did you know about Diego and Rose?"

She laughed. "Almost from day one."

"I like it when you laugh."

Her smile faded. "Sir?"

"Don't 'sir' me, Steph. We've been past that for years. You're family."

A strange look passed over her face and he wondered what it meant, but then she was smiling again, and he thought he might have imagined it. "I'm Ceci's cousin, that's all. We're not blood relatives."

"No," he said quietly. "We're not."

And the strange feeling he'd had while dancing with her returned. Like his skin was somehow shrinking, taut with…damn, he couldn't be feeling attraction. That would just be wrong.

And yet… He dropped his gaze to her lips. They were plump and red, fuller than Ceci's had been, and right now they opened just a little as Stephani inhaled sharply.

"Raoul," she cautioned.

He dragged his gaze back up to her eyes, expecting to see disapproval, but instead they were wide with what he could only figure was equal awareness. He stepped closer, testing her, and watched as her pupils dilated.

"Raoul," she repeated, an edge of desperation in her voice. But not fear. He was clear-headed enough to recognize that wistful sound of longing, and when he lifted his hand and placed it along her cheek, her breath came out in a rush against the pad of his thumb.

And then he kissed her.

She tasted like dry champagne and a trace of almonds and citrus from the cake earlier, plus a darker flavor that was sultry, sexy woman. The little dress she wore was utterly appropriate, even conservative, but the woman inside it was so very alive and responsive. Her tongue met his as he deepened the kiss, and with a sigh of surrender she curled her arms around his shoulders and melted into him.

His body responded, and he was just man enough—just drunk enough—to be grateful. For the first time since Ceci's death, he was happy he hadn't died with her.

Ceci.

He stepped back from Stephani, breaking the kiss and putting a few feet between them. Her chest rose and fell rapidly, her lips were slightly swollen and parted. It would be so easy to step forward and take her in his arms. Press her against the stone wall, feel her body beneath his.

But she was Ceci's cousin.

And she was too valuable...no, too important for him to treat her in such a cavalier, self-indulgent way. She was Stephani. The person he counted on most.

"I'm so sorry," he murmured, shoving his hands into his pockets. "Steph, I...I have no excuse. That was so wrong of me."

Her lips closed and she lifted her chin, though he thought, for just a fleeting second, that her lower lip quivered a bit. "Think nothing of it, sir," she said firmly. "It was the Scotch talking, that's all."

"Yes, the Scotch..." His voice trailed off for a moment. "Forgive me, Steph."

"There's nothing to forgive." Her voice sounded oddly thick, but he thought maybe it was because they were still ensconced within the stone walls of the alcove.

"You put together this wonderful party. You always

have my back. You must know how I appreciate all you do."

She met his gaze and smiled a little. Was she sad? Why wasn't she angry? He took a breath, then remembered the little sound of acquiescence she'd made as she wrapped her arms around his neck and the words he had been going to say stuck in his throat.

She had welcomed the contact. Wholeheartedly. What the hell did this mean?

He wasn't sure how to ask, and after too long of a hesitation, she put her hand on his arm and gave a little squeeze. "It's my job," she said softly. "Try to sober up. I'll see you in the office tomorrow."

Then she slipped away, her footsteps echoing on the stone steps.

Raoul had no desire to go back to the party. Instead, he picked up his dusty jacket, made his way into the garden—Ceci's garden—and found a vacant bench.

Then he took the little silver flask from his jacket pocket, unscrewed the cap, and took a big swig.

Stephani was off-limits. Tomorrow he'd reset the boundaries and they'd go back to normal. And if he ever did decide to…have a romance again, it wouldn't be with his assistant.

No matter how alluring she'd turned out to be.

CHAPTER 2

*S*ix months later

Stephani had planned many events at the palace over the years, but none of this magnitude. A royal wedding was not your run-of-the-mill state dinner or ball, and the last one had been a small, intimate affair with only family present. Of course, some of the chores were the same no matter what the function: fretting over guest lists, menus, decorations, staffing. But there was also security at the church, press access, transportation to and from the cathedral, and honeymoon arrangements for the happy couple—Diego and Rose.

It was a long way from the small coastal town in Greece where she'd grown up. A royal wedding, put into her hands. She wondered if her parents would be proud of her if they were still alive.

She'd grown up a fisherman's daughter, and it was the sea that had taken both her parents when she'd been away at school.

Stephani printed out the final guest list and tucked it

into her folder. Diego's new assistant, Sofia, was wonderful and a hard worker, but she was still learning. And the bride, though easily pleased, had no experience with planning such a large event. She communicated her preferences, but Steph and Sofia were left to work out the logistics.

As a result, it was now three days before the wedding and Stephani wasn't sure she was going to make it without either falling asleep at her desk or getting an ulcer. She reached into a drawer and grabbed an antacid, popped it into her mouth, and let out a huge sigh.

"Stephani, can you find an extra hour in my schedule today for the tourism minister? The latest incident in Germany could have a ripple effect on travel and I want to be proactive."

She looked up and cracked down on the antacid. "Let me check," she replied, taking a deep, slow breath to keep the feeling of being overwhelmed at bay. "I'll see what I can do to set something up with her office for this afternoon."

"Thanks." He smiled. "You're a gem."

He went back into his office and she crushed the tablet to smithereens between her teeth, wondering if it would still work if she didn't do the slow dissolve thing.

This was how it had been between them for six months. Like nothing ever happened. The morning after his birthday party, Raoul had acted utterly professional and…platonic. Not a hint of awkwardness or, well, attraction. It had stung that she was actually that forgettable, but despite the disappointment, she figured it was for the best. Particularly when the tabloids had become involved in Raoul's personal life, and the first priority was avoiding a scandal.

The problem was, she was tired of being his assistant. She worked twelve, sometimes fourteen-hour days quite often. And she was thirty-two, for heaven's sake. The proverbial clock had started ticking and she couldn't get it to shut up. When the hell did she have time to actually date? And she might like to plan her own kid's birthday party instead of Max's or Emilia's, though she loved them dearly. She mentally ticked off a timeline in her head. Dating, a suitable time for the relationship to develop, then planning a wedding, then getting pregnant—assuming she got pregnant right away, of course, and nine months later...Thirty-five at least. And that was if she met the right person like...now.

Like that was going to happen.

And this hadn't even truly been on her radar until last summer, when Raoul had kissed her. All her feelings that had been riding beneath the surface came bubbling up, and she'd had to shove them back down again. Added to that the engagement and wedding planning for Diego and Rose, and romance seemed to be everywhere.

Except for her. A few weeks ago she'd discreetly started putting out feelers for other jobs. Maybe it was time to move on. She certainly had the experience to be incredibly versatile.

She scheduled the tourism minister for four o'clock and put the order to the kitchen to prepare a proper tea for the meeting in the blue salon. She finalized the seating plan for the reception meal after the wedding, got the church seating plan from Sofia and made a few adjustments, and touched base with the new nanny, Imogene, on Emilia and Max's schedule for the wedding day. A headache started behind her eyes and she chased it with a couple of painkillers and a strong coffee. When the staff delivered the tea service at four fifteen, she realized she hadn't eaten since eight that morning.

No wonder she had a headache and her stomach lining felt as if it had a hole burning through it.

Raoul came out of his office, took one look at her, and came to her desk, kneeling beside her. "Steph, are you all right? You're awfully pale."

She smiled weakly, touched by his concern, feeling vulnerable because of it. "I'm fine. I just…it's silly, really. I forgot to eat today, and the coffee I had a while ago isn't sitting well."

He immediately got to his feet, went to the tea cart, and put some things on a plate. "Here. You need to eat."

"Oh, no. That's for you and Señora Munoz."

"She's not here yet, and we won't miss a few sandwiches and tarts. You need to look after yourself."

Concern shadowed his eyes, and she felt the stupid glimmer of hope that he actually cared flicker in her breast.

Then he smiled gently. "I mean, we can't have you run-down. We can't manage this office without you."

And poof. Flicker extinguished. Replaced by a huge weight of guilt that she was thinking of doing just that—

leaving the office and palace business to someone else. God, she was going to have an ulcer if she kept this up.

She dutifully took a triangle of sandwich from the plate and nibbled on it. "I'll be fine, really."

"Maybe you should take tomorrow off."

She was in the middle of chewing and started to laugh, and lifted her fingers to her mouth to both cover the awkward moment and to avoid spitting out any sandwich. How mortifying. "Two days before the wedding? Not likely."

"After the wedding, then. Some rest and relaxation. You haven't taken a vacation in months."

Of course not. Because Ceci had died and every-thing had been in an uproar. Raoul had needed everyone to be behind him. And then there was the whole Diego and Rose fiasco, and firing Diego's assistant, and training someone new. It had been nearly a year and the only time she'd taken off was three days over the Christmas holidays.

A vacation sounded heavenly. And also impossible. It also distracted her from the fact that she was currently actively looking for other employment.

"We'll see, shall we?" She sat back and took a bite of lemon tart. She was just brushing the crumbs off her blouse when a footman appeared with the tourism minister just behind him.

And she had crumbs on her fingers and a mouth full of pastry.

Raoul stepped into the gap and greeted Señora Munoz personally. "Julia. How lovely to see you again. I've ordered tea. Please come in." He actually took the cart and wheeled it himself. But then, the Navarro men weren't always sticklers for protocol. In fact, other than the very proper and appropriate Cecilia, the Navarro men had a habit of loving in surprising places. Except Raoul. He was the rule follower. The "what's best for Marazur" member of the family. It had been good—for Marazur. Not so good for Raoul's personal life.

When they were gone, she leaned back in her chair and finished the lemon tart. No one did pastry like Señora Ortiz. Between that and the sandwich, she was starting to feel remotely human again. Which was good because she still had several hours of work left before she could go home for the night.

The tourism minister left at six. Raoul went back into his office and then came back out again, frowning at her. "You should go home," he advised, his eyes dark with concern.

"I will. I don't have much more," she lied. "See? I have everything on a schedule. Just a few more items to cross off." She turned her computer monitor toward him, then back again. What she had showed him was only one page of her task list.

"I'm off to have dinner with the family. Why don't you join us?"

Her horrified reaction must have shown on her face because Raoul's frown eased, and he laughed a little. "We don't bite, you know."

A staff member—no matter how "friendly"—simply did not have dinner with the family.

"No, thank you, sir," she said quietly, turning back to her screen. "I'm fine." She was tired and yes, a little cranky. The idea of sitting in the massive dining room with Raoul and the king and Diego and Rose and Raoul's children…it was too much.

"Lucy arrives tomorrow. Maybe she'll be able to convince you to take it easy."

Stephani looked over at him and raised an eyebrow. She loved Raoul's half-sister, but Lucy's energy wasn't always of the relaxing variety. "I doubt it."

Raoul laughed and put a hand in his pocket. "Suit yourself. Please leave at a reasonable time, though. Burnout is a real thing, Steph."

She nodded quickly, wishing he'd leave already. She didn't want him to see that little tears had pricked the corners of her eyes at his concern.

And it was time she admitted that she'd never stay this late or go the extra mile quite this much for anyone other than Raoul. He needed her, and so she stayed. At great cost to herself.

RAOUL CAREFULLY CARRIED THE TRAY THAT SEÑORA Ortiz had prepared for him. He'd known Stephani for many, many years. And he knew when she was lying. Tonight, when she'd said she was almost ready to go home, she'd been lying. The look on her face when he'd asked her to join them for dinner had been as honest as it could get. She'd been startled and intimidated by the very idea.

Since she was perfectly comfortable with the family, he figured there was only one reason for her reaction.

She was stressed and tired, and rightfully so. If she wouldn't come to dinner, he'd take dinner to her.

Sure enough, she was still sitting at her desk, squinting at the computer screen, the soft click of her mouse absurdly loud in the silent office.

"Steph," he said, and she jumped, her mouse flying onto the floor as she gasped in alarm.

"I didn't mean to scare you." What he'd said about burnout earlier seemed more and more likely, from the look on her face. "I brought you dinner."

"But I said I was leaving soon."

He laughed. "An hour and a half ago. And I knew you were lying." He put down the tray and took the cover off the plate. "Señora Ortiz made stuffed salmon this evening."

"It smells amazing." He was gratified when she sat back in her chair and sighed. "I'm sorry, Raoul. I know I've been snippy."

"Don't apologize. If you needed more help, why didn't you say something? We could have brought in someone temporary. Or you can have your own assistant. You have a lot to handle here."

"I can manage," she said, and looked away from his gaze again. Hmm. What wasn't she saying?

"Come. Let's move this to the seating area and table. There's no need for you to eat at your desk." He moved the tray to a small, round table and pulled up a proper chair. Thankfully, she didn't fight him. She sat, took the napkin from his hand, and placed it on her lap. He watched as she took her knife and fork and sampled the first bite, then he pulled up a chair himself. "Steph, what's going on? Are you truly all right?"

She nodded as she put another piece in her mouth and chewed. "I'm fine. I really am just tired, Raoul. The wedding is a big deal. Even bigger than Lucy's was. Diego's more visible. More popular. And there are different security needs now than there were when Lucy and Brody got married here at the castle."

It was true. For a long time, no one had even known Lucy existed—his half-sister was a product from a whirlwind romance shortly after Raoul and Diego's mother had passed. And she married a Canadian rancher and now lived in Alberta. All in all, that royal wedding had been more low-key than the production taking place in a few days.

She dabbed at her lips. "Don't you want to say good night to Max and Emilia?"

He smiled. "I will. They are upstairs with Imogene for now. I told them I had to make sure Tía Stephani had some dinner first."

"I'm not their aunt, Raoul."

"You're their cousin, and they've always called you Tía Stephani. They love you. You're family. I wish you'd join us sometimes."

He watched as Stephani played with her rice. "The thing is, Raoul, I'm Ceci's family, but first and foremost I'm an employee. And blurring the line between the two is not a good idea."

He met her gaze and felt the little jolt he often felt when they looked at each other. For a long time he'd been able to ignore the feeling, that little flicker of recognition, of awareness. But he hadn't been so successful since his last birthday and the kiss they'd shared. Now that flicker had context. Now he knew what she tasted like, felt like in his arms. He'd spent the last six months trying to ignore it, knowing it would only complicate things.

The line was already a bit blurred.

He got up and got her a glass of water, then sat again and waited for her to finish her dinner. When she was done, he handed over another smaller covered plate. When she looked up at him with a questioning expression, he grinned. "Coconut flan."

"Oh, that's my favorite," she said, longing in her voice. "But I shouldn't."

"Yes, you should."

"But my dress for the wedding..."

"You haven't eaten properly in two weeks." He knew, because he'd noticed and worried far earlier than today. "If you don't eat the flan, the dress will fall off you and create a spectacle. I'm certain that's not what you want."

A smile teased her lips. "You're making fun of me."

"I'm trying to say that the last thing you need to worry about is your figure. Eat the flan. There should always be room for flan."

If being a widower had taught him one thing, it was to enjoy the small moments. While responsibilities weighed heavy on his shoulders, he did try to make time for what was important. Bedtime stories with the children. Morning coffee with his father.

Watching Stephani eat flan. She put the spoon between her lips and that flicker came to life again.

"You're better now?" he asked, then cleared his throat.

"Much." She smiled at him. "Thank you, Raoul. For making me take the time to eat. A little hydration and food is exactly what I needed."

She needed more than that. She needed to get out of the palace for more than sleeping hours. He was going to see about hiring her an assistant, even if it was only part time. He'd see to it, right after the wedding was over and Diego and Rose were off on their honeymoon. He rather envied their trip, though he knew Diego was blending it with business, as well. They were off on a Tanzanian safari and then spending a few weeks at one of Diego's charity projects in the area.

Once upon a time he would have liked a trip like that with Ceci. Just the two of them, and it wouldn't have mattered where they were, as long as they were together. He'd hold her in his arms through the night and they'd hold hands during the day and share secret smiles. He looked over at Stephani, who was finishing her dessert. Intimacy. That was what he missed the most. He missed having that certain someone at the end of the day. He envied his brother more than anyone could guess.

"I'm going to head up and say good night to the children," he said, and pushed back his chair. "Just send word to the kitchen when you're done. Someone will collect your tray."

"Don't be silly." She smiled at him. "I'll take it down myself. And I promise I'll leave the rest of my work for tomorrow, Raoul. Now that I've stopped working there's nothing I want more than a glass of wine and a hot bath."

Dios mío. He did not need that image burned into his brain right now. He stood rather abruptly. "Then I'll say good night and see you in the morning."

He was nearly to the door of the office when her voice stopped him. "Raoul?"

He turned half around.

"Thank you for dinner. It was very sweet."

"You're welcome," he answered.

CHAPTER 3

Two days before the wedding Steph had a hesitantly optimistic feeling it was all going to come together. After last night's meal she'd gone home and had her wine and bath and a solid nine hours sleep. Today she'd come into work feeling more rested and energized than she had in several weeks. The checklist was well in hand and she'd made the brave, yet smart decision to do a little extra delegating. At some point she had to trust people to run their sections and do their jobs.

Lucy arrived at noon, coming into the office with a boundless energy that Stephani envied, as well as a splendid waterfall of red, curly hair. She looked nothing like the Navarros, but she had the same stubborn mind and ineffable charm.

"Stephani!" Lucy cried out, and came around her desk to pull her into a hug. "You look exhausted. Where's Rose? Isn't she planning all this stuff?"

Steph laughed. "Rose is being bridal. Today is spa

day. Body wrap, mani, pedi, facial, massage…the whole works. Then she has her final fitting and dinner with the bridesmaids."

Lucy shuddered. "I'm glad Brody and I kept things really simple."

Steph laughed, really happy Lucy was here. The youngest of the Navarros, she seemed to spread sunbeams everywhere she went, and not just because of the color of her hair. "Brody and the kids? They're settled?"

Lucy nodded. "And sleeping. We flew most of the night. I brought noise-cancelling headphones and slept. Brody didn't, and dealt with the kids." She sent Steph a wicked grin. "Sucker."

They were both laughing when Raoul came out of his office.

"Luce!" He came forward, a broad smile on his face, and enveloped his sister in a hug.

Steph couldn't remember the last time he'd smiled quite that big or so easily. When he did, his face transformed, and it was a glorious, beautiful thing. No lines of grief or responsibility etched there. Just happiness.

"Hello, big brother. You're looking well."

"So are you. You brought Alyssa, too, along with Alex?"

Lucy nodded. "At this age she's super easy. She just started sleeping through the night but she's not mobile yet." She laughed. "I left the children with Emilia and Max in the nursery. Alex and Max were planning some sort of battle on the grounds and Emilia and Imogene were fussing over Alyssa. I like the new nanny."

Raoul nodded. "Rose recommended her, and the children adore her."

Lucy stepped back from Raoul and looked at Stephani. "I expect you could use some help right about now. What needs doing?"

Stephani let out a breath. "You're a lifesaver, but you're not here to work. You're family."

"Oh, for Pete's sake." Lucy laughed while Raoul grinned at his sister's eye-rolling. "For that matter, so are you."

It echoed a little too closely to what Raoul had said last night. There was no denying that she'd always enjoyed a "familiar" relationship with the Navarro family because of Ceci. For a long time it had been wonderful, but now it added a layer of complication to what had once been fairly straightforward.

She'd always found Raoul attractive; when he and Ceci had started dating Stephani had been more than a little awestruck. Once they'd become engaged, she got to know him better and liked him as a person and not just as a king-in-waiting. But it had been when Emilia was born that she'd fallen for him.

It had been a strange, defining moment. She'd gone to visit her cousin and discovered Raoul in the nursery. Ceci was asleep and Raoul was holding the baby in his arms as Stephani peeked in the door. The conversation he'd had with his baby daughter had been so tender, so heartfelt, that he'd ceased to be a prince in that moment. He'd been a husband and a father and a man, and she hadn't been able to turn off her feelings since.

She couldn't tell Raoul how she felt, and certainly

couldn't "make a move." But she wasn't quite ready to say goodbye, either. Because Lucy was right. This was her family. Both the Navarros and also the household staff. To leave would mean starting over in so many ways.

"Yes, but I'm on the payroll," she said lightly, trying to cover the turmoil of her thoughts.

Lucy laughed again and linked her arms with Stephani. "Payroll, schmayroll," she argued. "Show me your to-do list and I'll see what I can take off your plate. I've got about two hours before I need to be at the nursery again."

Raoul disappeared into his office and Stephani opened up her spreadsheet, too glad for the help to turn it away.

"My brother looks good," Lucy remarked quietly. "Is he doing okay?"

Stephani's pulse took a little jump, surprised that Lucy would ask her such a question. "Um, as far as I know, I guess."

"Don't sound so surprised that I asked. You know him better than anyone, including Father or Diego. And he trusts you." Before Stephani could absorb that statement, Lucy continued. "He was really, well, dark for so long. He looks...I don't know. Lighter, somehow."

Stephani shrugged. "Maybe it's wedding fever?"

"Or maybe it's letting go of some of his grief. He has to move on sometime."

Stephani's fingers paused over her keyboard. Raoul moving on...of course he must. Marazur needed a queen when the time came for Raoul to sit on the throne. He couldn't remain a bachelor forever. And the idea of seeing him with someone else made her stomach tangle up in knots.

"Something wrong?"

"Oh no, of course not." Steph clicked on one of the task lists and brought it up on the screen. "What would you like to help with, Lucy? We have Rose's family arriving from Heathrow tomorrow morning. Maybe you can help with that?"

Lucy nodded. "Rose has a niece, right?"

"She does. A little older than Emilia. And there's Rose's sister, brother and sister-in-law, and parents."

"No grandparents?"

"None that could make the trip, no. And Diego's friend Ryan and his sister are flying in tonight."

"Give me the details. I'll organize their welcome and get them settled and make sure they're where they need to be for tomorrow. The day of the wedding, though, I'll be trying to get my own family whipped into shape."

"That would be fabulous." Steph printed off the details and schedule for Rose's family. "There's also a family dinner tomorrow night. Formal but not overly so."

"You're attending, of course?"

Steph looked up to find Lucy's gaze steady. "Well, I wasn't planning on it."

Lucy frowned. "Stephani, I know you're Raoul's assistant, but you're also Ceci's cousin. You meant a lot to her, and you've been with this family for what...seven, eight years? But you're always in the background."

"Where I belong," Stephani asserted.

"Not always. Look, at public functions, that's one thing. But you've been through it all with us. You should be at the dinner to celebrate, too. I insist."

Stephani reached for the papers coming out of the printer, then spun her chair back to face Lucy. If she were honest with herself, she'd love to go to that dinner. It would be relaxed, and far less structured than the official reception the next day. Rose and Diego would be happy and nervous. There would be children, and lately she hadn't had much time to spend with Max and Emilia. She missed them. All things she loved about the Navarro family and enjoyed vicariously since she had no real family of her own.

Lucy touched her hand. "Come on. You know you love us." Stephani choked out a laugh as Lucy added, "And we love you, too."

"You are so used to getting your own way."

Lucy smiled softly. "It's being a baby sister that does it. And having a husband like Brody. But seriously. I'll have your name added to the list and seating plan. Leave it all to me. In fact, leave the rest of the dinner to me. I'll check with Señora Ortiz and all you have to do is put on a pretty dress and show up."

She should say no. After all, it wasn't Lucy's job to show up and go straight to work. But the offer meant taking several items off her list for tomorrow. And it meant actually enjoying at least part of what was to be a joyous occasion for both the family and the principality. A new princess.

"I shouldn't, but I'm going to let you do that. Though if anything comes up—and I mean anything—

I want you to let me know. You have the children with you, and jet lag, and you need to enjoy the wedding, too."

"Leave it to me. Do you have a dress for tomorrow?"

Stephani raised an eyebrow. "I think I can find something in my closet."

There was a sound from Raoul's office and Lucy looked at his door for a moment, and then turned back. "Make it pretty. None of those straight, businessy lines you're used to. And no black. That's fine for state dinners but this is different. Make it...celebratory."

Stephani laughed. "Usually I'm the one playing fairy godmother." She'd picked out the dress Rose had worn to Raoul's birthday party, as a matter of fact, and that night had ultimately led to Rose and Diego's engagement. It was also the party where Raoul kissed Stephani senseless and then run away with his tail between his legs.

A kiss could only sustain a girl so long. And the Versace still hung in her closet, but she wasn't about to wear it again.

"Blue," Lucy suggested. "Raoul loves blue."

The knots tangled up again. "What difference does that make?"

Lucy met her gaze. "Oh, no difference at all, I suppose. Hand me the lists and I'll get started."

When Lucy was gone, Stephani sat back in her chair and pondered the last twenty minutes. Lucy was different than the rest of the family. She hadn't grown up with the protocol, nor lived in it for the past years since she'd discovered she was a real princess. Inviting

Stephani to a family dinner was no big deal to her, but protocol-wise, it was a precarious line. Then again, the situation had never been black and white, because of Ceci.

But the comment about Raoul liking blue...Stephani knew that already. Which was beside the point. Lucy had suggested she wear blue. Why? Because Lucy might play fairy godmother, but she surely wasn't playing matchmaker.

Steph wasn't about to wear blue just because Raoul liked it. He'd made his feelings plain enough six months ago. And trying to pretend otherwise was just punishing herself.

RAOUL MADE HIS WAY TO THE DINING ROOM WITH A bounce in his step. Tomorrow his little brother was getting married. Despite his own personal heartache, Raoul was happy for Diego. Rose was a spectacular woman, strong as steel but with a softness that spoke of compassion and understanding. Despite her commoner upbringing, she'd be a wonderful princess. And the fact that Diego had finally left behind his questionable behavior was an added bonus.

And Lucy was here, too, with Brody and their children. He'd looked outside his window today and had seen all of them—Emilia, Max, Alex, and Rose's niece, Alice, playing in the garden. Imogene was watching over all of them while the baby napped in a stroller. This was what the palace had been missing. Laughter. Home.

And if there was a little ache in his heart that he was going through this without Ceci, that was okay. At least now it was an ache and not an emptiness that brought him to his knees.

He stopped at the threshold of the dining room and simply watched.

Everyone was dressed up. Rose and Diego were here already, looking radiant, and holding wineglasses as they chatted to another couple Raoul assumed were Rose's parents. Lucy and Brody chatted with a couple about their age—Rose's brother and sister-in-law, he assumed, and a woman who looked younger than Rose, but with similar features and hair. Instead of Rose's easy smile, she had a strained expression around her lips. Ah. The sister who was a bit of a wild card. Should be fun.

"Bit of a full house tonight, *¿sí?*"

Raoul turned to see his father standing just behind him, a soft smile on his face. "It's good, I think."

"Me too. All of my family here together, and Rose's, too."

"And lots of children."

Alexander chuckled. "I'm hoping Rose and Diego will add to that number, too."

"Add to what number?"

Stephani's soft voice interrupted, and Raoul momentarily lost his capacity to speak.

Her dress was the color of a peacock's feather, a bright blue that shone against her bronze skin. The satin fell in a straight sheath, draped from one shoulder by a jeweled brooch, while her other shoulder was bare. And the hem… *Dios mío.* It fell to the midpoint of her thigh, showcasing her long legs.

His gaze lifted to her face again and she raised an eyebrow. "Add to what number?" she repeated, and he realized he hadn't answered her question.

"Grandchildren," Alexander supplied. "Four is good. But a half dozen or more would be better." He put a hand on Raoul's shoulder. "We should probably go in."

"I'll be in shortly," Raoul answered. In a more formal setting, there'd be protocol to follow. But for tonight, they'd put all that aside and had decided to treat the evening like a big family dinner.

He turned to Stephani. "You look beautiful. New dress?"

She met his gaze, a soft smile on her lips. "I've had it a while but haven't worn it. It's a little bright for official functions, when I'm supposed to be more invisible."

"Shame. The color is perfect."

Her cheeks colored and his heart gave a solid thump against his ribs in response. For six months now he'd ignored his…well, if not attraction, his awareness of Stephani. It hadn't been easy. He saw her every day. And he'd never forgotten the sweetness of her kiss in the alcove, even if he had been a little too deep into his bottle of Scotch.

"I'm glad you approve. It's not too much? Lucy said it wasn't formal, but a cocktail dress was required."

"It's perfect. And I'm glad you handed off some of the duties to Lucy. She's a great organizer and a little less official as far as the palace is concerned. Perfect for making Rose's family feel at home."

Imogene arrived with the four oldest children. "Papa!" Max came forward, bouncing on his toes. "Alex and I had a sword fight today!"

"Is that what you were doing out in the garden? I saw lots of commotion."

"It was fun."

Emilia was standing close to Stephani. "Oh, Tía Stephani, your dress is beautiful."

"Thank you, Emilia. You look lovely as well. Is that new?"

The girl nodded vigorously. "And I have a new one for the wedding tomorrow, too." As an aside, she reached over and pulled Alice closer. "And so does Alice. And she has shoes that look like ballet slippers."

"Oh, that sounds beautiful. I hope you're enjoying your time here, Alice."

Alice answered and the little girls then exclaimed over Stephani's rather high heels. Raoul couldn't help staring at her toned calves as she turned her heel this way and that. He also noticed that Emilia said something funny, and Stephani dropped an easy kiss on his daughter's head. She cared for his children, and they loved her, too.

Because she was family. And too often he treated her as an employee.

"Shall we go in?" he asked, and offered her his arm.

"Oh. Of course." She smiled up at him, then turned to the children. "Gentlemen, perhaps you could escort the ladies to the dining room?"

Max and Alex rolled their eyes but stepped forward. Alex immediately held out his arm for Alice, which left Max with his sister, but other than a put-upon sigh, nothing was said. Raoul laughed and nodded at Imogene, who would retire to the nursery with the baby over the dinner hour.

He put his hand over Stephani's as it rested on his forearm. "Nice work. Do you suppose Alex and Alice have a budding romance?"

She chuckled. "At their age? I doubt it. Alice is still at the 'boys have germs' age."

Raoul was laughing as they entered the dining room, and several pairs of eyes turned in their direction.

He hesitated for a moment and looked down at Stephani, who was smiling and beaming. Beautiful.

It felt very right having someone on his arm again.

CHAPTER 4

Lucy had seated her next to Raoul.

Stephani didn't make a fuss or move any place cards around. She simply took her seat after all introductions had been made with Rose's family. Raoul was on her right, Alexander at the head, and across from Raoul was Mr. and Mrs. Walters, lovely people who were still obviously agog at their surroundings. Alice and Emilia sat with them, along with Rose's siblings and Rose and Diego. On the same side of the table as Raoul and Stephani were Lucy, Brody, and the two boys.

At first it was slightly awkward, but then Diego fired up his charm, the second course arrived with more wine, and everyone loosened up a bit. Stories of the bride and groom popped up with regularity, and even Alexander chimed in with tales of Diego's antics as a small boy. Stephani laughed with the rest, though she caught some rather intense stares from Rose's sister across the table. Rose had warned her that Hayley was a tad resentful of others' good fortune when she'd become a single mother as a teen. Regardless, Stephani found Alice to be a lovely child, she clearly loved her aunt, and she and Emilia had already forged a friendship. It wasn't worth worrying about.

"Having a good time?" Raoul murmured in her ear.

"It's like the big family dinners we used to have, remember? Only a bit more formal."

He nodded. "Ceci's family was good that way. Lots of food, wine, teasing."

"Do you never hear from her father?" Ceci's mother had passed on years earlier, just after Emilia's birth, from cancer.

Raoul shook his head. "The odd phone call. I've invited him over many times, but I think he finds it too hard without Ceci here."

"But he's missing out on the children."

"I know."

"His loss, Raoul. They're wonderful."

He smiled at her. "And they feel the same about you. I hope that remains, Steph. You're the one bit of family from their mother's side that they still have."

The words stabbed like a knife to the heart. And she was thinking of leaving. How could she do that, knowing she'd leave the children behind? But then, she wouldn't be like their grandfather. Of course she'd visit. If she was the only family that the children had left, the reverse was also true.

The conversation had a sobering affect, and Stephani was quiet through her coffee and dessert. After dinner, Lucy took the children back to the nursery while everyone moved to the drawing room for after-dinner drinks and socializing. Wedding plans were in the air. Diego and Rose would soon say goodbye and Rose would depart for the seaside hotel where her brides-maids waited and where they'd all get ready for the wedding tomorrow. So much celebration, and Stephani found herself on the perimeter of the room, watching it all.

"So," came a voice beside her. "That's a nice frock."

Rose's sister, Hayley. Stephani pasted on a smile. The compliment didn't quite sound genuine.

"Thank you."

"Bet it cost a lot."

Stephani didn't know how to answer that, so she merely smiled and offered, "I hope you're having a nice visit. Rose said she doesn't see you often."

Hayley merely shrugged. "So you and the crown prince…how long have you been having it off, then?"

"Having it off?" Stephani frowned, puckering her brows together. But then Hayley raised one eyebrow with a knowing glint in her eye and Stephani resisted the urge to sigh at the girl's crassness.

"His Highness," she emphasized firmly, "is my boss. And he was also married to my cousin. I'm fortunate to have a close relationship with the entire family, which of course does not include 'having it off' with him." She wasn't generally up on Brit slang, but the meaning had been made plain enough.

Hayley laughed. "No need to get so defensive. It's clear to anyone who cares to look." She tossed back whatever was in her glass.

"I'm afraid you're mistaken. I do hope you enjoy the palace's hospitality while you're here. If you'll excuse me, I have a few more details to attend to before tomorrow's event."

She maintained her pleasant smile; after all, she'd spent many years working in a delicately handled world of diplomacy. This one, though, had been unexpected and personal. It was inaccurate but not entirely incorrect. Tonight, the look on Raoul's face when she'd shown up in her dress had been utterly gratifying. He'd been tongue-tied for a few moments. And when he'd offered his arm, she had felt ridiculously like they were a couple. His equal, in everything except perhaps official titles.

She belonged here. And that was what bothered Hayley, wasn't it? Thinking of it that way, Stephani was able to put her feelings aside. She knew what it was like to be on the outside looking in.

Lucy returned with the baby on her arm, and everyone ooohed and aahed appropriately. Still, it wasn't long before Rose and Hayley disappeared with the other bridesmaid, Becca, heading to the hotel. Diego and Brody made a late-night trip to the stables, probably to look over the latest additions to the polo stock and Imogene gathered the children and saw them to the nursery suite. Lucy took her jetlagged self off to bed, and as the staff cleaned up, it left just Raoul and Stephani.

"Nightcap?" he suggested. "Or do you have to leave, too?"

She didn't. She'd brought everything she needed for

the wedding day and had requested one of the smaller rooms so that she could be up and on duty first thing in the morning. "I'm actually staying in the north wing tonight. I thought it would be easier seeing as tomorrow's an early start."

"I won't keep you, if you want to get some rest."

She knew she should go. But she didn't want to. Now that the palace had quieted, she found she needed a little time to unwind before trying to sleep. If she went to bed now, still keyed up, she'd start running to-do lists around in her head.

"A brandy might be nice."

His smile was so warm she nearly melted. "Perfect," he said, and went over to a table, took two snifters, and poured a generous amount of brandy in each. He handed one to her, and she took a deep inhale of the bowl before touching the liquid to her lips. After the wine at dinner, this one drink would be enough to lull her to sleep when she went to bed.

"Mmm," she murmured, and let out a sigh.

Raoul took a similar sip. "Come," he invited, "let's sit for a bit. Tomorrow will be chaotic enough."

She smiled and sat in a plush armchair, crossed her legs, and rested her wrist on her knee, the snifter dangling casually from her fingers. "Tomorrow will go off like clockwork. The chaos will be contained to my brain. That's how it works. Crazy on the inside, outward appearances run smoothly."

"And you're incredibly good at it, Steph. I don't know how we'd run things without you."

She wondered if now might be a good time to tell

him she was considering other employment. But then he'd ask her why, and she'd have to come up with an excuse that didn't hinge on her feelings for him. Tonight she was too tired to do that, so she let it go.

"You'd find someone," she said quietly, taking another drink. "No one is irreplaceable."

"I don't know about that." He leaned forward in his chair, rested his elbows on his knees. "I meant what I said about you having your own assistant. I've been relying on you too much."

Ah yes. Ordinarily, that would be the perfect opening, but she was too tired, too languorous, to broach the topic. And if she were honest with herself, nights like tonight made her question what she really wanted. Moving on would mean giving up a lot.

"It's my job, Raoul. It's what you pay me for."

"Is this really just a job to you?"

She met his gaze, felt her heart catch a little as his dark eyes searched hers. "Of course, it's not," she murmured, before biting down on her lip.

"What happened last year…we never talked about it."

Forget her heart catching. Now her lungs felt cramped, like she couldn't possibly get enough air. Still, she forced herself to appear relaxed. She'd had lots of practice, after all. About seven years' worth.

"I assumed you wanted to forget about it. You were drunk, you know?"

"I was embarrassed. And didn't want you to hold it against me."

"I wouldn't." She softened her voice. "Raoul. I know

you. I know you were…" Her throat caught a bit and she stammered. "You were lonely," she finished.

"I was. I am. But I took advantage of your friendship, and I'm long overdue in apologizing."

Was his memory flawed? Because he didn't seem to remember that she'd been there too, as an active and very willing participant. "Then I should apologize as well," she said firmly. "You weren't alone."

The admission didn't ease the situation, however. Instead, it was an acknowledgment that she'd been just as involved in the kiss as he had, that she had wanted it as much as he. And now that realization hummed between them, and heat crept up her cheeks.

"I may have had too much brandy," she said quietly, leaning forward and putting the half-empty snifter on a little table.

"Well," Raoul said, clearing his throat, "I had an idea yesterday. After the wedding, we're going on a business trip. The tourism minister gave me some interesting ideas the other day, and I want to meet with some hoteliers and hospitality experts. I'll need an assistant to travel with me, of course. And a minimum of security. Plus, I intend to keep a light schedule and spend a few more days than necessary, so we can both have a mini vacation out of it. Both of us have been cooped up in this castle for too long."

She stared at him in surprise. Vacation? Raoul? The last time he'd done that, he and Ceci and the children had gone to Switzerland for some skiing and time in a mountainside chalet. He'd been nose to the grindstone since her death.

"And where would we be going?" she asked, tilting her head as she looked at him. He was utterly earnest. And excited. His eyes lit up and the lines around them melted away.

"The Riviera," he answered smugly. "There are some investors I want to meet, and resort owners. Our economy needs a boost, and while we've got a solid tourism industry here, we're missing some five-star opportunities. It's time we situated ourselves as a world-class destination."

The Riviera. She pursed her lips, trying not to drool over the idea of all that opulence and glamour. "Do you have anywhere in mind? Nice? St. Tropez? Monaco?"

"We can work out the details once the wedding's over. But what do you say? A week of fine dining, some spa treatments, lying on the beach?"

She laughed. "That doesn't sound much like work, Raoul. Is this your way of making me take a holiday?"

He put down his glass and his expression sobered. "We both need it," he said quietly. "Neither of us has had a break since the accident. And it's not like we wouldn't be working at all. I really do want to meet with investors and developers to try something different here." A small smile touched his lips. "Consider sampling the amenities as research."

"Massages and body wraps?" Her body nearly sighed, just thinking about it.

"And saunas and delicious food...not that there's any shortage of that here, but something different. I was looking at one resort and they coordinate heli-tours for their guests, or evening yacht excursions."

It did sound heavenly.

"You're looking to entice someone to build a new resort here?"

"Possibly. We'd have to look at environmental impact, of course, and what sort of partnership any developer would want to make with the government. I think it's worth exploring. So does Señora Munoz."

Ah, yes. The tourism minister. This had been on Raoul's mind a while, then. The idea that this was a luxury getaway for two melted away, and just as well. Raoul might think she needed a vacation, but she knew he didn't mean for them to take one together. He was as practical as she was. Combining a work trip with a little rest and relaxation was simply efficient.

"Well, it sounds like a terrible hardship," she teased, leaning back in her chair again. "I'd suggest waiting for Diego and Rose to return from their honeymoon first. That way you can enjoy Lucy's visit, too."

"They're all happy, aren't they?" he asked, and once more she picked up on a wistful note in his voice.

"Yes, I believe they are," she answered softly. "Lucy and Brody are perfect for each other, and Rose is just what Diego needed. They have it, Raoul. Just like you did with Ceci."

His eyes, nearly black in the dim light, met hers. "Do you think it's possible to have it more than once?"

She thought of their kiss in the alcove. Thought of the times he'd made her laugh, of the little considerations like bringing her a meal when she was working late. She thought of how she catered to his preferences without him even realizing, not just because it was her job but because she cared about him so deeply. If he gave her a chance, maybe they could see if there was something real between them. But even tonight, he brought up the kiss and then moved on. If there was another it out there for Raoul, he probably wasn't envisioning her in that role.

"I think it's possible, for sure," she answered. She picked up her snifter and downed the rest of the brandy in one burning gulp. After a small gasp, she looked up. "You're thirty-seven, Raoul. You're too young to be alone for the rest of your life."

The brief silence that followed her statement was slightly awkward. Raoul finished his brandy as well and put the glass down with a faint clink. "And what about you, Steph? You never mention your personal life. Do you want marriage, children?"

She got up then, uncomfortable with the questions, afraid of the responses sitting on her tongue. "It's getting late, and when we start talking about my love life it's clear we've exhausted all interesting topics." She laughed lightly, though inside she was churning. Was it wrong that she wished he'd take the hint? That he'd see what was right in front of him and maybe, just maybe, feel the same?

Or was it that she simply couldn't live up to Ceci's legacy? Even if Raoul did care for her, would she always be in her cousin's shadow?

Could she settle for that?

"I'm sorry if I overstepped," Raoul offered, rising from his chair and coming toward her. "I just want you to be happy. I'm afraid this job hasn't just worn you out, but it's kept you from living your own life." He frowned. "I was born into this family and into the responsibility. This is my duty. But it's not yours."

She lifted her chin. "I think I can decide what is and what isn't my duty, and I have as much right to love Marazur as anyone else. Even if I was born elsewhere." After all, Ceci hadn't been born in Marazur, either. But she'd loved her adopted country, and its people had loved her, too.

Of course, Ceci had always fit in better than Stephani. Her side of the family had been wealthy and connected. Stephani's family had been…well, not poor, but certainly lived a very different life from Ceci's. Not that it had ever mattered to the cousins. They'd spent a summer together when they were twelve and had been like sisters ever since.

"Of course you do. Are we arguing about something?"

She shook her head and let out a breath. "No. I'm just tired, and feeling the brandy, I think. I need to get out of these shoes and into bed so I can deal with tomorrow."

CHAPTER 5

Wedding day dawned gray and gloomy, with a steady rain falling. But by nine, the rain stopped, the clouds cleared, and the island of Marazur was clean and sparkling for the third royal wedding it had seen in a decade.

Stephani looked out her borrowed bedroom window and sighed, wistful but happy. Two people she cared deeply about were heading to the church today. The wedding was to be deceptively simple and elegant, but it had taken an amazing amount of planning for it to be so. An early breakfast buffet had been set up in the dining room so people could eat as their schedules allowed. A fleet of cars waited to transport guests and family to the cathedral. Security was already in place. The wedding party was small and intimate, with Raoul and Rose's brother standing up with Diego, and Hayley and another close friend, Becca, as bridesmaids.

Lucy and Imogene were in charge of getting the children ready. Both girls were standing as flower girls, and the boys were escorting them up the aisle. Diego and Rose had insisted that since Max and Emilia had been little matchmakers, they needed to be part of the day.

Flowers had already been delivered and were in place. Stephani had been downstairs already to oversee the ballroom and the preparations for the feast that would happen later in the day. Marco was on standby for driving Diego, Raoul, and King Alexander. Now Stephani just had to get dressed, redo her makeup, and get to the church ahead of everyone else.

She'd picked a more subdued dress for the wedding, a sheath-style in classic navy, with matching heels and sapphire earrings and a necklace that Ceci had given her for her thirtieth birthday. Elegant and appropriate, but not flashy in any sense, and suitable for remaining in the background.

The face that looked back at her in the mirror frowned. She should be happy. This was a glorious day. Wonderful for the family and for the kingdom. Instead, she was standing here feeling left out, like she wanted to belong as she had last night. Raoul could say all he wanted about her being family. Behind castle walls was one thing. The face they showed the world was quite another.

Lately it had caused more dissatisfaction than she was comfortable with. To be overly intimate in public would spark rumors. The media looked for any opportunity. She understood it completely, but nights like last night in the library underscored the loneliness she tried to ignore.

She changed her frown to her work-smiley-face and hoped it didn't look fake. Then she grabbed her jeweled clutch to head downstairs to the back entrance, where she'd leave for the cathedral, ensure everything was working like clockwork, and do her job.

She met Raoul in the corridor and stopped short, catching her breath.

Seeing him in a tux dozens of times over the years should dampen the effect, but it didn't. He looked utterly dashing—suave and powerful and sexy and with a presence that was both alluring and a little intimidating. "Raoul," she said abruptly, pressing a hand to her chest. "I didn't expect to see you."

"I was coming to look for you. Slight kink in the works. Hayley has apparently come down with some sort of virus. She's saying she can't possibly attend."

Her eyes widened. "And they sent the crown prince as a messenger?"

He shrugged. "Rose called Diego in a panic. Diego called me and we came up with a fix. Rose is totally on board."

"A fix for a maid of honor? Really?" Her heart thudded. Of all the things to go wrong, losing a bridesmaid was huge.

"You," he stated simply. "You're nearly the same size as Hayley. You are going to stand up for Rose today."

Oh, no. This wouldn't do at all. Her stomach churned as she thought about it. "It shouldn't be me. It should be someone close to her. A family member, a good friend."

"She has a good friend with her, but even so, you

two are friends. And you are family, Steph. Not sure when you're going to believe it, but everyone knows how much you helped Rose and Diego find their way to each other. Rose is sending the dress to the church, and you can change there."

"The dresses are champagne-colored. I need other shoes..." She looked up into Raoul's amused eyes. "I can't do this. I have to make sure everything else runs smoothly. It's my job."

Raoul reached down and took her hand, and she was momentarily stunned as his fingers squeezed hers.

"Stephani Savalas. You have planned this down to the minute and tiniest detail. Everyone knows their jobs. Trust them. Besides, we both know this isn't about your job. It's about you feeling as if you don't belong. Everyone here says you do. Maybe you should start listening."

Problem was it hurt too much to listen. It gave her hope for something that could never be and that she could never truly voice for fear of ruining the relationship they already had.

He squeezed her hand again. "Go change your shoes. I have Marco on standby to take you to the church right now and come back for us."

"Okay." She switched into crisis management mode and slid her hand out of his grasp. "Okay. Right. Bridesmaid down, filling in. Dear God, I hope that dress fits."

Raoul chuckled. "It will. And honestly? I have a strange suspicion that Rose's sister did this out of spite. Having the situation fixed so handily gives me a strange sort of pleasure."

His eyes twinkled at her and she let out a breath. "She's not a happy woman, is she? And doesn't seem all that happy for Rose."

"Which you are. So go. And I'll see you at the altar."

She turned to go back to her room, hoping he didn't see how her mouth had fallen open at his last words. Good God. See you at the altar? It struck her that she would be paired with Raoul now, since he was serving as Diego's best man. Every time she tried to keep her distance, something kept throwing them together.

Navy pumps were substituted for yesterday's neutral slingbacks that would match the bridesmaid dress. She hustled to the back entrance and slid into the limousine. Marco smiled at her. "Beautiful day for a wedding, ¿*sí*?"

"It is. Thank you, Marco, for accommodating our new schedule."

"It's no problem. We always expect something to go a little sideways and we make adjustments. Everything will run smoothly, don't worry."

Maybe she did need to loosen her grip a bit.

She got to the cathedral in record time. The press and security were already present, and she scanned the area to make sure everyone was in their places. Marco was right—everything was running like clockwork. Once inside, Diego's assistant, Sofia, was waiting with a garment bag. "Your dress." She lifted an eyebrow. "And if that cow is sick, I'll give up my salary for a year."

"You have a copy of the day's plans, right?" Stephani asked the question as she took the garment bag.

"I do. Between us this will be a breeze. Now go put

this gown on. I have pins if we need to make any quick adjustments." Her smile was just a little bit catty. "Hayley is a little hippier than you."

The dress did end up being a little big through the waist and hips, though not much. A few deft safety pins from Sofia had the gown fitting nearly perfectly, with a few tiny puckers that would only be noticeable to anyone who knew to look. Her shoes matched fine and Sofia said the sapphire and pearl pendant was perfect. They emerged from the room in time to see the first of the guests being ushered inside.

"Your bouquet is coming with Rose and Becca," Sofia said, referencing Rose's friend. "You look gorgeous, Steph. So glam."

"Thanks. I'm nervous."

Sofia laughed. "You planned this whole thing without turning a hair, and this has you nervous? Relax. It's going to be lovely."

Sofia gave her a quick hug and left to check in with the ushers. It would normally be Steph's job, but she forced herself to take a breath and loosen her death grip on the reins. Delegating wasn't something she was always good at, but Sofia was proving herself equal to any task she was given.

Thirty minutes later the guests were nearly all seated and families started to arrive. Rose's sister-in-law was seated, then her parents. Brody went up the steps carrying baby Alyssa, Lucy and Imogene beside him, as well as the four children who would soon walk up the aisle as well. Alice and Emilia were dressed in sweet white dresses with champagne-colored sashes, little bouquets in their hands. Max and Alex were in miniature tuxes, their shoes shined perfectly. Before the day was out they'd likely be covered in dust, but for now they were pristine.

"Tía Stephani! You are beautiful!" Emilia came forward, her eyes shining. "I'm so glad you are here."

"Me too, darling. Your dress is so pretty." She gave the little girl a hug, knowing she must be missing her mother on such an occasion. She kissed Emilia's cheek, then snuck a little glance at Alice, who looked uncomfortable and unhappy. "I'm sorry your mum isn't feeling well," she offered gently. "But you look lovely, Alice."

Alice smiled a little. "Thank you."

"Let's go inside the doors where we can wait for the big moment, okay?"

She held out her hand to the girl. She knew what it was like to feel like you didn't quite belong, and Alice was among strangers except for the small number of Rose's family in attendance and the other children, who seemed to have easily accepted her. Annoyance slid through Steph. If Hayley wasn't really sick, she was inconsiderate not just to Rose, but to her daughter as well, for leaving her alone on such a day.

Once inside, even the children were awed by the soaring ceilings, the crowd, and the profusions of flowers. Imogene knelt down before the four of them. "I'll be sitting with Brody and Lucy, so I'm not far if any of you need anything, okay? You all look brilliant."

Then she was gone, following behind Brody and Lucy to one of the front pews, leaving Stephani in charge of the lot.

It was only moments until the bride arrived, along with her bridesmaid, Becca. Steph took a moment to watch, entranced, as Rose emerged from the car, looking resplendent in her white gown. The cut was simple but the gown itself was not, with lace and pearls adding a timeless quality. Her veil drifted around her in the slight breeze, feather-light and magical. But most magical was the look on her face. It was a look of utter joy and excitement.

Becca helped her with the small train, then stood and handed the bride her bouquet. She reached back inside the car and took out two more—hers, and presumably Stephani's as well.

Rose climbed the steps, then gave a half turn, waved at the gathered press and public, and laughed a little. She was so artless, so genuine. The press loved her, and so did Stephani. In a way, Rose's kindness and strength reminded her of Ceci. The Navarro men did tend to choose strong women.

"You are stunning, but then, I knew you would be."

Raoul's voice tickled her ear, sending shivers down her spine. She took a breath, preparing herself to turn around and see him in all his tuxedoed glory. Still, the breath wasn't enough. It wasn't the suit that momentarily stopped her heart, though it was certainly a flawless cut, now adorned with an official sash of royal purple and red. It was his eyes that did it, warm with approval, never leaving her face.

This would be so much easier if she didn't love him.

"Likewise," she managed to say, offering a smile though inside she trembled. "Diego is here? Ready?"

"He is. Nervous and excited and shockingly ready for marriage. It's very, very odd."

She laughed a bit. "I think it's lovely."

Raoul rolled his eyes. "Right. It's also a bit disconcerting. When someone is getting married, they think everyone else should as well." He shoved his hands into his pockets. "This morning, Diego suggested that I consider marrying again."

It felt as if someone punched her right in the solar plexus, but it wasn't the first time, so she merely shrugged. "A king needs a queen, I suppose."

His brow furrowed. "I suppose, but that's not what Diego said. He said I was too young to never love again. And that I should find someone to fall in love with and be happy." His laugh was short but held a wealth of pain. "I'm afraid that's over for me. I was extraordinarily lucky to have had it once. I'm not really looking to have it again."

She couldn't torture herself like this any longer. It wasn't fair or healthy, and while she'd miss the Navarro family, she needed to make her own start. Cecilia was gone. Stephani would never be the one to capture his heart, and it had been utter foolishness to even entertain the slightest bit of hope.

But she would not think about it today. Today she would enjoy the wedding and celebrate being with the people she loved. Tomorrow would be enough time to check up on her inquiries and make further plans.

"Rose is here, just behind the closed doors." She looked over her shoulder to make sure. "You should be with Diego and Devon, ready to take your place with the priest."

"Yes, ma'am." He smiled. "I'll see you up there."

He turned to walk away, taking her heart with him. It hurt, but the last five minutes had solidified her decision to leave and it felt…right. Difficult, but right. She couldn't get over him when she saw him day in and day out. And she had to get over him or live in limbo for the rest of her life.

Stephani snuck out the large doors to where Rose and Becca waited with the children. "Oh, Rose. You look so gorgeous." A wistful sort of feeling swept over her. There was nothing quite like this moment, just before a bride took her walk down the aisle.

"Thank you," Rose said quietly, her smile shaky. "I'm so nervous, Stephani. In less than an hour I'm going to be a princess. It's suddenly so surreal."

"It's the press. They have that effect." Stephani smiled, both at Rose and Becca. "Looks like I'm standing in today."

Becca lifted an eyebrow. "I wish you'd stayed with us at the hotel last night, Stephani. It would have been more fun."

Rose snorted. "This is typical Hayley," she whispered, so that Alice wouldn't hear. "I decided I won't let it ruin a thing."

"Good for you. And as far as the princess thing…" Stephani thought back to Raoul's words, about Diego and marrying for love. "You're becoming Mrs. Rose Navarro first. That's all you need to think about today."

One of the ushers gave her a nod, and she reached for her bouquet. "All right. It's time."

Rose inhaled sharply, and Stephani reached out to squeeze her hand. She was going to miss this family so much.

Becca carefully guided the children into their proper pairs and started them up the aisle at the correct intervals as a choir sang. Then Becca gave a smile and started up herself, clutching her bouquet and walking at the precise speed they'd rehearsed.

Then it was Steph's turn.

She stepped to the door, saw the eyes on her, felt her stomach quiver with nerves. Her fingers tightened around the bouquet—she'd never been in a wedding before, not even Ceci's. On that day she'd been a special guest, but not a bridesmaid. One step on the runner, then another. Step by step up the aisle, knowing deep down that today she was simply filling in and not a first choice.

Diego was at the front, Raoul beside him, and her knees wobbled just a bit as his gaze met hers down the long expanse of aisle. He was so strong, so determined, with such a good heart. Loyal to a fault, with broad shoulders to handle the responsibility he was born to and never asked for. He was, and likely would always be, her ideal.

But not hers.

No matter how much she wished it. His loyal, loving heart had been given away years ago, and the real kicker was that the very reason she couldn't have him was one of the reasons she loved him so much. He was the kind of man who gave himself completely—to his kingdom, yes, but to his wife, to his children. She admired the ruler, but she loved the family man.

And still she couldn't look away. Not until she got to her place at the altar, next to Becca and facing the back of the church again.

The pipe organ swelled and Rose stood to the door, her father beside her, his chest expanded with pride. A collective "oooh" went up from the guests as she stepped forward, a picture of bridal perfection. The procession was dignified and stately until she heard Diego clear his throat beside her, and she looked over. His lower lip trembled just a bit, and his eyes were suspiciously shiny. When Stephani looked back at Rose, she saw a wide, wonderful smile and blue eyes that glittered with happy tears.

A stinging started behind her nose, but she wouldn't cry. She wouldn't.

Rose reached the front and Stephani turned just a bit, only to encounter Raoul's soft gaze. For a moment she wondered if he'd cry if she walked up the aisle, wondered what it would be like to meet him at the altar and take his hand.

Foolish dreams she'd held onto for too long.

The ceremony began with prayers and kneeling and blessings, moved on to vows and rings and a final kiss. Stephani held Rose's bouquet when she took Diego's hands in hers, then handed it back when it was over and they were preparing to leave the church and pose on the church steps before heading back to the palace for official pictures.

Rose clutched Diego's arm and looked up at him as if he'd hung the moon and stars.

Stephani stepped down and Raoul held out his arm, waiting for her. She took it, feeling the fine, stiff cloth of his sleeve beneath her fingers.

"They're happy."

She nodded, tears fluttering against her eyelashes. "Very," she replied as they began the walk back down the aisle.

Once on the cathedral steps, they stayed in the background while the press snapped pictures of Diego and Rose. After a few minutes, Raoul, Lucy, and Alexander joined them and posed as a royal family. Just for a few moments, then they would all head back to the privacy of the palace for more intimate photos.

Once the family photo op was over, Raoul returned to her side. "Are you ready to head back to the palace?"

She nodded. "I should change and check on the preparations for the rest of the day."

He took her hand. "Let Sofia handle it. If she has questions, she'll ask. You've trained her well, and this is an opportunity for her to step into a bigger role. She needs the confidence."

"But…"

"But nothing. I want you to enjoy the day, Stephani. Not as my assistant but as someone who means a lot to me and to our family."

She bit down on her lip. Maybe she should. Take this one day and etch it on her memory as a bit of a goodbye. If she left, there wouldn't be any more royal invitations to balls or parties or state dinners, would there?

"As you wish," she murmured, taking her hand out of his grasp.

He looked away and lifted his hand, signaling to Marco. Within seconds they were hidden away in the limo, sitting across from Diego and Rose who were beaming with happiness. Diego popped the cork on a bottle of champagne, making them all laugh, and poured the fizzy liquid into glasses.

"To happiness," Diego toasted, lifting his glass. "And love."

"To happiness and love," they echoed.

As Stephani sipped the champagne, she wondered if it was possible for her to have happiness, since love didn't seem to be in the cards.

CHAPTER 6

Raoul was, for the first time in a very long time, in the background.

He sipped a second glass of champagne and watched as Diego and Rose circulated through the grand hall, speaking to guests and smiling the whole time. He was happy for his brother; it also brought back memories of his own wedding day to Ceci and how he'd been so happy and hopeful for the future. The feeling centered in his chest was oddly bittersweet.

Lucy appeared at his side, her red curls bouncing as she rose up on tiptoe and kissed his cheek. "Everyone says a bride glows, but I think it's the groom in this case. Diego...he's completely lit up," she remarked. "And you're over here being a wallflower."

"It's his day," Raoul said easily. "I've had many of my own where I was the center of attention. Today the spotlight's on him." He grinned and winked at Lucy. "And this time it's not because of some scandal."

"Those days are behind him," Lucy agreed.

Together they watched as the children scooted around the edge of the crowd, Rose's niece, Alice, close behind, and a frazzled Imogene trying to keep up. Raoul shook his head. "Do you think they'll ever get tired?"

Lucy laughed. "Did you at that age?"

Raoul seriously tried to recall and couldn't. For as long as he could remember, he'd been aware of his future as king and the gravity of the position. Not that Alexander had totally sheltered him. He'd been allowed to be a boy, but there had always been a nanny, and security, and a risk analysis for any major activity.

He wondered if Emilia felt the same way. He hoped not. She was in line for the throne after him. She also deserved a chance to be a kid.

There'd always been Ceci to make sure the children had a real childhood. He wasn't as good at that, though he was trying. He thought back to Diego's words this morning. The idea of marrying again was inconceivable. But then, the idea of being alone for the rest of his life stretched out before him, bleak and empty. Equally inconceivable.

"Where'd you go? You got quiet all of a sudden." Lucy nudged his elbow.

He chuckled. "Oh, lost in some thoughts. Nothing serious."

She was quiet for a few moments, then nodded toward the curving staircase. "Is there anything Stephani can't do? She organized all this, and then stepped in as bridesmaid without batting an eyelash. And looks gorgeous doing it."

He looked over. Stephani still held her bouquet in one hand, but she was looking over something on a tablet with Sofia. Their heads were together, and Raoul couldn't help but notice the way her dress hugged her shoulders then tapered down her back to the hollow of her spine before flaring out slightly at her hips.

Gorgeous was a very accurate word. He swallowed roughly. He also knew what it was like to hold her in his arms, even if it had been briefly and he'd had too much Scotch. It had felt so good, so right, that it had terrified him. He had to keep thinking of her as one of the family. As Ceci's cousin. She was family, not…

She turned around, caught him staring at her, and a blush stained her cheeks.

Mierda. How were they supposed to get through the weeks and months ahead if he kept thinking of her this way? He'd meant what he'd said earlier. He wasn't interested in marrying again. But dammit, he wasn't dead.

He hadn't died with Ceci, and it was time he faced that truth.

Lucy coughed. "Raoul, you and Stephani, are you…" She let the thought hang.

He turned back, startled. "What? No." He let out a breath as he met Lucy's gaze. "No, of course not. She's my assistant. She's Ceci's cousin."

"So?"

He didn't need this. It was bad enough that his thoughts strayed from time to time. If anyone in the family knew he'd even imagined Stephani as something other than his assistant, they'd hound him mercilessly.

"So, I don't think of her that way." His lips thinned.

"I know you're my sister and you care, but I don't need anyone making trouble. I depend on Steph and we don't need any undertones in the office, okay?"

Lucy stared at him for a long moment. "Okay. Fine. But someday you're going to have to open yourself up again."

"People keep saying that. It's getting tiresome. Maybe everyone can find another topic. My personal life is off-limits."

Her eyes widened. "All right. I'm sorry, Raoul. I didn't mean to stick my nose in. Particularly when you're still obviously quite raw."

He nodded. "I know. And I know you all care. I just… I need to do things at my own pace. On my own timeline. Everyone pushing doesn't actually speed up the process."

"Fair enough."

He tried to smile. "Besides, this is Diego and Rose's day. The focus should be on them."

At that moment Brody came up to them, a sleepy Alyssa in his arms. "I thought I might put her down for a while, up in our room." He kissed Lucy on the forehead. "I know you have family obligations, so I'll come back down after she's fed and changed."

Lucy peeked into the baby's sleeping face and her features softened. "I'll come with you. I can sneak away for twenty minutes or so."

Raoul nodded at Brody, then watched as his sister and her husband walked toward the stairs and the family wing that housed their suite. They passed Stephani and Sofia on their way. Steph looked over at him and smiled, and he smiled back, though his heart wasn't in it.

Attraction was inconvenient, but it would pass eventually. He figured the only reason he felt it at all was because Stephani was both beautiful and familiar. He saw her nearly every day, and she was safe. She knew him well. Understood his moods. He didn't need to try to impress her or be someone he wasn't.

Well, except for hiding this awkward fascination that came over him from time to time.

She caught up with him five minutes later and touched his arm.

"Are you all right? You've been standing over here frowning for half an hour."

His arm tingled where her fingers rested on his tuxedo jacket. For heaven's sake. There was no reason for him to react so strongly to her.

"I'm fine."

"You don't look fine. You look annoyed. Did something happen? Is something not going well? I can address it."

"Everything's perfect."

She blinked and remained silent. He realized his voice had been rather sharp and he added regret to the other emotions running through him. "I didn't mean to snap. I'm sorry."

Her voice was cool. "It's fine. As long as the event is running as it should. If there are any issues, let me or Sofia know. With me pulling double duty, she's taken over my list."

She turned to walk away.

"Steph?"

His heart thudded behind his ribs. Was he actually nervous about talking to her? This was so ridiculous!

"Yes, Your Highness?"

"Oh dear. I really did make you mad." Ironically, her snooty tone made him relax slightly. Perhaps because her irritation was a genuine emotion. No hiding or dancing around.

Her lips twitched a little. "You're grouchy."

She had no idea, and he was glad. He would be incredibly embarrassed if she knew how he was reacting to the sight of her in that dress, with Ceci's sapphires at her throat and mile-high shoes cradling her feet.

She trusted him. His thoughts definitely betrayed that trust. He'd already made a mistake once and kissed her. To do it again could—probably would—make it impossible for them to maintain their working relationship. And he needed her.

"I am, a little. But I'll try hard to be happier." He sent her a false smile, and made her laugh.

"We're seated together, you know. At the banquet." She leaned in conspiratorially. "That means you won't have to make conversation with Rose's horrid sister." As maid of honor, Hayley would have been next to Raoul. Now that Steph had stepped in, she would be seated to his left.

He looked down at her, leaning so close, close enough that he could smell the light, sexy scent of her perfume. "It's always lovely to have you as a dinner partner," he said softly. "And you can slide me your pâté, since I know you don't like it."

"You know me so well," she teased.

"I've known you a long time."

"Nearly ten years," she replied, looking up into his eyes.

He swallowed. Held her gaze. Realized no one on earth—not even his brother or father—knew him as well as Stephani did. She knew his likes and dislikes. His moods and how to cajole him out of them. His routine and schedules. All the things that Ceci had once known as easily as breathing.

"You're disappearing again," she cautioned quietly. "Are you really okay?"

"I am. I promise." And he was. The truth was, Ceci was gone, and he remained. The truth was, he was a man in his thirties who was attracted to a woman, and a relationship with that woman would be fraught with complications. But Diego's counsel this morning had started a chain reaction of thoughts that he couldn't seem to control. The reasons why he should walk away from his impulses were the very reasons why he was attracted to Steph in the first place.

And there were times he really just didn't want to walk away. Why did everything seem to come with a truckload of ramifications and consequences?

"I've got to go, but I'll see you soon. Save me a dance later?"

Dancing. Raoul's body tightened at the thought of holding her close in his arms, but he merely smiled. "Of course. As best man and maid of honor, it's expected."

Her smile was bright and her eyes lit up, then she turned and walked away, heading toward the bride and groom. Raoul watched the subtle sway to her hips, lifted his glass to his lips and then realized it was empty.

Positively fraught with complications. He handled dealings with governments all over Europe, but he had no idea how to handle this.

He'd been watching her all night.

Stephani couldn't stop the fizz of awareness that skittered across her skin. First it had been at dinner, over toasts to the bride and groom and then the delicious meal. His fingers had brushed hers accidentally when he slid his dessert over to her, simply because he knew she had a sweet tooth, and the dark chocolate ganache was a particular favorite. Once, he'd leaned back to ask a passing server for more wine and put his arm along the back of her chair, the material brushing against her exposed skin.

More than once, as she'd tried to eat, she'd felt his gaze on her, and it had taken all her fortitude not to look back at him. It didn't matter, anyway. She didn't need to look at him to feel the energy running between them, around them. Why now? Why on earth had Hayley pulled this immature trick, throwing them together? Why did she hate it and love it at the same time?

When the dinner was finally over, Imogene appeared with Max and Emilia. "The children wanted to say good night, sir."

"Of course." Raoul turned in his seat. "Max, you have chocolate around your mouth."

Max's tongue swiped around his lips, but it was no good. The chocolate was there to stay until a washcloth could clean up the mess. "Dessert was good," he said.

"I know." He leaned forward and whispered, "Stephani had two."

Max looked at her with something like hero worship in his eyes, and she laughed. "I confess. I did have two, because I love chocolate."

Emilia hung back a bit, but she did look at Stephani with a smile. "Your necklace is very pretty."

A little pang went through Stephani's heart. "Your mother gave it to me. It's very special."

Emilia touched the little strand of pearls around her own neck. "These were hers, too."

"She would be very proud of you two today. You were wonderful during the wedding."

The compliment didn't impress Max as much as the chocolate confession, but Emilia's eyes glowed.

"Come, give me a hug before Imogene takes you up to bed." Emilia came forward and Steph gave her a squeeze. How they must miss their mother. No cousin or nanny or aunt could make up for it, though they all tried.

"You too, Max. I need a hug before you disappear." When the little boy put his arms around her neck, she whispered in his ear, "I'll have Señora Ortiz put aside a spare dessert for your tea tomorrow."

Raoul looked over at her as the children prepared to leave. "I'm going to go up with them for a few minutes. I'll be back, though." His dark gaze held hers. "To claim the dance you owe me."

And *boom*. The butterflies in her stomach returned in full force.

She spent the next forty-five minutes checking in with Sofia, but the day was winding down and the list of things to do was dwindling. There was dancing to come, and more food, and Marco was on standby to whisk Diego and Rose to the airport, where they'd take a private jet to a resort on the Spanish coast for a few days of privacy before heading to Tanzania.

She managed to spend a few moments with Rose's family, as well. They were a little wide-eyed at their surroundings, not to mention the guest list, but Stephani found them charming, with the exception of Hayley. Hayley had arrived just before the meal, in time to sit with her parents and brother and sister-in-law. Her eyes shot little daggers at Stephani from time to time; after all, Steph was wearing what was meant to be Hayley's dress, and sitting with the crown prince. Now that the dinner was concluded, she told anyone near that she was sure she'd picked up some sort of food poisoning at the hotel and thank goodness she was feeling much better now so she could be there for her sister's big day. It was a big load of manure, as far as Stephani was concerned, but Rose shook her head and gave Steph a smile. A few minutes later she was at Steph's side and giving her a hug. "Thank you for everything you did today."

"It was my pleasure. Truly."

"I should have asked you in the first place. But sisters..."

"Are family." Steph smiled. "I get it."

"Hayley's all right. Most of the time. She's resentful

about how things turned out, is all, and I'm not sure she'll ever learn how to be happy."

"Well, I think you learned. You're beaming."

Rose laughed. "I am, aren't I? I can feel it. I'm so happy."

Diego came up and slid his arms around her waist. "There's my beautiful bride."

They did make a rather stunning couple, and their happiness shone for everyone to see.

And Stephani was still going back and forth in her mind, knowing she had to leave Marazur and let Raoul go, but craving his presence like he was an addiction.

When the dancing started, the lights dimmed, and Diego took Rose in his arms for a romantic slow dance. Raoul still wasn't back, but Steph stood at the edge of the dance floor and watched what fulfillment looked like. Diego and Rose never took their eyes from each other. Once, Diego said something and Rose laughed, and Stephani saw his hand tighten at her waist. She didn't realize her own arm was half wrapped around her middle until Raoul came up behind her and put his arm over hers, so that they were in a very loose back-to-chest embrace.

"Sorry I took so long," he apologized, but Steph couldn't think. She simply froze at the intimacy of the contact. If she leaned back by only two inches, she'd be cradled against him. Even this much was incredibly familiar, particularly in public.

Thankfully—or not so much—he slid his arm away and came to stand beside her.

"The children got to bed okay?" she asked,

suddenly unsure of what to say. It was strange. Normally they were never at a loss of things to talk about.

"Max might pay the price for all that sugar," Raoul said, "but otherwise, yes. They've had an exciting day."

Again, an awkward silence fell between them, the quiet saved only by the music playing.

When the next song began, Raoul held out his hand. "Shall we?"

"Of course."

Being ensconced in his arms was heaven. He still wore his tuxedo jacket, and she marveled how he could still look perfect, with not a hair out of place, when she'd already freshened up twice during the day and felt as if her hair were coming out of its pins and her lip stain wasn't as long-lasting as she hoped. She forgot about most of that, though, when Raoul reached up and tucked a very small piece of hair behind her ear and smiled. "Let's show them how it's done," he said, then smiled. And she was a goner.

Smooth, sexy, and confident. That's how she'd describe Raoul as a dancer. He navigated the floor with the same surety that he worked a boardroom and took her with him. One hand was warm on the hollow of her back, just above her tailbone, while his other hand clasped hers firmly. Their bodies brushed rather than clung, each graze lighting little flickers of desire until her whole being was attuned to his.

His dark gaze captured hers, and she couldn't look away.

She bit down on her lip, and his gaze dropped

momentarily to her mouth, then back up again. Her lips tingled; it almost felt as if he'd kissed her.

The song was nearing its close, and as he navigated them in a turn, her breasts brushed against his jacket. When had they gotten so close? Why was her heart beating so fast? What were they going to do?

She didn't realize she'd voiced that question out loud until he answered it. "I don't know," he said roughly, his eyes never leaving hers. "I don't know."

With that simple question and answer, Stephani realized they were both on the same page. All the times that he'd said he wasn't interested, that he'd never marry again, that she was "family"—they all faded to the back of her mind. In this moment, they were touching in at least five points of contact, and admitting that there was an attraction they could neither prevent nor control.

The song ended and he released her, taking a half step back. Nothing would happen now. Not here, not in public. And maybe in an hour or two this crazy feeling would wane, and they'd come to their senses. She knew that would be the right thing, but the need for him was overpowering.

Diego came up to them, wearing a big smile. "Rose wondered if you'd each dance with the other member of the wedding party during the next song. You don't mind dancing with her brother, do you, Steph?"

"Of course not." She forced herself to smile brightly. "I'd love to."

They went their separate ways, but somehow they always found each other across the floor. She danced a faster song with Rose's brother, Devon, while Raoul danced with Becca. Then they lost each other momentarily as she danced with Rose's father and then with Diego, and Raoul danced not only with Rose's mother, who blushed furiously, but also took Hayley on a turn around the floor, who Steph took as trying to be unimpressed but unable to hide her secret triumph in her smug expression.

Then there were guests, and duty once again reared its head as she made the rounds so no one would feel slighted. She danced with their finance minister and then paired him off with a visiting dignitary from Andorra. Finally, near midnight, she made her way outside the ballroom to the terrace. A handful of people were out in the fresh air, and she slid off to a corner to catch her breath and make sense of everything.

The air was perfumed with the heady scent of flowers from the gardens, mingled with the freshness from the nearby Mediterranean. Stars had popped out in the inky sky, and she focused on a particularly bright one, wondering if it was a planet and not really a star at all. Wondering where she'd end up next, and what the view would be like. If there'd be a terrace like this one, or a high-rise with a view of the skyline.

Either way, there would be no Raoul, would there?

"It's a beautiful night," came a deep voice behind her.

The sound shivered over her nerve endings as a sense of inevitability enveloped her. She'd slipped away; he was out here because he'd sought her out. Wasn't that what she wanted? Memories of kissing him last year in the alcove came rushing back. Up until six months ago, she'd managed to keep her feelings locked down, but once the door had been opened, she'd found she couldn't go back to before. Everything had changed.

She wanted it all, and was afraid to even step forward into the remotest possibility of having it. As much as it was going to hurt to leave, it would hurt worse to fall deeper into love and then have to go, wouldn't it?

"You're shivering," he observed, and took off his jacket. He put it over her shoulders and she grabbed the lapels, holding it close. It was warm from dancing, and his scent rose from the fabric, swamping her senses.

"Thank you," she murmured. She turned around and faced him, his features illuminated by the lights coming through the ballroom windows. "Why did you come out here?"

She half hoped he'd say he wanted to get some air and saw her as a pure coincidence. The other half of her hoped he'd come out to find her.

"To find you," he answered.

Oh. Oh.

The doors to the terrace creaked, and then closed. Whoever had been out here before had gone back inside and closed the doors behind them. The laughter and music were muffled now, and instead Stephani could also hear the soft sound of the breeze and the mesmerizing shush of the water in the garden fountain.

"I asked a question earlier and you said you didn't know. Maybe I should ask it again." She lifted her chin, scared to death, yet filled with rich anticipation. "What are we doing, Raoul?"

"I don't know." His voice was hoarse. "I shouldn't be out here. I shouldn't have held you so close when we were dancing, or looked into your eyes. I shouldn't have kissed you at my birthday last year. I shouldn't want to kiss you right now, but I do."

She could barely breathe. "Why shouldn't you?" She wanted him to say it. To either put an end to the madness or surrender to it.

"Because you're my assistant. Because you're Ceci's cousin. Because I'm not over her."

That was it, wasn't it? Steph was almost ready to back away when he finished, "And because I want you so much I can't think straight."

ios mío.

Heat rushed up her body into her face and she clutched the jacket lapels tighter. She'd known Raoul for a decade, maybe a bit longer. Her fascination with his title and status had long faded until she saw only the man and not the monarchy. But just now, hearing him say those words, she was momentarily struck by the fact that a prince—the crown prince, no less—had just admitted that he wanted her.

That he desired her.

That he was so clouded by it he couldn't think straight.

Impossible. Only…it wasn't. Because he wasn't some two-dimensional Prince Charming. He was Raoul Navarro. Her boss and her—dare she say it—best friend, now that Ceci was gone. They worked together. They'd mourned together. And right now he was touching her face with gentle fingers while her eyelids fluttered closed.

"It's not just me, is it?" The uncertainty in his voice reached into her heart. Him, insecure? If she weren't already so overwhelmed, she'd laugh. Instead, she leaned into his touch.

"It's not just you. Not even a little bit."

He kissed her then. The last time he'd had too much Scotch and wasn't thinking straight at all. Maybe this time they were swept away in the day or whatever spell had bewitched them, but a few glasses of wine weren't enough to cloud anyone's judgment. She was fully aware of who she was, where she was, and who she was with. And so was he.

His lips were soft, warm, and seductive. While she knew it was in his power to be commanding, to take charge, this was a side of Raoul that few ever saw or could appreciate. There was tenderness and patience. A willingness to explore that made her head swim with delight. He was a man who knew how to be decisive, and also knew when to step back and let things unfold. This moment was one of the latter, and she was ever so glad. The way he kissed her was so swoon-worthy she thought she might have to let go of the lapels and hang on to his shoulders just so she didn't melt into a puddle at his feet.

He nibbled at her lower lip. "Mmmm." His mouth slid over her jaw until he nipped at her earlobe, which sent several points of arousal to full attention. "Oh," he murmured, his voice rich and warm. "I see."

Then he nipped at it again and Steph swallowed a groan. She had to be quiet. No one could know they were out here.

As if he sensed her thoughts, he pulled her with him so they were shadowed by a tall potted tree. In the process he tugged on her hand and she pitched forward, her body pressed against his, clenched fists still between them.

Then she dropped her hands; the jacket slipped off her shoulders and tumbled to the terrace stones. She wrapped her arms around his neck and pulled him forward, just enough that they were kissing again, with less restraint and patience than before.

His hand slid over her shoulder, warm against her bare skin, and goose bumps ran down her arms. Their breaths grew short as urgency grew, and Raoul's palm slid over her breast. She pressed into his hand, needing to feel close to him, to feel connected. To reach him in some way, and make him see it was her. Steph. She was the one here, flesh and blood, in his arms, kissing his lips, moaning into his mouth as he touched her.

More than anything, she wanted him to finally, finally see the woman she was. Below the surface of job titles and casual relationships. She wanted him to see her the way she saw him.

"Steph," he whispered, slowing the kiss a little, running his lips over her forehead. "We shouldn't be doing this out here."

She swallowed her fear and leaned back just enough that she could look him in the face. "Then do you want to take it somewhere else?"

The naked yearning on his face gave her the answer, but his words contradicted it. "I can't. Not that I don't want to, but…" He lifted his hands and cupped her face.

"It's too soon. I don't want to…" He frowned. "I don't want to make a mistake."

Ouch. It hurt to hear he thought being with her would be a mistake. But he must have seen her reaction, because he quickly amended, "Not a mistake being with you, but a misstep. I don't want to be careless with you."

For a brief second, Stephani wished she was the kind of woman to inspire a man to make missteps and mistakes. The kind of woman to awaken a great passion, rather than a strategic response.

But then, this was Raoul. He thought about all his decisions and weighed the options. It wasn't in his nature to throw caution to the wind.

Which also meant that he made a conscious decision to come out here tonight. And that meant something, too.

"You have never been careless with me, Raoul."

The warm breeze ruffled the tendrils of her hair that had escaped the pins, and she hooked a piece with a finger and pulled it away from her mouth. His chest rose and fell rapidly, as if he were still catching his breath. She reached up and pulled on the end of his bowtie, and it unraveled in her hand. Then she undid the top button of his shirt and wet her lips at the simple sight of the hollow of his throat. There was something about a man in formal wear loosening up and looking a little rumpled.

"I was careless, once. On my birthday."

"No, you weren't. Drunk, yes." She smiled a little. "Careless, no."

He sighed deeply. "I don't know what to do

anymore, Steph. I don't know what I want. I don't know if I'm afraid or dead inside. And I don't know how to figure it out, when everyone analyzes every single thing I do. Like they have to watch each action to make sure I'm not going to break. That I'm...hell. Moving on with my life on a family-approved calendar."

"You can't really grieve on anyone else's schedule," she answered, though it hurt. Deep down she wished he didn't have to grieve anymore at all. That'd he'd be at the point where he'd be ready to move forward without reservation. But neither would she lie. There was more than attraction between them. There were years and years of friendship.

A round of laughter echoed through the terrace doors, and they both turned toward the sound. The party was still going on, but she had no desire to rejoin it. Even though she really should, and so should Raoul. She would rather stay out here and feel the breeze and smell the sea and flowers and look at the stars and pretend that royal duty and the familial microscope didn't exist.

"What happens now?" she asked, then shivered. The air cooled at night, and her shoulders were bare. Raoul noticed and tucked her into his arms. She closed her eyes and soaked in the sensation. They could never embrace like this anywhere else. Maybe never again.

"I wish I could tell you. Feeling like this, about you...it's damned inconvenient. You're my assistant. You're close to the family. There are deeper ties than if you were some stranger or something. I don't want to hurt you. I don't want a bunch of questions and well-intentioned advice."

"You want privacy."

He nodded; she felt the movement against her hair. "I do. I'll be honest with you, Steph. I meant what I said about marrying again. The idea scares me to death. I'm in no position to make any promises. And I especially don't want to string you along and give you hope for something that might not happen."

Tears stung the backs of her eyes, but she said nothing.

"All that is in opposition to the attraction I'm feeling right now. I didn't lie when I said I wanted you. Kissing you and holding you…that's the most alive I've felt in a very, very long time."

The words sat on her tongue. The ones telling him that she'd cared for him for such a long time, that he was her ideal and she wanted him, too. But she didn't say them. It was sure to send him running in the other direction, erasing any chance they might have. The last thing he needed was for her to declare her undying love when he was so unsure.

And despite her earlier determination to remove herself from the situation, she knew she would always regret not giving this a chance, even if it was a slim one. To get this close and then walk away… No. She worked in a world of risk assessments and calculated moves. Right now she was doing her own risk assessment and she knew that she had to at least give this a shot. The possible reward was worth it, wasn't it?

Music started up again, a slow song that she recognized. Raoul adjusted his embrace until they were in a dance hold again, only this time she was pressed tightly against his body rather than the respectable distance they'd maintained in public. She sighed, happy and yet burdened with the knowledge that something this amazing had to be so complicated.

Their feet shuffled along the textured surface of the terrace, the music quiet behind them. Raoul kissed her hair. "Are we going to be all right?" he asked, a thread of worry darkening his voice. "I wish I could give you assurances. I wish…" His jaw tightened against her temple.

"I don't want assurances right now," she admitted honestly. "I wouldn't believe them if you gave them to me. I'd prefer the honesty, even if it's difficult and painful. Raoul, if you weren't so conflicted, I wouldn't care about you so much. It shows the kind of man you are. It shows your heart." She put her palm against his chest, feeling the strong beat there. "You loved Ceci as beautifully as any man could love a woman. It takes time to get over that. I have my own reservations too, you know." She looked up, moved her feet in the shuffle-circle even though they weren't really focusing on dancing anymore.

"You do?"

"Of course I do. Surely you know now that this attraction isn't one-sided. But Ceci was my cousin. There are times I wonder if I'm betraying her by caring for you in that way."

"Of course you're not. Nothing happened until Ceci had been gone for months."

Stephani didn't answer, but stared at his shoulder instead.

"Unless…" His feet stopped moving and he tipped a finger beneath her chin, forcing her to look at him. "Unless you've felt this way since before that night."

"I can't answer that. Don't make me."

He stepped back a little. "While we were married?"

"Yes. No." She put a hand over her eyes, trying to sort her thoughts. "Raoul, you were married. I would never have said or done anything to come between you and Ceci. You loved each other perfectly, you see? I didn't want to care about you so much. I just…" She chanced a look up at him, but his face was unreadable. "I worked for you. I saw the kind of man you were every day. I knew when you were happy and when you were worried and when you were hurting. I saw how you loved her and the children and… I don't want to say that I thought you were perfect, because you're not. No one is. But feelings are feelings, and I've had them for you for a long time."

"I see."

She could tell he did, and he was definitely stepping back. Of course he was. There was a big difference between a sudden mutual attraction and discovering someone had had feelings for months, even years.

"This is too complicated, isn't it? I should go in."

"You surprised me, that's all."

But his voice was still cool, and the hot energy that had flowed between them earlier had fizzled away.

"It's okay," she said finally, straightening her shoulders. "Seriously, Raoul. I've been dealing with my feelings for a long time. I'm fine. If you want, we can forget this ever happened."

It was a courageous statement, but not entirely brave on her part, because she didn't wait for an answer. Instead, she passed by him and went to the terrace doors to rejoin the party.

THE CASTLE HAD AN EMPTY FEEL TO IT, RAOUL REALIZED. He walked the quiet hallway to the part of the palace that housed the offices, his steps echoing dully on the carpeting. Rose and Diego were on their honeymoon. Rose's family had all departed back to England, and Lucy and Brody had taken the children—including Max and Emilia and Imogene—to Disneyland Paris. Alexander was around, and Sofia was in the office, since she was managing things for Diego in his absence. But it was uncharacteristically quiet as he left the family quarters behind and entered the foyer to the business wing.

Stephani was already at her desk.

The wedding had been on Saturday, and she'd stayed home on Sunday. Monday, he'd spent with the children, wanting to have some quality time with them before they left on their trip. Tuesday, he'd been booked to play polo in a charity event, though his skills were inferior to Diego's. When he'd returned, late in the day, Steph had gone home.

All completely valid reasons for not seeing each other. Nevertheless, he knew he'd been avoiding her, and he suspected the same was true for her. The way they'd left things Saturday night was awkward.

She looked up, glasses perched on her nose. "Good morning."

"Good morning."

It made very little sense that he wanted to go to her desk, pull her to her feet, and plant a kiss on her unsmiling lips. He'd always prided himself on his self-control, but he had started to realize that Steph could run circles around him in that regard. He'd never had a clue, not once, in all the years she'd been his assistant. She'd been his friend. She'd been his trusted and incredibly efficient assistant. She'd been his wife's cousin. He'd never had an inkling that she'd harbored any sort of romantic feelings toward him.

But he knew now. He thought back to the days after the drunken kiss in the alcove. They'd carried on as if nothing had happened.

A kiss was apparently easier to ignore than confessions.

"You have a call scheduled for nine thirty," Steph advised him. "Then nothing until eleven, when you meet with your father. Two thirty is the meeting with the committee regarding the environmental impact study that's being done for the proposed resort site." She gave a slight smile. "You and Señora Munoz weren't playing around when you met last week, were you?"

It was a rhetorical question, so he merely smiled in return. "A light day, then," he said easily. "Thank you, Steph."

"Of course. Do you want coffee?"

"I'd love some."

He went into his office and frowned. Was ignoring everything the best course of action? It felt like the coward's way out. At some point they had to deal with what had happened and decide what came next. It wasn't as if feelings had just disappeared, after all.

The thump of his heart when he'd seen her sitting there this morning told him that.

She tapped on his office door and then came in, carrying a tray with his coffee and a little plate with two rolls and some cheese. "I heard you didn't have breakfast this morning, so I brought something to hold you until lunch."

He met her gaze and admired the way she could stand before him and remain so calm and impassive. Had she perfected that look over the years?

"Why don't you get a cup for yourself and come in? We should talk."

There. A flicker of uncertainty. He was relieved he wasn't the only one freaking out a bit on the inside.

"Oh…of course. I'll be right back."

He wasn't really hungry, but while she was gone he bit into a soft roll. He washed it down with the strong coffee and then sat down behind his desk. By the time Stephani came back, he'd eaten half the roll and was feeling slightly calmer.

She sat down across from him, crossed her left leg over her right, and cradled the coffee cup in her hands.

"So," he said, leaning forward. "We've been avoiding each other."

She blushed and looked down before taking a sip of her coffee.

"It's okay." He folded his hands. "I'm as guilty as you are of hiding. I needed some time to process everything that happened on Saturday."

"Me too," she admitted. She put her cup on his desk. "Raoul, what I said…I know it was awkward. I loved Ceci like a sister. She got me this job. It's bothered me all this time. This isn't how you repay family, you know?"

Oh, he understood the idea of duty and loyalty very well. He had his own to deal with. He'd also had the thought that having feelings for Stephani was somehow dishonoring Ceci's memory.

"Family doesn't require payment," he replied, "and Ceci would have been mortified if she thought you felt you needed to pay her back. Family looks after each other."

"I know that, deep down." She smiled sheepishly. "I think this falls under the umbrella of 'this is a me problem' and a product of my own guilt complex."

"Well." Raoul steepled his fingers and thought about how to say what had been plaguing him for the better part of three days. "I guess what this comes down to is deciding where to go from here. Do we go back to normal, and maintain a professional relationship? Or do we consider exploring what this is?"

She stared at him so long he started to get worried. "What's wrong?"

"I'm just surprised, that's all. That you'd even…"

She broke off, swore in Spanish under her breath. "Sorry. I'm feeling a little overwhelmed. And raw."

He let out a breath. It was much better when she dropped her guard and was honest. "Me too," he admitted. "This wasn't what I planned. There are so many mixed feelings and complications. But the one thing I came up with for sure is that I don't think this is going to go away. We need to deal with it head-on." He took a breath and met her gaze evenly. "I'm also aware of the imbalance of the situation. You work for me, and so I need you to know right now that there is no pressure on you in any way."

Her face softened. "Oh Raoul, I know that. You've never been one to throw your weight around."

"Well, it needed to be said. We've never had a typical employee-boss relationship, you and I."

"No," she said softly, "we haven't."

He got up and went around the desk, pulled over a chair and sat at a right angle to her. "What do you want, Steph? Do you want to forget about it and move on? Or do you want to see where this leads? I can't make any promises. I just can't." He reached out and took one of her hands in his. It was shaking. "But I don't think I can just walk away, either."

They were both staring at their joined hands. Steph slowly moved her thumb back and forth, over his knuckles, a small but important caress.

"I don't want to walk away." Her voice was a little hoarse, and she cleared her throat. "Not yet. Not when..." She looked up at him. "Not yet."

He nodded, his throat suddenly tight. This was more

than the desire that had swept over them at Diego's wedding. More than a drunken impulse in a shadowed corner. This was a real acknowledgment of feelings, and it felt important.

The phone rang out at her desk and she stood. "We'll talk more about it later," she said, letting go of his hand. "We need to keep this away from the office, you know?"

She hurried away; he heard her answer the phone and the creak of her chair as she rolled it closer to her desk.

He took her still-warm coffee and put it at her elbow, then grabbed a pen and wrote on her message pad. Then, despite her last instruction, he kissed the top of her head and went back into his office.

CHAPTER 8

Stephani smoothed her hair with her hands, then rubbed her lips together and rolled her shoulders. She wished she could have gone home and changed clothes and then returned, but that would have taken over an hour. She had on the same navy pencil skirt and silk blouse she'd worn to work this morning, only now she was having dinner with Raoul in his suite.

He'd put her coffee at her elbow and then scribbled *Dinner in my suite at 7* on the little notepad she kept on her desk. Would this be construed as a date? Their actual first date?

It wouldn't be her first time in his private rooms. She'd had to come up here now and again when she'd needed him to attend to an urgent matter. This was different. This was a dinner for two.

Her. And Raoul.

She pressed a hand to her nervous stomach and counted to three, then lifted that same hand and knocked on the door.

Raoul opened it, and her mouth went dry.

He'd changed out of his suit and into a pair of jeans and a button-down shirt, open at the collar and untucked at the waist. His feet were bare. This was the most casual she'd ever seen him, and it was utterly sexy. And here she was in her wrinkled skirt and blouse with a tiny dot of coffee on the cuff of her sleeve.

"Come in," he said, and stepped back, a smile lighting his face. "I did something crazy and ordered in for us."

She laughed as she stepped into the living area of his suite. "But you have a whole kitchen staff."

"I also know where Señora Ortiz's talents lie, and it's not with your favorite."

She was intrigued now. "My favorite?"

He nodded. "I sent Marco off to pick it up for us. It's a surprise."

He looked so pleased with himself she couldn't help but smile in return and feel a little bit special. She didn't really have a favorite; she'd traveled extensively and enjoyed several kinds of foods. But clearly Raoul had put some thought and effort into this, so she'd go along and enjoy it.

"Prosecco?"

He held up a bottle that he'd had chilling and she nodded. One glass only; she had to go back to her apartment after dinner, but that was probably a few hours away. Raoul popped the cork and then handed her a glass. He poured while she held, and when he had a glass of his own, he touched the rim to hers. "I don't want to sound trite or cheesy, so I'll just say cheers, Steph. Thank you for coming to dinner."

It was so lovely and genuine that she clinked back at him and said, "*Yamas,*" before taking a healthy sip.

"I sometimes forget you're half Greek," Raoul said, sipping his own. "You hardly ever speak it."

"That's because we use mostly English and Spanish here. It's still the language of my home, though."

"Have you considered going back?"

She nearly bobbled her glass and wondered for a split second if he knew how to access her private email. Of course he must, because they'd hired someone to do just that when Diego's former assistant had leaked photos and information to the press. Did Raoul somehow know that she'd received a reply just today from a member of the Greek cabinet? Working on her home country's education portfolio would be a wonderful job, wouldn't it?

Except it wouldn't be here. Greece was her home country, but it wasn't home anymore.

Another knock sounded at the door, preventing her from responding to Raoul's question. He answered it and then returned with a large bag in his hands. "Are you ready?"

He put the bag down on the table and started taking out dishes. It only took a moment for her to realize he'd ordered sushi, something that was never served at the palace and was, indeed, one of her particular favorites. "Oh, yum!" she exclaimed, peering around his arm and into the rest of the bag. "You got so much!"

"We can take any that's left and put it in the fridge

downstairs for tomorrow's lunch," Raoul suggested. "If there's any left. I'm starving."

She sat at the little table and began opening containers. They started with miso soup, hot and tasty. Then once that was gone, she picked up her chopsticks and selected from the tray of maki. Flavor exploded in her mouth and she closed her eyes. "Oh, that's good," she murmured, before reaching for another roll. "And you got sashimi, too."

"I got a little bit of everything. If there's something you don't like, I probably will." He grinned. "You know, when I was at university, my guilty pleasures were sushi and really good curries."

"No pizza or late-night hamburgers for you?"

He laughed. "How about you? Did you go on any late-night food runs?"

Ceci had been studying in Barcelona and Stephani had gone to see her and stayed a whole month. "Ceci and I would go out and on the way back to her flat, there was this churro guy. We stopped every single time." She smiled softly at the memory. "I guess I've always had a bit of a sweet tooth."

"You really had some good times together."

"The best."

She toyed with a piece of tuna, then looked up at him. "This is really nice, Raoul. Thank you."

"You're welcome. I wanted something private, and I wanted you to be comfortable. I hope you are."

She nodded, watching as he swirled his California roll in wasabi. "Is that why you ordered in? So it would be private?"

He lifted his gaze. "Partly. Marco can be utterly trusted, but I'd be lying if I didn't admit I've been thinking about how to do this without the staff seeing and talking." He put down his chopsticks. "Sometimes the lack of privacy here is a real pain."

She laughed a little. "Well, you could ask Rose and Diego, but they didn't do a great job of covering their tracks, either. I don't like the idea of being a topic of conversation, but I'm not sure how we're going to be able to avoid it, especially if I keep having private dinners in your suite."

He held up the prosecco bottle, but she shook her head. "I have to drive," she said.

He refilled his glass, then went to a little fridge and took out a bottle of water, uncapped it, and handed it to her. "I'd say Marco could take you home, but you'd refuse, wouldn't you?"

She took the bottle. "I would."

"So sneaking around here isn't an option."

"I can't see it being successful."

Maybe this wasn't going to work after all. Rose and Diego had thought they'd fooled everyone, but in reality, the entire staff knew that he'd been going to her room each night after the children went to bed and then leaving some time before midnight. Or that he'd taken her to the battlements for a moonlight picnic...Things got around. Either they'd have to make peace with that, or find another way.

"Let me think about it," Raoul suggested, and they got up from the table. "I'm really great at problem-solving when I put my mind to it."

She snapped the lid back on one of the dishes. "Oh, so now I'm a problem to be solved?" she teased.

"The best kind." He stacked the dishes but left them on the table and instead reached for her, pulling her in close. "I wish we could just disappear for a while and figure out what all this is, and how we feel, and what we want. I've always known what it was to live in the public eye, but I've never wanted privacy any more than I do right now."

"I wish we could do that, too," she replied, winding her arms around his neck. "It's new, and scary, and wonderful, and fragile." She took a breath, decided to trust him with her feelings. "I'm afraid that if people start putting in their opinions, we won't stand a chance, and this will be over before it really begins."

He frowned. "But everyone loves you."

Having him say so warmed her heart because she loved the Navarro family, too. "And they love you. But well-intentioned meddling would happen, and we're already on shaky ground."

He dipped his head and kissed her, soft and slow, until her head swam with it and she was dazed when he backed away.

"Does that feel shaky to you?"

She shook her head.

"Let me think about it for a while. See if I can't come up with something so we can explore what's happening without taking out a royal proclamation."

She smiled then. She was afraid. He was, too. He'd had his heart absolutely crushed, but he was beginning to move on, and he was being considerate of her feelings. Of all his qualities, his sense of honor was her favorite. Some considered Raoul a bit cold, particularly in comparison to the charismatic Diego. But those close to him knew that his reserve hid a huge, giving heart, and he would do anything for those he loved.

He looped his hands at the base of her spine. "So. Do you want to stay a while? We can talk. Watch something on TV. Maybe a movie?"

She nearly laughed. It was easy to see that Raoul hadn't been on a first date in a while. He sounded so hesitant, and that wasn't his usual style. He was always decisive, in command. But he'd dated Ceci in the public eye. Married her and had been married for nine years before losing her. Stephani found his uncertainty sweet and endearing.

"What would you normally do after dinner?"

"I'd normally say good night to Max and Emilia, but they're in Paris with Lucy."

"Oh." She rather wished they were here, too. They were great kids, and Raoul seemed younger when he was around them.

"Do you…happen to play chess?" he asked hopefully.

And so it happened that they ended up in the library, seated at a chess table, trying to anticipate each other's moves and indulging in a shocking amount of trash talk. When she took his knight, he cursed so fluently her mouth dropped open and then she burst out laughing, the sound ringing to the high ceiling. The game got more intense and the talk gave way to furrowed brows and trying to anticipate the next move. Raoul finally had her in check with no way out, and she tipped over her piece to end the game.

"Dammit," she muttered, leaning back with a sigh. "I nearly had you."

"Yes, you did." He grinned, elated at his win. "You're a worthy opponent, Savalas."

"I'll get you next time, Navarro."

"I look forward to it. But not if I get you first."

The banter had turned to teasing, and something wild and wonderful expanded in Steph's chest. For this one split second, he wasn't Ceci's Raoul, or even just Raoul. For a brief moment, he'd become her Raoul, and fleeting as it was, it was a feeling she'd cherish for a long time.

STEPHANI LOOKED AROUND HER APARTMENT ONE LAST time and bit down on her lip. Seven minutes to go and Raoul would be here. She knew it would be seven minutes because he was accustomed to being precisely on time, and perhaps a little early.

The place was spotless. Her cleaning service had come yesterday and given the place a top-to-bottom scrubbing, and this afternoon Stephani had made sure everything was in its place. Still, she worried what Raoul would think of it. Her taste was nothing like the decorating at the palace. There it was rich and worked to impress. Her style was more what she'd call cozy chic.

Three minutes.

Maybe it had been a dumb idea, inviting him here

for dinner. To keep herself from going crazy, she checked on the dish in the oven one more time. The stuffed eggplant recipe had been a favorite of her childhood, and her grandmother had made it when she went to stay. Stephani's béchamel was never as good as yaya's, though it was passable. She just hoped Raoul liked it.

Her phone rang and she nearly tripped over herself, rushing to pick it up. "Hello?"

"We're just pulling up."

"Third floor, second door on the left off of the elevators."

"See you in a minute."

She raced to the balcony and looked down, saw one of the plain sedans pull up outside. No official limo. It felt a bit dangerous, sneaking around. But the press seemed to pop up without warning. Even last year, a picture had shown up following Raoul's birthday, of him and Rose in the palace gardens. That, though, had been an inside job.

Marco, she knew, could be trusted. And she doubted anyone else in the household knew where Raoul was tonight. After all, that was the job of the security team and, well, her.

She opened the door just as he was about to knock and laughed at the look of surprise on his face. "Come in," she offered, pushing her nerves away. Nothing could be changed now.

He stepped inside and dropped a kiss on her cheek. "I was going to bring you flowers, but I didn't want anyone to ask any questions."

"It feels a little strange, sneaking around." She

squeezed his hand. "Kind of exciting, but also… I don't know. Like we're doing something wrong."

"It's not wrong, it's private. And speaking of, did you want to shut the door?"

She laughed and closed it with a firm click. "Sorry. And welcome to my home."

He looked around, then back at her with a smile on his face. "It suits you. Simple, not overdone, but inviting. It's nice, Steph. Really nice."

"Thanks." She went to the kitchen and got glasses for the bottle of red she'd uncorked earlier. "I decorated it a piece at a time. Nothing really matches, but somehow—"

"It all fits together." Raoul smiled and followed her, then stood across the counter from her. "That's one of my favorites." He nodded at the bottle.

"I know." She grinned. "My job has its privileges. Knowing your preferences is one. That doesn't apply to dinner, by the way. I made one of my childhood favorites." She handed him the glass of wine. "Tonight you get a taste of my Greek upbringing."

"I look forward to it."

They touched rims and drank of the rich, ruby wine. There was no question of him driving; Marco would be back to pick him up whenever he called. Steph also had a bottle of his favorite Marazurian brandy in her cupboard for after dessert.

Raoul put his glass down and came around the counter. "Come here," he said, holding out his hand. "I've been wanting to do this all day."

She took his hand and he pulled her into an

embrace. "Every day at the office I have to watch what I say. How I look at you." He kissed the hair just above her ear. "It's not even a matter of keeping it professional. I would never do anything inappropriate."

"I know that. It's been driving me crazy, too."

"I keep thinking, what if Sofia or my father walks by? Or one of the security team or staff? How are we supposed to be real with each other if we self-monitor every word and action?"

"I know," she repeated, unsure of what else to say. Maybe she should tell him she'd had other job offers. She'd been sitting on them, not wanting to turn them down but not in a place where she could accept just yet, either. If she didn't work at the palace, maybe it would be easier. But then, all the offers had come from off-island. Right now, leaving meant leaving Marazur altogether. That wouldn't make dating any easier, would it?

"The children are back tomorrow afternoon." He rubbed his hands over her back and she closed her eyes, luxuriating in the sensation. "So are Lucy and Brody."

"You must have missed them," she murmured.

"I have, but it'll mean even less privacy for us, Steph."

She pulled back. "What are you saying, Raoul? Is this too difficult for you? I don't like the sneaking around either, but I don't know what else to do. We need to sort this out on our own time." Despite her deep feelings for him, she didn't want to rush anything. They both needed to be sure, and ready.

He met her gaze. "It's difficult, but not too difficult. We'll figure it out, okay?" He brushed a thumb over the crest of his cheek. "I'm still getting used to the idea that I can hold you, kiss you. That there's something more than work and friendship between us."

"I know you're unsure of your feelings."

"Not unsure. Cautious. I want to have a few things figured out before I try to explain it to anyone else, that's all." His thumb traced a path from her cheekbone to the soft spot just in front of her ear. "And I want to make sure you don't get hurt in the process."

"I'll be fine. I've been taking care of myself for years."

"Yes, you have. And I admire you for it." He kissed her lightly. "Now, whatever is in your oven smells delicious. When do we eat?"

She laughed a little, kissed him, and then stood back and reached for her oven mitts. "It should be ready anytime," she answered. "Why don't you take the wine to the table?"

While he was gone, she took the eggplant out of the oven and put the dish on the stovetop to let it rest for a few minutes. She grabbed the salad from the fridge and put it on the table while Raoul lit the candles. When she came around the corner with the main dish, Raoul was topping up their wineglasses.

"That smells wonderful." He waited for her to put the dish on the table before holding out her chair. "I didn't know you could cook."

"Are you kidding?" She laughed up at him. "Before working for you, I was on my own. It was cook or starve. Besides, my family used to be close, and we'd have these great Sunday meals. Cooking feels like comfort to me."

"Now everyone is spread out."

"Or gone," she said quietly. "She straightened and smiled. "Well now, that's just depressing. Let's eat instead and talk about happier things."

"Like what?"

"Oh, like what sorts of souvenirs Lucy will let the children bring back." She served him a section of the stuffed eggplant. "And what they'll bring you. I bet it's Mickey Mouse ears and they'll make you wear them."

He grinned. "Lucy will do something to make me look ridiculous."

"And you'll secretly enjoy every moment."

"I will."

They managed to make small talk over the meal. Raoul took a second helping, more wine was poured, and Stephani got up to make the strong, dark coffee she would serve with dessert. To her surprise, Raoul helped clear the table and rinsed dishes while she loaded them in her dishwasher. She poured the coffee from the press and cut slices of samali cake, another one of her childhood favorites. Raoul took one look at the syrupy cake and his eyes lit up.

"I know what that is! Ceci's mother made it once, when we were dating. It's semolina cake, with that weird flavor."

Stephani laughed. "Yes, it's called mastic. Not everyone likes it, but I love it. Especially when there's lots of syrup soaking through."

They drank coffee and ate the sticky dessert, then Stephani took the dishes to the kitchen and came back with both the bottle of brandy and more wine for herself. "To round out the meal," she said, "I have brandy. Why don't we go out on the balcony?"

"That sounds perfect."

Her balcony was covered, so the bright evening light was shaded from their eyes as they sat in wicker chairs, looking out over the city. The location of her building was on a hilltop, and on a clear night, such as this one, she could see right down to the sparkling water of the harbor. Pots of geraniums brightened the little space and added a spicy, floral smell to the air. She sipped at her wine, looked out at the skyline, looked over at Raoul, and realized that her life had turned out pretty amazing, no matter what the future held.

"You look happy," he remarked.

"I am happy." She held his gaze. "You're here. I have a full belly, a lovely place to live, a fantastic job. My life is feeling rather charmed at the moment."

"*Tranquilo,*" he murmured.

"*Sí,*" she replied, reverting to his native Spanish. "*Estoy muy contenta aquí.*"

"I'm glad. You deserve to be happy, Steph. No matter what happens, I want you to be happy."

"I'm happy right now, and that's all that matters. The future will take care of itself."

As soon as she said the words, she felt a calm descend. Why was she so worried about what people would say or how things would end? All that did was color the experience of the moment.

He let out a short laugh, a puff of skepticism but without any teeth behind it. "The future rarely takes care of itself."

"Granted, sometimes things don't go as planned. But I think that looking after the present is the best preparation for the future, and a whole lot less stressful."

She finished the wine in her glass, felt the liquid slide down her throat, the little woozy rush in her head that told her she'd had enough, but not too much. Raoul was still sipping on his brandy, but the date had gone well, and she was getting impatient. They'd kissed on their date at the palace, and he'd made her weak in the knees in the library after the chess game, then put her in her car to go home. It had been five days since then, with no kisses, no touches, no nothing. She was tired of waiting, and the little kiss in the kitchen had only whet her appetite.

She put her glass down on a little table and stood, then moved over to his chair and leaned over just a little, so that her hair fell over one shoulder and she could see the black ring around his chocolate brown irises.

"What are you doing?" he whispered, clutching his glass.

"Being in the moment. Do you mind?"

He shook his head, his throat bobbing as he swallowed. "Not at all."

"Good." She took his glass from him and put it beside her empty one, then returned and slid onto his lap. She was taking the lead and it felt amazing. "Raoul?"

"Yes?"

"Kiss me."

CHAPTER 9

Maybe she had taken the lead, but it didn't mean she was in total control. Steph gasped when Raoul cupped his hand along the back of her neck and drew her head down, meeting her lips with his. The kiss was strong, sure, and devastating; a clash of mouths and tongues as they let desire sweep in. After only a few moments Stephani shifted, so that she was no longer sitting on his lap but straddling it, her knees pressed against the back of the chair and her bottom resting on his thighs. His hands cupped her there and she threaded her fingers through his hair. It was so thick, so soft. She'd always wondered, and now she knew.

His lips slid from her mouth to the hollow of her neck, and she gave a little cry as he nipped the tendon running from her neck to her shoulder. The chair was rather limiting for movement, but Raoul tilted his hips anyway and she strove to meet him.

Confused, cautious, whatever he wanted to call it—

there was no mistaking what they were feeling right now. Desire. Turned on. She knew in her heart that Raoul hadn't made love to anyone since Ceci's death, and it had been even longer for her. She wanted him so badly she nearly wept with it.

But weeping would definitely be a mood killer, so instead she kissed him full on the mouth again before whispering, "We need to go inside."

She gave a little squeak when Raoul didn't answer but grabbed her bottom and stood, keeping her legs wrapped around his waist. "Open the damned door," he growled, and she blindly reached behind him and hit the handle on the French door.

He backed them into the living room and then kicked the door shut with a definitive rattling of the glass. When he put her down on the sofa, she looked up and saw his nearly black eyes glittering at her. A dark thrill shot through her body, full of anticipation and want. Raoul dropped down on a knee on the cushion beside her, bracing himself up on his hands as he kissed her. It only took a few seconds for him to lower his body, the delicious length of him pressing her into the sofa.

She welcomed his weight, reveled in it. Hips to pelvis they rocked, mimicking the act she wished for so much but knew could not happen tonight. But she wasn't going to stop yet. It felt too good. She'd waited too long.

Raoul sat up and made quick work of the buttons on his shirt, peeling it off his shoulders and discarding it on the floor. Stephani's heart raced at the sight of him, and she scrambled to undo her own buttons until her blouse gaped open, revealing her barely there bra. Over and over her mind repeated that he was there for her. She was the one turning him on. She was the one he wanted to be with. It didn't stop being surreal, no matter how often she thought it. She was overwhelmed with it not because of what he was but because of who he was.

No title. Just Raoul. Strong, sexy, capable. Her dream man that she'd thought she'd never have. And right now he was so totally hers.

When he lay on top of her again, it was to the sensation of skin to skin, warm and smooth. He flicked open the front clasp to her bra, baring her breasts to his gaze and then his mouth, drowning her in delight. He shifted on the sofa, slid his hand beneath her skirt and touched her. She lost all rational thought and simply went with the sensations created by his talented mouth and fingers.

Until they built to a peak and she crested, releasing a sharp, glorious cry.

When she opened her eyes, he was watching her with a soul-searing intensity. Her skirt was hiked up around her waist, and he reached for the button on his trousers. Stephani ached with wanting him, but she'd told herself over and over that this wouldn't happen tonight.

"No, Raoul. We're not ready for that."

A muscle ticked in his jaw; she understood that he was extremely aroused and she was asking him to stand down. She couldn't blame him; the lovely boneless feeling in her body right now was glorious. But for them to truly make love…he wasn't ready. She wasn't sure she was, either.

He let out a slow breath, adjusted himself, and sat down on the end of the sofa.

"I'm sorry," she murmured, sitting up and pulling her blouse over her naked breasts. "I let myself get carried away, and I got to…you know. And you didn't. And that's not really fair."

He looked over at her. "I'll be all right in a few minutes. Fairness doesn't enter into it, Steph. You say stop, we stop." He smiled a little and raised an eyebrow. "Though maybe you might want to fix your clothes. Seeing you like that isn't exactly conducive to…deflation."

The little wry grin was half amused, half chagrined, and Stephani laughed a little in return. She sat up, smoothed down her skirt, and turned a little bit away from his gaze to re-hook her bra and button her blouse.

When she turned back around, he'd reached for his shirt and was putting it on. He didn't button it, though. Instead, he leaned back into the cushions and spread one arm over the back of the sofa. "Come here," he said quietly. "Let's just sit for a bit."

They did. She curled into his embrace and he toyed with her hair, playing with a few strands over and over until she got sleepy with the warmth and comfort of it. The silence should have been odd, but it wasn't. Instead it inspired an intimacy even greater than the one they'd just shared. Tenderness. How she'd craved it.

When his fingers stopped moving in her hair, she turned her head a bit and discovered he'd fallen asleep, his head back against the cushion, lips closed. He looked peaceful. Relaxed. In a way she'd rarely seen since he'd become a widower, single parent, and future king.

She closed her eyes and decided to let him sleep.

RAOUL STEPPED INSIDE THE GREAT HALL ONLY TO HEAR his father's voice echo from the library. "Raoul, is that you?"

He sighed. He'd hoped to sneak up to bed. It was nearly midnight, but he'd fallen asleep on Stephani's sofa and had slept for over two hours while she got up and cleaned up the dinner mess, then sat on the other end of the sofa with a book.

It had been disturbingly domestic, particularly on the heels of their earlier activity. He was still feeling a bit off balance from it all.

He stuck his head inside the doorway. "It's me. Sorry. I didn't mean to disturb you."

Alexander smiled. "You didn't. I'm sixty-two years old and sometimes I have trouble falling asleep. I decided to come down here instead."

Worry worked its way into Raoul's heart. "Are you feeling all right?" His father had slowed down lately, and there were times Raoul wondered about his color. There was a vitality that was sometimes missing.

Alexander nodded. "I'm fine, really. Just thinking, mostly." He gave Raoul a sharp look. "And you're out late."

"I was in the city for dinner," he explained. "I was just going to head up to bed."

"Before you do…" Alexander got up from his plush chair. "Lucy called this evening. The children wanted to say good night to you."

Raoul tensed. His father was fishing, as if he knew something was up. "I'm sorry I missed them, but I'll see them tomorrow afternoon."

"Diego checked in as well."

Raoul frowned. His brother was on his honeymoon; why would he feel the need to phone? "Is everything all right?"

"I believe so. He wanted to get approval for some side program you two talked about, but I think Sofia is going to come see you about it tomorrow."

"I'm sorry you ended up acting as my secretary, Padre. I'll look after everything tomorrow."

Alexander casually went to a table and poured himself a splash of Scotch. "Out for dinner, you say. What's her name?" He smiled, raised an eyebrow, and gave Raoul a knowing stare.

This was why they wanted privacy. Raoul's neck heated. Was he blushing? How embarrassing. He wasn't a schoolboy. He was a grown man. He'd been married once before, had two children. Surely he could go on a dinner date without having to ask permission.

"It's not like that," he lied.

Alexander sipped at the amber liquid. "Of course it is, and I'm glad. You need to start dating again. As I've told you before, it's better to rule with someone by your side rather than do it alone. You need to get married again. Have a queen."

Raoul's annoyance flared. "Better to rule alone than

marry purely for the sake of marrying. I loved my wife. I may never love anyone that way again. It was just dinner. Let's leave it at that, *¿sí?*"

"I've made you angry."

"It's a sensitive topic. And one I don't care to discuss at the moment."

Alexander lifted his hand. "Okay. If I promise to back off, could you just let someone know where to reach you? Even Stephani. She has both your work and your social calendar, *¿sí?*"

Raoul prayed his expression hadn't changed at the mention of her name. She had his social calendar, all right. She'd been in charge this evening from start to finish, and he'd enjoyed every moment.

He nodded. "If it's urgent, Marco always knows where I am. He knew tonight as well. Good night, Papa. I'll see you tomorrow."

"Good night, Raoul."

He strode off in the direction of his rooms, went inside, and stripped down to take a shower. Afterward, dressed in a simple pair of blue boxers, he lay down on top of his bed and looked at his phone.

Messages from the children, via Imogen's phone. He sent them a reply, apologizing for missing them and that he couldn't wait to see them when they got home. He signed it with hugs and kisses.

An email from Diego, which required a longer response and that he'd answer in the morning.

And another text came in, the phone buzzing in his hand. He thought maybe it was Imogene, but when he tapped on the little envelope, he saw it was Stephani.

Are you still up?

Yes, he typed back. *Ran into my father. He asked questions.*

What did you say?

He hesitated for a minute, then tapped on the little keyboard. I said I was out for dinner. He didn't need to tell her about the rest of the conversation. She'd only get paranoid.

There was a bit of a break, and then another message came through.

You're very cute when you sleep.

He chuckled a bit, as he highly doubted anyone had ever described him as "cute."

I must have been comfortable, he replied. Maybe a little too comfortable. He liked her apartment. Liked her cooking. She was slightly different in her own environment. More at ease, perhaps.

He wondered if she'd disappeared, it took so long for her to answer. When she did, it was simply two words; a question left hanging.

About earlier…

Raoul's body tensed, simply from the memory of holding her in his arms. She'd been warm and sweet, like Señora Ortiz's dulce de leche, and amazingly open to him. His earlier thought came back to settle in his mind. He'd liked how she'd taken the lead. Admired her confidence. He also knew she'd been right to stop. His brain was already crowded with thoughts; if they'd slept together it only would have compounded his confusion. His body had demanded satisfaction, but she'd correctly recognized that they needed to take things slowly.

You were right, he typed. *It's too soon.*

Once again, she didn't answer right away, and he wondered if that had been the wrong response. Damn, it had been years since he'd had to worry about saying the wrong thing to a woman. He added, *When it happens, I want it to be right.*

When it happens. Did that mean it was a foregone conclusion? He rather thought it was. Rationally, he knew he should be able to date, to possibly even have a relationship, without marriage being an inevitable result. They could take their time. It wasn't like there was a rush on for heirs, either. He'd satisfied that duty with Emilia and Max.

He flipped over to his side. Dating had to be so much easier when a person was ordinary. Most of the time the pressure that came with being next in line didn't bother him so much. But sometimes, like tonight, he wished he could just be a regular man with a regular job trying to navigate the dating scene.

His phone buzzed again.

I want that too, she answered. *Good night, Raoul. I'll see you in the morning.*

Yes, yes she would. And he'd lie awake for a long time, thinking of how on earth they could maintain a secret relationship within the castle walls.

CHAPTER 10

Stephani held down the mouse button and slid the email over into the "responses" folder. That made four replies now, and she was starting to panic over how to answer. Did she go for interviews? How could she manage that without Raoul knowing what she was doing? How could she ask for time off right now, when their relationship was just getting going?

And the biggest question: Did she still want to leave?

It felt as if moving forward with the job-hunting process would create a self-fulfilling prophecy that the relationship would fail. On the other hand, if it did fail —and of course there were no guarantees—she needed to have a plan.

What frightened her most of all was that she'd walked into the office this morning, dying to get her first glimpse of him. To see him smile at her. It made her feel unfocused, and she didn't like that. At all.

Raoul was at a meeting in the city and she should be

taking this opportunity to catch up on the things that got behind during wedding week. Instead, she heard running feet coming down the hallway, and a decidedly girlish giggle.

It was Emilia, dragging a gigantic gift bag, with Max and Alex trailing behind.

"Tía Stephani! We're back from Disneyland and we brought you a present!"

Lucy was with the boys and sent Stephani a grin. "Wait'll you see. Emilia picked out the big present."

"I did." Emilia rushed over to her desk. "We got home a while ago, but Tía Lucy said we had to do things before we could come see you."

Stephani was ridiculously pleased that Emilia had not only picked out a souvenir for her but that she was in such a hurry to present it. "Well, let me see!" she exclaimed, getting up from her desk chair.

The bag was nearly as big as Emilia. Stephani wondered how she'd managed to run along the hall without tripping. The little girl danced from foot to foot as Stephani knelt down and removed tissue paper from the top of the bag.

Inside was a dress. A princess dress in a bright, golden yellow.

She held it up and truly didn't know what to say.

Lucy burst out laughing, then covered her mouth, her eyes sparkling. Oh, she was enjoying this too much, wasn't she? Stephani raised an eyebrow in Lucy's direction, then dutifully did a half turn, swirling the skirt in front of her. "Emilia, I am going to look just like Belle!"

She'd never been one for Disney movies, but the

recent remake of Beauty and the Beast meant that she was familiar with the iconic gown.

"Do you really like it?"

Her heart melted. "Of course I do, pequeña."

"Will you put it on? I want to see!" Emilia's dancing from foot to foot had turned to full on jumping.

Stephani looked at Lucy. "Did you feed her candy for the whole flight?"

Lucy laughed. "No. I might have, but Brody would have killed me. Max, you give Stephani your gift now. Emilia, Stephani can try the dress on later."

"Aww." Emilia pouted, but Max stepped forward and took a little bag from behind his back.

She opened it and found an adorable Christmas ornament of the castle.

"It's Sleeping Beauty's Castle," he informed her. "It has sixteen turrets. Our castle only has four."

"*Dios mío!* Sixteen!" She turned the figure over in her hands. "*Gracias,* Max. I'll put it on my tree this year." Then she looked up at Alex. "Did you have a good time, Alex?"

He nodded, then grinned at Max. "Max and I went on rides. Emilia did at first but then she got sick."

"Only because I ate pizza first!"

"We all had pizza," Max pointed out. "You were the only one who—"

"Okay, we get the idea," Lucy interjected, still trying not to snicker.

Emilia looked up at Stephani with pleading eyes. "Tía Stephani, will you please put on the dress? I want to see so bad."

How could she resist? There were no further meet-ings or visits scheduled for the day, so it wasn't like anyone outside the family would walk in. And Raoul was downtown. "I'll put it on, but just for a minute, okay? I'm supposed to be working."

She came out of the staff bathroom five minutes later, feeling ridiculous but knowing she'd do just about anything to see the smile on Emilia's lips. The poor child had spent months with barely a smile. It was only when Rose had come to the household that she'd perked up. Now she laughed and played as before, with only moments of somberness when they spoke of Ceci.

"Here I come," she announced, thankful that the dress was at least of a decent quality. The skirt swooped around her ankles and she'd put her hair up in a loose bun, holding it with the golden ribbon that had been attached to the dress.

"Tía Stephani! That's so pretty! Isn't it pretty, Tía Lucy?" Emilia was nearly beside herself, and Stephani felt both girlish and silly. She turned in a circle for Emil-ia's benefit.

"What do you think? Do I look like Belle?"

"Very much," came a deep voice.

She froze, her mouth falling open as she looked up and found Raoul standing behind Lucy and the boys.

"Papa!" Emilia forgot all about Stephani and rushed to her father. "We're home!"

He scooped her up in his arms. "So I see. And looking like you had a wonderful time." His gaze settled on Stephani again. "And you brought Tía Stephani a dress?"

Emilia nodded. "Yes, Belle's dress! Because Tío Diego says you are always grouchy and a beast to work for. And that Tía Stephani deserves a medal for working for you." She wiggled in his arms. "We got you something, too, but it's upstairs."

Stephani tried not to laugh. The description sounded precisely like something Diego would say.

"Hmm. I think I'm going to have a chat with Tío Diego."

Emilia's face fell. "Uh-oh. Am I in trouble?"

He kissed her cheek. "Not at all. Were you good for Tía Lucy?"

She nodded. He looked down at the boys. "And you two? Did you have fun?"

"The rides were the best," Alex said. "And the fireworks."

"I liked everything," Max stated firmly. "We should have a Disneyland here, Papa. But the castle would need more turrets."

Raoul laughed, and so did Stephani, though she was still feeling conspicuous in the dress. "Well, I don't think we can turn this place into Disneyland, but there might be some exciting things in store for Marazur."

Stephani met his gaze. "The meeting went well?"

He nodded. "Very. There's a lot I want to talk over with you."

Lucy stepped in. "That's our cue. Come on, kids. Let's go up and have something to eat. We'll see your papa at dinner tonight."

"Aww," Max grumbled. "I wanted to show Papa my light sabre."

Raoul knelt down in front of his son. "We'll have dinner, and then I'll come up and you can show me everything you got and tell me all about your trip."

"Promise?"

"Promise." He held out his hand for a fist bump.

Max grinned and bumped it back, then turned to his cousin. "Come on, Alex. I bet Señora Ortiz made cake."

They dashed off, Emilia not far behind. Raoul looked at Lucy. "Does he always think with his stomach?"

She laughed. "They both do. Alex is even worse."

"Thank you, Luce. For taking them. They needed it, and I haven't done something fun like that with them for a long time."

"It was my pleasure." She looked over at Stephani. "No hard feelings about the dress? Emilia was pretty single-minded about it, and I didn't have the heart to say no."

Stephani laughed. "No hard feelings. Though I don't think I'll be wearing it to the next state dinner."

"Aw, why not?" Lucy teased, and threw Stephani a wink. "I'd better go after them or they'll stuff their faces full of cake and spoil their dinner."

When she was gone, Stephani made for the bathroom to change back into her work clothes. But Raoul's warm voice stopped her.

"Where are you going?"

She looked over her shoulder. "To change."

"I think you should leave it on." His lips held a twitch of humor. "Belle."

"Don't be silly." She was embarrassed, but at the

same time, she liked a teasing Raoul. It was a side that she'd glimpsed often when he'd been happy before, but one that had been absent for months. She'd missed it.

"I'm not silly." He stepped forward and reached for her hand, then tugged it, spinning her into a dance hold. "Now, I've watched a few of these movies from time to time, and it seems to me that when the dress appears, it's usually a dance scene."

"Yes, and usually at a ball. This is an office."

"But also a castle. And I am *el príncipe*, am I not?" He pulled her close. "Should I put on my official sash and medals?"

She swallowed tightly. "Raoul..."

He started humming and moved his feet. "A ball gown is made for a dance, is it not?"

She had no choice but to follow. She took little steps until he spun her around, and her stride accommodated the movement naturally. A smile played on her lips as he kept humming, something she didn't recognize but she suspected was slightly out of tune. "Now who's being silly?" she asked, then caught her breath as the spun her under his arm, her skirt swishing behind.

"I am. Because I solved a problem today." He pulled her back in, close to his chest. "We both want a chance to explore this without family interference, and I found the perfect solution."

She lifted her eyebrows. "You did?"

He nodded. "Remember when I suggested you needed a vacation at the wedding? It's all set. We're going to the Riviera."

Her feet stopped moving. "We are?" Confusion

rushed through her veins, cramping her chest. "You mean France? When?"

"I've been officially invited. The resort developer we've been working with has several properties on the Riviera and has offered to host us for a week. It's a chance to see the things that are working there, what we'd like to do differently, meet with his development team about potential designs, and run figures. It's a working trip, but you have to admit, the location is second-to-none and naturally, I'll need an assistant."

It wouldn't be the first time she'd traveled with him on a business trip. But to use it as a smokescreen for their relationship…

"It feels a little clandestine, doesn't it?" Maybe it was wrong, but the idea of it was a teensy bit exhilarating. She'd always been a rule follower. Crossing her t's and dotting her i's, making sure protocol was followed to the letter.

"A bit. But no one will give it a second glance, and it gives us a little time. Not much, but a little." He reached for her hand. "Just last night my father was asking who I was with and why I wasn't reachable. Diego called and wondered why I wasn't here. The children missed saying good night to me. Forgive me, Steph, but when do I get to have a little freedom? When do I get a chance to do something without it being on someone's daily agenda? It's not a perfect solution, but it's the best one that will prevent a lot of intrusive questions."

The idea of spending a few days in a five-star resort on the Med wasn't a hardship. Particularly spending it with Raoul. "How long would we be gone?"

"Just short of a week. We'd leave the day after tomorrow. I still have to take a security detail. I'm sorry about that, but I'll take Marco to be our driver and have him choose a few people from the team."

"I can be ready by then. I'll delegate some of the work from here to Sofia. It gives her an undue burden, though."

"It's only a week." He squeezed her fingers. "But you'll come?"

She met his gaze and shrugged, feeling ridiculous once again in the rustling, golden gown. "I work for you. You say I go, I go."

But he shook his head. "No, Stephani. Not this time. I'm asking you to go with me. Not commanding."

Why did he have to be so perfect? "All right, then. I'll go. I'll work on a handover for Sofia tomorrow and pack tomorrow night. And I guess I'll reschedule your appointments for the next week."

"Perfect."

She pulled her fingers from his grasp. "Now may I please change out of this dress? And get back to doing my job?"

"By all means."

She was nearly to the bathroom when he called out behind her, "That's a great color on you, by the way."

Her cheeks flamed the whole way to the door.

CHAPTER 11

This business trip wasn't like any other she'd taken with Raoul before. They boarded the royal jet and zipped off at mid-morning, after saying goodbye to the children.

Normally, they'd have coffee on the plane, then go over the itinerary and any documents that needed reviewing before any meetings or engagements.

Instead, Raoul popped a bottle of champagne and presented a plate of pastries and fruit for them to munch on as they made the short flight. She'd spoken to the resort owner's assistant yesterday and had discovered that Raoul had been given a suite and that her smaller suite was next door to his. She was glad to have her own space; not only was their relationship not at a "share rooms" level, but for discretion's sake, this was better.

"You're quiet," he said, as he topped up her champagne glass. "We're spending a week away in one of the most glamorous places in the world. I thought you'd be happier. You've needed a vacation for a long time, Steph."

She looked up at him. "I'm sorry. I've just been deep in thought, that's all." A smile touched her lips. "Confession. I've never been to Cannes, or Nice, or Monte Carlo."

"I haven't been there in years, either. I'm looking forward to it." He leaned back in his chair. "Perhaps we can head over to Monte Carlo, play a little roulette or try the dice."

She chuckled. "Now you're getting carried away."

"When was the last time you took a real holiday?"

They both knew the answer to that. The job was a busy one and had only gotten more so in the months since the accident and Raoul had been deep in his grief. Then there was the whole incident with Diego's former assistant, and training Sofia...

"Still," she said, reaching for a piece of melon. "That might be a little conspicuous. Isn't the idea to fly under the radar?"

Raoul grabbed a plump berry and popped it in his mouth. "Let's keep an open mind, then. We've got a basic itinerary, but there are lots of windows of opportunity for...other activities."

Her cheeks heated, and she looked out the window at the layer of clouds beneath the plane. She was sure he hadn't meant any innuendo because that wasn't his style. Still, intentional or not, the possibilities were before them. There were no meddling family members around now. It was just the two of them.

Marco popped in from the cockpit, where he'd been

sitting with the flight crew. "Excuse me, sir. I thought we could go over the transportation arrangements one final time before we land."

"Certainly, Marco."

While the two of them talked, Stephani looked out the window. They'd started a slow descent, and the clouds got closer, then they were in them, the wing disappearing in a swirly, soft mess. A minute later and the clouds were above, and little drops of moisture showed on the window. A spring shower? The coastline was visible now, and it wouldn't be long before they arrived at the Nice airport and then the short drive to their hotel.

"We'll be on the ground soon." Raoul's voice broke through her thoughts. "It's cloudy now, but the forecast is good for the rest of the week." His smile was wide. "And despite your protests, I do have a few little surprises up my sleeve."

Warmth spread through her body at the intimate way he looked at her. Maybe part of her problem today was that this didn't seem like it should be real. She'd wished for this for so long, it had become a dream that played on a continuous loop in her head, but one she'd been sure she would never have. Now she felt as if she might wake up at any moment, or that the tenuous grip she had on the future she wanted could slip out of her grasp at any moment.

He cared about her. He wanted her. Both of those had been impossible only a few weeks ago. Was it possible that he could fall in love with her, too? Or was that a wish too far?

They landed with a small bump and a smooth glide down the runway. For better or worse, they were here. And in a week they'd likely know which direction their relationship would take.

RAOUL WATCHED AS STEPHANI SURFACED THROUGH THE clear water of his personal pool. He ran a hand over his chin, a familiar tension taking over his body. She was more beautiful than she realized. She wore these conservative, totally appropriate suits and dresses to the office. She was impeccably dressed for every official engagement. But the aqua-colored bikini revealed honey-gold skin that he longed to touch. And so far he hadn't, even though they'd been here two days already.

She rested her arms on the edge of the pool. "You coming in?" she invited, water glistening on her lashes. "It's lovely."

"I thought I might. A morning swim is a nice way to start the day."

So is something else, he thought to himself, but didn't say it. Clearly the chemistry between them was good. The dinner at her apartment had made that plain. This trip was for more. It was about compatibility. About romance.

She smiled. "Join me. We have time before today's meetings."

He'd intended to anyway, so he untied his robe and dropped it on a nearby chaise, then stepped down into the cool water of the pool.

Her smile widened and she pushed away from the side, floating on her back. He couldn't look away from the twin points her breasts made out of the water, or the way her long, dark hair spread out around her. Watching her the last two days had been gratifying to say the least. She greeted every little thing with wonder, even though she was no stranger to opulence. She'd sighed with happiness at her suite, even though it was only half the size of his. The balconies outside the rooms looked over the cerulean sea, and she couldn't seem to get enough. They lived in their own corner of paradise on Marazur, but Stephani was anything but blasé.

She was appreciative. She found enjoyment in the smallest things. She reminded him to take pleasure in moments, something that hadn't happened in a long, long time.

They had only kissed since arriving, sweet little stolen kisses. They hadn't slept together, and even so, Raoul was starting to feel as if she was giving him back himself.

"Where did you go? You're lost in your head."

He blinked and met her gaze. "Sorry. Just thinking."

"Well, don't hurt yourself."

He smiled. "I like it when you tease me."

"It's easier when we're not in the office. I wouldn't want to be insubordinate." She flashed him a saucy grin, then dove under the water, giving her toes a little flip that splashed water up and over his face and chest.

Scamp.

He got the rest of the way in and swam a bit, though it

wasn't big enough of a pool for him to do laps or anything. Still, it was refreshing, and he got the pleasure of being near Stephani. Once he reached out and pulled her close, felt her cool skin rub up against his. He kissed her and then let her go, but the hazy look in her eyes told him all he needed to know. Maybe later. He had something special planned, in her suite where she'd be sure to have privacy.

"We should probably get ready for the day," she said, rather reluctantly, he thought.

"If you want to take some extra time, why don't you? I can handle this one."

She shook her head. "No, I want to be there. I'm being indulged sufficiently, Your Highness." She put a sassy little inflection on the title. "The least I can do is my job."

"Fair enough." He moved to the steps and got out, dripping water while reaching for a towel. She followed behind, and he swallowed at the sight of her skin glistening with water, then the way she efficiently used the white towel to dry off.

She paused and looked out over the terrace. "It's beautiful here, isn't it? I mean, I spend the majority of my time in a palace, but this…maybe I needed a vacation more than I thought."

"You look more relaxed," he offered.

"So do you." She went over to him and touched his cheek. "You needed to get away, too. You've shouldered everything for years now. It's better now that Diego has stepped up, but he's also been busy with his charity and getting married." He held his breath as her fingers stroked his skin. "No one really understands how hard you work, and how much you worry."

"Apparently you do," he replied, his voice sounding strangled. He couldn't think straight when she touched him this way.

"I've noticed. I just wasn't at liberty to say anything before."

He held her gaze, then dipped his head and kissed her cool, soft lips. They tasted like salt from the pool, and a little bit of sweetness that was uniquely hers.

When the kiss ended, she licked her lips and sighed, another one of those replete sounds that he loved so much.

"Make sure you eat something before our meeting. I'll come get you in forty-five minutes, okay?"

"Perfect."

She walked back through the sliding doors to his suite, her damp feet leaving little prints on the terrace floor. She'd go next door and shower off, he realized. He'd do the same. And they'd dress in different suites...

Yes, maybe it would be tonight. He only had so much restraint, and the waiting was beginning to affect his thinking.

THE MEETINGS FILLED THE DAY UNTIL NEARLY FOUR IN the afternoon, but for Stephani, it wasn't hard work. They spoke with the architect of the resort, who agreed to work up a proposal for a resort on the Marazur west coast, among the limestone cliffs and with spectacular vistas over the ocean. They had a delicious lunch, sampling chef specialties until she couldn't possibly eat another bite. Particularly when Raoul kept insisting she try something else and she would love it. Invariably she did, though she avoided anything with the word "tartare." It was a taste she'd never managed to acquire.

The mango sorbet, though, was the perfect finish.

She took notes with regard to services offered to guests, the shopping available on site, and the pricing structure. It was the latter that stopped her up every time. While the resort was solidly booked, the sheer number of euros required nearly stopped her breath. She was enjoying herself so much, but she also knew she could never have an experience like this without Raoul footing the bill. He wanted a five-star exclusive resort. She wondered if he'd be open to something a little less glamorous and slightly more affordable. With the current economy, perhaps having a slightly lower price point would bring in more people.

During the afternoon, they toured one of the two villas on the property, both with three full bedrooms and all the amenities. The other, they were informed quietly, was not available for touring, since it was occupied by a certain famous actor and her family.

By the time they finished, Stephani had taken several pages of notes and wanted to get back to her suite to put them in some sort of order, filling in blanks and recording full thoughts and impressions. It was three thirty and she was ready to take off her heels and sink her bare feet into the thick carpet of her room. Raoul left her at her door with an intimate smile and an assurance that he would see her later for dinner. She put her keycard in the door and stepped inside.

She had taken off her shoes and opened a bottle of water when there was a knock on the door. She assumed it was Raoul, and she hurried to answer, wondering if he'd decided he couldn't wait until the evening to see her. Her heart pounded an excited tattoo, but instead she was greeted by a lovely French woman who smiled and offered a quiet "Bonjour, Mademoiselle Savalas."

"Bonjour," she replied, then noticed the foldable table at the woman's side.

"You ordered a massage, *oui*?"

She hadn't, but she knew who had. She tried to feel badly about not transcribing her notes and couldn't. "Please, come in."

"May I set up on the terrace? It is so beautiful this afternoon."

It felt as if her whole body sighed at the mere thought of a massage while the soft Mediterranean air caressed her skin. "Oh, that would be fantastic," she replied. The notes could definitely wait. "Shall I put on a robe?"

In less than five minutes she found herself face down on the massage table, a sheet covering her from feet to tailbone. Her face rested on a soft pad, and the masseuse, who she'd now determined was named Mariel, opened a little bag and took out a selection of oils.

"What scent do you prefer, *mademoiselle*?"

"What do you suggest?"

"I do love the lavender. It's a special blend made just for us from the fields in Provence, and is very calming."

"That sounds perfect."

What followed was a solid hour of bliss. At one point, she nearly fell asleep as Mariel kneaded and soothed the muscles of her lower back. She gave a little start when the masseuse shifted the sheet and worked on her buttocks, down her thighs and calves, but it was utterly blissful. She rolled over and groaned as the muscles in her neck released beneath capable fingers. The perfume of the lavender oil teased her nostrils. Why had it taken her so long to do this? If she could, she'd book a massage every week for the rest of her life.

"There," Mariel said, standing back from the table. "Take your time getting up. You might feel a little light-headed at first. I will wait inside."

Stephani sighed, wishing it wasn't over. Still, her body felt so limber. So soft. She sat up and reached for the robe that Mariel had left at her feet, pulling it up over her shoulders and belting it loosely around her waist.

She went inside and retrieved her water, drinking the rest of the bottle in short order. Mariel was packed up and gone as quickly and quietly as she'd arrived, but just as she was leaving another woman arrived at her door.

Raoul was giving her the royal treatment, and she was starting to feel rather princessy about it all.

This time it was a facial and a pedicure. She knew that the spa offered such things, of course, and she'd planned to tour those facilities as well this week. But this room service was incredible. By six o'clock, her face glowed when she looked in the mirror, and her toes were a delicious shade of deep red. She chose a dress for dinner, a little ivory dress that she loved. Pearly white sandals accentuated her calves and showed her newly painted toes, and she put her hair up, a combination of braids and twists that looked more complicated than it was.

Once it was anchored with pins, she frowned. It was missing something. Jewelry? The boat neckline required something long, but she knew she'd failed to pack anything that would suit. Instead she dug in her case until she found the half-dozen gold bangles she'd packed. Then, with a flash of inspiration, she plucked a showy hibiscus blossom from the bouquet of lilies, hibiscus, and plumeria on the side table in the living room. She tucked the crimson petals into the side of her twist, then anchored it with an invisible pin. It gave an exotic flavor to an otherwise simple outfit. Satisfied, she tucked her key card and her tube of lipstick into a red clutch. That, with the flower, was the dash of color she'd been missing.

Instead of waiting for Raoul, she left her room, took the ten steps to his door, inhaled sharply for fortification, and knocked.

CHAPTER 12

She looked stunning.

Raoul was momentarily speechless when he opened his door and saw her there. He recognized the dress; she'd worn it before to some luncheon function or something. But there was something different tonight that he couldn't put his finger on. Something that made her glow from the inside out. He'd like to think it was him, but he knew more realistically it was probably from the spa treatments he'd set up as a surprise for her.

Apparently that had been a good move on his part.

"You look beautiful," he said quietly, standing aside. "I'm nearly ready." He'd showered and changed after their day, choosing a tan summer suit with a white shirt and no tie. He wondered if he should reconsider that and pick one from the selection he'd brought, but then Stephani smiled at him and any thoughts of neckties fled.

Anticipation curled through his belly, taking him by

surprise. These feelings—excitement, anticipation, even carnality—he'd never expected to feel them again. He pushed any guilt aside. It felt good to be alive. It felt good to be with her. Nothing else really mattered tonight, did it?

"I had a table reserved for us on the veranda," he said, trying to sound normal when inside he was quaking. Quaking! Like a schoolboy on a first date. "Do you have a wrap?"

Her face fell. "I never thought. Can we stop by my suite first?"

"Of course." He held out his hand. "And I can have the table moved if you like. We can sit inside."

"No, I like the veranda." She smiled up at him. "We're almost always in formal dining rooms. The fresh air feels like freedom, doesn't it?"

He knew what she meant. And yet, the moment they stepped outside his suite, he dropped her hand.

They stopped for a moment as she went inside to get her wrap. When she came back out, a light ivory wrap covered her shoulders and looped around her elbows.

She was all class. She smiled up at him and put her hand at his elbow. Together they walked to the elevators and traveled down to the second floor where the restaurants were situated.

The veranda seating was elegance and comfort together. Wicker chairs provided a light, tropical vibe, but the candle lamps and white flower arrangements on each table provided intimacy and romance. They'd barely been seated a moment when a bottle of champagne was delivered to the table.

"Is champagne all right?" Raoul asked.

Her eyes lit up when she saw the bottle. "Is there ever a bad time for champagne?" she asked. The bottle was popped, the fizzy liquid delicately poured into crystal. The remainder of the bottle was nestled into a silver bucket of ice beside the table.

Raoul met Stephani's gaze and lifted his glass. "To a beautiful night."

Her cheeks flushed just a little, and when she reached to touch the rim of her glass to his, her shawl slipped off her shoulder. She was so beautiful. He was really starting to realize how much she'd been there for him. In the early days it had been her job. He'd barely known her, after all, and was just happy to help someone in Ceci's family by giving her a job, and happy to have someone so very capable running his office. It had been a win-win situation.

Somehow, over the years, they'd become friends. It had been in part because she'd attended some of the family functions, too, at Ceci's insistence.

Then, when Ceci was gone…suddenly Stephani wasn't family anymore. Except she was, and she stepped in and shouldered so much of the load. At the time he hadn't seen it, but looking back now, he knew he'd been mired in grief and she'd kept things afloat.

Because she cared about him, expecting nothing in return.

It had taken all this time for him to see her. To really see her. And the vision was breathtaking.

They began with a delectable shrimp salad and artichokes with truffle ham and black olives, followed by more champagne. Their mains came—beef filet for him, braised lamb for her, and a bottle of full-bodied red. They chatted and laughed, made eyes at each other over the glimmer of the candle, and tasted each other's dishes.

He loved how she seemed to enjoy the simple pleasures. The beef was tender and flavorful, and she closed her eyes as she tasted it from his fork. When she opened them, her tongue swept over her lips, licking away the butter and shallot sauce, and her pupils re-adjusted to the light. He swallowed tightly. Did she know what such an innocent gesture did to him?

"I haven't said thank you for this afternoon," she said quietly, toying with a roasted fig. "It was amazing, Raoul. Simply amazing."

"You are welcome. And that's just a sample of what the spa has to offer. We have three full days left, Steph. I want you to book yourself for one new treatment each day." He winked at her. "Sometimes being a guinea pig is a pretty good job."

"I will if you will," she countered, surprising him. "There are men's treatments too, you know. And if we're supposed to be mixing business with relaxation, you deserve some pampering, too."

He laughed. "Me?"

"Well, I haven't looked at their services, but you're probably spared from a body scrub or a get-rid-of-cellulite wrap." She grinned and took a sip from her wineglass. "But a facial feels so good. And you could do a massage, or a manicure."

"I'll consider it."

Then he refilled her wineglass and they chatted longer, lingering over their entrees until they were finally cold and the candle on their table had burned low. Raoul was surprised to see they were the only ones left on the veranda. They'd certainly lingered over their meal.

"Dessert, Your Highness? Mademoiselle Savalas?"

"What do you think?" he asked.

She looked up at the waiter. "I've been longing to try the blackberry vacherin since I arrived."

"My favorite, *mademoiselle*." He smiled at her.

"And I'll have the lemon tart," Raoul said, giving a nod. "And we'll each have a glass of Sauternes. *¿Sí, Stephani?*"

He was so used to making decisions that he'd forgotten to defer to her, but she didn't seem to mind at all. He certainly hadn't meant to speak for her.

"That sounds lovely. *Merci.*"

When the waiter was gone, Raoul apologized. "I didn't mean to order for you. I'm sorry."

"Don't be, it's fine." She gave a little shrug. "Raoul, I've known you long enough now that if I didn't want it, I would have simply spoken up and said so." She reached across the table and put her hand over his. "You have never been autocratic with me. And I have never once felt I couldn't speak my mind if I really needed to."

"Except to tell me your feelings."

"Telling you my feelings wouldn't have been helpful. That was a matter of discretion, not intimidation. They are two very different concepts." She squeezed his fingers. "And far more complicated than whether or not I wanted a dessert wine."

"You're very good for me, you know," he said, turning his hand over and twining his fingers with hers. "It can be lonely, being seen as the title. But you see me as a person. As a man."

"More than is appropriate," she murmured, keeping her voice low and intimate.

Dessert arrived and he slid his fingers away from hers, somewhat reluctantly. They still needed to be discreet, and despite the lack of diners around, it was no secret among the staff that he was here. He scooped up some of the tart, but barely tasted it as their eyes met time after time, and it seemed as if the lingering part of dinner was over. Now there was a different energy, a desire to finish, a need to move on to whatever came next.

Because something was going to happen tonight. He wasn't sure what, but something was. He'd been utterly appropriate ever since their arrival, but now he wanted to move forward. But only if she was on the same page.

When their dishes were cleared, he held out a hand. "Shall we?"

"Of course."

She stood and wobbled a little. Her eyes widened as she picked up her little purse. "Oh my. I do believe the wine has gone to my head."

"Maybe a walk on the beach?" It was nearly dark now, and the stars were starting to poke through the indigo sky.

"I'm afraid of slipping in the sand," she confessed. "But I wouldn't say no to a stroll through the gardens."

She took his arm once more and looked up at him with a tenderness that made him want to say the hell with it and sweep her up in his arms. Such a spectacle was out of the question, though, so he stroked a finger over the hand that rested on his elbow.

The gardens would prolong the evening, but Raoul was surer than ever that it would end with the two of them in his suite. What happened after that was up to her.

Stephani tried to ignore the way her pulse quickened every time Raoul touched her, but it was no good. She'd had a little too much wine at dinner but figured a walk in the resort gardens would be a good way to clear her head.

Only she'd been so wrong.

Their steps slowed as they made their way along the cobbled paths. The rosebushes, hedges, and shrubs were no doubt beautiful, but in the evening light, they cast secretive shadows. It was secluded and hardly anyone was there. One moment they saw another couple, the next they were completely alone.

"It was a good day," Raoul said softly. His shoulder brushed against hers.

"Yes, it was." She couldn't look up at him. Couldn't meet his gaze and let him see the temptation, the longing she knew had to show. So she kept her eyes straight ahead on the path, focused on remaining steady on her slim heels. "I've never felt so pampered, Raoul. Thank you so much."

"I wanted to do it for you."

His words sent a thrill through her. A boss would say "you earned it." But wanting to do something for another person…that came from affection.

"You never realize just how much tension you're holding in your body until someone works it out," she replied, but immediately was aware of the innuendo of her words. Or maybe that was just because she couldn't get him off her mind. All evening she'd been thinking about sliding that suit jacket off his shoulders and unbuttoning the white shirt. She'd seen him shirtless before, like this morning in the pool, and she wanted him with a yearning so intense it sometimes threatened to overwhelm her. Until last week, everything had been in her imagination. But she'd tasted him now, touched him. Knew the texture of his skin and the sound of his sigh in her ear.

Too much wine. She'd definitely overdone it.

"Steph," he said, and halted.

They were in the shadow of a hedge, the little green leaves nearly black in the growing dark.

"We shouldn't…we're in the garden, Raoul. We still need to be discreet."

"I know. I just…one kiss. Just one to get me through until we get upstairs to some privacy."

Whoosh. The flames she'd tried to keep banked throughout the evening flared to life. He murmured something in Spanish, but she couldn't make it out because he was pulling her close at the same time, pressing his mouth to hers. She opened her lips to him, inviting him in.

"Mmmm." His lips vibrated with the sound, and desire rushed through her limbs to her core. Even though she was in heels, he was taller than she, and she stood a little more on tiptoe to nibble at his mouth. Her wrap slipped off her arm and dangled to the grass, but she didn't care. All she wanted was to taste him, to feel the urgency pounding between them.

He pulled away, breathing hard, his lips slightly swollen. "You were right. This isn't wise. One kiss isn't going to satisfy me and I'm not into public displays of… well." He cupped her jaw. "There are stolen kisses and then there's playing with fire."

"I know," she replied. "I knew it would be like this. I knew—"

He cut her off with another searing kiss, then tugged on her hand. "Stephani, I know you said you wanted to be ready, so I'm going to ask you and I want you to be honest with me."

Her heart clubbed so hard against her ribs she could hear it in her ears.

"Will you come to my suite tonight? Stay with me?"

She nodded dumbly, her chin bobbing up and down. He reached over and snagged the end of her shawl, tucking it back up over her shoulder.

"Okay, then," he said, letting out a huge breath. "Okay."

She got the feeling he was trying to measure his steps so that they didn't appear to hurry, but they were failing miserably. Her sandals tripped over the stones as if she were dancing, and once inside they headed straight for the elevator bank. They rode up alone, and Stephani had the crazy urge to kiss him while the doors were shut, but she also knew there were probably cameras feeding through to a security room somewhere. She also knew that guaranteed privacy was rarely ever really guaranteed.

The doors opened with a subtle ding.

Before they ever got to their hallway, Raoul was fishing in his pocket for his key card. She stood back while he inserted it in the slot, then waited as he swung open the door and pulled her inside.

The door shut with a definitive click, Raoul tossed the key card on a nearby chair, and then pressed her against the closed door as he kissed her thoroughly.

Never in her life had she been kissed this way. Not even the other night when they'd made out on her sofa. This was desperation and desire and naked need, and she gave herself over to it. Her shawl slipped to the floor in a puddle of ivory silk. Raoul plunged his hands into her hair, scattering pins and tearing the petals on the fragile hibiscus blossom. When his mouth glided up her neck, her eyes slammed shut and she half gasped, half moaned with delight.

He put his hands in hers, then pinned them against the door as he deliberately devoured her mouth.

She wilted, succumbing completely to the pleasure rushing through her body. She pulled her hands away from his, then pushed his jacket off his shoulders. "Need to touch you, too," she rasped, ripping his shirttails out of his trousers. He reached behind her, between her and the door, and found the little hasp of her zipper. It slid down, down, down to the hollow of her spine, until his hand slipped just inside and touched the indentation just above her tailbone.

The time had passed for modesty or even restraint. Now there was only room for honesty, and Stephani took a step away from the door, slipped the dress from her shoulders, and let it drop to the floor.

Raoul's breath came out in a rush. *"Dios mío,"* he breathed. "You're beautiful."

She'd kept her underwear simple but pretty for the evening—a bra and panty set in ivory satin. It wasn't just that he said she was beautiful, she felt beautiful. She still wore the sandals on her feet, and she took a few steps toward Raoul until she could reach the buttons on his shirt. One by one she slipped them through the holes.

"You're sure?" she asked quietly. She didn't want to keep going if he had reservations of any sort. "I know it's the first time since…"

She couldn't finish the sentence. Truth was, she couldn't know for certain if it was his first time since Ceci's death or not. She only assumed because of the man he was. He wasn't the type to have casual sex. Particularly not when he was nursing a broken heart.

He smiled tenderly at her. "Are you asking for consent, Stephani?"

"I guess I am."

"Then I'll answer. I'm sure. I'm sure that I want to do this, and I'm sure because it's with you, and I know I'm safe. I trust you, more than anyone in the world. I want you so much I ache with it. Is that what you wanted to hear?"

The urgency was now mixed with an emotion she found hard to define. There was a gravity now, a depth that terrified her and made her incredibly happy all at once.

"More than you know," she whispered, as she moved into his arms.

CHAPTER 13

Raoul twisted in the sheets and realized he was alone.

A little slip of paper was folded on the pillow where Steph had laid her head. He picked it up, unfolded it, and read the words.

Raoul, I woke up early and thought it would be best if I went back to my room, so I wasn't seen leaving yours. Want to come over for breakfast?

He flopped onto his back, still holding the note. She was right, but he hated that they had to sneak around. It was better than trying to keep things secret at the palace, but not much. The paparazzi popped up at any moment, as he knew all too well.

But waking up alone…he wasn't sure if he was let down or relieved. At least now he had some time to sort through his thoughts.

In the moment, it had been incredible. Steph was beautiful, responsive, sexy as hell. There'd been a connection between them, too, that went beyond satisfying physical needs. But was it love? He wasn't sure. He'd only ever really been in love once in his life, and he wasn't sure he'd ever find that grand kind of passion again.

Did he want to? He thought he did. Then why was there this hesitation every time he considered being in a public relationship?

The bedside clock said it was nearly eight, so he got up and showered and dressed in tan trousers and a blue shirt and tie. No jacket today; yesterday had been far too hot, and he and Stephani were going to be sitting in a conference room for most of the day, working through numbers. He wanted to go back to Marazur armed not only with impressions but also hard data. But first, breakfast. He needed to see Steph, get an idea of where her head was at. Last night had showed him that he wanted to pursue something with her. But perhaps he wasn't ready to make a relationship public. There was nothing wrong with taking it slowly, was there?

She answered the door, already dressed in dove-gray trousers, a navy silk sleeveless top, and gray shoes. Perfect attire for his assistant, right down to the tidy bun keeping her hair scraped back from her face. She looked businesslike and capable, but a smile curved her lips, so he ignored his awkward nerves and stepped inside.

"I'm sorry, Raoul. I've already eaten. Our meetings start at nine thirty, and I didn't want to be running late or risk getting food on my outfit." She gestured to the room service cart. "But there's plenty. Do you want me to fix you a plate?"

"I can fix my own," he replied, keeping his voice easy but feeling inexplicably grumpy.

"I'll pour you a coffee, then," she offered, and moved to the silver pot on the cart.

He took a small plate and added a pastry, smoked salmon, yogurt, and fruit. When he sat at the table, she placed his coffee in front of him, then returned with a glass of orange juice. As she moved away, her hand grazed his shoulder in an intimate gesture. It should have made him feel better, but it annoyed him further.

He looked over his shoulder. "It was strange waking up and finding you gone this morning."

Her cheeks colored. "I woke up early and thought about it for a good half hour before I got out of bed." She poured another cup of coffee and added cream before coming back to the table and sitting across from him. "I just kept thinking, what if I ran into housekeeping or someone in the hall if I stayed? It's one thing to have dinner in the restaurant, but something else entirely sneaking out of a bedroom wearing the same clothing as the night before."

He nodded, chewed thoughtfully, and swallowed. "My head knows you're right. It just… God, I don't know."

She raised an eyebrow. "Feels cheap?"

He met her gaze evenly. "Never. Secretive, sure. But never cheap, Steph. There's more between us than that."

She nodded, took a healthy gulp of coffee. "And we should probably talk about that, but not now. We're due downstairs in fifteen minutes, and you need food to get through this morning's schedule. Our lunch isn't scheduled until nearly two."

She got up from the table and took her half-empty coffee cup to the cart. Then, as he hurried through the selection of grapes and berries, she stuffed files into her slim case.

He admired her so much. As wonderful as Ceci had been, her forte had been charitable events, being the face of the monarchy, capturing the admiration of the people. It had been important, and she'd been good at it. He'd loved the way she'd embraced his people and they'd embraced her in return. But Steph…she was smart and efficient, calm and collected in a crisis, and he knew she was the one who really kept the business interests of the Navarro family in line. Perhaps he hadn't appreciated her enough over the years.

He wiped his lips with his napkin and then pushed the plate aside, washed everything down with two big swallows of coffee, drank the juice, and stood.

"I guess we should get going, then," he said, rolling his neck.

They went to the conference room and found the team already assembled. Meetings went late, finishing around two thirty; they grabbed a quick lunch and then went on a drive up the coast. Marco did the honors, while a guide showed them the different four- and five-star resorts along the stretch between their hotel and Monaco.

Raoul remembered mentioning taking Stephani there on their flight from Marazur, but they had a full itinerary for the rest of the week. As they wandered through the grounds of a resort even grander than the one where they were staying, Raoul wondered if they might extend their visit by a day or two, and zip away for some fun.

And so it went for two more days. A jam-packed schedule meant no time to talk during the day, and when they were finally alone at night, he couldn't bring himself to bring up the subject of their relationship. Instead, they made the most of the stolen hours, either in his suite or hers. He did a video call with the children one evening before dinner, and when he might have had a few free hours during an afternoon, he ended up on the phone with Sofia and then Diego, leaving instructions for issues left hanging at home.

On their second-to-last morning, Stephani remained asleep until the sun was up. He, on the other hand, had awakened several minutes before. Maybe he should have woken her, let her slip back to her room before the hotel was up and bustling. Then again, their floor was quiet. The chances of her running into anyone were slim at best.

Besides, it was the first morning he'd awakened with her tucked in his arms, and he wasn't sure what to do about the feelings rushing through him.

It was different than other mornings. She was in his bed, in his embrace, in his life. Tomorrow they would fly back to Marazur, and they had to figure out what to do about their relationship.

Despite how close he felt to her, he realized he

wasn't prepared for his personal life to be dragged through the press. Hell, last year a single picture that wasn't even incriminating showed up in the rags and he'd had to endure website headlines like "A new mother for the prince and princess?" Or his personal favorite, "See ya, Ceci." That had been in huge block letters in a particularly scurrilous rag out of England.

The photo had been deliberately misleading. It had been of him and Rose in the garden on his birthday, when Rose and Diego were just finding their way to each other. It had also caused further trust issues, since Diego's assistant had been the one to take the picture from inside the palace, and then sell it. The last thing he wanted was private pictures splashed on a tabloid. The press had a way of making the most innocent of situations appear sordid, and he had the children to consider.

So a public relationship was out. What about personal? Did he want to bring the family into the loop?

He thought of Diego, Rose, his father, the children... Ah, that stopped him up every time. They loved Stephani, but he'd seen Emilia's face at the wedding, when Steph had recognized the pearls. She was not ready for another mother, and neither was Max. His son still had nightmares about the accident. How could Raoul truly move forward when his children still needed help?

And that brought him back around to his original worry. The last breach had been from within his staff. As much as he wanted to trust the people inside the palace, there was always a chance that if he told the family, it would get out into the world at large.

Goddamn his life anyway. Normal people didn't have to deal with this stuff.

Stephani stirred in his arms, and he looked down at her face. Her dark hair was a tangle over her shoulder, and her lashes lay on her cheeks as she slept. They twitched a little, as if she were on her way to waking. Tenderness swept through him, and a protectiveness that was unexpected cramped his chest. She deserved better. She deserved someone who could give themselves unreservedly. Someone not bound by protocol, someone who didn't have to worry about their smallest misstep being in the papers. She deserved babies, and he was thirty-seven. He'd been there and done that already.

The cramp turned into an uneasy tumbling in his stomach. Was he really thinking of ending something this good? He thought back to the night before. They'd had a quiet dinner, then had finally taken that moonlight stroll on the beach. Everything had felt so perfect. But maybe that had been his miscalculation. This week had been a fantasy. What waited for them back in Marazur was reality.

She stirred again. "Good morning," she murmured, curling into his shoulder.

His heart ached. He couldn't make this decision now. It would have to be when they got back to Marazur, back to reality, and he could put everything into context. They had twenty-four hours to spend together, so he would put aside his misgivings and enjoy it.

"Good morning," he replied softly. "You didn't make it back to your room this time."

She turned her head and smiled up at him sweetly. "I guess I got too comfortable. Or you wore me out."

It would be so easy to pretend they could stay like this forever. But they couldn't, and that little fact kept hammering at his brain. He'd thought this week was to decide if they wanted to pursue something, but it hadn't quite worked out that way. Instead he'd realized what he was ready for…and what he wasn't.

"Raoul?" She braced up on an elbow. "What's wrong? It's like you're a million miles away."

He tried to smile. "Not a million. Maybe just in the hundreds. We go home in the morning."

Her smile faded. "I know. It's been a lovely week." She sighed. "But we can't expect it to be like this forever."

"Real life has a way of intruding," he agreed. "But we do have today. Our schedule's a bit lighter, as well. What do you say to finishing up this morning, then taking a side trip? We'll go to Monte Carlo. Try our luck at the tables. Leave work behind."

He was surprised when Stephani sat up in the bed, gathering the sheet around her. He thought she'd be happy about some off-the-clock time, but the pucker in her eyebrows said not so much.

"Raoul, that would be lovely, but don't you think we should talk about what happens next? We've put it off all week, and it was easier to leave it alone and enjoy ourselves." She put her hand on his arm. "And I have. Oh, I have. It's been magical. But we've avoided talking about the big things. I don't think we can do that any longer."

"We can't leave it until tomorrow?"

The pucker in her brows deepened. "The only reason to put it off is if you're going to say something I don't want to hear. And if that's the case, I'd rather hear it now, before I…before we…"

His stomach churned and he struggled to find the right words. "Stephani, this last week…" He paused, looked down, then back up again, meeting her troubled gaze. "It's been incredible. I've sat in meeting rooms with you and marveled at how smart and intuitive you are. Watched you interact with people and caught myself smiling when you smile at them. I can talk to you more than anyone else I know, and being your lover…" He reached for her hand. "Holding you in my arms has been the most unexpected, incredible gift. Do you blame me for wanting to pretend the rest of the world doesn't exist for just a little longer?"

Her frown had softened, but the worried expression still darkened her eyes. "It's been amazing for me too, Raoul. I can't begin to tell you how much."

He leaned over and kissed her gently, then pressed his forehead against hers. What would happen if he threw caution to the wind and just went for it? The very idea terrified him. It simply was not his way. For a week, maybe. But as a long-term strategy, it sucked.

"I sense a 'but' coming," she said quietly.

He took a breath.

And was interrupted by his phone ringing. The ring tone was a special one, reserved for one number only: the secure line inside the palace.

He reached for his phone and answered.

When he hung up again, he felt as if the strength had left his body.

"It's my father," he said sharply. "He's suffered a heart attack."

CHAPTER 14

Stephani sat stiffly in the limousine that carried them from the airport to the palace. Worry for Alexander tightened her chest, and frustration with Raoul was giving her a headache. She wished he would just talk to her, tell her what he was feeling. Instead he'd closed himself off, his face locked in a grim expression she recognized.

His defense against grief.

As soon as he'd received the call, she'd called Marco with new travel arrangements, gone to her room to pack, and cancelled the morning meetings. Raoul had packed his own things and spent most of his time on the phone with Sofia, who was still at the palace, and his father's physician, who had accompanied Alexander to the hospital. There was no chance of the news not getting out, so as soon as they got to the palace, she and Sofia would work on crafting a press release for immediate distribution.

That she could do without any trouble; it was her job and she'd been doing it for years. What really nagged at her was the look in Raoul's eyes this morning. There'd been resignation, and despair. If anything happened to Alexander, he'd become king. The pressures he felt now would increase. It didn't take a rocket scientist to figure out what he'd been thinking before the phone call. He wasn't ready for anything official. With Alexander's illness, he'd be even less so.

He'd suggested a trip to Monaco, but she'd known, deep down, it was a last hurrah. A man who had decided to carry on with a relationship didn't put off talking about it or speak about avoiding the real world. She knew in her heart he'd made his decision.

This had been the risk she knew she was taking. She was good enough for an assistant, and even good enough to be his lover. But beyond that, no. He'd decided that either he wasn't ready or that it wasn't what he wanted in the long run.

She should be filled with anger, or regret, but she wasn't. She'd known the risks, known the rewards. She didn't need a trip to Monte Carlo to take a gamble, and she'd lost. But the regret would have been if she hadn't played at all. Now she knew. They'd tried.

Raoul was 100 percent focused on his father right now, and rightly so. She reached over and took his hand, the only solace he seemed willing to allow. Presently he was speaking to Diego on the phone, who was in the middle of having his own travel plans adjusted so he and Rose could fly home from their honeymoon a week early. By late tonight the two brothers would be together, and she'd be back home in her apartment, licking her wounds. Until then, she'd be where she belonged. Beside him.

That was the kicker, wasn't it? She knew they had no future, but she still belonged at his side. As his assistant; as his friend. On the flight she'd insisted he eat something, and he'd gone through the motions. As he'd spoken on the phone to Sofia—again—she'd linked her fingers with his and tried to be strong and reassuring.

But still he didn't let her in, so she'd help in the only way she knew how. She'd look after palace details and whatever business was waiting, so he'd be free to stay with family.

Once back at the palace, Raoul had his bags sent to his rooms while she wheeled her case to the offices. She'd take it home with her later, but there was no time to waste. "Raoul, please have Dr. Sanchez call me right away with an update, and I'll get to work on an official release. We've already lost a lot of time, and with no official word from the palace…"

"I'll do it right now."

She sat at her desk and called Sofia over to give her a debrief. The phone rang and she got the update from the hospital. It was indeed a heart attack, but a small one, and Alexander was expected to make a full recovery. Raoul went upstairs to change, then left for the hospital.

By three in the afternoon, Sofia went home, as she'd been called to the palace at five in the morning and had been going nonstop ever since. Stephani sat at her desk, fielding queries from the press and sorting through her materials from their trip. Raoul had hardly said a word to her before leaving for the hospital. She knew he had to be worried, but in a true relationship, you leaned on each other in times of trouble. That he'd shut her out spoke volumes.

The tender man who'd held her, who'd made love to her so thoroughly…he was gone.

At eight she heard from Rose that they had landed and were going straight to the hospital. Raoul hadn't returned. Stephani thought about going to see the children, but she couldn't face them right now. She was too raw, too worried to put on a happy face for their benefit. And she'd be lying if she hadn't thought, once or twice during the week, what it would be like to be their stepmother. Instead she met with the housekeeper and cook about the needs of the family over the next few days, and then unpacked Raoul's briefcase and her own. Tomorrow she'd work on putting together an analysis of their meetings during the trip. Raoul wouldn't want the project to be delayed. If it was all he'd allow her to do to help, she'd do a top-notch job.

Marco was back at his post and offered to drive her home. "You've got your suitcase and you've got to be tired," he said gently. "Let me take you home and take your bag up for you, Stephani."

"I should say no, but I'm not going to argue with you tonight, Marco. I'm exhausted. Thank you."

They were quiet as they left the palace, but then Marco looked at her in the rearview mirror. "Stephani?"

"Yes?"

"About what happened this week…you and His Highness can count on my discretion."

Her throat clogged as she met Marco's kind gaze. His face blurred as tears stung her eyes. "No need," she whispered. "I don't think it's going to happen again, Marco. But thank you." She blinked the tears away. If there were crying to do, she'd do it at home, in private.

He watched the road, then glanced back at her again, his face a little harder. "If that's the case, then I'm very sorry. You are both good people who deserve happiness. I had hoped maybe you found it in each other."

"Me too, Marco, me too." She sighed, bit down on her lip, regained control. "He was married to my cousin and now he's married to the monarchy. He didn't have to say it for me to understand what he was thinking today. If anything happens to Alexander, he steps up. He wears the crown."

"Begging your pardon, but he does that anyway," Marco countered. "King Alexander has eased off the day-to-day duties substantially over the last few years."

They were both quiet for a few moments; his assertion was correct, after all. It didn't make her feel any better.

"We're here," he said quietly, and pulled up outside her building.

He opened her door and she stepped out, and he retrieved her suitcase from the trunk. She moved to take it from him, but he shook his head. "No, ma'am. I'll take this up for you and see you to your door."

"Marco…"

"I insist."

His kindness touched her. He was Raoul's most trusted staffer but he'd always shown a genuine affection for the family. He'd been the one driving in the accident that had killed Ceci and Mariana, and everyone knew he'd blamed himself. Now he was trying to care for her, and it made her feel a little less alone.

He waited while she unlocked her door, and then stood back as she reached for the handle of her suitcase. "Thank you, Marco. For this and for everything you said."

"Maybe you need to give it time," he suggested helpfully.

But she shook her head. "I don't know. And right now things are a little too hectic to be making demands. Don't worry about me." She smiled. "I always land right side up."

He smiled back at her. "Well, good night, Stephani."

"Good night, Marco."

She wheeled her case inside, kicked off her shoes, and headed for the sofa. She didn't unpack or even think about something to eat, though she hadn't eaten since the hurried meal on the plane this morning. She simply sank down into the cushions, covered herself with a blanket, and fell asleep.

~

STEPHANI LET IT GO A WEEK BEFORE SHE SAID ANYTHING. By that time, Alexander was home from the hospital, with strict instructions as far as diet and activity, Diego and Rose were settled back in, and Lucy made do with calls from Canada each day or so to check up on her father. Alexander wasn't working, though, and Stephani often arrived at work to find Raoul already in his office. By Friday she was both annoyed and worried. He was working too hard, putting himself under greater pressure than was necessary, while keeping all his feelings to himself. It was business as usual, and now it was starting to make her mad. He was singularly focused on the resort project, and Stephani was working on it with him as well as keeping the office running and fielding inquiries about Alexander's health. She was exhausted.

She understood him not delving into their personal relationship right now. She didn't like it, but she understood. But an acknowledgment of her help and support might have been nice. Prince or not, she deserved better than this.

She was battling with a spreadsheet when Diego strolled in. "*Buenos días, bonita.* Happy Friday."

She grunted in reply, then looked up. "*Lo siento,* Diego. I'm grouchy this morning." She tried a smile. "The correct response would be, good morning, Your Highness."

The easy smile fell from his face. "You know I hate it when you call me Your Highness. What's going on?" He pulled up a chair. "You've been looking stressed all week."

She considered being truthful, but Raoul was behind

his office door and she really didn't want to get into it in detail. "Oh, just a lot of work since coming back."

He lifted an eyebrow. "You're a terrible liar."

"Thank you, Your Highness."

He chuckled then. "Okay, so you don't want to talk about it."

"I'm fine, truly. Just trying to sort some things out."

"Things meaning my big brother?"

Her cheeks heated. "Raoul's been too busy working to be any bother." And that was the truth.

Diego slid closer. "You care about him." He looked her in the eyes, his expression kind as he kept his voice low. "Rose figured it out weeks ago. It puts you in a tough position, doesn't it? We all loved Ceci, but she's gone. You'd be wonderful for him, if he'd just open his eyes."

She gave a bitter little laugh. "Oh, his eyes were open. It just didn't make any difference, Diego. Please, let's change the subject. This isn't the time or the place."

"Fair enough. Listen, why don't you go find Rose in the library? She's having coffee there, and we were talking about her asking for your opinion on something. Go have a cup of coffee and maybe a slice of Señora Ortiz's cake. It almost always puts things right." He frowned. "You've been working too hard and need a break."

The words, coming from Diego, were nice, but not the same as if Raoul had spoken them. She shouldn't leave her desk, but she'd barely seen Rose, either, and the office was starting to feel incredibly oppressive. "Actually, that sounds very nice." A tap of a few keys and her phone was forwarded to Sofia's line, and she set off for the library.

She found Rose curled up on a sofa, a book in her hand and a cup of coffee at her elbow. "Diego said I would find you here."

Rose's smile was broad, and she wore the glow of true happiness. "Oh, I'm glad you stopped in! I've barely seen you since we got back."

"You said the honeymoon was lovely, but that's it," Steph chided. "I was hoping for some details."

"Of my honeymoon?" Rose faked a shocked expression. "Really, Stephani..."

They laughed then. "I meant the charity work. Diego is so excited about it, and he and Raoul have been talking about expanding the program? Did you have anything to do with that?"

Rose nodded. "We're adding a women's health program to the education one. Ryan O'Toole—you know, Diego's friend from university? He and his sister have been working there for months. Brenna is a whiz at administration, so she's going to be our coordinator on site. It's very exciting."

Steph agreed. It sounded exciting and innovative and important. She rather thought she'd like to be a part of something like that. Wondered briefly if she could offer her expertise for a while. Maybe it would be better if she could get away for a bit, put some distance between her and Raoul. Do some hard thinking about what she wanted. When he was close, she lost all perspective.

Rose patted the seat beside her. "Come, sit. You look like you're in need of cake."

"I seriously wouldn't say no."

Cake and coffee were delivered and devoured. Rose talked extensively about the program, and the more Stephani listened, the more she was interested. She'd been doing the same job every day for nearly a decade, and it was a great job, but a change of scenery and a new challenge might be just what she needed.

"Rose, do you think you could use my skills over there? I'd love to help out. Maybe not permanently even, but with start-up? I could work with Brenna, help with hiring staff, set up a records database, whatever."

Rose looked at her keenly. "Are you looking to help, or looking to get away from Raoul?"

Since Diego had said Rose suspected her feelings ran deeper than a work relationship, she wasn't all that surprised by the question. "Both. I think I need to go somewhere where I can clear my head. I want my own happy ever after, Rose. If I'm not going to find it here, I have to start figuring out my life." She swallowed thickly. "As much as I love this family, I can't sort that out if I'm with Raoul every day. It's too hard."

Rose nodded, though she looked sad. "I'll talk to Diego, but I'm sure he'll say yes. What will you do about your position?"

That was easy. "I'll promote Sofia and bring in someone new to train for her job. Plus, it'd be easier on the new person with me handling the charity stuff abroad."

"That's true." She met Stephani's eyes. "You're sure

about this? We were kind of hoping the trip last week would nudge you two into something more."

There it was, the little bump of pain caused by the reference to their trip to France. There'd been a lot of nudging from both sides. They'd experienced the connection she'd longed for. When he touched her, kissed her, said her name…it had been sublime. But Raoul's continued silence hurt worse than any words he might have said at the end of the week. To her, they showed a lack of respect and care. Regardless, she deserved an explanation. And felt like a heel for feeling that way, because he was dealing with a lot right now. Was she being unreasonable? Or was she just hurt that he hadn't turned to her in his time of trouble?

"I'm sorry," Rose said quietly. "I've touched a nerve, haven't I?"

Stephani looked into her eyes. "I love him," she confessed. "I have for years, when it was completely wrong to do so. Now both of us are free, and there are feelings there, Rose. There are. But not love. Not for him. I thought I could be okay with whatever he would give me, but I'm not. I'll never be Ceci, and I'll always second to Marazur. Oh, I know the duty and responsibility thing, and I'm not unreasonable. I've lived here and worked here long enough. Still, look at you and Diego. You made it work. Together. We don't have that. And I don't think we ever will." She hesitated, then added, "It's not about what the country demands of him. It's how he views his life that's the problem. Ceci was it for him, and his feelings for me aren't strong enough to bump me into the number-one position. I'll never be his grand passion, and it's time I accepted it."

Rose didn't answer. She just gave Stephani a sad smile.

Steph sighed, but then lifted her chin and met Rose's eyes. "You got your fairy tale. It just isn't in the cards for me."

CHAPTER 15

Raoul stared at Stephani, unsure he'd heard her right. "You seriously want to leave here and go to Africa?"

"You make it sound as if it's the moon. It's not. I asked Diego if I could help him with the new phase in his project, and he said yes. It's only for six months. Sofia can handle things here, and hire an assistant to work with her. With me handling the project administration on site, it'll cut Diego's assistant's workload by about a third. Quite manageable."

A knot formed in his chest. "You've got this all figured out," he replied, his voice cold with fear. Leaving? He knew he'd handled things badly between them, but leaving? Impossible. She was Stephani. He relied on her. He couldn't have got through the last few weeks without her running the office.

"I do, yes," she said quietly. She uncrossed and then crossed her legs again, the only indication she was nervous. "I need to go, Raoul. I need a new challenge.

Something different. And maybe I can help change the world a little bit while I'm at it. This is a good thing."

Good for her, but not for him. She'd been his right hand for so long he didn't know how he'd manage without her. "I've taken you for granted," he replied, folding his hands on top of his desk. "I'm sorry, Steph. You've been here so long, I think I always just thought of you being here forever."

She flinched a little at his words, and he realized what a poor choice they were. "What I mean to say is—"

"I know what you meant," she interrupted. "But I can't stay. Not now. I need to put some space between us, Raoul. This will be good for me."

"But I need you." It hurt him to say it. He didn't like being needy. He was the one who held things together, not the other way around. But the idea of her leaving Marazur filled him with an inexplicable fear. He had to convince her to stay. "I know I've taken you for granted. You've never asked for a raise, for anything, really. Let me make this up to you."

Her pink cheeks turned a deep red, and her eyes flashed. "Do you seriously think this is about a raise?" Her fingers clenched into fists so tight that her knuckles turned white and she let out a flurry of what he could only assume was Greek cursing. "Taken for granted? What planet are you on, Raoul? How can you sit there and pretend that what happened between us wasn't important? You're acting as if it didn't happen at all!" She bit down on her lip, but before he could reply, she continued. "I gave myself to you. You told me that our week away was a chance for us to see how we felt without being in the public eye. The morning we left, I knew you were going to try to let me down easy. I'm not stupid. And your refusal to speak of it since our return says all I need to know. I wanted to be there for you. To help you. And when you froze me out, I did the only thing I could to make it better. I worked. But it hurt that you shut me out so completely. After what we shared, did you really expect me to stick around?"

She took several deep breaths while guilt crawled over him.

"You're right," he finally answered, feeling slightly sick. "I was a total coward. I didn't want to hurt you. I didn't know how to say what I wanted to say, so I said nothing at all."

"But you hurt me anyway. Do you get that I loved you? That our week away I kept telling myself not to get my hopes up but I couldn't help it, because being with you was so…so…"

She looked away.

He'd felt it, too. And that was what had scared him.

"It was for me too. It's just…I'm not ready, Steph."

"Then you should have said so, instead of acting like nothing happened. Like I didn't matter."

His head snapped up as he met her gaze. "You do matter! Of course you do!"

"How would I know?"

Tears had formed at the corners of her eyes now, and he felt panic mix with the guilt. He wasn't sure what he'd do if she cried. All the emotions of the past few weeks pummeled him. His feelings for her, his fear, his conflicting vision of the future, the sobering incident of his father's heart attack, and what that meant for him personally… Now this. She was right. He hadn't offered her one thank you, one bit of extra praise for taking up the slack. He'd been so stuck in his own head he'd ignored the one person who was always, always there.

He pushed out his chair and paced to one end of his office, and then back again, running his hand over his hair. "Do you know how much I feel pulled in every possible direction? Everyone wants something from me! And there's no way I can make everyone happy. What the hell am I supposed to do?"

She stood and faced off against him. "You were always so quick to judge your brother, but maybe you could try taking a page out of Diego's book. You could put your happiness first and realize that the rest will fall into place. But I don't know if you can ever do that, Raoul. You're too afraid. And until you can face that fear…"

She swiped at her tears. "I can't sit around and wait for something that might never happen. I deserve better. I deserve to put my happiness first, too. So I'm either going to Africa to help Diego and Rose or I'm putting in my notice and leaving."

His stomach dropped to his feet. He'd always admired her stubborn streak but not this time. "Leave? Where would you go?"

Silence fell in the office. She lifted her chin and God, she was beautiful. That warrior look was one of the reasons he admired her so much. She was a woman who got things done. Who committed and saw it through. He knew that her words weren't idle threats. If she said she'd leave, she'd do it.

"I've had four job offers in the last month. A few might have expired, but I have options, Raoul. I've worked a very high-profile job and my qualifications are excellent."

He sat back down in his chair.

"Go to Africa," he said weakly. "Take some time."

She stared at him for another moment, then gave a quick nod. "I'll bring Sofia up to speed until I go. It'll take a bit for arrangements to be made."

She left and closed the door with a firm click.

Raoul put his head in his hands. How had he screwed this up so badly? He knew how. He'd been a coward, told himself he didn't want to hurt her, so he avoided talking about things altogether. He'd been utterly unfair, and the longer he'd remained silent, the harder it had been to imagine having that conversation. So he'd ignored it, pretending their problems would just go away.

She was right to be angry. And he was ashamed. He'd definitely counted on the fact that she would always be there.

And yes, his father's sudden illness had been a jolt, making him realize how much the family and the people of Marazur relied on him. But that didn't excuse his behavior.

He went after her, unsure of what he would say but knowing he had to say something to try to set things right. Or if not right, at least honest.

She'd wasted no time leaving. By the time Marco

had brought the car around, Raoul figured she was already home at her flat. To his credit, Marco said nothing on the trip into the city. And when they arrived, he simply advised Raoul that he would wait in the car.

Raoul climbed the stairs to her floor and knocked on her door.

She answered it, but he couldn't read the expression on her face. She'd shut him out. He deserved it.

"May I come in?"

"Of course."

She stood aside, and he stepped into her apartment. He was immediately assaulted with memories of his other visit here. The dinner, the balcony, the sofa. Their relationship had really started here.

"I have no excuse for how I behaved, Steph. I'm sorry. I can make excuses, tell you what was going through my mind at the time, but the truth is I was wrong. I protected my own feelings at the expense of yours, and that was completely selfish and cowardly."

Her face softened a bit. "I don't hate you. How could I? But I have to do what's right for me. And I can't figure that out if I stay here. I need some time, Raoul. Truth is, I was thinking of leaving long before we went to France."

He didn't know what to say to that. He'd had no inkling that she was unhappy.

"Sit down," she suggested. "I'll bring you some water."

When she returned from the kitchen, he'd found his voice again. "I can't change your mind?"

She shook her head. "You might have, once. If you'd

told me what you were feeling, even if you'd asked me to be patient while you thought things through. I could have worked with that. But you shut me out, and you put my feelings and our relationship at the bottom of the list. I understood those first days that your father was in the hospital. But after that…it was avoidance, pure and simple. And that's not good enough for me."

"I was going to talk to you when the call came about my father. You do realize that, right?"

She pulled up a chair and sat across from him. "I know that's where it was leading. I love you, Raoul. It's because I love you that I have to do this. I gave you opportunities. And the only time you came forward with your feelings was because you had to. Because I said I wanted to leave."

He put the water on the table beside him. "Then I think you should go. Maybe we both need to think about what we want. How we feel."

"I know how I feel. I don't think you can say the same. And until you can, I need to start living for me."

He nodded, feeling oddly like crying himself. She was a special woman and he was throwing his chance away. *Dios mío,* she'd said that she loved him, and it humbled him and scared him all at once. But she was right. He hadn't treated her as she deserved. And that had happened because he wasn't ready to fall in love and he'd been too afraid to admit it. His father's illness had only been an excuse. She would have stood beside him if he'd allowed it, and they both knew it. Because Steph was the kind of woman who would be there, no matter the consequences.

He thought back to how she'd made sure he ate and how she'd tried to hold his hand on the plane and in the car. How she'd taken over the resort report on their return, and even made adjustments within the household for Alexander's return home.

She did deserve better, and he hadn't given it to her because he was too afraid.

He looked into her eyes and said the words he should have said that morning in his suite. "I'm not ready, Steph. I care about you and the time we spent together was so amazing. But I'm not ready to love anyone. I thought about our relationship being in the press or even within the family and staff and I just froze."

"Thank you," she whispered. "And as disappointed and hurt as I am, I do understand." She reached up and touched his face. "Now let me go."

He nodded. "Okay."

They sat that way for a few moments, because leaving meant leaving whatever potential they might have had behind. Finally he got up. She did too, and he leaned forward and kissed her cheek.

"Whatever arrangements you need to make, do it. We'll accommodate."

"Thank you, Raoul."

He nodded, then turned to leave.

Marco was waiting in the car, saw Raoul approaching, and got out to open his door. Once Raoul was inside, he slumped against the seat.

"Home, please, Marco."

"Yes, sir."

The car pulled away from the curb. They were out of her neighborhood and on a main street when Marco spoke again. "This will be completely out of line, sir, but you're an idiot."

Raoul wondered if Marco expected him to disagree or be angry. Instead he met his driver's eyes and simply said, "I know."

STEPHANI'S DAYS WERE JAM-PACKED WITH arrangements. There was handing things over to Sofia, setting up interviews for a new assistant, getting up to speed with the project in Tanzania, travel arrangements. She felt tired all the time, and at the end of the day she often felt like crying as she ate a late dinner before falling into bed.

She credited the fatigue to both the long work days and the emotional toll it took to be in the same office with Raoul day after day. She'd said she loved him; he hadn't said it in return. He focused on his work and the children and his father's recovery, but barely spared her a glance or a word.

Three weeks had passed since they'd jetted off to Nice. She'd been taken right to the top of the roller coaster and then plunged to the bottom again.

There was a reason she didn't like roller coasters.

Before she could make her trip, she needed a physical. Dr. Sanchez, the palace physician, set up an appointment for her at his office. She walked in at three in the afternoon on a Wednesday and was immediately ushered into an exam room. The nurse gave her a soft cotton gown and she lay down on the bed, a thin sheet covering her.

She woke when Dr. Sanchez entered the room.

He smiled at her. "Working too hard again?"

"Long days. It's a lot of prep, getting ready to move for six months."

"But exciting." He moved to the side of the bed, and his face turned serious. "Stephani, I think you should reconsider your trip."

His statement was surprising and she gaped at him. "What? Why?"

"Well, your records show that you're not up-to-date with some of your vaccines."

Relief flooded through her. "Well, that's part of why I'm here."

He nodded. "And some of them I could give to you safely. But not yellow fever, and the anti-malaria medication approved for you isn't as effective in areas of Africa."

"Why do you mean, approved for me? Why aren't they safe?" She sat up on the bed.

He looked at her evenly. "By the look on your face, I'm going to assume that you don't know that you're pregnant."

The room swirled around for a moment or two, and she saw black dots. "Put your head between your knees," Dr. Sanchez advised. He rubbed her back for a few moments, then went to the little sink and got her a paper cup of water. "Drink this, and we'll talk."

She nodded and took the cup from him. The water

was cool and revivifying, and she took a deep breath while the word ran on repeat in her brain. *Pregnant. Pregnant. Pregnant.*

"I didn't know," she said weakly, then leaned back against the pillow again. "It's only been a few weeks. I haven't even missed my period yet. I'm due in a few days."

"I always do a test on a checkup urine sample," he answered. "We can confirm it with a blood test, but I'd trust it."

A baby. Raoul's baby. Oh God. This was horrible… and wonderful…and if she thought things were complicated before, they'd just be ratcheted up to about nine billion.

"And so the problem with the vaccine is that I'm pregnant?"

He nodded. "A lot of vaccines are safe, but some aren't, or some lack the data to support it either way. I can't stop you from going, but if you were to get sick, it wouldn't be just you. It would be the baby, too." He looked her square in the eye. "If you are going to keep it, that is."

Of course she was. This wasn't how she'd planned it, but she wanted children. "I am. But wow. This just… changes everything."

He smiled again. "Babies usually do." His voice was warm and calming. "I'm sorry about your trip, though."

"Me too." She looked over at him. "Dr. Sanchez, you're the royal physician. Will my condition be…that is, I mean to say…"

He took her hand. "No. I am still bound by confidentiality, and anything we discuss here is safe."

She looked into his kind face and let out a breath. "Okay. The baby is Raoul's."

If he was surprised, he didn't show it. "I see."

"I don't quite know what to do about that, to be honest. It's highly possible I'll be leaving the palace. If I do…if I end up away from Marazur, could you recommend a doctor for me?"

"As long as you're here, you're my patient," he said. "And I've known Raoul since he was a teenager. Even if the two of you aren't together, he'll want the best of care for your baby. You'll be taken care of, Stephani. I promise. Shall we get on with the rest of the appointment? We want you as healthy and happy as possible."

He wrapped a blood pressure cuff around her arm, while Stephani scrambled to make sense of her thoughts. Healthy? Maybe. Happy? How could she be completely happy when her personal life was in such a mess?

CHAPTER 16

The last thing she wanted to do was tell Raoul the news, but since her plans were all going to be cancelled right away, she couldn't wait. She parked her car at the back of the palace and entered through the servant's door, stopping at the kitchen first. It was nearly eight and she hadn't eaten since noon; she'd been so out of sorts after seeing the doctor that she'd driven down to the ocean and sat on the beach, watching the waves break on the shore. She'd needed time to think.

In reality, she should probably be panicking. She and Raoul weren't together. She'd thrown a monkey wrench into the operations of the monarchy and was about to turn it upside down again. The crown prince was about to have an illegitimate baby. Even if she didn't reveal the identity of the father, there would probably be speculation.

She should be panicking, but she wasn't. Because deep down she was happy. Oddly, she kept telling herself she shouldn't be. She was single, her relationship with the father was in tatters, and all her plans were changing. But she was. Come what may, she was happy that she was going to have a child. Be a mother.

The kitchen staff was still bustling around, but Señora Ortiz took one look at her, grinned, and fixed a plate. The chicken and salad was delicious and exactly what she needed. She turned down dessert, thought of the bottle of vitamins she now had in her purse. Even the way she ate was about to change.

"Is the family still at dinner?" she asked.

"They're just finishing dessert."

Nerves bubbled around in her stomach. She had to simply get it over with, didn't she?

She gave Señora Ortiz an unexpected peck on the cheek. "Thank you for dinner."

"Of course. You come to my kitchen anytime."

Stephani went upstairs then, toward the dining room. Raoul and Diego were still seated at the table, chatting, when she stepped to the doorway. Her heart tumbled a little. Her feelings for Raoul hadn't changed. There was no question he'd disappointed her, but that was added pain. It had done nothing to stop how much she loved him. Now she was going to tell him they were going to have a child together, all the while knowing they would be raising him or her apart.

"Raoul? May I speak to you for a minute?"

He looked up and his face immediately fell into an expression of concern. "Of course. Are you all right?"

She tried a smile, but nerves seemed to be getting

the better of her. "I'm fine, but if we could talk in the library, that would be great."

Raoul looked at Diego, who also wore an expression of alarm. Did she really look so bad?

"I'll catch up with you later, Diego," Raoul said, rising from the table.

She led the way down the hall to the library, which was just about as neutral a territory as could be found in the palace. When he was inside, she shut the door behind them.

He was at her side immediately. "What is it? Are you okay? You look scared to death."

She nodded. "I am, a bit. But I'm okay, I promise."

"I know you saw Dr. Sanchez today. If you're sick…"

The fear on his face was real, and it made her feel better—and worse—that he truly did care.

She took his hand and led him to a plush settee. Once they were seated, she dropped his hand and clasped hers together on her knees.

"I did see Dr. Sanchez." She lifted her gaze, her chest constricting as she forced out the words. "I'm not sick, Raoul. I'm pregnant."

All the color drained out of his face.

"That was my reaction, too," she said dryly. "Dr. Sanchez thought I was going to faint."

"Pregnant? But we were careful."

"Not careful enough, it seems. There's been no one else, Raoul."

The blood rushed back into his face. "Of course not.

I mean, not that you couldn't… Oh my God. I can't speak. I can't think right now."

"Take your time," she suggested softly. "I spent the afternoon sitting on the beach, working up the nerve to come here tonight."

"A baby." He let out a huge breath. "Did you have a feeling? Ask for the test?" He frowned. "Miss your period?"

She shook her head. "He did a test for my checkup. Routine, apparently. I can't go to Tanzania now. My shots aren't up-to-date and it's too risky to go without and not safe for me to have a few of them while expecting."

"I'm sorry," he offered, surprising her.

"You are?"

"I know that you were looking forward to it. It wasn't planned under the best circumstances, but it was going to be a new adventure for you."

"Well, it looks like I have an adventure of a different sort coming in the future."

They sat in silence for a bit, then Raoul nudged forward. "You know, Steph, I keep thinking about the things you said when we talked. About me avoiding making a decision about us. I was a coward, and I know it. It's not like me to run away from my problems. I make decisions. It's what I do."

"I'm not sure what you're getting at."

"You deserve someone who's going to be decisive. Someone who is going to follow through. Now we're going to have a baby together, and it's not the time to be ambivalent about anything. It's a responsibility we'll bear together."

Unease rippled through her veins. "What are you saying, Raoul?"

"I'm saying I think we should get married."

She nearly fell off the settee. What once would have filled her with joy now filled her with a mix of sadness and frustration. For years she'd daydreamed about Raoul popping the question, but there'd been no question here, just a statement, and only because she was carrying his baby.

It was wrong, all wrong.

"No," she heard herself say.

"We can do it quietly; no one will think it terribly odd if my second marriage is a smaller, private affair."

"No," she repeated. "Raoul, did you hear me?"

"And if you're only a few weeks along, the sooner the better. Even if there's speculation, we can simply say we'd planned it for a while but didn't want to overshadow Rose and Diego's big day."

He stood now, started pacing. "But first we'll have to tell father. And Diego. You can move into my suite."

She stood, too. "Stop talking. Just stop."

He halted. "What?"

"Raoul, I said no. I will not marry you."

He laughed. "Of course you will. I know things have been screwed up, but we both need to let our pride go. It's the right thing."

She clenched her teeth to keep from crying. "Raoul, for a smart guy, you can really be very stupid. I don't

want to do the right thing, don't you see? I want... I
want..."

He stepped forward so that they were face to face.
"What do you want? Because I'm really trying here. My
God, Stephani. I'm willing to make you a queen."

The tears she'd held back started to choke her.
"You're a bastard," she cried out, unable to keep her
cool any longer. "Willing to make me a queen? Did you
just say that? Why are you not the man I thought you
were? Why aren't you the man who—"

She stopped. The words sat on her tongue, so thick
she was choking on them. Raoul's brows had pulled
together, his cheeks red with...anger? Was he angry
at her?

"The man who what?" he bit out.

"The man Ceci loved!"

She turned away then, ashamed. She had never
truly coveted what Ceci had. Or if she had, she hadn't
ever wanted to take it away from Ceci to have for
herself. It wasn't like that. But what she'd wanted was to
have him look at her the way he'd looked at Ceci once
upon a time. She didn't want to be a replacement. She
wanted to be loved for herself.

"What do you mean?" he asked, his voice danger-
ously low.

She took a breath. Turned back around.

"You said you weren't ready. I accepted that. And I
don't know all the details about your relationship with
my cousin, but from what I saw, you always treated her
with respect, and love, and affection. Tonight you
offered me your kingdom but you didn't offer yourself,

Raoul. That's not respectful, loving, or affectionate. I'm not a replacement for her. I'm my own person, and I deserve to have someone love me the way you loved her. You didn't even ask. You just informed me we'd be married, that the wedding would be some slapped-together private affair, and the sooner we did it, the sooner we could make the world think that this baby was conceived after the wedding."

Her voice shook but she was determined. "In all the years I've been here, Raoul, until tonight you have never made me feel cheap. But I do. I'm a problem to be solved, and I'm telling you right now, I won't have it. I'll have all of you or nothing. I can't spend my life trying to live up to what she was to you."

She lowered her shoulders, surprised at herself for delivering such a speech, glad she'd done it, terrified of the result.

He ran his hand through his hair. "You don't know what you're asking!"

"I know exactly what I'm asking. And you being so freaked out gives me my answer. So here's my counter offer." Her stomach turned and she willed the nausea away. "I'm going to inform Diego about the change of plans. I'm going to work with Sofia to bring in the new assistant. Then I'm going to take some time off and enjoy my pregnancy."

"That's not an offer. That's a statement."

"It's as much of an offer as you made to me, Raoul. And just about as emotional."

He spun away. "Dammit, Stephani." He put his hand on the back of a chair, clenching it tightly. "You want all of me. I don't have all of me to give. Not anymore."

Her throat tightened. "I know that now. I do, Raoul. That's what I'm saying. You told me the truth about your feelings, and I've accepted it. So let me tell Diego about the change of plans. And everything else we'll do one day at a time."

She put a hand to her stomach, seriously afraid she was going to throw up now, needing to get out and get some fresh air. When Raoul didn't answer, she turned on her heel and left the library, then headed to the back of the castle where her car was parked.

Marco was there, closing up the garage for the night. He took one look at her and came over, his dark eyes concerned.

"Stephani. Are you all right?"

She shook her head. "Yes and no. I need a moment."

"Do you need me to drive you home?"

She shook her head once more. "No, I..."

The sickness became overwhelming, and she rushed to a hedge and threw up.

Marco was there by her side, holding out a handkerchief. "Wipe your mouth. It'll help get the taste out."

She took the square of fabric and did what he said. His big hand was on her back, anchoring her as she gulped in big breaths.

When she was better, she stood up straight. "I'm so sorry."

He watched her carefully. "Ceci wasn't often sick with the babies, but if she got worked up..." He leaned down a bit to look straight into her face. "I'm guessing you're in the same situation."

"That's a pretty big leap, Marco."

"I have sisters. Four of them." He smiled a little. "I'm sorry, Stephani. It's complicated, isn't it?"

She nodded. "Incredibly. He'll 'do the right thing' by me, but he doesn't love me, Marco. And I don't think I can marry someone who doesn't love me. Or who will always love someone else better."

He gestured with a hand, motioning toward the garage. "Come with me for a moment. I want to tell you a story."

He led her inside and to a desk area. She'd never been inside Marco's personal "office," and it was plain but comfortable with a desk, computer, filing cabinet, and not much else. She sat in a sturdy chair and he grabbed a rolling stool and perched on it.

"I was driving the night of the accident," he said softly, regret hanging on his words. "I can't tell you how many times I've wondered what I might have done differently. If I'd taken a different route, or gone slower, left a few minutes later… Ceci would still be here. Mariana, too. And the children…they were so scared. It was the worst night of my life, but it's nothing compared to the pain Raoul felt.

"I know you saw him after. We all watched him go from shock to grief to, well, months of going through the motions. He made a big show of having a stiff upper lip. Not that he fooled anyone, but did you ever see him cry?"

Stephani shook her head. Not once. She'd known he

was holding it all inside, but he'd never broken down in front of her.

"I did," Marco said, his voice hoarse. "When he came to the hospital, and she was gone, and I was alive. And he hugged me and cried, Stephani. Sobbed like a baby on my shoulder and said he didn't want to live if he had to live without her."

The pain in her heart was real and stabbed at her like knives. "I know he loved her, Marco. I can't compete with that."

He shook his head. "See, that's where I think you might be wrong." She opened her mouth to protest, but he held up a hand. "Hear me out. The thing is, I've known Raoul for a long time. Longer than you, actually, and when he falls in love, he goes all in. Then he lost her in the blink of an eye. No chance to say goodbye, no nothing. Just a phone call saying his world had collapsed. Tell me, how eager would you be to love like that again, knowing how it feels to lose that one person who was everything?"

She sat silently, unsure of what to say.

"Stephani, I watched the two of you in France. What you have is real, but he's scared to let himself care too much. It's not that he can't. Or that he doesn't. It's that he won't let himself. I'm not saying you should marry him for the baby. But I guess I'm saying, don't give up."

"I can't hold on to an impossible dream forever, Marco."

"Then maybe just take a breath and let things unfold over the next few weeks or months. He'll figure it out."

"And if he doesn't?"

He smiled. "My eldest sister runs a design business right here in Marazur. She's stubborn and also brilliant. Having a partner to run the administration would be perfect, and I have leverage."

She laughed then. This really was home, both the Navarro family and the people who worked here. "Thank you, Marco. I needed the chat to get out of my own head a bit."

He stood up and held out his hand, helping her rise. "You're welcome. I care about both of you, you know. I think you would make him very happy, and you'd make a wonderful queen, too."

He walked her to her car and she made the drive home in the dark, thinking about what Marco had said. Maybe Raoul really did love her. Maybe it wasn't that he wasn't ready, but that he was afraid to lose again.

But until he could admit it, she was no further ahead than before.

CHAPTER 17

Raoul met Diego up on the battlements, as per his brother's request. He had a feeling he knew what the conversation was going to be about, and also why Diego had chosen it. Every single time Raoul had given Diego a lecture on behavior and responsibility, he'd taken him to the top of the castle where they could survey all of the royal grounds, and much of the surrounding island.

That he and Diego had seemed to have switched places was disturbing.

Diego was waiting, his hands resting on the stone wall and the wind ruffling his hair and he looked south toward the ocean. When Raoul approached, his shoes clacking on the rooftop, Diego turned.

His brother looked happy, and grown up. It made Raoul proud, and also, for the first time, a little out of his depth with his brother.

"I'm glad you came," Diego said, holding out a hand. Raoul shook it, felt a reassuring connection there.

Diego had become a man he was comfortable with, and he was glad of it.

"I figured you'd want to talk after you met with Steph. She told you everything?"

"Congratulations," Diego offered dryly.

Raoul pulled his hand away and went to the wall as well, needing to feel the wind and sun on his face. "I've messed things up in a big way. And I'm sorry about your project."

"Don't worry about that. Brenna's still keeping things going and she's going to look at hiring. I'm more worried about you."

"Don't worry about me. Worry about Steph."

Diego sent him a sideways glance. "Steph has her shit together. You don't."

Raoul bristled, said nothing. The lecture was starting, it seemed.

"Stephani will have this baby with or without your help."

"She knows I'll help her. *Mierda*, Diego, I would never shirk my responsibility."

"She doesn't want your responsibility, brother. You're always responsible. You take care of things and she knows you'll make sure neither she nor her baby want for anything. Except your love."

Raoul turned sharply to look at Diego, only to find his brother watching him with a mild look in his eyes.

"I offered to marry her."

"Begging your pardon, and correct me if I'm wrong, but you offered to minimize the scandal with a slapped-together wedding."

Raoul rubbed a hand over his face. "For God's sake, it's not that simple."

"But it is," Diego replied. "Do you love her?"

"Again, not so simple."

"And again, that's bollocks."

"You've been spending too much time with your British friends."

Diego laughed. "Actually, that's too much time with my British wife, and there's no such thing, because I adore her beyond reason."

Raoul's heart thumped. "I know you do."

"That's right. Because you loved Ceci that way."

"Ceci's gone."

"Yes, she is, *hermano*. And you're alive. And you have a woman who loves you, who is carrying your child, and you are too afraid to love her back."

Raoul's insides trembled.

"I'm not ready," he answered, his voice barely a whisper above the breeze.

"No one is ever ready. It just happens. And either you reach out and grab it or you mess it up and regret it for the rest of your life. Steph doesn't care about a crown or a palace or any of the things you offered her. She wants you, and just you. She wants you to look at her and say you love her, and to mean it. She wants you to make her feel like she matters, more than any crown or royal duty. She's looking for a partner, Raoul, and you have to prove yourself worthy of her love. Because make no mistake, that woman loves you. She loves you for the man you were and the man you still are, in here." He thumped a hand on Raoul's chest. "But you can't have her and protect your heart at the same time."

"I'm scared," Raoul admitted finally, letting out a long, shaky breath. "I never want to go through something like that again. And the children…how do I tell them I'm going to love someone else? Max has nightmares still. Emilia clings to the memories she has left."

"You stop doing what you did to me."

Raoul looked up sharply. "What do you mean?"

"You stop trying to shelter them from anything bad or try to make everything right for them. You did that after mama died and I felt utterly useless. You grab at life, and you live it. And you teach them to live it, and you teach them that you embrace the love and embrace the fear because locking your heart up in a box for safekeeping is no way of living at all."

Tears formed in Raoul's eyes and he blinked them away. Sniffed, blinked again. Diego was right. It killed him to admit it. He'd always tried to do everything right, he realized. "After mama died, I tried to be perfect," Raoul said. He looked out over the palace grounds, so expansive that he couldn't see where they ended and public land began. Beyond was the capital; inland was another city teeming with people who depended on the Navarros and their government. "I tried to be the best son and brother to spare you and Papa. And then I met Ceci, and I didn't have to try so hard. I never wanted you to feel the pain I felt. And when Ceci died, the pain was back and I swore I'd never do it again."

"I know. And it's not wrong, Raoul. It's just that you have to choose which life you want, and live with the consequences. Unless you're willing to open your heart again, you're going to lose her forever." Diego put his hand on Raoul's shoulder.

He walked away, leaving Raoul alone on the ramparts to think things through.

STEPHANI DIDN'T TAKE MUCH FROM HER DESK. THERE were her special pens, and she was keeping her laptop, so she could work from home if either Sofia or the new assistant, Marcella, needed help. But today was her last day working full time at the palace. She was going to go home, take a week or two's vacation, and then take it from there. She was planning on spending a little time in Corfu. With all the upheaval lately, the idea of going to her childhood home held a wistful appeal.

She packed the pictures off her desk—ones of Emilia and Max, another of her with Ceci on her cousin's and Raoul's wedding day. She touched the glass with a finger and felt tears well up in her eyes. "I tried," she murmured, her voice catching. "I'm sorry."

She sniffed, put the photo in the box, and folded over the flaps.

Then, with a heavy weight in her stomach, she went to Raoul's door and knocked.

"Come in."

She opened the door and stepped inside. "I just wanted to let you know...I'm going now."

His gaze held hers for a long moment. Then he held

out a hand, motioning to a chair. "Please, sit for a minute."

She did, wanting to leave, wanting to prolong the moment at the same time. Today felt very, very final.

"We've been through a lot in this office," he said quietly. "And you have always, always been an asset to this monarchy and to Marazur."

"Thank you, Raoul."

"Don't thank me for that. Please, don't. Because while it's true, I've done you such a disservice, Steph. And I am so, so sorry that I hurt you."

She put her hand to her abdomen without thinking. Their child rested there. She was eight weeks along now, not showing, but feeling a change inside her, nonetheless.

"We were friends long before we were lovers. We'll sort it out. It's okay."

He got up from behind his desk, went to her, and as he had once before, moved a chair so he could sit facing her. "It's not okay. The truth is, I started having feelings for you and I got scared. So scared that I put up road-blocks that didn't need to exist in order to protect myself. And by doing that, I hurt you."

She didn't know what to say and didn't quite know where he was going with it, but she also sensed he felt the need to get whatever it was off his chest. Her fingers twisted together in her lap. "What are you scared of, Raoul?"

"Losing you," he answered simply. "Not like I've already lost you, but like I lost Ceci. Afraid of giving you my whole heart only to have it crushed again."

"But Ceci's death was an accident. The chances of that happening again…"

He paused, then inched a little closer until he could reach out and touch her knees. "My mother died when I was just a boy. I watched my father grieve for her. I listened to Diego cry himself to sleep at night. I decided that I was going to be the best prince I could be. I'd help my father and protect my brother. I fell in love with Ceci and vowed I'd be the best husband. But I lost her, too. Like my mother. And I told myself I would never love like that again."

"I understand, Raoul. I really do. But I'm not sure how this changes anything."

Nor would she allow herself to hope. He wasn't the only one who'd been hurt, after all.

"I've spent the last few weeks doing a lot of soul searching." He took his hands off her knees but rested his elbows on his own so that he was leaning toward her. "I've thought about the kind of king I want to be. The kind of father I want to be. I've thought over and over about some things Diego said to me, because my little brother has grown up far wiser than anyone gives him credit for. And the truth is, I have a choice. I can choose to be afraid, to keep my heart under lock and key, to never get hurt again, and to never experience pure joy."

Her pulse began to hammer, despite her resolve to stay unmoved.

"Or I can open myself up to loving again, take a risk by knowing life sometimes deals us horrible blows, but accept that a chance at joy and happiness is worth it."

Her breath caught in her chest. "And what did you choose?"

He held her gaze. "It came down to asking myself, if I'd known what lay ahead, would I have still married Ceci? And the answer was yes. All the pain, all the grief… It was still worth it. And if I'm lucky enough to find that kind of love again? Well, I'd be a fool to let it slip through my fingers because I'm too much of a coward to own it. To give it."

There was no stopping her pulse now, or the quickening of her breath. "Raoul…"

To her utter shock, tears filled his eyes. They shone at her as he said, "I love you, Stephani. I love how smart you are and your confidence and your intuition. I love how you laugh and how you love my children and talk to them as if they matter. I love your sweet tooth and your apartment and the way you feel in my arms."

He sniffed and two tears dropped out of the corners of his eyes. "And I love that you're carrying my baby and that you're so beautiful it hurts. Please, reconsider. Marry me. And not because we need to legitimize this baby or throw together a quiet wedding, but because I love you and you love me and we need to be a family. We can take out a headline in The Sun for all I care. If the world knows this baby was conceived two months ago, so what? I'm tired of being the perfect prince. I want to live again, Steph. And I want to do that with you. Just you."

She nodded, swiping away tears of her own. "I'm sorry," she said, her voice tight as she tried to keep control.

"What on earth for?"

"I don't even know." She cried a bit and laughed at the same time. "Just that this ended up such a mess. I've loved you for so long, and when you shut me out and pushed me aside, it hurt so badly. I wasn't patient with you, when I promised myself I would be."

"I didn't deserve your patience," he countered, smiling a little. He reached over to his desk for a tissue and wiped her eyes with it. "When Papa had his heart attack, all I could see was how I was going to have to step up and that our trip had been so self-indulgent. So out of character for me. I felt guilty because of it, like I should have been here."

"But being in France didn't cause his heart attack."

"I know that."

She gazed into his eyes. "I wouldn't trade those days for anything," she answered. "Not a moment."

"Me either."

He patted his knee. "Will you come over here, please, and let me hold you?"

She got up from her chair and slid over onto his lap. Oh, it felt good to have his arms around her again. He snuggled her close and the put one wide hand over her belly. "I didn't even get to tell you that I'm happy about the baby," he whispered. "Or how beautiful you are carrying it." He looked up into her face. "You tell me how you want to proceed, and that's what we'll do."

"I want us to be a team," she responded immediately, touching his face. "I want us to make decisions together. I want to rely on you and oh, Raoul, I want you to rely on me. For all things. For work and for play and for raising a family. I love Em and Max. And I think they would want you to be happy. It doesn't mean forgetting their mother. She'll always be a part of all our lives."

"Consider it done." He turned his head and kissed her palm. "Now, there's just one thing left for you to do."

"What's that?"

"Answer my question."

The hope she'd tried to tamp down blossomed fully in her heart, along with a wide smile. "Your Highness, el Príncipe Raoul Navarro a Marazur, I have very good recall. And a question was not asked. I was, however, issued a command."

"Then allow me to rephrase. Stephani Savalas, will you marry me? Will you be my wife, mother to my children, queen of my country?"

Oh my. The gravity of it reached in and grabbed her, but she took a deep breath and nodded. "Yes," she replied, hugging him tightly. "Yes, I believe I will."

CHAPTER 18

The wedding was held five weeks later, a private ceremony properly administered by the priest at the cathedral. Rose and Diego stood for the bride and groom, while the rest of the Navarro family sat in the first two pews. Max and Emilia were beaming —Max in his tux from Diego's wedding, and Emilia in a new dress and shoes with just the tiniest little heel. At the bride's request, several of the palace staff attended as well, including Señora Ortiz, Marco, Sofia, and Marcella.

Stephani wore a Ferretti empire-waisted gown that suited her perfectly and hid the tiny bubble that was beginning to form at her waist. When she reached the top of the aisle, she turned to the children and gave them each a rose from her bouquet and a kiss, awed that she was going to be their new mama and so very happy to be taking on the job. After the vows, her hand shook as she held it out, but steadied when Raoul put her fingers in his and slipped the wedding band over her knuckle. To her delight, he lifted her hand and kissed it before letting it go.

After the ceremony, they went back to the castle for a private celebration. The event was not kept from the public, but was rather more low-key, which was fine with Stephani. She'd never been in it for the big production or flash; instead she had the wedding she wanted with the people she loved. It didn't get any better than that.

And when the day was over, she and Raoul went to the nursery and tucked the children into bed.

"Good night, Max. Good night, Emilia," Raoul said, leaning down and kissing their foreheads one at a time.

"Good night, Papa."

"Good night, darlings," Stephani said softly.

Emilia sat up. "Tía Stephani..." Her little brows pulled together. "Is that what we should still call you?"

"If that's what you like."

Max sat up, too. "We wondered if you wanted us to call you mama," he said quietly.

She sat down on Max's bed and looked over at Emilia in hers. "I love you both very much, and I would love to be your mama. But you don't have to call me that if it feels wrong. I loved your mama very much. And we're always going to remember her, okay?"

Emilia nodded quickly, and Max let out what sounded like a relieved sigh.

"Now, you two have had a busy day. Get some sleep, and your papa and I will see you in the morning."

Once they closed the nursery door, they went hand in hand to his suite. "What you did just now..." Raoul said, shaking his head.

"It was okay?"

"It was perfect. They love you too, Steph. Giving them time and acceptance is just what they needed."

They shut the door behind them. "And how about you? Do you need time?"

He shook his head, his dark eyes glittering. "I think I've wasted enough time being a fool, don't you?"

She reached up and untied his bowtie, tugging on the ends gently, watching as his throat bobbed as he swallowed.

"So, Señor Navarro. *¿Como estas?*"

He smiled down at her. "*Muy bien, gracias,* Señora Navarro. *¿Y tú?*"

She cupped his face in her hands and drew him down for a kiss. "*Yo soy completa, mi amor.*"

"Me too," he whispered. "Me too."

Find your next great Donna Alward story at www.donnaalward.com/bookshelf

ABOUT THE AUTHOR

While bestselling author Donna Alward was busy studying Austen, Eliot and Shakespeare, she was also losing herself in the breathtaking stories created by romance novelists like LaVyrle Spencer and Judith McNaught. Several years after completing her degree she decided to write a romance of her own and it was true love! Five years and ten manuscripts later she sold her first book and launched a new career. While her heartwarming stories of love, hope, and homecoming have been translated into several languages, hit bestseller lists, and won awards, her very favorite thing is when she hears from happy readers.

Donna lives on Canada's east coast. When she's not writing she enjoys reading (of course!), knitting, gardening, cooking…and is a Masterpiece Theater addict. You can visit her on the web at www.DonnaAlward.com and join her mailing list at www.DonnaAlward.com/newsletter .

Find your next great Donna Alward read at http://
www.donnaalward.com/bookshelf

9 781989 132326